Jezebel

Titles by Katherine Sutcliffe

Jezebel

KATHERINE SUTCLIFFE

JOVE BOOKS, NEW YORK

JEZEBEL

A Jove Book / published by arrangement with
the author

ISBN: 1-56865-558-4

A JOVE BOOK
Jove Books are published by The Berkley Publishing Group,
a member of Penguin Putnam Inc.,
200 Madison Avenue, New York, New York 10016.
JOVE and the   J   design are trademarks
belonging to Jove Publications, Inc.

PRINTED IN THE UNITED STATES OF AMERICA

Jezebel

One

❧

THE TEXAS PANHANDLE, 1870

Obviously, Hell had actually frozen over. So had his butt, not to mention his shivering horse.

Rafael de Bastitas, his back against the frigid, howling night wind and driving sleet, did his best to focus on the mirage that had materialized through the freezing curtain of ice pummeling his shoulders. A house, if one could call it that. More like a shanty, by the looks of it; a dilapidated structure with a collapsed porch and a solitary light glittering intermittently through the downpour. Obviously, someone occupied the pitiful dwelling. Surely they would not be opposed to offering a grateful stranger refuge against the icy storm.

The wind tore at his coat and bit at his face as Bastitas stiffly slid from the icy saddle and wrapped the reins loosely around the pommel. He cautiously moved toward the house, pausing momentarily at the questionable steps leading to the hazardous front porch. Deciding that a foot through a rotten board or two was preferable to freezing to death, he ventured toward the first precarious step, then stopped abruptly.

Had he imagined it, the wail—the long, suffering sound of pain that lifted the hairs on the back of his neck and made him momentarily forget the freezing rain? Glancing over his shoulder, he removed a glove and slid his hand beneath his slicker to rest lightly on the butt of the revolver strapped low on his hip; he could just make out the blurred image of his horse and nothing more. The wind, no doubt. Barreling across the rock-strewn countryside, it could produce sounds that could make a grown man believe that all the demons from hell were gnashing at his heels.

Christ, he was cold. He would happily dance with the demons from hell for the privilege of wrapping his numb fingers around a cup of hot coffee.

He eased around the black pit of broken lumber in the center of the porch and lifted his fist to rap soundly when the scream erupted again—clearly this time. He leaped to one side and, with his back flattened against the wall, grabbed his gun. Memories came winging at him like bats from a cave—a woman and child screaming, pleading for mercy, wailing in pain and rattling in death.

Closing his eyes, Rafe counted backwards—ten, nine, eight—anything to erase the memory—concentrate on the present, not the past, at least, not at this moment; he would continue to deal with the past later.

He swung toward the door and kicked it open with a force that rocked the walls. Knees bent, gun gripped in both hands, he pivoted on one heel, swung the gun toward the shadowed form in the corner of the room and opened fire.

The culprit toppled to the floor, riddled with bullet holes, ravaged threads floating like feathers in the air. Crouched, the hammer of the gun still cocked and ready,

Rafe focused on the mangled sewing mannequin and felt his face go from cold to hot.

Silence slid like a death pall around him.

The parlor, of sorts, with a scattering of formal furniture and stained-glass lamps with dangling crystal prisms, felt bitterly cold and suffocatingly musty. A solitary shaft of dim light spilled over the nearby threshold leading to a hallway flanked by a scattering of closed rooms.

Carefully, Rafe moved down the narrow corridor, senses alert, gun raised, aimed, and ready for the slightest movement or sound. Coming to the kitchen, he paused and scanned the room, which was lit by a solitary oil lamp on a crude wood table draped with a red-and-white checkered cloth. A dish of barely touched food had long since grown cold. A blue-and-white speckled coffeepot remained on the stove, obviously forgotten. The stench of scorched coffee made his empty stomach turn over.

There came a sound, a muffled groan from a room at the end of the corridor. He eased toward the open door, paused to one side of it, fingers tightening on the trigger, blood buzzing in his ears and his heart hammering at the base of his throat. He dove into the chamber, hit the floor and rolled to a crouched position, prepared to fire at the first indication of threat.

With his back pressed against the foot of the iron bedstead, he squinted through the shadows at each corner of the cramped but cozy little bedroom with its multitude of colorful rag rugs on the floor and frilly curtains on the window. Nothing, then . . .

A squeak of the bed, a moan so quiet he might never have heard it had the wind battering the house not slackened at that moment. Slowly, slowly, he turned, eased his way up to his knee so that he just peeked over the top of the high feather mattress.

Briefly, he closed his eyes, then reluctantly opened them again.

A hag of a woman with wild, colorless hair lay sprawled before him, her legs bent at the knees and spread wide apart, her skirt hiked well above the enormous mound of her very pregnant belly. Her head raised, her eyes wild with obvious fear, she glared straight at him while blood oozed from a bite laceration on her lower lip.

She made a hissing sound at him.

He stood, his gaze shifting from her face to that place between her legs that was swollen with the crown of a child being born.

"Damn," he uttered, just before she raised the barrel of a shotgun straight at him. He ducked. She shot. He dove toward the door while she shot again, the buckshot blasting into the wall behind him and winging him across the back of his neck.

Stumbling into the kitchen, plowing into a chair and sending it crashing to the floor, Rafe grabbed his burning nape and swore through his teeth.

"Perverted fiend!" the woman shrieked. "Thieving malfeasant! Get out of my house before . . . before my husband kills you!"

Husband. Christ. He needed to face down a rampaging husband as much as he needed to become involved with the goings-on in that bedroom.

Fine. He'd get the hell out. Let the witch lie there and stew in her misery. He didn't have the time or the inclination to become embroiled in this sort of annoyance.

Gun still gripped in his hand, blood trickling down the back of his neck, Rafe made his way back to the parlor, stepped over the maimed dummy and reached for the door, hand resting on the tarnished brass knob but not turning it. What the devil was he waiting for?

"Get out!" the woman screamed from the back of the house.

"Right." He threw open the door. The icy blast struck him so hard he stumbled back.

The sleet had turned to snow falling in so thick a blanket that he was forced to shield his face with a forearm. He leaped from the porch and stumbled to where he had left Jake.

The horse was gone.

"Shit." He kicked a clod of frozen dirt, crammed the gun back into the holster and pulled his hat down over his brow. He took a reluctant look back at the house as he moved off into the drenched darkness in search of shelter, discovering the barn some hundred feet out back of the house. The structure was more like a lean-to, with warped and rotting boards affixed haphazardly so that the building looked on the verge of tumbling at any moment. Sure enough, his horse was there, nestled between a solitary cow that was in sore need of milking and a swine that did little more than grunt at his intrusion. A mule stood buried in the shadows, chewing hay and staring at his horse balefully.

The horse snorted, swung his butt to Rafe and stuck his head in the corner of the makeshift stall. It would be no easy task coercing his companion out into the weather again, but by Rafe's estimation, they were no more than an hour out of Hell. Once in town he could board the weary animal in the local livery, and he himself could take a room at the hotel, order up a hot bath and a little companionship for the night . . . not to mention a meal that consisted of something other than hardtack and beans.

The horse pinned its ears and cocked one back leg threateningly as Rafe approached. "Don't even think it," Rafe sneered, but he was careful to keep well away from the animal's rear anyway as he collected up the reins and tugged the disinclined horse toward the door.

There were dusty, molding harnesses and lines on the walls and a sorry-looking buckboard with a broken axle wheel. Rafe frowned, uneasy with the picture painted by the poorly maintained equipment scattered around the miserly lean-to; even more uneasy about the distress that made him hesitate to mount Jake and ride as hard as he could for town.

The house in the distance seemed minuscule and frail against the onslaught of the worsening storm. There wasn't a hint of smoke coming from the stovepipe, and precious little firewood was stacked near the back kitchen door.

There was no husband. He knew it all the way to the pit of his aching belly.

He unsaddled and unbridled the horse, tossed the tack into a pile of hay and trudged back to the house through shin-deep snow, entering this time through the rear door straight into the kitchen, where he stood shivering while he allowed his eyes to adjust to the dim interior of the room, knowing even as his gaze was drawn to the chipped enamel kettle on the stove and the wire basket of onions hanging from a hook near the washbasin that his willpower wasn't strong enough to deny the flood of memories roused by his surroundings.

It had been a hell of a long time since he'd stood in a kitchen with his senses swimming in the scent of onions and coffee and . . . female.

No doubt about it; he would get the devil away from here. But first he would see what he could do—if anything—to make certain the banshee in the other room had enough firewood to keep her from freezing to death.

The house was silent and felt a hell of a lot colder than it had before; the fire in the stove had gone out completely. Another half hour and even the water in the basin would begin to freeze.

Rafe removed his hat and tossed it on the table with its scattering of dirty dishes, then shrugged out of his slicker, which was dripping water on the plank floor. He wasn't about to give up his gun. Hell no. If push came to shove, he was liable to shoot the crazy woman if she lifted that shotgun at him again.

Situating the Colt evenly in his hand, finger resting lightly on the trigger, Rafe moved to her bedroom door. She appeared to be sleeping. Surely she wasn't dead. There was no baby . . . *yet*. Thank God for that. While he *might* consider sitting at hand throughout the night, just to make certain nothing too terrible transpired, he wasn't about to involve himself in the birthing of some hysterical woman's no doubt ill-begotten offspring.

She groaned. Her head rolled from side to side on the damp feather pillow. "God oh God," she whispered. "What did I ever do to deserve this?"

Rafe raised one eyebrow. "By the looks of your belly, lady, I got a pretty good idea."

The woman gasped. Her eyes flew open, and she weakly lifted her head and fumbled for the shotgun, which had fallen to the floor.

Rafe entered the room, pointing the revolver to a spot above her head. "Just in case you decide to pull another gun out from under your pillow, Miss Whatever Your

Name Is. I don't normally take to being shot at without doing a little shooting of my own. And *I* don't miss."

"Is that right?" she hissed through her teeth.

"Damn straight. I could put a bullet between your eye sockets before you could blink. And I'd not give it a second's thought."

"Oh fine. It's not enough that I'm dying with a baby between my legs refusing to be born—now I've got some murdering cutthroat who wants to—oh. *Oh!* It's starting again. Oh, God. Just shoot me. Put me out of my misery. *Please.* If you have a decent, compassionate bone in your disgusting body—just put the gun to my head and shoot."

She grabbed the bedstead behind her head and clenched her teeth. Her face turned red and twisted. Her fine, colorless hair spilled down over her eyes and her back bowed into the bed. Her legs flailed open further and her heels dug into the mattress. A scream worked its way up her throat.

As the contraction eased, the woman collapsed into the mattress, body sweating and limp. "God, oh God," she breathed raggedly. "Something's wrong."

"You're fighting it." Rafe slid the gun into its holster, his gaze never leaving her frightened, tortured face, which looked much too gaunt considering that she was so far along with child.

She rolled her head from side to side again, and, for the first time, focused her blue eyes on Rafe with something other than anger and suspicion. "What would you know about it? You a doctor?"

"Do I *look* like a doctor?"

"You *look* like a saddle tramp come begging for a handout or an opportunity to steal a helpless woman blind."

He smiled thinly. "I know that you're supposed to *push* with the contraction. The object is to get the baby born, not keep it in there long enough for it to walk out on its own."

She made a feeble attempt to close her legs and shove her skirt down over her pelvis as he moved around the bed. "Don't bother," he said. "There's nothing there that I haven't seen before."

"You haven't seen *mine* before." Lifting her chin, she regarded him with a haughty look.

"Guess I have my lucky stars to thank for that, Miss . . . ?" He began to roll up his sleeves.

"*Mrs.* And what do you think you're doing?"

"Long as I'm here I guess I should—"

"Don't you *dare* touch me! I'll—"

"This supposed husband will come crashing out of nowhere to shoot me, huh?"

"I *am* a married woman, you filthy, uncouth bastard."

He glanced around. "Lady, the only hint that a man might have ever visited this house is that baby doing its damnedest to be born, despite its hysterical and irrational mother."

She hissed at him again, and then contorted in pain.

Rafe retreated to the kitchen, grabbed up the last of the firewood stacked near the foot of the woodstove and tossed it into the bed of embers. Then he proceeded to pour water from a white enamel ewer into the kettle.

There was a partially full bottle of whiskey tucked behind a flour tin, a swig or two of which might help the woman through the worst part of the pain that was to come. Might relax her some, too. Not to mention him. What was he still doing here, playing midwife to a woman who was obviously afflicted with lunacy?

He took a swig; then he took another.

If he were smart, he would leave, ride into town and confiscate some midwife to see the woman in the other room through the ordeal of birthing a baby. What the blazes did he know? He'd witnessed the birth of only one other child; he'd been precious little help, other than to whisper support and pray to the Almighty that all would work out in the end. It had, thank God . . . for a little while, anyway.

No doubt about it, he was wasting valuable time by remaining here. One night in town and his objective would be realized—at long last. Then he could move on, before he was forced to come face-to-face with the man who would execute him for the bounty on his head . . . a price that would triple as soon as he put a bullet between Sheriff Frank Peters's eyes.

Shadows distorted the woman's shape and made the knees jutting from beneath the soft blanket Rafe had laid across her belly look like little amber nodes. He dunked a dishcloth into a basin of cool water, then wrung it out. Her lips were dry and cracked; she hadn't made a sound in half an hour. Only an occasional movement of her belly assured him that all was as it should be, regarding the baby. He wasn't so certain, however, about the woman.

Her eyelashes fluttered as he touched the damp cloth to her lips. She stirred. "Is it over yet?" she asked weakly.

"No."

"Something's wrong, I know it."

He brushed a strand of hair back from her brow.

"What are you doing in my house?" she said. "And who are you?"

"Just a man looking for a warm stove and a hot cup of coffee."

"So you just sashay into a person's home without being invited."

"Desperation and an empty belly make devils of us all." He wiggled his eyebrows at her, making her smile weakly before she caught herself. Her lids fluttered and her hands clenched as a spasm went through her. Rafe lay one hand on hers to comfort her for a brief moment, but her fingers closed around his, clutching like a frightened child struggling to be brave. He wondered how someone so frail and weak could hold on so fiercely.

She lay still and quiet, her eyes closed as the wind howled louder outside. Then she roused and her fingers twisted more tightly around his. It seemed as if she focused on something beyond him—her face, for a brief instant, becoming almost serene and without pain.

"Do you believe in angels?" Her eyes shone like dew and her lips curled as if in amusement. "Do you?" she prodded.

"I guess if I was to believe in angels, then I would have to believe in God."

"Don't you believe in God?"

"Once." He tried to tug his hand away. She held it tighter.

"You don't anymore." She turned her gaze on him, and it was penetrating. "Just before you came . . . I prayed to God to send help."

"That's called coincidence."

"I prayed that he would send me an angel to help my child survive."

Rafe shook his head. "Lady, I ain't no angel."

She was either dying or totally insane. Either reality

made Rafe turn his face away; it was one thing to watch a man die . . . but a woman was something else.

Her hand touched his cheek. Her fingers were cold and slightly blue. "Where do you go from here?" she asked.

"To Hell."

She managed a brief laugh that made her wince and catch her breath. "You sure found it, mister. You've come just about as close to it as you're ever going to get without burning the bottoms of your feet. If you're smart, you'll ride off in the other direction; maybe toward Fort Worth or such, or maybe even up to Kansas. But I wouldn't give Hell a second thought. Not unless you're a man hungry for trouble. Then again . . . you look like a man who's seen his share of trouble. Maybe even looked for it. If I weren't lying here half dead I might be afraid. As it is, I'd welcome death at this point. Anything to stop this misery." A smile toyed with the corners of her mouth. "I sure could use a sip of water. My throat's feeling as dry as this Godforsaken countryside."

Rafe watched her a few more seconds, hesitant to leave her. All this talk about God and angels was making him uneasy. So was the ashen pallor of her face. If she and the baby died, what was he supposed to do? Bury them amid a lot of sand and rock and prairie grass?

Rafe swallowed hard and turned away.

In the kitchen the ewer was empty. When he tried the water pump over the washbasin, it did little but sputter air and spit mud; so, sweeping up his hat from the table, he headed for the door.

The driving snow stung his face; it robbed him of breath and made his lungs ache, but that was all right. He needed something to slap some sense back into him. Feeling pity for another human being was an emotion that he had long since dispensed with. Compassion could mess up a man's mind; make him second-guess his motives, not to mention his objectives. Sympathy made bad men soft . . . and too slow with their guns.

It took a good ten minutes before he stumbled over the well pump in the snow. A thick film of ice coated it. Rafe was forced to give it a few hard kicks with his boot heel in order to break the pump handle free. An icy slush gushed into the pitcher, and in that instant the night erupted with a scream.

The ewer fell from his hands. He drew his gun and pivoted on his frozen heels. The dark yawned endlessly before him, around him, rolled over his head with a vastness that made him dizzy. Or perhaps it was only the blood rushing in his ears and his heartbeat slamming against his ribs. For an instant he'd thought . . .

Another scream, snapping him back from reality. He sprinted toward the house, skidded across the kitchen floor, then made his way to the bedroom. The woman was partially sitting up; her face looked like fire and her eyes were as round and glazed as bottle bottoms. A puddle of water and blood lay between her legs . . . and what looked like a cheesecloth-covered forehead protruded from her vagina.

"Do something!" she wept, then glared at him and growled, "Don't touch me. This is all your fault. God, what was I thinking? Why didn't I listen to my mother? I could be married to Chester Muesler right now and living in Boston, but no—I'm stuck out here with a lot of rattlesnakes and spiders big enough to saddle, not to mention scorpions with a penchant for my petticoats!"

His gaze locked on the emerging baby. A rock seemed to have settled in his chest; it felt a hell of a lot like bitterness and white-hot anger, not to mention resentment. He should have been in Hell by now, minding his own business and getting laid by some big-bosomed woman who'd dunked her body in cheap toilet water to hide the smell of the last man who'd bedded her.

"Well?" she shouted. "Are you going to stand there all day and gawk, or are you going to put me out of my misery?"

Rafe aimed his gun straight at her head. "Any woman with a temperament like yours *deserves* to be shot."

Her eyes grew as round as two blue china plates.

Rafe moved toward the bed, his eyes narrowed. "I'm not in the habit of shooting women and partially born babies, but in your case I'd do the world a big favor by shutting you up. However, I'll make you a deal. You stop fighting this baby and I won't put a bullet down your gullet."

Blond hair plastered to her head, she nodded.

"Now you swing your butt to the edge of the bed and prop yourself up on your elbows. Good. The next time you feel the pain coming on, you take a deep breath and push as hard as you can."

"The baby will slide right out on the floor!"

Grabbing up a pillow, he flung it onto the floor. No way in Hades was he touching that baby, or the woman. Soon as the kid hit the floor he was out the back door and on his way into town, blizzard or no blizzard. He wanted nothing to do with this apparently mentally disordered female, her baby, or the frilly, homey collection of gewgaws and lace doilies scattered throughout the house.

"You're crazy," she cried.

"What do you know? Indian women squat in a pile of

leaves and the baby tumbles right out on its head. If it was so bad for the baby, there wouldn't be a hell of a lot of Indians around, now would there?''

Her eyes widened; her teeth clenched; her hands, small but obviously work-roughened, twisted into the sheets so hard that her knuckles stuck out. Rafe raised the gun and pointed it at her again. "Push," he demanded.

"Go to hell."

"I'm already there, remember?" He cocked the hammer. "Push."

She pushed. Her face turned five shades of red and blue. The infant emerged another few inches and no more. Again. There came the child's forehead, its eyes, its nose, all covered in a filmy white tissue, then the shoulders— it was a long way down to that pillow, after all.

"Ah, hell." Rafe fell to his knees and dropped the gun on the floor. "Push," he said more softly. "One more time—a good hard heave and it's over. Come on, sweetheart, you can do it."

The baby slid into his hands.

The sudden silence and stillness were as reverberating as a dozen church bells ringing. "Don't you die," he whispered, tipping the little body slightly down and shaking it. "Don't you die, or . . ."

The baby stirred, kicked; its arms flailed and the quiet erupted with a sudden trembling squall.

"Damn, oh damn," he groaned to himself, and closed his eyes. "It's a boy."

Two

⚶

CHARITY BELL OPENED HER EYES. SHE HURT BAD ALL over, but especially between her legs. But that wasn't what bothered her most. She'd felt despair before—intense despair, like the first time she set eyes on what was to be her new home in Texas, but nothing like this abyss of hopelessness. She never, ever had wanted to die so badly as she did in that moment . . . not even on her wedding night.

As if that weren't bad enough, someone was tugging at her shoulders and forcing her to sit up. Someone with hard hands, someone who smelled like sweat and leather. She tried to protest, but the words lay flat and lifeless on her swollen tongue.

"Listen to me," came the deep, impatient voice near her ear. "This baby needs feeding, lady. I can do a lot but that's one area I can't help you with."

Baby? Dear merciful Lord in heaven, perhaps if she closed her eyes and sank into blissful sleep again she could wake up and discover that this had all been a horrible dream, that the last nine months had never happened—that the last two years had never happened.

Maybe she would wake up and discover she was back in Boston, living with her parents and—

He shook her, that stranger with big dark hands that were sprinkled lightly with fine black hair. Those hands were yanking at the buttons on her blouse, exposing her left breast; then they deposited onto her lap a squirming, swaddling-wrapped little bundle that latched onto her swollen, sensitive nipple with such suction that she cried aloud and shoved it away.

"Is that any way for a mother to act?" the stranger demanded and did his best to nestle the baby to her again.

"Take it away. I don't want it." She pushed the baby away once more, refusing to look at it.

"*It* happens to be a boy, lady, not a platter of old beans. And in case the thought hasn't occurred to you, *he* is your *son*. Now I'm telling you one last time, give up that titty or . . ."

"You going to shoot me?" She grunted and closed her eyes. "Be my guest. Just leave me the hell alone and get out of my house. I . . . want to sleep. Understand? I just want to . . . sleep."

The baby rooted at air, its blotched, squinted little face screwing into a silent cry of hungry protest. Frowning, Rafe removed the infant from the bed, holding it away from him as he moved to the kitchen, where he deposited the child on the table near a plate of forgotten food.

Now what?

Just get the hell out and don't look back.

Right.

Ride into town and drag some midwife out into the blizzard and let *her* deal with the unseemly situation.

He glanced at the squint-eyed infant, whose scrawny little arms were flailing wildly, his feet thrusting at their bindings. The child looked on the verge of squalling again.

It was then that Rafe noticed the book on the floor beneath the table. He picked it up.

Queen Charlotte's Textbook of Midwifery by Wilfred Gibbens, F.R.C.S., F.R.C.O.G., Formerly Examiner to the University of Cambridge; Formerly Examiner to the Central Midwives Board.

He opened the book, his eye catching the title, "Puerperal Insanity"; he read it aloud, and swallowed. If there had been any doubt that he should haul his butt out of here before this incident got any uglier, he suspected that the following passage would alleviate that.

> *There may be a curious and unreasoning dislike of husband, doctor or nurse, and she may show a complete lack of interest in the baby. After a day or two of this difficult behavior the patient may suddenly become wild and maniacal.*

His eyebrows went up and he cautiously peered toward her bedroom door. "A day or two my ass," he said to himself. "This one's crazy as a loon already."

> *She may come to threaten both herself and the baby. Another type of insanity is melancholia. In this condition the woman sinks into a state of completely dull apathy, refusing to take food or any interest in those about her. Insanity is commonest after a pregnancy of fear and anxiety as may happen in the unmarried.*

Fine. Just fine. That's all he needed. A lunatic on his hands and a baby that looked on the verge of wailing its head off for a mother who didn't want any part of him.

And all he'd wanted was a warm spot out of the storm and a hot cup of coffee.

The fire in the stove took hold at last. He made coffee, cleared the dishes off the table and sat down, sipping, doing his best to avoid looking at the squirming infant, perusing the book with his senses attuned to the escalating storm outside and the silence emanating from the bedroom.

There is a condition of deep and dangerous collapse which may occur within two or three hours after labor which, though uncommon, may be of great importance to the nurse in charge inasmuch as she may have to treat the patient before there is time to summon a doctor.

A perfectly normal labor may end in tragedy by the sudden death of the mother caused by pulmonary embolism. The uterine veins easily become thrombosed after labor, and if for any reason a fragment becomes separated it will escape into the blood stream and be carried to the heart and thence to the lungs where it will block a small artery and throw out of action the mass of lung supplied by the vessel. The result is sudden deep distress, inability to breathe, coughing of blood, and heart failure. Death may occur within a minute. Any slight exertion such as sitting up in bed may cause sudden heart failure. The preventive treatment of clotting of blood in the veins is movements of the limbs, or better still, set exercises and spells of deep breathing during every day after delivery. In this way circulation of blood is stimulated and the veins of the limbs are thoroughly emptied.

Setting down his cup, Rafe rubbed his eyes and the back of his sore neck. He left the table and wandered to the hallway, glancing back at the baby, then to the infant's mother, who lay still as death in her tangle of sheets and blankets.

"Hey!" he called to the woman. "You still breathing?"

No reply.

He moved into the room and to her bed. Her face looked as white as the pillow under her head. Bending, he focused hard on the blankets over her chest. Yes, yes, she was breathing. Maybe.

He poked her.

Nothing.

He lifted her hand and let it fall, limp and heavy as a wet rag.

"Look," he whispered near her ear. "I got no time or patience for this. I'm gone from here soon as the sun comes up so you'd best get it through your head that you've got a baby here who's dependent on you. Just you. It's up to you if he lives or dies, not me. I want no part of this. Understand?"

Nothing.

Cursing, he returned to the kitchen table, to the book he had left open and the infant, who had turned his face toward the lantern and appeared to be staring at it through the slits of his swollen eyelids.

Rafe gulped his tepid coffee and flipped through the pages in mounting frustration.

The average weight is about 7 lbs. but normal children vary between 6 and 9 lbs.

He glanced at the baby, measured the plumpness, or lack thereof, of its arm with a gentle squeeze of his thumb and forefinger, lifted the bunting from its bulbous little belly and protruding stump of an umbilical cord and decided there was no way in hell that the wrinkled little creature could come close to tipping the scales at a whopping six pounds, much less nine.

The normal loss of weight of 8 ozs. or more during the first four days is of no importance, provided that the child can feed normally. Undue loss of weight can be partly if not entirely prevented by correct feeding and by not allowing the child to become chilled at delivery. It is a much better practice than the bath to anoint the child with olive oil for the first two days, and perhaps give it an ordinary bath on the 3rd day. If the breast is inadequate, teaspoonful feeds of cow's milk (1 in 4) should be given while waiting for full establishment of lactation.

Wonderful. Not only was there no "lactation" going on, there probably was no olive oil within a continent of this damned shanty in the middle of nowhere.

He rummaged through the cupboard. There was flour, sugar, baking assortments and jarred vegetables, as well as pickled pig feet and snouts. There were giant cans of molasses, rice and lard; pepper sauce, salt, vinegar, coffee, fruit-jar rings, a tin of salted crackers and the remainders of a round of yellow cheese wrapped in a checkered cloth. There were squares of soap too, reminding him that he hadn't last dipped his backside into a tub of hot water since he'd celebrated killing Billy Bonner by buying a bottle of J.D. whiskey, a cigar, and a tub of water and cake of soap, which were supplied by a red-haired woman with the biggest titties he had ever seen. For a dollar he'd coerced her to join him in the tub out back of Kansas City's finest hotel, where they'd both got roaring drunk and he'd been forced to fish her out of the bottom of the tub before she drowned attempting to perform an oral service on him.

Yep. A hot bath would feel pretty good right about now.

The baby slept on the table while Rafe stewed in the big galvanized tub he'd found hanging from a nail on the side of the house. He was way too big to fit in it properly, so he took turns with body parts, washing his head and torso first, then his feet and legs, before settling his butt into the soapy, chilling water, allowing his long legs to drape over the sides of the tub as he leaned back as best he could and ate heated-over beans with cold cornbread crumbled into them.

He decided that things could be worse. Not much, but some. At least he was out of the storm. His belly was full, and for the first night in a month he would sleep on something other than the cold, hard ground. First thing in the morning he'd saddle up his cantankerous horse and make his way into Hell. He'd find some midwife for the crazy woman in the other room, take care of business, then mosey down to San Antone to spend a little time with his parents and brothers before he hightailed it to Mexico, then maybe to South America. Let that son-of-a-bitch bounty hunter John Wesley follow him into the flipping Amazon jungle, if he so desired.

There came a sound from the other room. Rafe stopped his scraping of beans and listened hard. A cough. A whimper. He chewed slowly and his eyes narrowed. What had that damned book said about coughing? Something about clots of blood settling in the lungs and causing instant death?

Jesus H. Christ.

Heaving himself from the tub, he draped his shirt over his front privates and tied the sleeves together at the back of his waist. Water and soapsuds streamed down his legs onto the floor as he eased to the bedroom door and regarded the sleeping woman. Her face was streaked with tears and sweat, her cheeks flaming with the blush of fever. She coughed again, harder this time, and rolled her head from side to side.

"Lord, oh Lord," she cried aloud. "What have I got myself into?"

It was frigid in the room. The fact that he was wet from head to toe didn't help. His teeth began to chatter and his feet to ache from the cold seeping up through the floor. He bent over to check her breathing again.

Her eyes flew open, her hands came up and latched like talons to the hair on either side of his head, causing him to stumble back and grab her wrists with a hiss of pain and surprise.

The shirt slid to the floor. He barely noticed. The woman's contorted face was thrust at his, and her eyes were those of a maniac, not to mention that she was working feverishly to yank every hair out of his head.

"You lying hypocrite!" she wailed. "I should've listened to my mama about you. She said you were no good

and not fit to wipe Chester's boots.'' She wagged his head
back and forth, causing him to grit his teeth and do his
best to unclench her. Impossible. She held on as fast as a
snapping turtle. ''I could be married to Chester right now
and living in a big house with servants instead of this
pigshit of a place. You and your holier-than-thou preaching and big dreams that ain't worth spit. You're not even
a man. I wonder what your precious congregation would
think if I told 'em about that? Be fruitful and multiply my
ass.''

He stumbled back until he came up against a rocking
chair that caught the rear of his calves, causing his knees
to buckle from the force of the banshee's momentum. He
dropped like a rock into it, still gripping her arms as she
wound up in his lap, her knobby little knees digging into
the tops of his thighs, her hands slamming his head
against the back of the chair.

Nose to nose, she stared into his eyes, her own wide
and puddling with tears, and whispered, ''It's not right
what you've done to me, Randy. It's not fair. I could
accustom myself to living like this if it wasn't for the
other. I'm your wife, after all. I deserve the privilege of
knowing my husband in every sense.'' She dropped one
hand to Rafe's lap and wrapped her fingers around his
organ.

Grabbing her wrist, he said through his teeth, ''Lady,
if you go yanking on that like you did my hair, I'm liable
to have to do something drastic. Let it go.''

Her eyes became drowsy.

''I said to *let it go*.''

She smiled, a sultry smile. The tiny lines at the corners
of her eyes turned up slightly and her lashes lowered even
more. Her tongue moistened her pink, full lips, and the

grip on his private part eased, just a little, enough to allow
him to take a deep breath of relief and relax a mite while
his mind scrambled for what to do next. That damned
medical book had said nothing about a lunatic turning into
a wanton.

Her hand softly stroked him, up and down. Swallowing,
he briefly closed his eyes, the realization striking him all
at once that he was actually aroused, or in the process of
it. She had finally let go of his head with the other hand
and was rubbing it fairly brazenly over his chest and down
his stomach. With a groan, he trapped her arms and
pushed her away, carried her at arm's length to the bed
and dropped her into it as if she were a sack of flour.

No sooner did her head hit the pillow than her eyes
were closed again. Her chest rose and fell raggedly, and
her brow glistened with sweat.

The dreams came and went. Good dreams about good
times. A pampered childhood. A soft bed with lacy curtains on the windows. There was her father, as always
dressed impeccably in his dark suits and white shirts with
collars starched so stiff they cut into the underside of his
double chin. He always smelled of soap and bay rum lo-
tion. His blue eyes always twinkled when he called her
"my sweet Charity." Oh, she did so love her father.

Claude Hesseltine was bright, Sunday afternoons spent
driving through Boston in an open buggy, the one with
spring suspension so you hardly noticed the rough,
bricked streets. "Only the best for my sweet Charity,"
he'd always declare with a puffing out of his broad chest.
"Only the best for the prettiest girl in Boston."

After their ride they would return home to be greeted
by her beautiful mother, Caroline, and the smells of Sun-

day dinner wafting through their three-story house over-looking busy Boston Bay. Servants darted here and there, seeing to the Hesseltines' every desire as the family enjoyed the splendid food and discussed their futures.

Her mother never failed to mention Chester Muesler and what a splendid match he was for Charity. How his wealth and position in society would make Charity the most envied and respected young woman in Boston. Caroline had been so certain that her daughter and Chester would marry just as soon as Charity completed her last term at the Fontaine School for Young Ladies.

Back in Boston she was never cold. Every room had a fireplace. The eiderdown bedcovers and mattresses smelled of the rose petals her mother collected from the masses of roses she grew in her gardens.

Back in Boston she was never hungry. Beebe, their cook, bought vegetables and fruit from the local market every morning. Their larders were overflowing.

Back in Boston there were no cows to milk, no stone-hard dirt to plow, no water to fetch from wells when it was cold enough to freeze the spigot. There was no soap to make, or candles to pour, or livestock to slaughter in order to survive.

There were no aching muscles. No sunburned noses. No hands grown so dry and cracked from the toil and weather that they occasionally bled.

There was no isolation. No loneliness.

No tears.

And no regrets.

Charity forced open her eyes, focused on the dark, solitary window covered with ice crystals. Outside, the wind howled. The walls rattled and groaned. Focusing on the oil lamp beside her bed, she listened to the sounds coming from the kitchen—pots and pans clanking together and the dull hiss of fire in the stove.

Then she remembered.

The baby.

Her water had ruptured as she sat at the table eating dinner and reading some medical book she had borrowed from Hell's only doctor. The pain had set in immediately, as if she were being torn apart inside. Randall Bell, her late husband and Hell's only preacher—the only preacher for some two hundred miles—would have declared the terrible pain a punishment for her conniving and manipulative ways. She could almost see him standing by her bed, his white hand on her enormous belly as he proclaimed, *"Child begot by lust will beget pain, for he is Satan incarnate."*

Thank God Randall Bell was dead.

Three

BY MIDNIGHT THE SNOW HAD PILED UP OVER THE BACK steps. Two hours later it had crept to the bottom edge of the back door and showed no signs of abating.

Twice Rafe attempted to rouse the woman in bed, gently, then not so gently tried to coerce her into feeding the fretful infant, to no avail. For hours he walked the floor, baby nestled in his arms, jiggling it up and down and rocking it back and forth each time it began to whimper. He rubbed molasses inside the child's mouth, which helped for a while, just long enough for the sweet to wear off; then the baby began squawking again until, finally, he fell asleep with his little sweaty head nuzzled against Rafe's throat.

The temperature continued to drop; the fire in the stove's belly diminished. Situated in the rocking chair near the woman's bed, Rafe fought sleep, thinking that if he slept they would probably all freeze to death. He hoped to hell his horse had found a cozy place between that cow and hog. With any luck the snowdrifts would cover the lean-to barn and insulate the animals from the cold. Then again, his horse had a problem with being closed in. Had never cared for it at all. The only time Rafe had ever attempted to stall the horse in an enclosed stable, the mule-headed gelding had kicked down the wall, which hadn't pleased the stable owner one little bit and had cost Rafe a week's pay to repair—more than the cantankerous horse was worth, for sure.

And thinking of cows. . . .

Someplace in that medical book he'd read something about feeding an infant cow's milk if necessary. The cow in the lean-to had surely needed milking. But it was damned cold outside and a long way to the barn.

Besides, feeding this baby wasn't his responsibility any more than his nursemaiding the child's feckless mother. Why should he freeze his butt off squeezing some cow smack in the middle of a snowstorm, deep after midnight when he should be coiled up in blankets asleep. He was tired, dammit. The bath, followed by warmed-over beans and cornbread, had allowed a lethargy to wrap around him. Still, he couldn't put the child in the bed with its mother because she would probably wake in another one of her fits and do something drastic. Now that he had time to dwell on it, he'd heard a few stories about new mothers going crazy and doing some harm to their babies. Any woman nutty enough to accost a man and threaten to damage his private parts could definitely be capable of knocking a baby on its head, or worse.

He glanced at the bed.

It was a nice bed. High. Plump. Warm-looking. (When had he last slept in an honest-to-God bed?) There was only one problem. *She* was in it. Looking at a bed with her in it was like gazing wistfully at a crystal-clear lake on a scorching summer day and thinking how refreshing it would be to take a dip . . . but knowing that just beneath the glassy surface roiled a bed of angry water moccasins. Chances were pretty slim that he'd crawl back out alive.

When had he last slept? Certainly not the night before. Or even the night before that. Hell, if he was honest with himself he'd admit that he hadn't had a decent night's sleep since he'd first cut a man's throat and watched his blood pump out into the dirt, turning it to mud.

A shudder passed through him.

At last he left the rocking chair and paced the room again, pausing at the window, which was mostly covered with ice and snow. His reflection stared back at him: a broad-shouldered slender man with hard, hollow eyes and gaunt cheeks who needed to shave and cut his shoulder-length black hair. Who was thirty going on a hundred years old. Whose Colt .45 on his hip had become as essential to his survival as the air he breathed.

Yet . . . there that image stood, cradling an infant to his chest . . . an infant he had helped bring into this world.

He blinked away the jarring picture and focused on the woman in bed, face turned toward the wall, pale hair strewn like dull yellow threads over her pillow.

Dammit, this wasn't going to work.

Rafe left the room and stood for a shivering moment in the little hallway while his wearied mind scrambled to divert the uprising of memories. It was then that he noted the closed door.

There was just enough light spilling from the kitchen to slightly illuminate the tiny windowless room, which smelled as musty as the inside of an infrequently opened clothes trunk. There was a solitary, cane-seated chair against the wall, a chest of drawers, and what looked like the shape of clothes hanging from pegs on the walls. But, most important, a bed. An actual bed. With a pillow, sheets and a quilt folded nicely along the bottom edge of the mattress. Maybe God hadn't finished with him yet after all.

The girl in the calico dress had honey-brown hair and the clearest green eyes he'd ever seen. They sparkled when she smiled. She had laughter like little bells ringing and he had fallen in love with her instantly. She had a way of looking back over her shoulder at him, a smile as alluring as it was innocent turning up her pink mouth. His heart squeezed painfully every time he looked at her, but it was a good sort of pain; the kind that radiated like warm sunshine through his entire being and filled him with a sort of weakness that most men wouldn't care to acknowledge, but kept to themselves like some coveted secret known and experienced only by them. Her name was—had been—Nora. Nora with the laughing green eyes.

"Nora? Nora, honey, I'm back and I've missed you like crazy. Where are you, baby? Nora?"

Nora?

"Nora!"

His eyes flying open, Rafe stared at the ceiling while his heart pounded so hard he could hear blood swishing in his ears. There was a weight on his chest that felt warm and wet. Cautiously, he raised one slightly trembling hand and touched it, his numb mind acknowledging it as a baby.

His eyes drifted closed again. The trapdoor of his memories eased open once more and the forbidden images seeped through like smoke from a genie's lamp.

He lay in bed next to Nora, her head resting on his shoulder as she slept. A baby nestled on his chest like a little frog, the fine spray of hair on the child's head tick-ling the underneath of his chin, and he realized at that instant how vastly the human heart could experience hap-piness, and love. He floated in it like a feather on a breeze.

But when he went to wrap his arms around the child again, it was gone.

And Nora was gone.

And the emptiness swelled back at him like a yawning black pit.

The day was a miserable pewter gray. Somewhere beyond the roiling clouds and sheets of driving snow was the sun, though a body would never know it.

The woman in bed had refused to rouse. The baby he'd cradled on his chest the last few hours had become un-responsive to his ministerings. Out of desperation, Rafe tunneled through the icy drifts at the kitchen door and slogged through the waist-deep snow to the barn, where he was forced to burrow through more drifts before reach-ing the dark interior. With his clothes sodden and his boots filled with melting snow, he felt his way around the cluttered building until he located a lantern, which he at-tempted to light three times with the matches he'd brought from the house, cursing at the thought of having to return to the house for more should these prove too damp to fire. He managed to light the final match and touched it to the lamp.

The gelding showed his teeth and pinned his ears at Rafe, no doubt thinking he was about to be dragged out into the weather. "If I was smart," Rafe stated aloud, his teeth chattering and his entire body shaking, "I'd do just that. I'd saddle up your ornery ass and ride the hell out of here—get as far away from this place as possible. But you and I both know I'm not always smart or I wouldn't be in this predicament now.''

The near-to-bursting cow gave up two full pails of warm milk and grunted gratefully as he squeezed the last drop from her tender teat. After forking a goodly amount of hay to each of the animals, he returned to the house and tossed more wood into the stove until the entire kitchen felt warm as an oven. Then he settled down with the weakening baby in the crook of one arm and attempted to spoon milk through its lips, just like the book said to do.

The child wasn't fully inclined to cooperate. More milk dribbled from the corners of the infant's mouth and off his chin than went down his throat. ''Drink,'' Rafe muttered, his lips tight with frustration. ''If you don't drink you die. *Comprende, muchacho?* I've got enough on my conscience without having to deal with that. At least open your eyes. Squawk. Do something.''

Don't just lie there and die on me—again.

''Do you like my bonnet?''

Rafe looked up.

The stark-naked woman stood in the doorway, her yellow hair as tangled as a bush and her face as white as the snow clinging to the windows. Her hands fluttered over and around the nonexistent bonnet on her head. Her swollen breasts bobbed up and down with each sway of her rounded hips as she glided into the room. There were pearl eardrops dangling from her lobes.

''Good God,'' Rafe muttered, and covered the child's eyes with one hand.

''Mama ordered it directly from Godey's. Papa says the daisies match the color of my hair perfectly and the streamers bring out the blue in my eyes. I saved it special for tonight. I've been looking forward to this opera for weeks, you know. Do you like the dress?''

She focused those wide blue eyes directly on him. They were as glazed as china. Her face had become flushed as pink as the underside of her son's little feet.

"I said, do you like the dress?''

His gaze slid down her white body, to the stretched and rounded mound of her lower belly, then down to the patch of pale hair at the juncture of her thighs, which were stained heavily with fresh blood. Slowly standing, he said, "Get in bed.''

Her eyes widened. "Why, Chester. How very bold and improper.''

"Get back into bed, and my name's not Chester.''

She pirouetted on her toes, offering him a generous display of her narrow back and firm buttocks. "Papa's quite certain this dress is the finest in Boston. He had it sent all the way from London, just for tonight. Do you care for the ruching on the petticoat?'' Pointing her toe, she went through the motions of lifting the hem of the gown. Her eyelids lowered. Her mouth smiled. "We're not leaving for the opera until you've convinced me that you like my dress.''

Rafe took a patient breath. "I like the dress. Now go back to bed before you—''

"What about the color? Does it suit me?''

Jeez. She was crazy as a Betsy bug all right, and getting crazier by the minute. He and the kid would be safer huddled up in the lean-to with his horse, the cow and the belligerently stubborn mule. Narrowing his eyes, his gaze drifting down the backs of her shapely knees, he said, "What color would you call that, exactly?''

Tipping her head in a saucy manner, lifting her chin just enough to cause the pearl eardrops to wiggle, she glanced back over her shoulder at him and tweaked her eyebrows. "White."

"White. Well, that's a right nice shade of white." He bounced the baby and patted its pink cheek. He tried to remember the last time he'd been in a room with a naked woman wearing only a pair of pearl earrings and carrying on a conversation about a dress—a nonexistent one at that.

"You could look a little more enthusiastic."

"My apologies. For some reason my thoughts are pre-occupied."

"I take it you don't like white."

"White's nice. It reminds me of bedsheets and virgins. And speaking of bedsheets, go back—"

"Papa won't allow me to wear anything but white. He says young ladies of my social station should always be cognizant of their reputation. Bright colors are for married ladies or the pariahs of the community . . . fallen women." She whispered "fallen women."

I'd give ten dollars for Papa to walk through that door right now, he thought.

She returned to the bedroom and Rafe breathed a sigh of relief, albeit briefly. In an instant she was back, with a closed frilly parasol resting against one thin pale shoulder. "I'm ready," she declared, as pompously as the Queen of England. Then she marched straight for the back door and flung it open.

The torrent of frigid wind and snow ripped through the room, scattering the curtains on the windows so that they leaped like startled rabbits. Rafe jumped from his seat, wrapping his arms around the baby. "What the hell are you doing now?'' he shouted, loud enough to cause the infant to bob his head.

With her hair flying straight back from her face, which was fast becoming damp, she smiled. ''What a glorious day! Perhaps after the performance we could take a ride in the countryside.'' With that, she walked straight out of the house and disappeared into a snowbank.

''Holy hell,'' he cursed through his teeth.

He laid the baby as gently as possible, considering the circumstances, in the bed on which he had rested fitfully, flanked him with pillows and blankets, then struck out for the open kitchen door. A goodly amount of snow had already mounded on the threshold. He slid on it before catching himself, then cupped his hand over his eyes to shield them from the driving wind and cold.

As if it were some glorious spring day, she stood thigh-deep in the snow, twirling the open parasol against her shoulder.

He sank to his knees in the snow before realizing he'd not taken the time to put on his boots. Still, he slogged his way off the porch, struggled through the drifts, ice stinging his face, plastering his hair to his head and his clothes to his body.

At least the woman had the good grace to look somewhat befogged as she stared up at the bleak sky, her earlier gay enthusiasm dwindling as her body began to shake and her skin began to go from milk-white to blue.

Rafe said nothing, just carefully removed the parasol from her hands lest she smack him with it, tossed it aside and swept the woman up in his arms. She was light as a feather and just about as thin. Her skin felt cold enough to shatter. Her breath slid through her purple lips in a vaporous stream as she fixed her attention on his profile and said, "You're not Chester Muesler. And this isn't Boston, is it?"

Stepping into the kitchen, he kicked the door closed against the storm. "No," he replied, and shifted her in his arms. "This isn't Boston."

"I was afraid of that."

Gently, he lowered her into the bed, snapped the blankets over her shoulders and tucked them under her chin. She looked like a child, staring up at him with round blue eyes. For the first time he noticed that her lashes were the color of golden honey. There was a beauty spot in the shape of a heart at the corner of her mouth.

"If this isn't Boston," she said in a thready voice, "then where is it?"

"Hell," he replied.

Her eyes drifting closed, she whispered, "I was afraid of that."

Four

IT SEEMED THE CRAZY WOMAN MAY HAVE BEEN TELLING the truth after all. There had been a man—a husband—not so long ago. Rafe found evidence of him in the spare bedroom. There was a trunk stacked with neatly folded clothes: trousers, shirts, coats—all black and somber. Hidden beneath them all was a collection of Bibles with heavily underlined scriptures, and tucked within the tissue-thin pages Rafe found a marriage certificate claiming that Charity Hesseltine and Randall Bell had been joined in matrimony on the seventh day of June in the year of our Lord 1868. There was a ring of keys, a pair of leather gloves, what appeared to be a deed to the house and property, and numerous papers on which had been scrawled rambling, ranting passages proclaiming damnation to sinners, not to mention the coming end of the world.

There was also a certificate, dated just six months ago, stating that God had obviously decided his disciple had done his time on earth and proceeded to drown him at Rattlesnake Gulch.

So. Randall Bell, the lunatic's husband, had been a preacher—which explained the extensive collection of religious artifacts scattered among the few furnishings and hanging from the walls, along with a scattering of spider-webs and long-abandoned mud daubers' nests, giving Rafe the impression that Mrs. Bell hadn't frequented the room since good ol' Randall was laid in the ground.

Hell's preacher. The idea made Rafe laugh, almost. He was too damned cold to find much humor in the situation. His clothes were drenched, his toes frozen. Firewood for the stove was buried somewhere outside under several feet of snow.

Since the only clothes he owned were the ones on his back, he had no choice but to drag out a few of the preacher's duds. The shirt barely fit across his chest and shoulders, and while the trousers' waistband was suffi-ciently ample, the legs hit him well above his ankles. No bother. He'd tuck them into his boots as soon as they dried. In the meantime, he'd take some of Randall's socks . . . two pair would do nicely to keep his feet warm, thank you.

The wind continued to pummel them. Snow mounded deeper against the walls of the house, inching over the north windows like frilly curtains, which was good. It sealed up the cold-seeping cracks and formed a barrier against the unrelenting gale, but in the process made lo-cating the dwindling firewood an exercise in torment, if not futility.

The day dragged on. Sleep no longer tapped on his shoulder, but pounded inside his head. To ward it off, he roamed from room to room, the baby nestled in one arm. Should he dare sit, even for a moment, he was certain to nod off and drop the weakening infant. Finally, Rafe lo-cated a blue-speckled roaster tucked behind some pots and pans in the bottom of a pie safe. After padding it with blankets, he tucked the sleeping child into it and wrapped him tightly.

He deliberated briefly over napping in the spare room or remaining near the baby's mother, perhaps sitting up in the rocking chair, knowing even as he paced by the preacher's room and glanced longingly at the bed that he would choose the chair. He placed the baby on the floor by the rocker, propped his feet up on the lamp table by the woman's bed, and rested his head back against the chair. His lids grew heavy as he watched the preacher's wife sleep.

Charity Hesseltine Bell had a very nice body, despite the fact that she had just had a baby: he'd noted *that* much as she'd paraded, naked, in front of him. There was something appealing about a woman's body after having a child. Curves became more rounded. Softer. Fuller. Even the most timid and helpless female became sanguine. How could a man not love—and respect—his wife more after she'd given birth to his child?

So how the devil did the preacher Bell drown at Rattlesnake Gulch?

Baptizing sinners, no doubt.

He grinned and shifted in the spindle-back rocker.

Maybe it was preferable to spending the rest of his life with a crazy woman.

But had Mrs. Bell been crazy before the troubled birth of her son?

Had to have been. Why would a woman whose husband had died choose to remain in this squalid little shack stuck out in the middle of scorpion heaven, especially in her condition?

• • •

He awoke with a jolt to pitch darkness and silence so heavy he could hear his heart beat. Only one other time had he heard such ominous quiet. . . .

What the hell had happened to the lamp? What time was it? Christ, he must have slept for hours. The room was as cold as a well. A frigid draft came swirling through the room, brushing his face and making him shiver. The back door. Oh, Jesus. The back door was open. . . .

Rafe jumped from the chair, his foot banging against the roaster-crib, causing him to freeze while his ears strained for any sound from the child. Dropping to one knee, doing his best to see in the dark, he searched like a blind man with his hands, at last locating the pan and its bundle, which lay very still under his touch.

His fingers stroked the tiny round head and the silken strands of fuzzy hair on the crown; he cupped the little cheeks and drew his thumb over the dry lips, getting no response, and deep in his gut a knot formed, driving the wind from him. Then . . .

A movement, slight at first, then the little head turned toward his hand and the lips latched upon the tip of his thumb and began to suckle. The breath left him in a rush.

Rafe left the baby and fumbled for the bed. It was empty.

Damn crazy woman.

He rushed toward the door, knocking his shin against a table, and made his way to the kitchen, hopping up and down on one foot and cursing. Just as he'd suspected, the back door was wide open—had been for some time, by the looks of the snow mounded on the floor.

The world outside the house was an eerie blur of black and gray; the wind had, at long last, ceased, as had the snow. The sky had cleared and sparkled with pinpoint

lights. Rafe searched the nonexistent horizon and saw little more than a deep dark stretch of emptiness. Where the
hell was she—the preacher's wife?

He discovered her tracks then, wandering aimlessly
away from the house. Sinking into the snow, he followed,
fighting his way along, expecting at any moment to stumble over her body frozen stiff as an icicle. There was a
tree in the distance; the tracks led straight to it. A moment
passed before he focused enough to realize that she was
there, stood up against the crooked trunk, rigid as wood
herself. She looked like an ice sculpture, glazed and crystalline.

A hundred thoughts flashed through his head as he
stumbled toward her. Strange thoughts. Disturbing images
as swirling and vaporous as the powdery snow that, raised
by the occasional gust of wind, roused like misshapen
ghosts around him. But they all narrowed to one: She was
dead. The child would die too, of course. He would be
forced to bury them together in a hole chiseled out of the
earth and rock, and pour dirt and pebbles over their innocent faces; he would lie in bed at night in a cold sweat,
fearing that, just maybe, he'd buried them too soon. What
if they had not been dead after all, but simply sleeping
soundly—too soundly to awaken. And he would fight the
urge to claw the sand away from their faces to make certain. . . .

The preacher's wife was sunk to her thighs in snow.
Her hair was glazed in ice. She stared out over the horizon
like some sailor searching desperately for a shoreline.
Rafe wrapped his arms around her and slung her over his
shoulder. She made no sound. There was no movement,
no sigh of breath or gasp of pain.

By the time he reached the house, all feeling had left

his legs and feet. He deposited her on the bed and wrapped her in blankets before searching out the lantern and fumbling with matches, his fingers too damn numb to manage easily. At last, he shoved the shimmery yellow light near the bed and focused on the woman who stared up at him like one in a trance.

She whispered. Her hands, like frozen claws, raked at his arm.

Bending near, sweeping her hair back from her brow, he said, "What are you trying to say?"

She tried again, her lips barely moving.

Rafe rubbed her face between his hands, then her arms and fingers. "The baby?" he asked. "Are you asking about your son, Mrs. Bell?" He rubbed harder, hope springing to life. Perhaps there was an iota of sanity rattling around in her head after all.

"Cat . . ." Her voice faded.

"Cat?" He shook his head. By now his feet and legs had begun to thaw. They felt as if a thousand fire ants were stinging him, and he was shaking so uncontrollably from the cold and wet of his drenched clothes that his teeth rattled. Gripping her jaw none too gently, he shook her and demanded, "Cat what? Speak to me, woman. Are you asking about your son? Cat . . . ? Catlin? Cat . . . ah . . . what the hell are you trying to tell me?"

She grabbed him with both hands, some of her old pugnacity returning. "Cat . . . tle."

Cat . . . tle?

"Cattle? You're worried about cattle?" Shoving her hands away and leaving the bed, he shook his head and pointed to the sleeping infant. "You got a hungry baby tucked into a pot like an Easter ham and you're worried about cattle?"

A seizure of cold overtook her. Her body began to shake so hard that the bed made bumping noises on the floor. There were tears in her eyes suddenly, and that unsettled him. He couldn't handle a woman's crying. Never could. His aggravation melted from him and he dragged off his clothes, tossed them into a sodden heap near the rocker, then peeled back the blankets from the woman's shaking body. A moment's hesitation passed, then, with a muttered curse, he climbed into the bed, dragged the quilts up over them both and pulled the woman into his arms.

Her skin felt as cold as marble. She squirmed at first, but he locked one hand onto the back of her head and held her still. "You're not going to like this any more than me, sweetheart, but I'm not about to let you lie here and freeze to death. You're going to pull through this for your son's sake, not for mine. If it's the last thing I ever do I'm going to see you nurse that boy. I'm going to see you hold him and smile into his little face and sing him a lullaby. A woman is never more beautiful than when she's smiling at her own child. It's enough to make a man's heart ache. Now be still. Quit squirming. You're freezing and I aim to warm you—and me, nothing more. I don't want your body. I don't even like your body. Not that it's a bad body . . ." No doubt it had been passably shapely before her pregnancy.

Rafe took a deep breath and slowly released it. Her head lay on his shoulder, her flesh warm against his. She had ceased fidgeting; her breath fell softly against his chest, and her hand lay on his belly, as warm as an ember. He stared at the ceiling until the first dim hint of daylight crept between the window curtains; then he slipped from the bed and quit the room.

• • •

At long last, the sun emerged and the temperatures warmed. Over the next three days the snow dissolved into icy clumps that sparkled in the daylight like tiny bits of crystal and diamonds. Along with the melting came the evidence that, once upon a time, there had been a working farm here. There were pens, albeit poor ones. Water troughs, a windmill, loafing sheds and discarded plowing implements. A chicken coop, housing a pitiful number of scrawny hens, was situated behind the barn. However, the most elating of his discoveries came when he dug through a waning drift of snow to find a sore excuse of a curing hut, in which hung a butt of pork and a salted side of bacon.

The realization that he would, at last, eat something other than beans and cornbread made his belly ache. With the butt slung over his shoulder, he hurried to the barn to milk the cow; then he tossed his horse, the pig and the suspicious mule a fork of hay and buckets of grain while his mind mused over the varied ways he might cook the ham. It was going to taste damn good for breakfast, for sure, fried with some of the biscuits he'd prepared for dinner last night. He'd stir up some redeye gravy too, using the remnants of this morning's first pot of coffee. He would try once again to get the preacher's wife to eat.

He returned to the house, removing his boots on the stoop and dropping them just inside the kitchen door.

Alex peered up at him from the blue-speckled roaster on the kitchen table. Rafe had started to call the baby Alex after his father, Alejandro. Why not? The boy could hardly go through life nameless, and as removed from reality as his mother continued to be, that's exactly what was going to happen.

Setting aside the pail of warm milk and butt of meat, Rafe winked at the wide-eyed infant. *"Amigo. Cómo está? Eh? Muy bien? Bueno."* The baby kicked and cooed in response, causing Rafe to laugh as he reached for an apron and tied it around his waist. He checked the oven heat, pumped water into a dishpan, then grabbed up a knife. "It's meat for the old man today, *bebé*. If we're lucky we might even convince the *mamasita loca* to join us."

He proceeded to saw away at the meat while the beans he had put on to cook earlier bubbled in the pot. The biscuit dough he had worked up just after dawn had begun to rise and in another ten minutes would be ready to punch and divide into a dozen rounds that would provide him with enough bread for the next two days.

Tossing a chunk of ham into the beans, he said, *"Amigo*, what say we work on that parlor after breakfast? After that I might scrounge up enough mud to pack into the crevices around the windows. By the looks of this place I suspect that the preacher Bell wasn't any better with a hammer and nail than he was at swimming. If this weather continues to thaw I might manage a nail or two in the barn as well. That roof leaks like an old sock. And there's a hole in the chicken coop big enough to—"

Click click.

He stopped sawing the meat. He'd looked down the barrel of a cocked gun enough times to recognize the click of a hammer being drawn back.

"Put down the knife," came the woman's voice, serious and steady as the Rock of Gibraltar. As he did as he was told, she said, "Raise your hands and lace them behind your head."

Arms raised and fingers laced, Rafe focused on a bubble in the windowpane. "Mrs. Bell, I presume."

"Who wants to know?"

"The stupid son of a bitch who saved your life, that's who."

"Watch your mouth, mister. The Reverend Bell doesn't appreciate foul language in his house."

"The Reverend Bell is gonna have to do a whole lot of earth shovelin' if he intends to wag the Good Book at me, now isn't he? Or maybe he and God have got some plan to strike me dead with lightning." Glancing over his shoulder, Rafe raised one eyebrow at the sight of the widow Bell, draped in a nightgown that pooled around her feet by a couple of inches, peering at him down the barrel of a shotgun. She appeared befuddled and more than a little crazy, and the realization struck him that she had no more idea who he was and what he was doing here than the man in the moon.

"One more move and I'll blast you to hell and back," she declared as he started to slowly turn to face her.

"Is that any way for the preacher's wife to talk?" He smiled thinly.

"You from the church?"

"I'm not sure. I guess it depends on whether or not you hold a fondness for your husband's congregation."

"I'd tell you exactly what I think about *that* lot of hypocrites but, regardless of what Randy thinks, I *am* a Christian woman."

"I don't think Randy gives a flying flip anymore what you think, Mrs. Bell."

A frown crossed her brow. The gun barrel sank a little. She looked, for an instant, as if she might faint. Her color turned as gray as ash. The thought of jumping her flashed through his mind, until the barrel snapped up again and her eyes narrowed. Her gaze took a studied journey up and down his person, resting at last on the apron tied around his waist. A smile flickered across her mouth before she set her chin and shoulders and raised one eyebrow.

"You're wearing my husband's clothes, not to mention my apron."

"You needn't remind me."

"This food. Who cooked it?"

"I did."

"Liar. Everyone knows that men don't have the good sense to boil water. Now you'd better tell me who you are and what you're doing in my house before I scream for my husband."

"Lady, unless the preacher Bell has been hiding under a bed somewhere for the last week and faked his own death certificate I do believe he's deader than the proverbial doorknob. And as far as who I am and what I'm doing here . . ." He glanced toward the table and the baby in the roaster. Reluctantly, her eyes followed, growing wide and disturbed at the sight of the infant. Her hands began to tremble. Her fingers tightened on the trigger.

Rafe slowly lowered his arms. His brow began to sweat. Obviously she was still crazy. By the look on her face he suspected she was about to get even crazier.

"The child is a boy," he said gently. "He's five days old. You had a rough time of it—"

"Oh God."

"We nearly lost you a time or two—"

"My son?"

"I call him Alex—"

Her wild gaze swept the room before returning to the infant. Her face became as red as the inside of the oven door before she swung the rifle barrel up his way again. "Get out," she hissed through her teeth.

Rafe backed toward the door, bumping the table and toppling a jar of blackstrap molasses in the process.

"How dare you come into my home and take up residence—"

"Careful, sweetheart, your gratitude is showing."

"And handle my child—"

"If it wasn't for me, you and that boy would be dead right now." He backed out the door, onto the frozen stoop and ice that cut through his socks like little knives.

Catching the door with the barrel of the gun, she slammed it in his face. Rafe counted backward before yelling, "You might stir those goddamn beans, lady. And while you're at it, go to hell!"

Five

A BABY. DEAR MERCIFUL LORD IN HEAVEN, SHE HAD given birth to a child. A boy. With ten fingers and ten toes and a head full of fine gold hair—and she could remember nothing more than snatches of images: someone poking and prodding at her, forcing food and liquid down her throat when all she had wanted was to sleep away the horrible heat burning her from the inside out. Why could she not remember?

Charity raised her eyes to the kitchen door. The man, the stranger who had occasionally occupied those brief memories stood with his hands cupped around his eyes as he attempted to look into the room through the mud-spattered window. Slamming the gun down on the table, she marched to the door—oh, yes, there were definite threads of pain stretching up and down her legs and coiling in her nether region as if every muscle in her lower body had been wound up tight as a steel spring—grabbed the open curtain with both hands and yanked it shut, obliterating the sight of the stranger's face, his unshaven jaw working and his dark, deep-set eyes blazing.

"Listen to me," he shouted. "I've worked my ass off

for you for the last week. You can't just toss me out like a sack of weevil-infested flour.''

Leaning back against the door, a weakness fluttering through her knees, she focused on the cooing baby. *Her* baby. Her *son.*

"Look," came his voice from the stoop. "At least hand over my boots and coat. Please. Before I freeze to death."

Her steps were hesitant as she moved to the table, her gaze locked on the child snuggled deep in a lining of quilts. "Oh my," she whispered, and touched his pink cheek with one fingertip. The little head turned in response, and his lips opened, exposing a rosebud tongue. The child gurgled and squeaked and kicked at the bindings around his legs. He made a tiny fist, which he waved in the air before finding his mouth and proceeding to suckle.

As if in response, her breasts throbbed. For the first time she realized how heavy they felt, and sore—dreadfully sore. Even as she stood there absorbing the presence of her son, her breasts began to leak, forming damp splotches on her gown.

The stranger, having moved to another window, tapped on a glass pane. "Mrs. Bell," came his muted voice, no less aggravated certainly. If anything he sounded more menacing.

"Go away," she responded, softly at first, then more loudly as he continued to rap. "Get the blazes away from my house." She snatched those curtains closed as well, only to have him move to another window.

"We have to talk," he yelled.

"No we don't."

"You can't just—"

"Certainly I can."

"How the devil are you going to take care of that baby? You're crazy."

"I'm not," she snapped, and closed the curtain in his face again. Spying his boots by the door and his coat hung from a peg on the wall, she grabbed them both, flung open the door just long enough to sling his belongings into the snow, then slammed it again. "Go away," she shouted, causing the baby to jump and begin to cry. "Now look what you've done," she shouted again.

The baby wailed.

The beans on the stove began to burn.

Milk seeped from her nipples and ran down her belly.

Where was Randall? Oh God... The maniacal idiot cursing her from the back stoop had been right. She remembered now. Her husband, Randall Bell, Hell's fire-and-brimstone preacher and most infamous whoremonger was, indeed, dead.

Thank God.

The stranger's breath fogged the windowpane, blurring his image before he turned away from the house and strode with an odd sort of animal grace toward her barn, his shins furrowing the fast-diminishing snow. Who was he? More important, what was he?

"Silly question," she said aloud, her words condensing on the same windowpane as his. "Any man who has business in Hell, Texas, has got only one thing on his mind, and that's trouble. He's trouble, all right. You can tell by the looks of him."

Her brow furrowed, and she turned away. A light-headedness made her sway; she leaned momentarily against the countertop, her fingers brushing a cup of cold coffee he had put there. There were traces of him everywhere, from the food simmering on the stove to the tidy pile of diapers he had invented from an old quilt. A stack of damp stovewood rested against the wall, drying. Dirty dishes soaked in a pan of hot water in the sink. Had she not known better, she might have believed that her mother had arrived sometime during her sojourn from reality. Then again, her mother would never have submerged her hands in dishwater, God forbid.

The baby squawked. Its face became red as it sucked hungrily on its fist and kicked at its bindings. For the first time Charity realized that the infant—her son—was tucked into a cooking pot. She hurried to the table, then hesitated; the realization that the baby was nearly a week old and she had never so much as held it—as far as she could remember—made her stomach flutter. Her hands shook. Gently, she eased one hand beneath his bottom, the other behind his head, and lifted him, her anxiety pacified by the sudden exhilarating surge of maternal instinct that brought tears to her eyes.

Oh, how she had anticipated this moment the last nine lonely months! At long last there would be a child to fill up her days and nights. No more sitting beside a solitary lamp writing letters to Boston that she would never send. He would be her best friend, her world, her existence. They would uplift one another. They would dream together. They would build an empire, and to hell with the rest of the world who thought them insane for remaining, solitary, in this bleak countryside.

She had long since decided there was something to being insane. It kept people at a distance. Like the Red Sea waters before Moses, the public parted to let her pass, their expressions solicitous but suspicious. They didn't trust her any more than she trusted them. She did not fit the image of a preacher's wife any more than the preacher himself had fulfilled their expectations of piousness. But because the Reverend Bell fell to his knees every Sunday morning and begged their forgiveness, they forgave. What choice did they have? In a place teeming with souls bound for perdition, Hell was forced to take what it could get and be thankful for it. But Charity never asked for their pardon, and therefore received none. They were welcome to think what they wanted, and to the devil with them.

The weather had been too damned frigid for Rafe to take much notice of the old barn, aside from its lopsidedness. But except for the occasional sliver of cold wind that oozed through the cracks between the rotting planks, the shed felt comfortably warm, due to the animals' body heat and the manure steaming on the floor. Pulling on his boots and doing his best to avoid a fresh pile of digested hay, mentally he scolded himself for wasting so many precious days on a woman and child who from this moment on would be nothing to him but an aggravating memory.

His feet were frozen solid; his socks were soaked and they squished inside his boots as he moved to his saddle where it lay on a heap of straw. The saddle weighed close to fifty pounds; it had been a gift to him from a saddle-maker employed by Rafe's father. Within the scrolls of tooled leather were Rafe's initials, as well as those of the home from which he had walked away—all with the intention of establishing his own dreams that had nothing to do with the raising of cattle, his father's passion. Rafe didn't want to think of his father as he easily swung the saddle up with one hand and headed for his horse. There was enough here and now to boil his blood. He needed no reminders of the past to add salt to this new festering injury.

He said to the horse, "It's not that I'm emotionally wounded over this. Hell no. Just because I delivered the crazy woman from death's door, not to mention her baby, doesn't mean I should expect and receive gratitude."

The gelding pinned his ears and swished his tail as Rafe dropped the saddle on the horse's back.

"I could've been done with my business and halfway to Mexico by this time. As it is I'll have to spend the next two days practicing my draw before I pay a call on our two friends." He reached for the girth and tugged it tight behind the horse's elbows, then stopped. "My gun," he said aloud. "That crazy bitch still has my gun."

"You're right," came the reply from the door behind him, followed by that all-too-familiar click of a hammer being drawn back.

Rafe looked over his shoulder. Charity Bell stood in the doorway, little more than a silhouette as she pointed his revolver at him with both hands. At least she was clothed this time, in an ill-fitting calico dress that barely covered up her fuzzy-stockinged feet.

"Why do I get the feeling this isn't a social call?" he said.

"You bastard."

"Many things I might be, lady. Bastard isn't one of them. While my father occasionally vowed to disown me, there was never any doubt of my parentage."

Moving into the barn, trailing bits of snow behind her, Charity briefly struggled to keep the barrel of the pistol leveled at him. Her chin quivered and her lower lip trembled. "What have you done to my baby?" she demanded, her voice breaking.

"Aside from delivering him? Or aside from nurturing him for the last week while you paraded around the house in your birthday suit and fantasized about being a lady?''

She raised the gun and steadied it. ''I said, what have you done to my baby?''

Rafe stared down the gun barrel. Her finger flirted with the trigger, causing him to swallow and take a step backward. She was pissed. No doubt about it. Best to humor her for the moment.

''Meaning?''

''He doesn't want any part of me. I touch him and he cries. I hold him and he squalls.''

''He's accustomed to being fed by now.''

''He's not hungry.''

''Could be a bellyache. Try laying a warm cloth over his stomach—''

''Didn't you hear what I just said?'' she yelled and the gun wavered from side to side. ''He won't eat. I . . . tried. He won't . . . have me.''

Her meaning nailed him.

Eyes welling, her chin quivering uncontrollably and her shoulders shaking, Charity did her best to hold the gun steady. ''Don't you see what you've done? My own son can't tolerate me any more than his father could. This child is all I have in the world and you've gone and taken him from me before I even had the chance to prove to him that I'm good and worthy of his love.''

''I haven't taken your son from you, Mrs. Bell.''

''You have! Now what am I supposed to do? Live out the rest of my life with *another* man who can't stand the sight of me? I could tolerate it with Randy. I didn't like him much anyhow—not after I got to know him. But this is my own flesh and blood.'' She swiped away tears with one shoulder. Her nose began to leak and she did her best to sniff it back, causing herself to cough. "I needed this child. I'm damn tired of being alone."

Rafe attempted to avert his eyes as she wept openly. His gaze stole back to her, to the growing damp spots on the overtight bodice of her dress.

"If your own child can't love you," she whispered, "who will?"

"He just doesn't know you yet," he offered, just as softly.

Quiet filled up the old barn. And stillness. Had the sky still been sugaring the countryside with snow, each little flake would have sounded like pebbles plinking on a tin roof. Rafe didn't care much for quiet, but he suspected that the preacher's wife had long since grown accustomed to it. Or maybe not. Definitely not. That's what this was all about. Her being lonely. Needy. She had sunk nine months of hopes and dreams into the child inside her, only to have him, in his ignorance, rob her of her precious maternal privilege.

"Tell you what," he said, forcing a smile. "If you'll allow me, I'll have a talk with him. Explain things. Then I'll go. I never meant to stay so long anyway." He shrugged, "I just stopped for a hot cup of coffee and a place to ride out the storm. I have urgent business in Hell, after all."

As if the weight of his gun had finally gotten the better of her diminishing strength, her arms fell to her sides, the one with the gun appearing slightly longer than the other as she turned, shoulders slumped, toward the house. His first instinct was to sweep her up in his arms and carry her back through the snow—as he had done twice before. But she was right. He had intruded. If she was to grow strong again—if he was to leave her to her drudgery of existing by herself on this bleak and desolate ocean of rock and sagebrush—then she must rouse and act; she must desire to survive even more than she longed to eat or sleep or cradle her beloved little boy.

He followed her to the house, putting his feet exactly where she had placed hers. The perverse thought flashed through his mind of him laying his entire body down on hers, skin against skin, belly against belly, the darkness of his flesh like a shadow upon her moon-light paleness.

Christ, he'd been barely more than a week without a woman (nine days to be precise—but who was counting?) and he'd grown desperate enough to imagine laying some preacher's widow whom he didn't find remotely attractive.

She climbed the steps and vanished into the darker interior of the house. The baby wailed somewhere beyond the threshold. He heard the widow coo and cluck, the sounds watery and desperate. He knew right then and there that he should leave—to hell with the gun, he could buy another revolver in town; one bullet was just as good as another when it came to blowing a sheriff's brains out—but he didn't . . . and he knew, eventually, he would come to regret it.

The preacher's wife hadn't exaggerated. The baby boy wanted no part of her. With a scream that could have cracked glass, the infant kicked and bowed his back, made angry fists that thrashed the air and his mother, too, as she attempted to soothe him. Rafe watched it all from just inside the kitchen door. Charity paced, the baby nestled against her shoulder as she gently patted her son's back and bounced him up and down.

"Hush now. Hush. I'm not going to hurt you. I'm your mother. Please, listen to me."

"You're too tense," Rafe told her.

"You're an expert, I assume," she snapped back.

"Babies are a lot like horses, I think. They can pick up on a person's state of mind with a perceptiveness that's spooky."

"Really. You talk like a man with children. Do you have children, Mr. . . . ?"

"Bastitas." He lowered his eyes from her flushed and sweating face. "And no. I don't have children."

"Then I suggest you stick to horses and leave the children to me."

A drollery nipped at his tongue, but he swallowed it and began removing his coat. After spending the last half hour shivering with cold, the mounting heat in the tiny kitchen felt suffocating. As he tossed the coat over the back of a chair, she turned on him abruptly.

"I wouldn't get too comfortable, Mr. Bastitas. You're not staying long enough for that to be of any benefit."

"I can leave now if you want." He reached for the coat as he turned for the door.

"Wait." The baby screamed louder and thrashed in her arms. In frustration, she hurried across the room and thrust the infant at him. He'd witnessed a man digging a bullet out of his own leg once; the look of pain carving the man's face had been only a little more intense than the anxiety twisting Charity's features. To add insult to injury, the instant Rafe wrapped his hands around the belligerent child, the baby stopped crying. He blinked his swollen eyes at Rafe and let go a noise that sounded like a dove cooing.

Charity picked up a pot off the countertop and flung it as hard as she could against the wall.

"Is that any way for a mother to behave?" Rafe shouted as Charity stormed to the bedroom.

"I wouldn't know," she shouted back, slamming the door. "I'm obviously not going to be given the opportunity to find out."

Rafe winced. With the contented infant nestled in the crook of his arm, Rafe raised one eyebrow and chucked the baby under his chin. "You're going to have your hands full with that one. I don't envy you any."

With that, he went to work cutting bits of dough and working it into rounds that he placed in a circular tin pan. As the biscuits baked, he finished slicing the pork butt and slapped a few slices into the iron skillet heating on the burner. The smells wafted. Soon he heard the bedroom door open and he reached for a clean cup and the pot of hot coffee.

But she waited, listening to the odd sounds of a stranger in her kitchen. Her stomach hurt with hunger as she tried to recall the last time she had eaten a breakfast prepared by someone other than herself. Certainly before she came to Texas, and that had been two long years ago; eternal years ago. Forever ago.

She leaned against the doorjamb and peered around it. The stranger—Bastitas—she mentally rolled the sound over her tongue—Spanish, not Mexican—moved expertly from the stove to the countertop, his free hand busy tending cups and a coffeepot while his other hefted her son as if he were little more than a corn sack full of goose down. Aside from Jake Callahan, a panhandler who'd set up housekeeping along the creek bed of Rattlesnake Gulch, she'd never seen a man cook his own food.

"What do you take in your coffee?" he asked, his back to her.

"How'd you know I was here?" she replied.

"Floor creaks. You want sugar?"

"One."

"Cream? It's fresh."

"Just enough to color."

He spooned cream off the top of the milk and eased it into the coffee. No doubt he had made the coffee thick enough to cut. Men did that. They liked to crow that it was stout enough to grow hair on their tongues. She'd always wondered why men cared to have hair on their tongues, but men were odd creatures. She'd long since given up attempting to figure them out.

After placing the cup of coffee on the table, he swung back to the stove, tossed a dishcloth over her son's face and proceeded to fork rashers of ham around the skillet. "Biscuits will be ready in a minute. You want an egg?" Glancing at her, one dark eyebrow lifted, he waited.

"Eggs make me sick."

"What about gravy? Gravy make you sick?"

"You needn't be so sarcastic."

He opened, then closed his mouth, prodding the crisping pork again before reaching with one foot for a chair and dragging it back from the table. "Sit."

"You have no right to order me about in my own house, Mr. Bastitas."

"Fine. If you desire to stand up and eat, you're welcome to do so. You may hang by your toes from a cave wall and eat if that's what you want."

Her eyes narrowed.

"Personally, I enjoy sitting while I eat. I also enjoy using both hands to feed myself. So, if you don't mind, you may take your son while I enjoy my breakfast.''

Her eyes widened as he dumped the infant into her arms. "He'll cry."

"No he won't."

"How do you know?"

"He told me." His plate heaped with steaming biscuits and ham, Bastitas sat at the table and reached for his cup of coffee, which he sipped cautiously, his gaze locked on her.

He had jet-black eyes, and long lashes to match. The fingers wrapped around the white chipped china cup were long and hard and brown—powerful hands, too powerful and menacing to administer comfort so adeptly to an infant. There was a sprinkling of dark hair and minute scars over the knuckles, remnants of fights, perhaps, like the thin scar that slightly nipped his upper lip. There was another on his chin, and still another that crooked up and out like a raven's wing over his right eyebrow.

The baby stirred in her arms.

So far, so good. No crying or wailing this time, only simple curiosity as the child sucked on his fist and stared up at her with midnight-blue eyes.

"You see," Bastitas said through the steam from his coffee. "He likes you."

She felt herself flush, and smiled tentatively at her son. "Do you think so?"

"Positive. Speaking from experience, boys are always slightly in love with their mothers, which is no doubt why we constantly look for a mate who most reminds us of the woman who gave us life."

Charity looked at him. He shrugged and cut his meat, stabbing it with the fork before saying, "Suffice it to say, we're in awe that a creature so . . . fragile can give birth to something that grows up to be as monstrous as ourselves.''

His self-deprecation bemused her. Odd man, sitting at her table as if he owned her kitchen, her apron tied around his waist, the smells of his cooking creating an aromatic swirl that tweaked some discomfiting emotion deep in her belly.

The baby squirmed and made an impatient sound.

''He's hungry.'' Bastitas pointed to a pan on the stove. ''I've warmed the milk. I've been feeding him with a spoon. It was the best I could do. Occasionally I let him suck on my finger; it seems to pacify him.''

''I don't need you to tell me how to feed my son.''

''No?''

The insinuation hovered in the air. Charity turned back for her bedroom, her cheeks growing warm with frustration. Just how much was she supposed to endure from this . . . interloper? He had taken over her house and her child. For the last two years she had survived on her own, for the most part—Randall had been little help in running the farm, too busy paving his way to hell, and suddenly she felt thoroughly helpless.

Rafe sat back in his chair as Charity slammed her bedroom door. He listened, jaw tight, fingertips firmly gripping the china cup as he waited for some sign that the child would, again, deny his mother.

Why?

Because he had become comfortable playing house. Because the checkered curtains, the larder that smelled like onions and coffee and molasses, had become too familiar. Because the child had filled up the emptiness and erased that pulsating void of pain in the pit of his heart. Because the woman and child had made him forget . . .

He sat for several silent minutes, watching a strand of sunlight slant through the kitchen curtains and pool on his plate of uneaten ham and honeyed biscuits. At last, he roused, scraped all the food into the skillet of congealed drippings and dumped in the coffee grounds; then, with the pan of scraps in hand, he left the house, pausing on the stoop to scan the yard. Here and there the remnants of plows and wagons and rotting fenceposts jutted up like old bones from the earth. The barn was in worse shape than he had first imagined. The house itself looked barely capable of riding out the next rainy season.

What the hell was he thinking? Here he stood on the widow's back porch with a skillet full of greasy scraps for the pig, his mind assimilating a list of chores necessary to keep her pitiful excuse of a farm from falling in on itself.

Returning to the kitchen, he dropped the skillet onto the stove, snatched his gun off the table where she had earlier placed it, and grabbed his coat from the peg. He moved to the stale-smelling living room where he had draped his gun belt across the shoulder of the mannequin he had blasted to hell the night of his arrival and, after sliding the revolver into the holster, slung the belt low around his hip and buckled it.

Good. That was more like it. The weight of the Colt grounded him to reality, reminded him just who and what he was—obliterated what he once had been. *That* Rafael de Bastitas would have fit comfortably in this setting—doilies and lace curtains and braided multicolored rugs on the floor, rooms that smelled both masculine and feminine. But he wasn't that man any longer, and the fact that he had fallen back into it so easily made him frown.

Nudging aside the living-room window shade, he stud-

ied the horizon. Empty for now. But that could change—
and would change. It was only a matter of time. The
bounty hunter Wesley wasn't an idiot. The son of a bitch
would come. He and Rafe would face off once again. One
of them, possibly both, would end up dead . . . but not
before he did what he came to Hell to do.

And hanging around some crazy widow's house wasn't
getting it done.

Six

STANDING AT THE KITCHEN DOOR, ONE HAND ON THE doorknob, the other resting on the pearl handle of his .45, Rafe focused on the floor between his feet and listened, and did his best to ignore the irrational sense of responsibility tapping him on the shoulder. There hadn't been so much as a squeak from the widow's bedroom in over a half an hour. All was obviously fine. A truce had been declared. The widow Bell and her son would live out the next years of their lives in harmony . . . until the lad's voice began to change and he suddenly realized he was not destined to make the same mistakes in life as his parents. Then he would pack up his few belongings and walk away, leaving his mother to weep softly into her delicate hanky and plead with him to write. And he would . . . occasionally. But not often enough.

His fingers turned the knob; the door shifted, allowing noon light and a stream of cold air into the room. The day was fast slipping away; he could have repaired the hole in the front porch by this time and maybe started on the barn roof.

It was stupid to leave a woman and her child alone this

far from town. Bad things happened to women and children who were unprotected. He should know. There were renegade bands of Comanche and Apache Indians. And outlaws. And Comancheros. Perhaps he could have abandoned a stranger with no compunction. But the widow Bell was no stranger any longer.

The least he could do was make certain she had plenty of bullets for her rifle. And enough firewood to tide her over in case another front blew through. And just to make certain, he would give the water pump a good going-over because it was all he could do to work it.

He walked to her bedroom door, listened with his eyes closed, heard her weeping softly. Nudging the door open with his boot, he peered into the dim room. The widow Bell sat in the rocking chair, which appeared to swallow her, her toes barely brushing the floor. The infant suckled on his fist, his face turned from her, ignoring his mother's engorged nipple.

Charity looked up, her countenance ravaged, though she tried desperately to hide it as she covered her breast with a flap of quilt. "He still doesn't seem to want me." A thin smile flickered over her mouth. "At least he's not screaming for you. I suppose that's some improvement. If he doesn't starve to death we might yet end up friends."

Rafe returned to the kitchen and grabbed the pan of warm milk. Charity frowned as he approached.

"Before you go getting violent again," he said, "listen to what I have to say. He's grown accustomed to the taste of this, and me. Maybe we just need to trick him a little. Let him think he's getting one thing while you're slipping him something else." He knelt to one knee beside the chair, dipping one finger into the milk, then rubbed it on the baby's lower gums. The little pink mouth puckered, then opened like a baby bird's.

"Now you." Rafe offered Charity the milk. "Try rubbing a bit on your . . . ah . . . well . . . just until he gets the hang of it."

"You're crazy," she told him.

"Maybe. You won't know until you try. Go on."

"Leave the room."

He almost laughed. "Sweetheart, you've got nothing hidden under there that I haven't seen before . . . several times."

Her cheeks colored, accentuating the cornflower blue of her eyes. The idea occurred to him that she had fine eyes, now that they were free of fever and insanity. With a sigh of impatience, he turned his head, and felt rather than saw her dip her finger in the cooling milk. There followed a symphony of coos, motherly clucks, soft pleading and whispered encouragements. Then—

A gasp. A groan. A swallowed sob.

He looked.

The infant, somewhat clumsily, suckled his mother's breast, his tiny red hands clasped upon the pale skin surrounding her nipple. Laying her head back against the chair, Charity closed her eyes and radiated her joy. Her face became luminous, her being weightless as sunlight.

She said, "I would scream in relief but I fear to do anything that might shatter this moment. Thank you, sir. Thank you for my son." In her exuberance, she thought nothing of touching his face with her hand.

Rafe backed away and stood huddled inside his long coat, the .45 pressing into his outer thigh, feeling heavy as a tombstone. The urge to touch the place where she had put her cool fingertips upon his skin rattled him.

Her eyes discovered the gun then and the light went from her face. All of her previous suspicions roused, forming deep lines between her brows. She clutched her son closer to her, coherent enough in that moment to feel afraid.

"What are you?" she demanded in a dry voice.

"You don't want to know, Mrs. Bell."

"I've seen enough gunslingers in Hell to know one. You wear that gun like a man accustomed to killing, Mr. Bastitas. Is that why you're here? Did George Peters hire you to get me off of this farm once and for all?"

"I don't kill women and children, Mrs. Bell."

The infant fell asleep, his lips still pressed against his mother's breast, a bubble of milk pearled upon his chin.

"But you're a killer, nevertheless."

He would have liked to argue that point. But couldn't, and his heart twisted a little. Not much, but enough to unnerve him. He had long since buried his conscience, or thought he had, along with the man he once had been.

The widow Bell said nothing more, just stared up at him and clutched her baby more tightly, her work-reddened fingertips stroking her son's head. He turned away and left the room, pausing long enough in the kitchen to remove the coffeepot from the stove burner and toss a couple of sticks into the fire. Then he left the house and took a long, studied look around the thawing grounds.

The water pump was a real bitch, so he pumped it a few times to prime it. When she came to get water, it would be ready. He tossed the chickens a few handfuls of corn, scratched the cow and pig behind their ears, bridled his horse and left the barn. Charity stood on the stoop, the door partially open behind her. The first thing he noticed was that she had brushed her hair. It lay like shiny corn silk over her shoulders.

Charity said nothing as he swung himself gracefully into the saddle and collected the reins in his gloved hands. The horse suited him: a big black bay with an exotic dished face. Its eyes flashed as it stomped and snorted, eager to get on with the journey.

How did one thank another for saving her life, and her son's life? He wasn't a man for sentimentalism. He was a killer, after all. He'd admitted as much. *Let him go. Turn away and don't look back.*

Yet it was the gunslinger who turned away. With a light touch of one finger to his hat brim, he rode off down the mucky road toward Hell. Charity considered whispering a prayer to God—just a small request that he watch over Mr. Bastitas—but with a sinking heart she realized that it was probably far too late for prayers to benefit the stranger disappearing in the distance.

Hell's bawdy district was no different than those in Fort Worth, San Antonio, Abilene or Denver. It consisted of a stretch of ramshackle wooden cribs—one-room shanties from which prostitutes worked. The cribs were a succession of wooden cubicles barely wide enough for a door and a front window, perhaps ten to twelve feet deep, which cost the "renters" twenty-five dollars per week. At twenty-five cents a lay, that meant one hundred clients per week just to satisfy the landlord—which explained the line of men outside each shanty door, their drunken hoots and hollers sounding like yapping coyotes in anticipation of a kill.

Rafe watched it all from his hotel window. "So what's your pleasure?" came the feminine voice behind him.

"Try bathing," he replied and took a swig from a bottle of bad whiskey. He was going to feel like hell tomorrow. His head already hurt.

The prostitute he'd hired for the evening was better-looking than most. She had wheat-colored hair and lips that were red and luscious. He hadn't asked her name—didn't give a damn, really. If he was still in Hell this time tomorrow night, he'd hire a different girl. Lately, he'd not been a man to form an attachment to anyone . . . so why did he continue to dwell on the preacher's wife and her son?

Frowning, he turned away from the window.

Unlike the crib girls, who covered their persons from neck to ankle in wool Mother Hubbard dresses, the "ladies" of Hotel Ambrosia sported brightly colored, low-necked, knee-length dresses covered in spangles. Black silk stockings accentuated their shapely legs.

With one foot propped up on the ledge of the tub, Rafe's companion rolled the filmy hosiery down to her ankle, cocked Rafe a seductive look, then peeled the silk slowly from her foot. She tossed the stocking toward him, then purred, "Now it's your turn. You might start with that mean-looking gun, unless you aim to use it. If so, I do require that you remove the bullets first."

He took a swig from the bottle, rolling the liquid fire around in his mouth before swallowing it.

The whore grinned. "I understand. You want me to do it." After peeling the other stocking from her leg, she sauntered to him, hips swinging, lips parted. Pressing her body against his, she draped the silk hosiery around his neck, brushed it against his unshaven cheek, lightly touched it to his lower lip and ran the other hand down the front of his breeches.

Her eyes lit. She laughed huskily. "Honey, you don't need no flippin' gun to prove your masculinity, not when you've got this damn cannon between your legs. Heck, *I* might be payin' *you* before we're done. Give me a swig from that bottle, sugar. I gotta feelin' I'm gonna need to be half drunk before this is over."

"You talk too much."

"Yeah? Well, you don't talk enough."

"I didn't pay you to talk. I paid you to—"

"We'll get to it. Just sorta got the idea that you were a man in need of lettin' off a little steam, is all. That's my specialty, you know. I can handle anything you want to dish out. The harder and faster and rougher, the better."

Her hand slid to his gun. He grabbed it.

She smiled, slowly withdrew the weapon from the holster and backed away, raising it to her lips. Her pink tongue flicked up and down the long barrel, swirled around the tip of it and dipped in and out.

Rafe's eyes narrowed; his body grew harder. "It's loaded," he warned her.

"I'm countin' on it," she replied, then slid her mouth over the barrel opening, moved her wet lips up and down as she backed toward the bed, allowing her dress to spill around her ankles.

Her breasts were pendulous. Her wild, thick pubic hair was the color of straw and wiry. As she lay back on the brass bed, she opened her legs and ran the gun down between them. She gasped. Groaned. Her hips writhed.

He moved to her like a stalking cat, slow and careful, fingers opening the gun belt, which dropped to the floor. Then his breeches, plucking buttons one by one until the pants slid to the tops of his thighs, but no further. His organ felt heavy and ready to burst. The ache sluiced like fire down his legs and up into the pit of his gut.

He flipped her over, pressing her face into the feather mattress. "I get it," she gasped as he moved between her legs, his dark hands like shadows upon her buttocks. "This way you can pretend I'm someone else."

He took the gun with some force and put it aside. Then he opened her up and drove inside where she was hot and wet. She squirmed against him, made little gurgling sounds in her throat as her fingers dug into the mattress.

"It's your wife, ain't it?" She gasped and squeezed her eyes closed. "You're pretending I'm your wife."

"Shut up about my wife." Sweat ran down his temples as he spread her legs a little further, thrust a little harder.

The whore gasped. "She's either pissed you off bad or she's dead—"

"I said to shut up about my wife, goddammit."

The bed bounced against the floor, sounding like rhythmic drums. Sweat burned his eyes and he closed them, tried to focus on what was going on between his legs instead of in his head—which was damn near starting to annoy him. He could will this ordeal to be over in a matter of seconds, but hell, it was a long night, after all. A man had to occupy his time, else he'd do something stupid like get himself shot before he could accomplish what he came here to do. Still . . .

He lay against her, his chest pressed to her flushed back, and raked her hair away from her ear. "I want to know about the preacher Bell," he said.

"You're a real sweet talker, ain't you?"

"Did he love his wife?"

"That piece of fluff from back East? Hell, Randy Bell never loved anything but little boys and whores."

"Then what was he doing with Charity?"

The whore did her best to look around. "This is the damnedest talk I ever had after sex."

"It's liable to get stranger if you don't cooperate."

"I'm startin' to wish I had that gun back. It was a hell of a lot more interested than you in what's between my legs."

Rafe took a deep breath, then slowly released it. With a groan, he drew away, rolled onto his back and stared at the ceiling.

The whore cleared her throat and moved to mount him. He shook his head. "Don't bother."

She lowered her head toward his crotch. He grabbed a fistful of her hair and dragged her back up, until her nose was pressed to his. "You didn't answer my question."

"I get it. You get off on talking. Ain't that a hell of a note."

"I want to know about the widow Bell."

With a huff, the whore flung herself against a pillow. Her breasts sprawled to each side like partially full gunnysacks. "She's pregnant."

"Not anymore."

"Had the kid, did she? Great. Maybe now she'll get the blazes away from Hell. She never belonged here anyway. Always held herself above the rest of us. Thought she was better than us. Used to put on all those frou-frou dresses and prissy hats and sashay down the street with her nose in the air. We all thought her marrying Randy was a real hoot. Guess she had some idea that being a preacher's wife was living in some quaint little house with a white picket fence. Reckon she imagined havin' the congregation in for tea and finger sandwiches and all that crap."

Crossing her thin legs, the whore scratched her belly and looked thoughtful. "She managed to play the part for a while. She come to church, sat there while her husband spouted on about the sins of gambling and lyin' and such. Then . . ." Her eyes going a little distant, the whore shook her head. "She began changing little by little, more remote. Always looked like she was in a perpetual state of the weepies. Then one Sunday the preacher Bell stood her up in front of the congregation and evangelized at the top of his voice about the sins of the flesh, and the wanton wickedness of the demon lust. He demanded that she go to her knees and beg forgiveness for her unrighteous behavior or else her soul was doomed to eternal perdition."

Rafe frowned and the whore chuckled. "There was speculation, of course. Ever'one figured the preacher Bell had caught his wife with another man. The question was . . . who was it?"

"Are you saying Alex isn't the preacher's son?"

"Alex?"

"The baby."

"Knowing the preacher Bell . . . I'd say you were right on the money." She patted the mattress and grinned. "Can we forget the widow Bell now and get down to business?"

Rafe looked away, the image of Charity Bell as he'd last seen her—hair brushed, cheeks flushed, and eyes sparkling blue as she stood on the stoop and watched him ride off—rising to stir something inside him. "Who is George Peters?" he asked, his voice going hard. "Her lover?"

"Lover?" The whore laughed. "Now I reckon that's one avenue that bastard Peters hasn't thought of yet."

● ● ●

Frank Peters reared back in his chair and propped his muddy boots on the desk. He scratched his crotch and narrowed his one good eye, first at his deputy and cousin, Lendon Hintz, then at his brother, George. "The two of you look like a couple of moon-eyed calves in a hailstorm. I told you I'd take care of the situation and I will, when the time is right."

"Ain't no time like the present," said George as he paced the floor. "Before you know it, summer will be on us and I'll be right back up shit creek. My cattle will be dying by droves and I'm out a flipping fortune . . . again. We got to act now. If we wait until my creeks are dry it's going to be damned obvious."

"George, you never was very smart when it came to making business decisions. If you was, you'd been bright enough to buy up Randall Bell's parcel before he did."

"How the hell was I supposed to know my creek beds would some day go dry? And how was I supposed to know that Bell's parcel was sitting smack on top of an underground spring?"

Sheriff Peters pared his thumbnail with a knife. "You could try buying the widow Bell out—"

"I done tried that a dozen times. She won't sell. Silly bitch has got some idea of raising cows herself. As if a woman has got the brains to know what to do with a goddamn cow. Hell, the last I heard she had contacted some breeder in England about importing stock to cross with her own. I'm telling you, Frank. She won't sell."

"She's got more to lose now."

"Meaning?"

"A woman will submit to a hell of a lot if it means protecting her kid. Ain't that right, Lendon?"

Lendon rubbed the back of his neck and frowned. His

brow had begun to sweat; his hands trembled as he glanced toward the empty whiskey bottle on his cousin's desk. "I ain't real sure I like the direction this conversation is takin', Frank. You know my feelin's on killin' women and children. Makes me want to puke just to think about it."

"What's wrong, Len? You back to having nightmares again?" Frank laughed and shifted in his chair, causing the rusty springs to squeal. "George, it seems our good cousin is eat up with a festering conscience."

"It ain't right what you done, Frank."

"What *I* done?" Frank raised his eyebrows. "You was there too as I recall. You had a piece of the woman, too, and right enjoyed it if my memory serves me."

"Taking a piece of pussy now and again ain't the same as killin'."

"The bitch deserved to die after what she done. She scratched out my right eyeball and kicked me in the nuts. A man's got a right to protect himself."

"What about the kid? That boy didn't do nothin' to you, Frank."

"He seen us, Len. He seen us cut the woman's throat."

"He seen *you* cut the woman's throat. Besides, he wasn't no more than three or four years old. He could never have identified us."

"Better safe than sorry is my motto. Better than spending the rest of your life looking over your shoulder."

"Gawd," Lendon mumbled and ran his hands through his limp hair. "I never figured you for a stupid man, Frank."

Frank exchanged looks with his brother before demanding, "What's that supposed to mean?"

Lendon pulled a folded piece of paper from his shirt

pocket and flung it on the desk. "That come in on the telegraph this afternoon. Delbert was shot dead two weeks ago."

"Our cousin Delbert?"

"How many Delberts do we know?"

Frank fiddled with the black patch over his empty eye socket. His cheek began to twitch.

Leaning on Frank's cluttered desk, Lendon stared hard at his cousin. "That's four of us dead, Frank: Jimmy, Lee, Billy and Delbert. That's a bit more than coincidence, don't you think?"

"What are you getting at, Lendon?"

"Each one of us was there, Frank. We all participated in murderin' that family . . . the woman, the kid . . ."

"And the husband." Frank dropped his feet to the floor and sat up straight. "I took care of the woman. Jimmy did the kid. And you, Lendon, put a bullet in the man's head."

Lendon backed away, shot a look at George before swiping the sweat off his brow with the back of one hand.

Pushing away from the chair, Frank rounded the desk. "There weren't no witnesses, Lendon. Ain't no way anyone could know it was us. By the time them corpses was discovered we'd scattered like sand in a wind squall."

"Then how do you explain Jimmy, Lee, Billy and Delbert?"

"Poor aim and slow draws. You know they never had the good sense God gave a horny toad." Frank opened a desk drawer and withdrew a full whiskey bottle. Lendon gawked at it like a pleading pup. "Why don't you run on to that cesspit you call home and drown your conscience in this. Tomorrow you'll see things in a different light."

"I shouldn't, Frank." Lendon licked his dry lips and

shook his head, his gaze never leaving the liquor. "It's been doin' crazy things to my head lately."

"Your head has always been crazy," said George with an impatient tone.

"You shut up," Lendon snapped. "You weren't there. You didn't see the look on that man's face when he was forced to watch his wife and son murdered. It haunts me, Frank. Ever' night for the last three years I've seen that look in my dreams and heard his wail of grief. I'm the last one who looked into his eyes and seen the pain. He wanted me to shoot him, Frank. He was a dead man before I ever pulled the trigger."

He swallowed hard and a sound of trepidation crept up his throat. "Somethin' come to me last night, Frank. Somethin' I ain't thought about since the killin's. The music . . ."

Frank's eyes narrowed. His lip curled. "What the hell are you talking about, Lendon?"

His voice dropping to a husky growl, Lendon rasped, "You made the man play that Indian flute. Remember? You made him play it when you was raping his wife. You told him that if he played real pretty you might not kill them."

"So?"

"I heard it again, Frank."

George made a sound of exasperation. "Damn, Frank. I come here to discuss important business and we got to listen to this idiot prattle about nightmares and Indian flutes."

"I heard it," Lendon repeated. "Sure as I'm standin' here now. It come to me in the middle of the night, light as a flutterin' moth. I thought I was dreamin' at first—like I always do . . . dreamin' about that kid tryin' to run to his papa before you put a bullet in the back of his head. Then I realized that my eyes was wide open, Frank, and I was still hearin' it—that goddamn music creepin' from every corner of my room."

"You're crazy, Lendon. Pure crazy. Ain't he, George? Ain't Lendon crazy?"

"As a flippin' loon."

Lendon reached for the whiskey bottle. "I'm thinkin' it's time we move on, Frank. Maybe head for Mexico before someone discovers us as frauds. We got no right to be wearin' these badges."

"Hell, Texas, don't deserve no better than us, Lendon."

Lendon shook his head, caressed the bottle and sighed heavily. "Maybe you're right. Maybe all I need is a drink and a good night's sleep. Maybe I'll drop by the Ambrosia first—see if Betsy is occupied. Sometimes a good poke before bed helps to clear away the memories."

"Good idea." Frank pushed his cousin toward the door.

Lendon stepped from the sheriff's office into the night that was black as pitch and bitterly cold. His eyes watered as he focused on the distant glowing windows of Hotel Ambrosia, and unable to wait, he uncorked the whiskey bottle with his teeth, then turned it up to his mouth, allowing the pleasure of the smooth liquor sliding down his throat to replace the sting of wind against his raw cheeks.

Judging by the number of horses tied outside the hotel, Lendon decided there was no point in calling on Betsy. She was Madam Sally's best whore and much in demand. Betsy was a real beauty, at least by Hell's standards. Her wheat-colored hair was always clean and smelled like a bouquet of French flowers. She had incredible tits. There was nothing she wouldn't do for a man if she liked him well enough. He ought to know.

There was only one other woman in town who could compete with Betsy and that was the widow Bell. There hadn't been a man in Hell who hadn't envied the preacher when he showed up with his ring on Charity's finger.

Lendon stumbled, fell against a porch post and, leaning there, took another deep drink. Heat sluiced through his veins, swept up the back of his head and thumped like a little hammer at his temples.

Aside from being pretty, the widow Bell was also nice. Too damn nice for Hell, Texas. Nobody cared for nice in a town made up of drunks, cheats, liars and thieves . . . not to mention whores and murderers. In the last ten years, every God-fearing, law-abiding sheriff who had taken office under the naïve assumption of making a difference in this evil infested den of iniquity had met his demise in a nasty manner, the last two being flung into a pit of rattlesnakes. Now Frank was sheriff and meaner than most of the no-account vermin who infested the town. No one in his or her right mind would cross Frank or his brother George.

Yet, the widow Bell was doing just that. And he, Lendon Hintz, would tuck his tail between his legs again and watch his cousins move in for the kill, like a wolf spider devouring a cactus wren. A damn shame, but what was a dickless coward like himself supposed to do?

Lendon staggered across the street in the general direction of the Ambrosia. Aside from the occasional feminine laughter emanating from the hotel, Main Street was quiet as a tomb . . . except for the low groan of the wind as it slid in and out of the alleys between the scattering of clapboard buildings with their sham facades. Mud sucked at his boots and spattered over his pants legs as he struggled toward the opposite boardwalk. Then he stopped.

He looked around.

The street behind him stretched into a tunnel of darkness.

The hair on the back of Lendon's neck stirred. He tried to focus on the dark, but the shadows from the buildings painted distorted images that made his eyes ache. "There ain't nothin' there, Lennie," he muttered to himself. "Frank said so. Frank's a smart man. Mean as a snake, but smart. It's just your own damn conscience gittin' the better of you."

Forgetting the Hotel Ambrosia and Betsy, he tottered down the mucky street, slipping and sliding, his stride growing faster until he broke into a run. Panic caused his chest to constrict. Hell, Frank would laugh his ass off if he saw him now, running from his own shadow, believing that the moan of the wind was the groan of a man watching his family die.

He ran down an alley to the back of Max Grove's General Mercantile, clutched the stair banister and made his way to the second-story room he rented from Max for a miserly fifty cents a week. Max let him have the room for half its worth simply to have the deputy sheriff living on the premises—as if anyone in this town took Lendon Hintz seriously when it came to law enforcement.

Slamming the door behind him, he sank against it, gulped for air and allowed his eyes to adjust to the sputtering yellow light from the kerosene lantern on the bedside table. The room was a twenty-by-twenty-foot cubicle with a solitary window and door. A chest of drawers occupied one wall, the single bed and side table another. A crucifix with a bleeding Jesus hung from a nail over his pillow. Lendon felt like a hypocrite sleeping under it, but to remove it would make him seem a bigger sinner.

There were times he wished he could close his eyes and never wake up. Spending eternity burning in hell seemed almost pleasurable compared to another night of reliving the murder of a family . . . especially since the music had begun. Haunting, haunting. Conjuring images of a man on his knees, doing his best to play a Kiowa flute while tears ran down his face.

"Stop it!" Lendon yelled to the four walls. "Just leave me the hell alone! Ya hear? It weren't none of my doin'! The woman gouged Frank's eye out—she shouldn't have done that. She should've just laid there and let him hump her and git it out of his system. He wouldn't have killed her then. Damn, damn. I need a drink. Right. Good. That's good. Damn good whiskey. Ah, Gawd."

Dragging open the top chest drawer, he rummaged through his sparse collection of wool underwear and wrinkled shirts, closed his fingers around a metal object and dragged it out, wobbled toward the bed and fell upon it, muddy boots and all. His tobacco-stained fingertips traced the delicate scrolls on the gold watch, the engraved script—"To R from N, With Love"—then he flipped it open.

The watch ticked in the silence.

Lendon's gaze moved to the tintype image of a woman's young face, her smiling eyes, her brilliant smile, her dark hair swept up in a coil around the back of her head . . . and the memories swept back, dank and fetid as wind from a grave.

A candle-lit table set for three. A home smelling of cinnamon apples and roasting fowl. A woman in a freshly starched gingham dress with her hair falling full and thick over her shoulders. A child with a sprinkling of freckles and bubbling laughter gripping a tissue-wrapped gift to his tiny chest. A shared cry of "Surprise!" as the woman flung open the door, expecting her husband.

Lendon groaned and closed his eyes. If he ever had a wife and children, he would teach them to never, *ever* open the door to strangers like himself.

Seven

SHE DIDN'T COME TO TOWN OFTEN, BUT ARISING THIS
morning before dawn, Charity had looked at the blue sky
and warming earth and decided she at last felt strong
enough to venture to Hell. There were supplies to buy.
Coffee was running low. The gunslinger who had occupied her life those few days had obviously indulged himself to extremes when it came to her staples. She needed
flour, and molasses. She hoped Max's mercantile would
have a new supply of thread so she could start on the
baby's quilt she had put off constructing for nine months.

Standing on the walk outside the mercantile, her bun-
dled baby cradled in the crook of her arm, she swept the
street with her gaze and wondered if Bastitas, the gunslinger, was still around. Not that she cared, of course. It
was good to have her house back to herself. Over the last
months she had grown accustomed to living alone. There
was something to be said for silence. Still, if she wasn't
so damn stubborn, she'd admit to herself that since Bastitas had ridden off into the sunset the once comfortable,
and comforting, silence had felt a tad suffocating.

"Well now, look who we have here. If it ain't the widow Bell lookin' right feisty and a whole lot skinnier than she did three months ago.''

Charity didn't bother to look around, just tugged the blanket more securely over her son and drew an impatient breath. "Syd Hayes. I could've sworn somebody told me you were bitten by a rattlesnake up at Copper Pass and died a painful death.''

"I'm here to prove I didn't.''

"But what about that poor snake? I'm afraid he came out on the short side of it.''

Hayes chuckled and moved around her, blocking her view of the street. "I declare, Charity, you're like a snappin' turtle when it comes to clampin' onto a grudge and not lettin' go. You still mad because of that little tiff we had?''

"I don't call trying to rape a pregnant woman a mere little tiff, Mr. Hayes.''

"Rape? Hell, that wasn't more than a little sweet talkin', sugar. If I'da wanted to rape you there wouldn't have been a whole hell of a lot you coulda done about it.''

Charity cut her eyes up to his. Syd Hayes stood six feet five inches in his stocking feet. He had shoulders like a bull, and a face to match. All that was missing was a brass ring through his nose.

He smirked at the baby.

Charity turned on her heel and entered the mercantile. At the far end of the long narrow room was an iron stove with fire glowing in its belly, surrounded by the usual collection of Hell's riffraff. They all gawked at her as if Medusa had unexpectedly popped out of the floor.

Syd followed on her heels. "I'm thinking you're going to need some help again now that the baby's here.''

"No thank you." She pasted on a smile for the glazed-eyed spectators. "Good afternoon, gentlemen. I hate to intrude. I can see you're positively swamped with responsibility, but I'm going to require a few supplies."

Max Grove picked his nose and said, "Looks like she had that baby, finally."

Bill Forester nodded and spat in the vicinity of a rusted tin can near his feet. He hit his boot instead. "Looks like it. Wonder who it looks like."

Jess Millford worked his gums before saying loudly behind his hand, "Two to one it don't look like Randy."

"Course it don't," returned Max. "My money's on Syd there."

They all guffawed and slapped their knees. Charity's face grew hot. "Hyenas, the lot of you. You disgust me with your asinine innuendoes."

"There she goes again, spoutin' them highfalutin words."

"Back East gibber jabber," said Bill. "Besides, I don't hear her denying nothin', do you, Max?"

"Such moronic and imbecilic defamation and character assassination isn't worthy of contradiction, Mr. Forester." Charity rested the baby on her shoulder and patted his back. He squirmed and burped, then proceeded to chew on her collarbone. "Now, if you don't mind, Max, I'd like to collect my supplies and be off."

"Can't do it, Mrs. Bell."

"I beg your pardon?"

"Got no more credit to let you until you pay me what you already owe me."

"But I was under the impression you would wait until this spring, when I sell a few head of my cattle."

"I reckon if you got the money to send away to England to buy some foreign-blooded bull, you got money to pay my bill.''

Her eyes narrowed. "How dare you. You've been reading my mail.''

"Maybe it's time to consider selling my brother them damn cows, not to mention your farm, and getting the hell back to Boston, Mrs. Bell—or is it Jeze-bel?''

Charity slowly turned and locked eyes with Frank Peters, who stood at the entry, his coat pulled back to expose his tin sheriff's star. She raised her chin a fraction and gripped her baby more tightly. "You can tell your brother that he'll get my farm over my dead body.''

"If I was you I wouldn't go around hatchin' chicks in front of hungry coyotes.''

"Are you threatening me in front of witnesses, Sheriff?''

"Just offerin' good advice to a vulnerable woman . . . and her little baby. Besides, you never know what could happen to your cows. Wolves are bad this time of year. You're liable to go looking for them one morning and discover the lot of them with their throats eat out.''

"Those so-called wolves would have to find my cattle first, Sheriff.''

Peters smiled; his single eye grew hard. "You'll have to bring them up soon, Charity, if you want to drive a few to Kansas. I'm just wonderin' . . . who you gonna get to round up them heifers now that you've got a baby?''

She glanced at Syd, recalling the stench of his breath on her face as he'd groped and fondled her that day three months ago. His tobacco-stained lips parted in a smile that made her breath catch.

"Perhaps Mrs. Bell forgot to inform you, Peters,'' came the familiar voice near the entry. "But the lady has hired *me* to take care of her cows . . . not to mention her farm.''

Everyone turned. Her heart leaping into her throat, Charity peered around the sheriff's form straight into Bastitas's dark eyes, shadowed by his hat brim. He filled up the doorway, his weight resting on one hip, his long coat drawn back behind the low-slung gun strapped to his thigh.

Frank's cheek ticked. He glanced at the gun, then back at Rafe's face. ''Is that a fact?'' he finally said.

''That's a fact.'' Rafe walked toward Frank, and Charity forgot to breathe. It was the look in the gunslinger's face—hate and fury in the purest sense. It popped like static electricity in the air around him.

Rafe stopped an arm's length from Frank. He didn't blink. His body looked hard as stone. ''I don't like bullies, Frank.'' His voice was a rasp that caused the men clustered around the stove to shove back their chairs and hustle to the rear of the store. ''Especially those who pick on women.'' He glanced toward Syd, then again to Frank. ''And children,'' he added with a coldness that made a spear of fear run through the pit of Charity's stomach. ''Any man who would threaten a woman and her baby is asking for trouble.''

''You threatenin' me, boy?'' said Frank.

Rafe grinned unpleasantly, his only response.

Frank's gaze shifted to Rafe's gun, then back to his eyes. ''Just who the hell are you?''

''Your destiny,'' he replied in a soft whisper that made Frank rock back in reflex.

Syd moved up then, stationing himself between Rafe and Frank. He stood several inches over the gunslinger and made two of him in bulk. There wasn't a man alive in town dumb enough to take on Syd Hayes. He'd been known to break a man's neck as if it were a stick of dry mesquite and toss him aside like a rag doll. Yet Bastitas didn't back down. Didn't so much as swallow in anticipation of what might follow.

Damn fool idiot, she wanted to scream. *What do you think you're doing? . . . and why?*

Syd smirked. "Funny. You don't look like no cowboy to me, mister. Looks to me like you do more talkin' with that gun than you do with a rope."

"You willing to find out?" Rafe replied softly.

"What if I am?"

A heartbeat passed—no more. As if time had ground to a near stop, Charity watched Syd's big arm lift to strike, swinging at air as Rafe stepped to one side and, in a blur her eye could not fathom, drew his gun and drove it up into Syd's flabby throat, the mouth of the barrel thrust against Syd's jugular.

Charity stumbled back, clutching the fidgeting baby to her breast.

A hoot of amazement erupted from the rear of the room.

Frank thumbed back the hammer; the double click shattered the sudden brittle silence. "As I recall, Hayes, a bullet entering your throat at this proximity and angle will splatter the top of your head over an area of some ten square feet. Max will be scraping your brains off the ceiling for the next week."

Frank wiped beads of sweat from his upper lip as his gaze shifted from Rafe to Syd to Rafe again. He took another step backward; one hand fluttered nervously around the butt of his pistol. His good eye widened as Rafe looked his way.

"What's wrong, Sheriff? You going to stand there all slack-jawed and pasty-faced and let me blow him away? Tsk, tsk. And here good ol' Syd was playing hero for you. Guess your choice of friends leaves a lot to be desired, Syd. What d'ya think?"

Syd swallowed.

"I suspect Frank's courage doesn't extend much beyond bullying helpless women and children. That's a pretty sorry requirement for a sheriff, if you ask me."

"Nobody asked ya," Frank sneered.

Rafe shoved the revolver harder into Syd's throat until the muzzle disappeared beneath a flap of flushed and sweating skin.

Syd whimpered and rolled his eyes back in his head. "Hot damn," he finally croaked. "Yore gonna get me killed, Frank, if you don't shut up. Jeezus, this bastard is crazy."

"And mean," Rafe added. "Don't forget mean. Mean and crazy make for big trouble because the crazy makes the mean get out of control real quick. Crazy can't rationalize. Crazy doesn't care about consequences. Crazy just doesn't give a damn about dying. That's what you've got to be careful of, Frank. The ones who don't give a damn about dying."

"Who the hell are you?" Frank barked.

"Jeezus," Syd groaned. "Who cares who he is. Just back off, Frank, so this crazy fucker don't blow my head off."

"Shut up, Syd!" Frank mopped his brow again. His lips looked pale and dry. "I've seen you someplace, mister. I can't reckon on where that was right now, but I will."

"I'm counting on that, Frank." With that, Rafe eased

the hammer closed and removed the gun barrel from Syd's throat. The mark on Syd's flesh glowed like a cherry. Rafe glanced toward the rear of the store, revolver balanced and pointing toward the ceiling. "It's my understanding, Max, that you promised Mrs. Bell that you would extend her credit until spring. I'd hate to think that a man of business would renege on an agreement he made to a widow and her baby. Tell me it ain't so."

Someone cleared his throat. Someone else shuffled his feet.

Rafe cocked the hammer again and Max made a squeaking attempt to speak.

"I bed your pardon?" Rafe said.

"Course Mrs. Bell—"

"What did you say her name was?" Rafe demanded.

"M-m . . . Mrs. . . . Bell?"

"Good. 'Cause I could have sworn when I was standing at the door that someone called her Jezebel and questioned her son's being lawfully begotten. I assume I was mistaken."

"Yes!" chorused several voices.

"And I assume that should any one of you encounter such comments in passing you'll do your best to quash such a stupid, not to mention dangerous, implication."

"O'course!" they chorused again.

Rafe smiled coldly. "Good. Now Mrs. Bell is about to hand you the list of goods she needs, then she's going to go wait in the wagon while you load up. Frank and Syd here are about to leave. Frank's going to walk directly to his hole of an office, knowing that if he so much as looks back over his shoulder or brushes his gun with his coat sleeve that he's going to bleed to death in the middle of the street, and Syd's going to waddle down to his brother

Ernest's blacksmith shop and hump his sister-in-law like he does every day good ol' Ernie plays poker at Jeremiah's Saloon. Do we all understand one another, gentlemen?''

Everyone but Frank nodded implicitly.

Rafe holstered his gun. He stepped around Syd, gently caught Charity's arm and pushed her toward the door. Her feet dragged. Every joint felt frozen by a terror she hadn't realized until that moment.

"Walk," she heard him mutter not nearly so gently as his hand felt encircling her arm. "For God's sake pick up your feet and get the devil out of this store before all hell breaks loose."

She complied, though it wasn't easy. Stepping from the store, into the street, the urge to break loose and flee momentarily overwhelmed her, as did the magnified sounds of rusty wagon wheels and the obnoxious hoots and hollers spilling from the saloon across the way. He took the baby from her, nestled him in the crook of one arm and with the other hoisted her partially into the wagon, planting his hand firmly on her butt with an insistent nudge. She dropped onto the wagon seat with a thump that made the mule's ears swivel and her head lift in mild surprise.

Someone stepped through the mercantile door just as Rafe handed the baby up to her. Their eyes locked for an infinitesimal instant, the realization of Rafe's momentary vulnerability sucking the world into a pinpoint of fear that stabbed something inside her. She snatched the child from his hands, a breath of ''Careful,'' slipping through her lips as he slowly turned back toward the mercantile.

Max stood in the shadows, mouth gaping, a fifty-pound sack of flour balanced on one shoulder. "You ain't gonna shoot me, are you?" Max asked.

"Maybe," Rafe replied. "I'm still thinking about it."

"Tell you what; you stay plumb away from my store from now on and I'll let these supplies go at half price."

Rafe narrowed his eyes.

"On second thought, she can have the damn supplies for nothin'."

Charity frowned and raised her chin. "I don't accept handouts, Mr. Grove."

Max's eyes brightened with relief; then he looked again at Bastitas and cleared his throat. "Ain't no handout, Mrs. Bell. Consider it a gift for the baby." He dumped the flour in the wagon bed just as Frank and Syd stepped from the store.

Rafe moved away from the wagon. Charity couldn't see his eyes; they were shielded by his hat. Something in her twisted, a sudden alarm that even she had not experienced when she herself had faced Frank and Syd's intimidations moments before. Dear God, Bastitas might outdraw one lumbersome hulk of a man . . . but what about Frank? What about them both?

Frank adjusted his hat over his eyes, and with a sneer on his lips, sauntered toward the jailhouse, with Syd following like a whipped dog. While no one else milling the streets would look at their sheriff's mood twice, Charity recognized the tenseness of his shoulders. The triangle of sweat bleeding through his shirt on his back, despite the bracing bite of the air, stamped Frank with nervousness, if not outright terror.

Frank entered the jailhouse, slamming the door closed in Syd's face. Syd took off running down the street, then disappeared into the blacksmith shop.

Rafe reentered the mercantile. In a moment men came trooping out, each loaded with the supplies Charity required. By the time the wagon was loaded, the old boards creaked and popped. The mule swished her tail back and forth, anticipating the laborious journey home and fuming about it. Having tucked the baby into a basket and covered him well with blankets, Charity grabbed the worn and moldy driving lines, her hands only now beginning to shake.

Rafe swung himself up onto the bench, his shoulder bumping hers. He reached for the lines.

She jerked them back.

He thumbed back his hat and raised one dark eyebrow. "Fine then. You drive."

"What do you think you're doing, Mr. Bastitas?"

"Aside from saving your pretty little ass again?"

Her cheeks flushed. The lingering pressure of his hand on her bottom made her draw back her shoulders. "You saved me from nothing, sir. If anything, you nearly brought about the demise of a half-dozen people."

"That's gratitude for you. And here I was thinking I was protecting a lady's honor. Damn, that was probably foreplay I saw going on between you and Syd."

Her jaw dropped. Her eyes narrowed. "Just when I get a tickling of fondness toward you I'm reminded that you're an ill-bred, blood-letting oaf."

"Ouch." He sank back and stretched out his long, mud-spattered legs.

"Get out."

"Can't."

"Why not?"

"I'm working for you, remember?"

She blinked.

"Unless of course you wish to have Frank, who's watching us through those tacky little curtains on his window, or Syd, who's working up a steam by now with Ernie's wife and imagining she's you, realize that you're a sitting duck on that pitiful excuse for a farm. Hell, you might as well jump up and down right now and invite them to shoot you."

"You're infuriating, Bastitas."

"So I've been told."

"Very well . . . I'll allow you to drive me home, on one condition."

"What?"

"That you not say another word the entire trip."

"That'll be my pleasure."

"And that as soon as you unload my wagon, you'll leave and never darken my door again."

"Best idea I've heard in *my* lifetime."

She raised her chin.

He grinned; then, looking over his shoulder, he gave a shrill whistle that caused a dozen horses to prick their ears and turn their heads. Jake came trotting, teeth showing and ears pinned.

Frank watched Charity Bell and the gunslinger roll down the street, the old wagon lumbering under the weight of their supplies. The stranger turned his head directly toward Frank, and though Frank couldn't see his eyes, shadowed by his hat, he saw his mouth, curled up on one side in a manner of arrogance and . . . something else.

"That son of a bitch is gonna be trouble," Frank said.

"You just got your nose outta joint 'cause he called your bluff," George replied as he finished peeing in a can. "Guys like him are all bluster, Frank. You see a dozen of 'em pass through here a week, flashin' their guns like it was their dicks."

Frank narrowed his eyes, returning the stranger's stare. "I got a feeling this one's different, George."

George joined him at the window, teeth clenched around a fat cigar. "I ain't interested in that damned gunslinger. It's that bitch next to him I want to strangle."

"Well she's gonna be a mite harder to budge now that he's around. Just think about *that* for a spell."

"There's two dozen men in this town who could take him out with a single bullet. And if that don't do it, then separatin' his head from his shoulders ought to."

Frank fixated on the disappearing wagon. "I got this feelin' we'd be doin' that bastard a favor."

"What the hell is that supposed to mean?"

"That we got ourselves a walkin', talkin' corpse on our hands."

George looked at his cousin. "You're gettin' crazy as Lendon."

"Am I?" Frank turned away, dragged his hat from his head and tossed it toward his desk. His mouth felt as dry as old wood shavings.

"Hell," said George. "If Lendon ain't spoutin' on about ghosts, he's rattlin' on about devils playin' Indian flutes under his bed at night."

"Somethin' about that gunslinger gives me the creeps." Withdrawing a flask from a desk drawer, Frank uncorked it and sat down in his chair. "I can't put my finger on it, George, but I had the feelin' when I was standin' in his face that I'd looked in them damned cold eyes before."

"Yeah? Well, we're gonna be lookin' in 'em again, Frank. Just before I stick a gun in his ear and blow his brains out. But first, I'm gonna let him watch me enjoy the preacher's wife. Yep, that's one fine piece of—"

The door flung open with a bang. Frank hit the floor behind his desk. George threw himself into a corner, tripping over his own feet and landing against the wall so hard that a windowpane shattered.

Lendon, breathing hard, stumbled into the room, his face as white as paste. "I seen him," he croaked, first to George, then to Frank, who cautiously peeked at him over the desk edge.

"I mighta knowed," Frank huffed.

"Numbskull," George muttered, standing up straight and kicking glass shards off his boots.

"One of these days," Frank said, climbing to his feet, "you're gonna come bustin' through that door and I'm gonna shoot you right between the eyes, Lendon. That's a promise."

"I seen him," Lendon repeated, wringing his sweating hands.

"Who?"

"The devil I tol' you about."

George rolled his eyes.

Frank settled back into his chair, heart thumping like a wild hare's. "Lendon, if you wasn't my cousin, I'd—"

"He came again last night. Just as I was driftin' off to sleep."

"Passin' out is more likely," George drawled.

"Maybe I had a nip or two. So what? I wasn't drunk. It came to me clear as pure daylight, Frank. First that damn music—"

"The flute again." Frank turned the whiskey flask up to his mouth, glad to be diverted from the gunslinger.

"Right." Lendon licked his lips as he watched Frank drink again. "It came to me in the dark like fog swirling over a gas bog—"

"Ain't we waxin' poetic?" George guffawed, hitched up his pants and walked to the door, shouldering Lendon aside in the process. "Sorry I ain't got time to hang around listenin' to more bedtime stories, but I got plans to make regardin' the preacher's wife."

"Fine," Lendon called behind him. "Don't listen. But I'm tellin' ya, a day of reckonin' is comin' real soon."

"And why is that?" Frank asked.

" 'Cause I seen him just now, ridin' out of town—with the preacher's wife."

George stepped back into the room.

Frank sucked on his lips before slowly recorking his flask and leaving his chair. He put the drink aside and stared at one of a dozen water rings branding the scarred and dusty desk top. The image of the gunslinger's eyes roused in his mind, and he felt the liquor he'd swallowed creep back up his throat.

Slowly turning his gaze back to Lendon, he said softly, "You're crazy, Len. Pure crazy."

"Crazy," George parroted.

Lendon took a step backward as Frank approached, his jaw clenched, his hands fisted. Like a snake, Frank's hand stuck out, twisted into Lendon's shirt front and with little effort slammed him against the wall. "Now let me get this straight, Len. You're tellin' me that the dirt farmer whose wife and kid we killed just rode off down that street with Mrs. Bell? You tellin' me that the bumblin' fool who couldn't hardly aim a gun as I raped his wife is the same man who outdrew me no more'n a half hour ago? Is that what you're tellin' me, Len? 'Cause if it is, I'd have to say that either you've gone plumb starkravin' crazy at last . . . or you been lyin' to me all these years."

"Lyin'?" Lendon blinked sweat from his eyes.

"Did I or did I not send you back to put a bullet between his eyes, just to make certain he was dead?"

"I—"

"I'd hate to think you'd leave such an untidy mess, Len. You did bury the son of a bitch like I told you, didn't you?"

"I dr-dragged his body right in with his wife's and kid's," Lendon stammered.

"And you shot him—"

"He was already shot, Frank. Remember? Delbert's the one who plugged him in the gut."

"You shot him again, right? Just like I tol' you to do. 'Cause cousin or no cousin, if I thought you'd left anyone alive that day, I'd have to kill you just on principle."

"Right." Lendon nodded and glanced toward the bottle on Frank's desk. "You're right, Frank. I reckon I'm just confused is all. I wouldn't lie to ya. That'd be stupid. It's just these damn dreams . . . they won't leave me alone. I keep hearin' that music you forced him to play while you was havin' his wife. It keeps comin' to me like—"

"Fog swirlin' from a gas bog," George taunted, and elbowed Frank. "He's twisted as a sidewinder, Frank. If that dirt farmer was still alive, would he have waited three years to come after ya? If he was alive and in Hell, Texas, he would've killed you by now."

Frank relaxed his grip on Lendon's shirt and backed away.

Lendon sank against the wall and released his breath.

"Git outta my office," Frank said, and Lendon nodded, pushed himself out the door and staggered into the street, his eyes fixed on the distant wagon, which was little more than a speck on the horizon.

"Course he was dead," he muttered. "Ain't no way he could have survived that bullet in his gut. Ain't no way."

Eight

∽

"I SUPPOSE YOU'LL BE WANTING TO EAT BEFORE YOU start back." Charity shifted the baby from one arm to the other as she stood in the doorway looking down on the back of Bastitas's dark head. He had nice hair—recently washed. It was thick and black as coal, and looked soft to the touch. A bead of sweat clung to the sweep of one side of his jaw, which was studded with beard. He shouldered it away before glancing back.

"You cook? I don't believe it."

"I'm a decent cook."

"I'll take your word for it."

Standing, he unrolled his shirt sleeves. The temperature was dropping with the sun.

"I suppose you have some reason for hurrying back to town. Her name wouldn't be Sally or Betsy, would it?"

He flashed her a sideways smile, flipped his hat up off the porch and dropped it on his head at a jaunty angle. "I don't ask 'em their names, Mrs. Bell."

"Bright red hair. Rouged cheeks."

"That about fits the description of half the women working in Hell."

"She specializes in preachers and married men."

"Well, I'm not married and I sure as the devil am not a preacher." He shrugged on his long coat, then reached for his holstered gun, which he had laid on the porch step. He draped it around his lean hips, then proceeded to tie the leather strap around his thigh. "You attempting to make conversation, Mrs. Bell, or simply trying to find out if I'm married?"

"Don't be absurd. Why would I care if you were married?"

Why indeed? she wondered as she watched his long brown fingers form a knot in the thin frayed leather. It made a slight dent in his leg—not much; the thigh was too hard to give much. The man himself was hard. She should send him away, like she had before. Get rid of him. He was trouble, pure and simple. A man with baggage. A man with hate. Too much hate to be safe.

"Just thought you might like to have a buttered slab of the cornbread I have baking," she said absently, her brows drawing together as she recalled the firmness of his hand on her backside. "It's a long ride back to town, after all."

He stood with his profile to her, eyes downcast. The soft shadow of dusk made his features sharper and hollow.

Charity stepped back from the door, one hand cradling the back of her son's head as she turned to the stove. Every square inch of her body tuned to the sound of his presence on the stoop—waiting. Then it came—a foot on the creaky old step. It had been months since she'd last heard that step creak. Always it had shouted like a bugle announcing Randy's arrival home. Company at last. Someone to talk to. Even if he did smell like a whore and cheap gin. *Ah, Randy, you sorry excuse for a human be-ing, robbing me of my youth and dreams.*

"Drag up a chair and relax," she called over her shoulder as she hurried to her bedroom. "I've put on a fresh pot of coffee. It'll be ready directly. You know where I keep the sugar. There's fresh cream, too. I churned this morning so there'll be good butter for the bread. Do you like your cornbread sweet or not?"

"Not," came the masculine response, and she paused, her cheek pressed against the baby's warm brow. One thing about the gunslinger, he was pointed if nothing else. Chester Muesler, along with most well-bred Boston men, her father included, would have rushed to assure her that any sort of cornbread would be fine—just fine, long as *she'd* made it.

"Good," she called out. " 'Cause I didn't make it sweet."

Placing the baby in the center of the bed, Charity tucked the quilt snugly about the tiny body and patted him lightly on the back. He cooed and gummed his fist. He kicked his bound feet. "Hush now," she whispered, and hummed softly until the babe's eyelids fluttered closed.

She hurried to the mirrored dresser and groaned at the sight of her disheveled image, dusty from the day's travels. The skirt still pinched a little too tightly around the waist. The blouse gaped at the buttons. Quickly, she pulled back strands of hair that had fallen around her face and fastened them with a tortoise-shell comb. She pinched color into her cheeks, licked her lips, and wondered aloud, "God, what am I doing? I must be desperate if I give a rotten fig what that unprincipled man thinks about my appearance."

But she did care, heaven help her. She'd cared from the moment he'd planted his hand on her backside to help her into the wagon. She'd cared the entire ride home with her body pressed next to his. In her mind she had planned tonight's dinner, imagined how she'd wear her hair, what dress to don: a cornflower-blue blouse exactly the shade of her eyes, a fawn-colored skirt scattered with minuscule beige daisies. While he unloaded supplies, she'd hurriedly chopped potatoes, onions and carrots; she'd seared chunks of mutton, being careful not to burn her fingers because every time he walked into the room with another load of supplies her entire body had begun to tremble. When he'd asked for a glass of water, she'd felt like some giddy adolescent on the verge of swooning. She'd washed her hair, claiming the ride to and from town had made it gritty.

Why?

Because before he'd saved her and her son's lives, she had existed in a vacuum of monotony and isolation. Over the long months of marriage to Randall Bell, she had gradually grown accustomed to aloneness, and loneliness. But the morning she'd stood on the porch and watched the gunslinger ride away, that once tolerable vacuum had again slammed down around her so fiercely that she thought she might crumble beneath the weight of it; and as the next slow days trudged by, she had been surprised to discover how much she missed him—not him, of course, just his company . . . and the feeling he had given her that as long as he was there, in her house, she was safe. When the realization had finally sunk in that he would no longer be there to see after her comfort and safety, the anticipated sense of relief had not come, but rather a foggy sensation of insecurity and loss settled into every dusty nook and cranny in her house.

He wasn't the sort of man she found attractive, normally. Still, if she was honest with herself, she'd acknowledge that there was something appealing about his ruggedness—nothing like Randall or Chester, or any of the dashing swains she had known in Boston, all of whom had never known a day's labor in the sun. Their skin hadn't been dark, or their hair shaggy, or their bodies hard. Their eyes hadn't reminded her of hot cinders. A solitary glance at their mouths had not made her skin flush.

Charity took a fortifying breath before leaving her room.

Bastitas sat somewhat slumped in a kitchen chair, legs outstretched and crossed at the ankles, fingers laced together on his stomach, eyes drowsy. He still wore his gun. He'd left his dirty boots by the door, along with his hat and long coat.

At her entry, his eyelashes lifted. Nothing else moved.

"I've made stew," she said, curling her fingers into the folds of her limp skirt.

"I know."

"Would you care for coffee?"

"Long as you douse it with some of that whiskey you keep in the upper cupboard."

"Obviously you've taken the liberty to learn your way around my house sufficiently."

"Yes, ma'am." His tone was droll enough to lift her eyebrows and agitate her nervousness.

The coffee was hot and thick—too thick for her, but she knew he liked it that way. She added the whiskey, then doctored her own with sugar and cream, and the whiskey too—just a splash to smooth away the bitter bite of the coffee. The daring of doing so made her smile a little. She and whiskey weren't compatible—so why was she indulging now, in the company of a man with trouble stamped on his features?

Her fingers trembled slightly as she placed the cup on the table and nudged it toward him.

He sat up, his gaze coming back to hers. "Something wrong?" He sipped the coffee gently.

"No." She shook her head. "I was just thinking ... how small this kitchen seems when you're in it."

"Not accustomed to sharing space, I assume."

"Not recently." She closed both hands around her hot cup. Steam tickled her nose and made her cheeks warm and moist.

"That'll change soon enough." He drank again.

"Meaning?"

"The boy, of course. What did you think I meant?"

"I didn't think. Of course, the baby will be scooting about underfoot in no time. I'll be wishing for more room by then."

"What have you named him?"

"Named him?"

"The baby. Remember him?"

"Of course." She gulped the coffee, burning the roof of her mouth. God, why had she invited him to stay? She simply wasn't good at this any longer. Chitchat was for delicate women exchanging gossip over tea and petit fours. "I ... haven't."

"Haven't?"

"Named him ... yet."

"Boy needs a name."

"You're right, of course. But I have to be certain. It

has to be right. I hadn't really counted on a boy."

"A woman alone needs a son. Someone to help run the farm. Take care of those chores that are too hard on the woman."

"I've done well enough on my own."

"What about plowing?"

"I manage, thanks to Connie."

"Connie?"

"My mule, of course."

He thought, *Leave it to her to name a mule Connie!*

"What will you do now, carry the baby like a papoose on your back?"

"If necessary." She shrugged. "Really, Mr. Bastitas, I'm not the first widow with an infant. I'll manage. I simply have no choice."

He shoved the empty cup at her. She refilled it with coffee and whiskey before topping her own. The kitchen felt unbearably hot, what with the oven roaring, the stew bubbling. By the smell of it, the cornbread was beginning to brown. Another few minutes and it would be ready to come out.

She sat down directly across from him and focused on her coffee.

"So tell me about this bull you're importing from England."

"Why?" She smiled dryly. "So you can laugh at me too?"

"I happen to know a few things about cows, or rather bulls. Depending on the bulls, of course."

"I intend to cross him with longhorns. I'll get more meat on the hoof, and better quality."

"Not if George Peters has any say so in the matter."

"I'm not afraid of George Peters."

"You should be. If I were you I'd pack up my clothes and baby and get the hell away from here."

The coffee had grown cool. She drank it down any way, the whiskey making her shudder. An open window might alleviate the warmth, she thought, and mopped her brow with the back of her hand, knowing even as she stood, weaving slightly, that there was no hope of prying open the window. She'd painted them in the fall and they'd sealed tight.

So she walked to the back door and swung it open. Cool wind rushed around her, tugged her hair from the comb and fluttered the hem of her skirt. "You sound like another one of Peters's bullies, Mr. Bastitas. I had not thought of that. Perhaps that's who you really are, a gunslinger he's hired to do me in. Perhaps all that bravado and gunplay this morning was nothing more than a ruse to disarm my suspicions."

"If I'd come here to kill you I wouldn't have needed a gun to do it. Not in the condition you were in when I found you."

"Oh, please. Must you remind me constantly that you're a hero? I've said thank you. What more do you want, aside from my leaving my farm to vermin like Peters?"

"It's not safe for a woman to be out here alone."

"Don't preach, Mr. Bastitas. It doesn't suit you. Besides, I've had a stomach full of preaching. Charity, don't do this. Don't do that. Telling me what I should or shouldn't do. How to talk. How to walk. How to dress. How to keep my eyes lowered demurely while in God's house. How to keep my body covered modestly while in the preacher's house."

Leaning against the doorframe, arms crossed tightly

across her chest, she searched the treeless horizon. "Believe it or not, Mr. Bastitas, I once was a beautiful woman." Her head fell back and she laughed huskily at the darkening sky. "Once upon a time in a place called Boston my skin was soft and white. My lips were moist. My hands were smooth as the petals of a lily. And my hair?" Flinging the comb away, she allowed her hair to spill. It danced like feathers in the wind around her face as she pressed her back to the doorframe, a silhouette against the expanding night. "My hair shone like candlelight, Mr. Bastitas. It smelled of heavenly perfume. It flowed like gold water through my fingers. Once. Once. Once."

She sighed heavily and looked at her companion at last. He sat in partial darkness, the red and yellow of the oven fire casting glints of color on his black hair. Something in his look was predatory. It made her heartbeat escalate, exaggerated the whiskey's sweet lethargy thrumming in her veins.

"Would it shock you to know that I was a miserable failure as a preacher's wife?" she said.

A hesitation, then a shrug—his only response.

"One would think a prim and proper young woman from Boston would make the ideal companion for a man of God. One would be wrong, however, to think that of me. I was never really prim and proper, not inwardly. I found my peers silly and boring. Spending a lifetime with a man like Chester Muesler seemed a lifetime of slow, suffocating death. Then again, when I look around . . ." She searched the hazy interior of the tiny kitchen, then looked again to the now nonexistent horizon and the stars winking to life in the indigo sky.

"Certainly, there are times when I would give my heart

for a solitary creature comfort. Perhaps it's simply unreasonable to believe a person could have the freedom she so craves, another human being to love, and wealth too. Then again, my father always said I was too greedy. 'Life is compromise,' he'd declare. 'If life were perfect there would be no need for heaven.' Still, a woman has needs and desires, just like a man. Should we be condemned for it?''

He remained silent.

"Am I boring you, Mr. Bastitas?"

"Hardly," came his simple response.

"Tell me, Mr. Bastitas. What are your needs and desires?"

"Typically?" He laughed softly and shifted in his chair. "A bottle of good whiskey in one hand, and a beautiful woman beneath me."

"That sounds simple enough."

"Not really . . . It's hard to find good whiskey."

"But not so hard to find beautiful women?"

He shifted again. She couldn't see his face now. The fire's glow formed an ocher halo around his head.

"Do you consider me beautiful, Mr. Bastitas?"

He slowly stood—silent as a big cat. "You asking out of curiosity, or shall I take that as an invitation?"

"Depends on your answer, I guess." A delicious exhilaration rushed through her at the wickedness of her actions. Randy would be rolling in his grave by now, spewing sacred scriptures condemning whores and harlots—seducers of serpents.

Bastitas moved toward her, and something inside her fluttered wildly. She hardly knew this man. She should deplore everything he represented, yet here she stood with some unbearable pressure building between her legs, her body vibrating, her breath ragged and thin.

At some time he had unbuttoned his shirt a little. She could see the dark triangle of his chest as he moved against her. His body heat permeated her skin. He smelled raw, like sweat and leather and horse. Of wind and sunshine.

"Beautiful?" he murmured, then stroked her cheek with his knuckles, ran one rough fingertip down the sensitive side of her neck to the hollow of her collarbone. "If I say yes, what will you do, Mrs. Bell? What would a prim and proper young lady from Boston do with a man like me? I'm hardly a gentleman about making love, Mrs. Bell. I'm afraid my lack of tender sensibilities would be too much for a woman accustomed to being handled like china.

"Beautiful? Yeah, you're beautiful. And lonely. And there's nothing more vulnerable than a lonely woman. You mix lonely and whiskey together and even a saddle bum like me starts to look pretty damn good."

His hips pressed close. Her hand touched his gun, fingered the trigger—cold steel against hot flesh. It made the ache in her pulsate. She wanted to gouge out his taunting eyes for thinking she was the kind of woman who would seduce just any tramp who passed through. She wanted to take his hand and press it to her feverish breast. She wanted to tell him that in that precise moment she was exactly the sort of woman who would seduce a man like him—and she wasn't china. Far from it.

"What are you telling me, Mr. Bastitas? That I don't quite measure up to your red-haired whores at the Ambrosia?"

"I'm saying that they won't wake up hating me—or themselves—for what happens tonight."

"My. A killer with morals. What makes you think I'm the kind of woman who would wake up in the morning hating herself? Maybe the only difference between me and your friend in town is that I, for a while, had a ring on my finger." She lowered her lashes, swayed her body against his, which felt hard as granite. He caught his breath, made a sound like pain or fury in his chest, but as she ran her hand up his belly he grabbed her wrist and twisted, forcing her back against the wall.

"You're drunk, Mrs. Bell. Too damn drunk to know what you're doing, or saying. Once you've slept it off we'll have this little discussion again. Then we'll see if you're still in the mood to get screwed by a saddle tramp. Now see to your cornbread. I smell it burning."

He shoved her toward the oven. Charity briefly closed her eyes. Funny. She didn't feel drunk. Not even a little. No more drunk from whiskey than she'd been when attempting to seduce her husband through the two years of their miserable marriage.

She grabbed a dishcloth from the table and clumsily opened the oven door. Black smoke boiled out, stabbing at her eyes and assaulting her nose. She fumbled clumsily for the iron skillet, wishing she could crawl in among the fiery wood ashes—a fate far preferable than having to face her guest over the dinner table.

Pain seared her hand, and she cursed.

Bastitas wrapped one arm around her waist and swung her away, then made for the blackened bread himself. Eyes swollen and tearing, hand throbbing, Charity bounced against the table, then a chair as she stumbled toward the hallway door.

"Not so fast." Bastitas grabbed her from behind, his fingers wrapping around her arm.

"Don't touch me."

"You've hurt yourself."

"Don't—*touch*—me."

"Shut up and let me see. Goddammit, lady, I'm just trying to help."

"Then help me by getting the hell out of my house." She struck his chest, then slapped his face.

He hissed an obscenity. "Stop crying, for God's sake."

"I'm not crying. The smoke—"

Gripping the back of her head in his hand, he wiped the hot tears from her cheeks.

"I don't cry!" she cried. "Not anymore. And certainly not over a good-for-nothing like you. No wonder you aren't married. No woman in her right mind would have you."

"Then I guess you're tickled pink because I didn't go sniffing under *your* skirts."

"Buffoon! Stinking, uncouth—God, I *must* have been drunk to think I would want you anywhere near me!"

The baby cried.

"Hush." He shook Charity hard. "You're frightening the baby."

Forcing her eyes open at last, she shouldered him away, clutched her seared hand against her breast and fixed him with a maddened look. "Get out of my house. Get off of my farm. If I see you here again I'll shoot you."

He backed toward the door. "You should see to that hand, Mrs. Bell."

"Out."

"Indian plant is good. Break it open and rub the juice on the burn."

"Out, and take those disgustingly dirty boots with you."

He grabbed his boots and quit the house. She slammed the door behind him and fell back against it, covering her smarting eyes with one hand.

"Crazy," came his voice near the door.

"Right," she said to herself. "I'm crazy as a loon or I sure as hell wouldn't have considered you for—"

The baby whimpered. Charity wrist-wiped her eyes again, then her nose. She walked to the bedroom door and looked down on her son's squirming little body, his bald head bobbing like a cork on rippling water. Only then did she notice that her breasts had painted twin wet spots on her blouse.

She maneuvered the little buttons with her uninjured hand and allowed the plain blue garment to fall to the floor, then her chemise—the last of the lingerie that had made up her trousseau. She'd stitched it together repeatedly the last year, hoping to save it as long as possible. It was yellow and frayed and was missing the tiny pink ribbon that had once adorned the simple ruching.

After plumping the pillows, she lay on the bed, her son cradled in the crook of her arm, his lips adhered to her breast. He pumped his little pink fingers open and closed, peering at her from the corner of his dark eyes with their sweep of pale lashes. Charity smiled at him unsteadily, and closed her eyes.

Rafe remained on the bottom step a long time, deliberating. If he walked back through that door, he'd be sorry tomorrow, and so would she. Besides, he had a gut hunch it wouldn't be so easy to walk away from Charity Bell after only one night. It was tough enough now, with his face still stinging from her slap. She was a hellcat, no doubt about it. Big trouble for a man like him.

Stars glittered in the velvet sky. The night was so still that he could hear the distant song of a coyote, and the sound of his own uneven breathing. Now was not the time to get sloppy. He'd come to Hell with a purpose, and that purpose was at hand. Had Charity not shown up in town today, he would have done the intended deed and by now would be riding Jake toward the Mexico border.

He'd already wasted too much time dallying with the preacher's widow and her son. He was a sitting duck on this farm. It was only a matter of time before John Wesley showed up with his "Wanted Dead or Alive" poster claiming Rafe to be a cold-blooded killer. With the two-thousand-dollar bounty on Rafe's head, Wesley could take life easy for the next few years.

Damn right he'd be crazy for remaining here another hour . . . much less another night.

Nine

RAFAEL REACHED FOR THE WOMAN WHO HAD OCCUPIED his dreams throughout the night—a blond woman with exceptional blue eyes—curled his fingers in her pale silken hair and made a drowsy hungry sound in his throat. Even in his dream he realized there was a difference to the usual scenario—his making love to a beautiful woman with long brown hair, laughing green eyes, and smooth white cheeks that flushed with timidity over making love during the day—and at night by candlelight—as if passion were something acceptable only under the obscurity of darkness.

As the musty aroma of old hay and dung sluiced to his brain he forced his eyes open to stare up at the dew-heavy spiderwebs draping from the barn rafters. "Wonderful," he muttered, squinting a beam of morning sunlight from his eyes.

"I thought I told you to get off my farm, Mr. Bastitas."

He looked toward the door. Charity stood at the entrance, her shotgun nestled in the crook of one arm. The sunlight spilling through her skirt silhouetted her shapely legs, planted a little apart. She was barefoot and had swept her hair to the top of her head, securing it with a comb.

"Guess I didn't make myself clear enough last night," she said.

"You made yourself perfectly clear, Mrs. Bell. So if you want to shoot me just go the hell ahead and shoot me." He rubbed the back of his neck.

"Why are you here?"

"I'm obviously a glutton for punishment."

"Or crazy."

"No, ma'am. You're crazy. Remember? I'm just stubborn. I have this aversion to riding off and leaving vulnerable women prey to lunatics like Peters."

"Unless you intend to move in permanently, I don't see what good your staying last night is going to do."

Rafe dragged his hands through his hair. She was right, of course.

"Guess you'll be wanting some breakfast, since you never ate last night."

"I can manage until I get back to town."

"I suppose it's the least I can do. Coffee's already made."

"Fine."

She bent and retrieved a basket of eggs, then turned back for the house, her hips swaying gently from side to side as she moved. He noted the sunlight dancing on her tendrils of pale hair, and he thought, *Fine. If she wants to pretend that last night never happened, so be it.* No need rehashing mistakes. That could make a man crazy. He should know. He'd eat her food, then get the hell out of here . . . again.

The water in the trough was cold enough to make him gasp as he plunged his head into it, then his arms. He rubbed his chest vigorously, allowing the water to spill in streams down his belly. He shook his head and ruffled his hair, mopping his face with his shirt as he regarded the lopsided barn, the holes in the roof, the mountain of manure, piled behind the old structure, that in the heat of a summer day would stink like death, not to mention drawing flies all the way from Juarez.

As he sat on the rim of the trough, allowing the morning sun to dry his face and shoulders, the smell of coffee and fried ham came to him. A dreaded memory tapped at his consciousness—images of lazing on the rim of a water trough after a long day of sweating in the sun, shoulders aching, hands bleeding, a woman's body next to his, drops of water on her naked breasts glistening like crystal beads in the sun.

Charity held the plate of ham and biscuits in one hand, the cup of steaming coffee in the other. In the distance, Bastitas had stripped off his shirt; she noted how the sun shimmered off the water glistening on his dark skin. She wasn't certain she had ever seen a man's chest so broad or hard. Or arms so muscular. She wondered what his skin would feel like to touch, if the hair on his chest would seem coarse or silken, if her hand would mold easily about his bulging chest muscles.

She tried to think of something else, to look someplace else, to the distant undulations of dirt and sand, and the far-off rising of low mountains where her cattle spent their arduous winters. But her gaze swept back to him, his low-slung breeches hanging on his narrow hips, exposing his navel and a slice of pale skin just beneath. His corded stomach muscles. The vague ridges of his ribs. His armpits and their dark hair, which shone as if it had been oiled. The rousing of desire crept upon her again—as it had last night. Only this time she couldn't blame the feelings on whiskey.

She put the cup and plate on the table, wiped her sweating palms on her skirt, and moved to her bedroom. As the baby slept peacefully, she checked her reflection in the dresser mirror, rubbing a streak of dust from her sunflushed cheek just as the back door opened and closed. She listened to him cross to the table; then she swept up a tendril of hair before returning to the kitchen, which was empty. Her heart stopped as her gaze jumped to the open door. He sat on the back stoop, eating. He had put on his shirt, which was damp between his shoulders.

Charity moved to the door. "There's more coffee and biscuits if you want them."

"No thanks. Time to move on."

"Why did you stay last night?"

"Why do you think I stayed?"

"Because you were worried about me."

"You can take care of yourself, remember?"

For a moment, he ate in silence. She noted how his breeches hugged his thigh muscles, which were slightly jackknifed beneath him, the material worn thin and pale over his knees. She noted too how his black hair waved over his shirt collar. She was about to turn away when he said, "That barn roof is in bad shape. Didn't the preacher know how to use a hammer?"

"The only thing my husband knew how to beat was a Bible. And . . ." Her voice trailed off, and she bit her lower lip.

He paused in chewing, slightly turning his head as if attempting to hear her better. "And?"

"Nothing." She shook her head. "It doesn't matter any longer."

"First good rain and the entire barn will cave in. What do you intend to do with that mountain of dung?"

"Till it into the dirt."

"I assume that's your garden over there." He pointed the fork in the direction of the distant plot of rough ground. "Would have been easier for you to have dumped the manure closer to the plot."

"Anything else wrong with the way I run this place?"

"We'd discuss it but I don't have all day." Rafe put the empty plate aside and wiped his mouth with his shirt sleeve. "I found a hammer and nails in the barn, and a few passably good boards. I could try to patch up the barn roof before I go."

"I can't pay you."

Bastitas left the porch and headed for the barn, his stride slow and swaggering. "Consider it payback for breakfast," he said without turning, then proceeded to roll up his shirt sleeves.

Charity called out, "For your information, you needn't have slept on the barn floor all night. There's a foreman's room buried behind the hay manger. There's a bed there as well."

"Now you tell me." Partially turning, he flashed her a smile that made her stomach flip-flop.

The baby cried. Charity hurried to the bedroom and swooped the infant up, dancing in a circle before planting a kiss on his cheek. As her head swam with elation, she wondered if she wasn't a little crazy after all.

Charity washed clothes while Rafe repaired the barn roof. The repeated thump of the hammer sounded like drumbeats in the clear air. And there was his occasional whistling. Charity found herself with her hands in soapy water,

her eyes closed, listening, thinking she'd never heard anyone who could whistle so beautifully. It sounded like birds
singing on a spring morning in Boston. Her mind grew
drowsy, her body languid. With the warm sun on her face
and shoulders, she thought how nice it would be to look
forward to such pleasantries every day.

After hanging the clothes to dry, Charity returned to
the house, stopping as she rounded the corner to discover
Bastitas sitting on the shaded stoop, where she had left
her son wrapped in blankets and tucked in the roaster,
which would soon be much too small for his growing
body. Bastitas talked softly to the child cradled in his
arms, his look one of such intensity that Charity could
barely breathe.

"Your mother is a saucy little thing. And stubborn.
And I suspect she's a lot crazy. But she's easy on the eyes
and cooks respectably well. A kid could do worse for a
mother. Just you show her respect as you get bigger. A
boy should always revere his mother even before his father. It's your mother who brought you into this world.
Who will lay down her life to protect you. Who will teach
you the difference between right and wrong. A man can
do those things too, but they aren't taught with hugs and
kisses and assurances of undying devotion. While a father
will pick up his child when he falls, it's the mother who'll
kiss away the hurt. It's a man's job to make certain his
son is tough enough to handle the crap life dishes out.
Living isn't always going to be fun or easy. Sometimes a
mother's kisses won't eliminate the wound, but they sure
as heck will lessen the pain."

Rafe looked up and saw her, and the recognizable mask
of indifference fell again over his features. He quickly
tucked the baby back into his makeshift cradle before

leaving the stoop. He said simply, "Time to go."

She opened and closed her mouth, saying nothing.

"I'm not sure how long that patching job will last. If I were you I'd have someone tear the whole barn down and build a new one."

As he started toward the barn, she called out, "You're welcome to stay. The cattle will need bringing up soon—"

"Can't do it," he called over his shoulder.

She hurried to the stoop and picked up the baby, patted his back and smoothed the fine hair on his head. He smelled like Bastitas, and she held him more tightly as she followed Rafael to the barn. "Where do you go from here?" she called.

"Town."

"And then?"

"Mexico."

Her step slowed. "No one goes there unless they're running from something. What is it?"

"You don't want to know, Mrs Bell."

Charity stopped as he moved inside the barn to collect his saddled horse. As he exited again, he said, "It's none of my business, but you should think about going home to Boston. You're much too pretty a lady to waste your life in this hellhole. Go back to Chester Muesler. If he loved you as much as you say, he'll take you back."

"And the baby?"

"No man worth his good name wouldn't take a shine to that boy. I suspect if the preacher were still alive he'd be proud of his son."

"Obviously you didn't know the preacher."

Rafael mounted, then adjusted his hat over his brow. "Try staying out of trouble, Mrs. Bell. You have a son to think about now."

• • •

Sometime in midafternoon, and after a bout of crying and feeling sorry for herself, of hating Randall Bell, of hating herself for once believing that she deserved something better than the traditional role of Chester's indolent spouse, Charity fell asleep, her son's head resting on her breast. It was nearly dusk by the time she awoke. With the infant beside her, she listened to the silence, thinking it had never sounded so deep or felt so still. It closed around her like quicksand.

She went through the motions of cooking, but found she had no appetite. Her gaze kept shifting to Rafe's empty place at the table, his discarded breakfast dishes near the washbasin. By now Bastitas would be back in town—taking care of business. Whatever that business might be. Killing, no doubt. He had that look about him— so much anger roiling in those eyes, so much hate. But unlike the scores of killers who rode through Hell every day, Bastitas's eyes did not reflect the same insanity as the others. That in itself was startling and somewhat frightening.

She tried to think of tomorrow's chores. There was ground to plow and the hen coop to repair. Perhaps in the next day or two she would venture out to find her cattle.

At last she wandered to the barn and fed the animals, feeling the dark close in around her. She jumped at every little sound until she gave herself a dressing down. For nine months she had lived on this farm by herself. George Peters had always been a threat—so why was she so nervous now?

The plow was propped up against the barn wall behind

a pile of old crates. The plow was rusty and heavy. As soon as she moved it, the blade fell off. Then the tears came, a salty flood that stung her sun-and-wind-abraded cheeks. Without the plow there would be no tilling. Without tilling there would be no food. If Randall Bell were here right now . . . she would kill him.

With his little belly full of milk, the baby Bell slept soundly in his roaster while Charity cracked a whip across Connie's broad backside and encouraged the stubborn mule forward. The leather straps crisscrossed over Charity's back bit into her body as the animal lurched ahead and the ragged plow blade dug into the hard earth, peeling back dirt that smelled as dry and musty as old dust. No sooner had the mule dragged them half-a-dozen yards than the blade tumbled off again, this time popping the pole in two with so loud a crack that Connie spooked and dragged Charity halfway back to the barn before she could stop her.

A number of hens came running from behind the barn, wings outstretched in a clumsy attempt to gain flight. Behind them came a dog, its ribs showing beneath its drab brown coat. From its mouth hung a limp chicken.

Charity scrambled for the shotgun she'd propped against the back steps and chased the scrawny thief toward the henhouse before planting her feet, taking aim and firing. The dog tucked his haunches under himself, but wasn't about to give up the bird. She focused her sights on him again and was prepared to lay him out when Bastitas appeared at the barn door, barely dressed, barefoot and bare-chested, pants sagging about his hips and unbuttoned. Charity stared at him hard before lowering the rifle.

"What the hell are you doing?" Rafe yelled.

"Putting a bullet in that dog."

"The hell you say. That dog is mine."

"Since when?"

"Since I found him half-starved out back of Max Grove's mercantile. I named him Jackson."

"Why Jackson?"

"He *looks* like a Jackson."

"He looks like a chicken thief to me."

"That damn chicken was already dead."

"That's a bald-faced lie. That hen was pert and saucy last evening."

Rafe frowned and scratched his chest. He glared at the hound with Charity's chicken hanging from its mouth. "I think a coyote probably killed that chicken," he said.

"Coyote? Coyotes don't go about killing hens for the pleasure of it."

"It could happen."

She shook her head.

Rafael shrugged. "I'll have a word with him."

"You're going to have a word with a dog? I guess I was wrong about you. You *are* insane."

Charity eased the hammer down and cradled the gun. "What are you doing here again?"

"I reconsidered the job offer."

She glanced toward the barn. "You find the room?"

"That's not a room. It's a scorpion pit."

"If you want comfort go back to Sally's."

Charity turned back to the broken plow, closing her eyes as she thanked God for the occasional small favor, not to mention Rafael de Bastitas.

She turned partially to look at him, hands on his hips, the pitiful excuse for a dog sitting beside him. "How long you reckon on staying this time?'' she asked.

"Just until I get that patch of ground plowed. And that roof fixed on the house."

"That could take a few days. What about your business in town? What about Mexico?"

"I figure my business will wait a while longer."

"Fine then." She took a deep breath and repeated, "Fine."

An hour into plowing, Rafe regretted his decision to stay—almost. The sun beat down on his bare shoulders like fire in a furnace. The leather straps dug bloody abrasions into his back, and his hands weren't much better. He'd swallowed enough dirt to piss mud by nightfall. How the preacher's widow managed to grow anything worth eating in the pitiful soil was a miracle, he thought.

Sweat running into his eyes, he glanced over at Charity. On her knees in the dirt, she carefully tucked potato eyes into the ground. The baby, lying in his roaster, cooed and gurgled and batted his tiny fists at the air while his mother sang to him softly. Then Charity looked up at Rafe and smiled, and Rafe found himself stunned by the image they made, mother and child aglow in sunlight. He grinned, despite the sharp rocks that cut into the bottoms of his boots and the dust so thick that it settled like river silt on the back of his tongue. His grin spread as Charity got hold of her son's tiny fist and wagged it up and down as if the baby were saying "Hello!"

He gripped the plow handles and sank his boot heels into the tilled earth. The blade sank a little deeper, the mule pulled harder. The sun beat down on him more intensely as he drove Connie up and down the sorry plot, rolling the piles of musty manure into the dirt, transforming sand into loam that, hopefully, would produce enough food for the widow and baby to survive next winter. But then what? Who would be here next spring to drive this cantankerous old mule?

And thinking of food . . . damn, he was hungry. For the last half hour, the smell of baking bread and roasting meat had made his gut knot. He'd forgotten how hungry toiling could make a man.

Frowning, glancing up through the sand swirling around him, he watched Charity emerge through the dust cloud, a quart jar of water in one hand. She wore a clean, starched white blouse tucked into a full, sweeping gingham skirt. Her hair had been washed. She'd tied it, still damp, with a red ribbon at the nape of her neck. Wrapping the lines around the backs of his hands, digging his feet deeper into the dirt, he hauled back on the mule and yelled, "Whoa, mule! Whoa!"

Charity carefully made her way over the furrows. Rafe wrist-wiped the sweat and dirt from across his brow as he focused on the sweating jar she offered him—and not on her.

Charity regarded him intently as he drank most of the cool water, then poured the rest over his face.

"You don't have to plow the whole plot all at once," she said. "It'll be here tomorrow."

Rafe closed his eyes and allowed the water to trickle down his neck.

Charity took the empty jar. "More?"

He shook his head. "I'll cramp."

Her gaze drifted over his sweating shoulders, across his chest, to his belly. She took a deep breath before swiping at a fly on his arm. "Those leathers are rubbing your back raw. You might do well to put on your shirt."

"Shirt won't help me now." He looked out over the turned plot. "I'm good for a while longer."

"You'll be hurting bad later, if you're not already. I can't quite fathom why men won't allow themselves to admit when they've had enough. But never mind. I'll prepare you a salve. It'll ease the discomfort you'll be feeling by nightfall." She turned for the house, then paused and threw him a look over her shoulder. "Food will be ready soon. I suspect you're hungry."

He nodded.

"I hope you like fried chicken."

"Mrs. Bell, I'd eat chicken raw right now, feathers and all."

Her gently curved eyebrows went up and she smiled, amused. "Mashed potatoes?"

He nodded, and doing his best to ignore some irrational tickle of warm pleasure in his chest, he shouldered the sweat from his jaw and focused on the plowed earth.

"And a cool glass of buttermilk. There's mince pie for dessert."

Rafe knuckled sand from his eyes and nodded again. He noticed that her feet were bare. Her toes peeked at him from beneath her skirt hem.

For a moment, she said nothing more, just stood there with her feet buried in the hot sand, her thin cheeks flushed by the heat, her wide blue eyes regarding him in that way she had of making him uneasy—an innocent but sultry look. She smelled like scented soap—lilacs or violets or something.

Finally, she inspected his plowing. Hands on her hips, her face a picture of discreet curiosity and amazement, she said with a touch of haughtiness, "You turn a straight furrow, Mr. Bastitas. You're to be commended."

With that, she returned to the house, leaving the hot air awash with the scent of flowers, until he reminded himself that he was treading dangerous waters. If he didn't get this damn job wrapped up quick he was headed for consequences he sure as hell wasn't prepared to deal with.

As the morning wore on the wind rose from the south, laying flat the emerging prairie grass and kicking up clouds of sand that scalded Rafe's raw back and shoulders as he finished yet another furrow and brought the mule around toward the barn. Judging by the mouth-watering smells wafting from the house, his meal should be ready soon. He'd unhitch and feed the mule and get himself cleaned up, he thought. It didn't seem right to sit down to a meal of fried chicken and mince pie with him smelling worse than the dung heap he had spread over the plowed plot . . . especially when she had gone to the trouble to bathe in lilac water and wash her hair.

Through the dust up ahead appeared a figure, then two. Then three. He focused hard, finding Charity's pale face among the collection of grim-faced intruders as he hauled back hard as he could on Connie's lines and cursed under his breath.

A man gripped Charity's arm, dragging her along as she kicked and clawed and spewed profanities that made the group hoot with laughter. Beyond them came another man cradling the baby in the crook of one arm.

The scene hit Rafe like a fist and he briefly closed his eyes, hoping to whatever god occupied heaven that this was simply a nightmare. But it wasn't, and he knew it. The sick fear expanding inside him was real—the men leering at him and the widow Bell were real. "Bastard," Rafe said through his teeth, but before he could move, a squat Mexican with a pock-scarred face pointed a gun at Charity's head and cocked the trigger.

"If I was you, *señor*," the man said, "I would keep my hands on that plow and don't so much as blink. 'Cause if you do, I'm liable to shoot the *señora,* and that would be too bad, *sí*?"

He nodded stiffly, then remained unmoving, lest he do anything that could be interpreted wrong. His palms began to sweat, and his throat constricted. If one of the sons of bitches so much as tweaked the baby's cheek, Rafe suspected he'd explode.

With no warning, Charity spun on her captor and raked his face with her nails. He howled in pain and backhanded her across her cheek, knocking her to the ground so hard that she lost her breath.

It was all Rafe could do not to act simply on reflex. Yet, what the devil could he do? With plow straps crisscrossed over his back and driving lines wrapped around both wrists, he was impotent. He barely managed to take in enough breath to say in a deadly calm voice, "Stay down and shut up, Mrs. Bell. Don't so much as look at them cross-eyed or *I'll* hit you . . . and I won't be so nice about it."

Her hair in her face, tears streaming from her eyes, she stared at him in disbelief. "Do something!" she cried. "How can you stand there so obviously unmoved when he's holding a gun to my son's head?"

"Shut up!" he yelled back.

"Coward!"

"What the hell can I do about it?! Do I look like a fucking magician?"

She continued to glare at him, her stunned eyes spilling tears and her shoulders heaving. Then George Peters stepped up, bouncing the baby gently and talking to the fretting infant in a soothing voice. He looked first at Rafe, then at Charity.

"I'd listen to the man, Mrs. Bell. He strikes me as an intelligent sort."

"Don't hurt my son," she pleaded. "Please—"

"Do I look like the kind of monster who would hurt a baby?"

Charity swallowed and managed to shake her head no.

George grinned and looked around at his companions. "The lady is reasonable after all, eh, *compadres*?"

The men grunted in agreement.

"Will it make you feel better, Mrs. Bell, if I remove the gun from his temple?"

She nodded and whispered brokenly, "Please."

"Would you like to have your baby back, Mrs. Bell?"

On her knees, her starched skirt spread in the dirt, Charity lifted her trembling arms out for her son. George knelt to one knee before her, his mouth more of a sneer than a grin as he continued to press the mouth of the gun barrel lightly to her son's head. "How much is your son's life worth, Mrs. Bell?"

"Everything," she whispered urgently, and began to sob.

Rafe glanced from one man to another. There was no hope of jumping anyone now, not with these damned straps holding him captive. With sweat burning his eyes, he tried to breathe evenly and concentrate. He focused on the mule, who was growing testier by the minute at having been diverted from her intended meal.

"Everything," George repeated. "Now that's the sort of answer I like to hear." He stroked Charity's cheek and hair, then slid his hand over one breast and gently squeezed.

Charity caught her breath, but didn't so much as quiver. George nodded approvingly. "I see you appreciate the situation, Mrs. Bell. Havin' a son of my own, I can understand how a parent would give up everything they own to guarantee the welfare of their child."

"You've come here to take my farm," she managed, in a voice as dry as the dust under her knees.

"I've come to negotiate, Mrs. Bell. I'll make you a fair offer. A place like this, with the proper handlin', could become a lucrative investment for the right person. But a widow on her own, with a tiny baby to manage? I don't think so."

George handed over the baby and Charity clutched him to her chest. She smoothed the sweaty hair on his head and pressed her trembling lips to his brow.

"I don't expect you to make up your mind right now, Mrs. Bell. Hell, I'll give you a week or two to stew on what kind of price you'd expect for the place, recallin', of course, that I ain't a rich man."

Standing, Peters fingered the hammer of his gun and stared down at Charity and her son for eternal seconds before slowly shifting his gaze to Rafe. George's eyes became serpentlike, and his mouth thinned. "I'm thinkin' to myself that your bein' around this place ain't doin' my cause any good, mister. I figure you've got three choices. You git on your horse this minute and ride for Mexico, or you come to work for me and we'll forget you've interfered with the widow Bell's plans to sell me this place."

"And the third choice?" Rafe narrowed his eyes.

"Or I kill you." George grinned at his cohorts, who grinned back.

The baby began to cry. Charity did her best to muffle the sound against her collarbone. She rocked back and forth and shushed him, to little avail. The fear in her eyes hadn't diminished since George had surrendered her son. Her eyes were like two glassy blue marbles in her china-white face as she stared at Rafe in anticipation. Just what the hell did she want him to say? To do, for that matter? Since this nightmare had begun she'd reacted to him as if he were part of George's little scheme to take this God-forsaken ranch.

George said, "I ain't expectin' an answer immediately. Take your time. A day or two at least. I think that's fair, don't you? But just in case you don't take my terms intently enough, I feel it's my duty to impress the seriousness of the situation. Pancho!"

The pocked Mexican ran forward.

George pointed to the driving lines wrapped around Rafe's wrists and entwined through his fingers. "Tie 'em good and tight. I wouldn't want 'em to come loose too soon. Then we'd defeat our purpose, wouldn't we?"

Blinking sweat from his burning eyes, Rafe remained cautiously passive as Pancho wrapped and tied the leathers so tight around his wrists that his hands began to throb almost immediately. What the hell was Peters up to?

Charity climbed to her feet as her son wailed more loudly. Her mouth fell open as if she were trying to find the ability to speak. Her face was the color of a fish belly and Rafe felt his gut turn over as Peters's intention became clear.

"Get in the house, Charity," Rafe said through his teeth. "*Now.*"

She shook her head and turned to George. Her lips formed, *No, please, no,* just as he raised his gun in the air.

Rafe braced himself.

Charity screamed.

Ten

HE FLOATED IN DARKNESS, WRAPPED IN A BLANKET OF fire ants and bull nettles.

"Mr. Bastitas? *Please.* Answer me if you can, just a blink of your eyes or a squeeze of your hand. Don't die. I could never live with myself if you died. Mr. Bastitas? Rafe? Oh God, you're dying and I killed you. It's all my fault."

Weeping. Sobbing. Coughing. The blanket of fire ants and bull nettles became rattlesnake venom that crept like molasses death through his veins. Through the slits of his swollen eyes, an image appeared. Vague at first, it slowly sharpened to a woman's tear-streaked face.

"Nora?" The effort sliced down his throat. He coughed and his body fractured in pain.

The woman came nearer, flooding his chest and shoulders with silken hair. "Don't move. Not yet. I'm not finished with your wounds. Lie as still as you can. I'm sorry about the pain. I'm sorry about everything. Had I not been so stubborn this would never have happened. I should have agreed to sell the ranch to George Peters long ago. No! Don't move. Let me lift your head, then I want you to drink as much of this whiskey as you can."

She pressed the mouth of the bottle to his lips. The whiskey pooled in his mouth, but he managed to swallow. Sinking into his pillow, he took a ragged breath and forced his eyes open. "What happened to me?"

Charity took a swig from the bottle herself. "The mule dragged you practically to Mexico and back before I could stop her."

He frowned as the memory took shape: some squat Mexican with a scarred face had tied his wrists with the plow lines, then George Peters had shot a gun, terrorizing the mule. The last thing he recalled was being hauled facedown across the rock-and-cactus-covered ground.

Charity bent over him again and tenderly touched his cheek. Her own face looked scraped and bruised. Her lower lip was swollen and cut. "I'm so sorry. I never meant—"

"Hush." Slipping his bloodied hand around her head, fingers lightly twisting in her hair, he pulled her close, so close he could smell the slight hint of whiskey on her breath. Her eyes looked tortured, and despite the gnawing going on inside, he felt a surge of fear more powerful than the pain. "What did he do to you, Charity? Dammit, don't look at me that way. Did he rape you?" He searched her face, saw her eyes well with tears before she struggled to pull away.

"Where's my gun? Get me my goddamn gun!"

Eyes wide, she frantically shook her head and did her best to stop him as he attempted to roll from the bed. Fierce pain brought him up short and he groaned.

"Stop this," Charity pled. "He . . . he didn't rape me."

"Liar." He fell back on the bed. "I'll kill that son of a—" Clutching his side, he searched the room. "The boy.

Did he hurt the baby? Ah, God. Tell me he hasn't—''

"No! Dear God, *no*, he didn't lay a hand on the baby, *I swear it*. Please, I fear your ribs are broken. If you don't lie still you'll make matters worse than they already are.''

Her words swam in his head as consciousness ebbed and flowed. He hurt too damn bad to fight it . . . Still—

"Rafe? Look and see. The baby is fine. He's just fine. He simply wants his . . . his Uncle Rafe to get better soon.'' With a trembling smile, she waved the infant's little hand, and Rafe sank like a stone into oblivion.

He awoke again to silence. And pain. It was the silence that disturbed him most.

Where were Charity and the boy?

Why couldn't he hear them? Or see them? Or smell them?

He would climb out of this grave and seek vengeance.

Except this was no grave, and death yielded no such pain as was cutting through his chest at that moment.

His chest bound tight, Rafe eased off the bed. His legs wobbled. His head swam. He struggled for breath before shuffling as quietly as possible into the dark hallway. A sound. Just the roaring of blood in his ears. Nothing more.

No sign of her or the baby in the kitchen. Not so much as a dish had been placed for supper.

He managed to crab his way to the parlor, where his gun and holster were slung over the mannequin's shoulder. With the .45 gripped in one hand, he eased through the kitchen, where he cupped his fingers around the lamp chimney and blew out the light. He moved to the open door.

The grounds were gray and going black. There was no sign of Charity or the infant.

He managed the steps, barely, then headed for the barn,

revolver raised, trigger cocked. It wasn't until he stepped into the musty stable that he saw the light spilling from his room. He heard Charity singing softly, the baby cooing in response.

She appeared to float around the transformed room with its newly appointed furnishings, consisting of a straight-backed chair, a collection of starched white doilies, and a rag rug on the floor. She swayed to music in her head, occasionally pausing long enough to swig from her bottle of whiskey and make certain that her son remained pacified on the bed, made fresh with clean sheets and a patchwork quilt.

He slumped against the doorjamb and released his breath.

She turned and saw him. Her movements stopped. The light behind her shimmered off her hair like a halo as she tipped her head and regarded him with slumberous eyes. A smile toyed with one corner of her moist, slightly swollen lips. "You're naked, Mr. Bastitas."

He glanced down his body. "So I am."

"As you like to say, don't worry, it's nothing that I haven't seen before." She smiled. He didn't.

"It's not safe to be out here alone, Mrs. Bell."

"With you, or generally speaking?"

"You've been drinking again, obviously."

"So I have." She approached and lightly placed her hand on his bound chest. "Does that bother you, Mr. Bastitas?"

He glanced at the sleepy infant, then back at her as she raised the mouth of the bottle to his lips. He reached for it, but she danced away. "What the devil do you think you're doing?" he asked.

"Do you like the room? One could hardly call it a

scorpion pit now, could he? You should be comfortable here . . . unless you'd care to move into the house . . . with me.''

"You're drunk," he said.

Charity laughed softly and shrugged. "Maybe. Maybe not. Maybe I'm just brazen enough to hope you'll take me up on the offer.''

"You don't even know me, Mrs. Bell.''

"You're standing in front of me right now naked as the day you were born. You've got a bullet hole scar two inches below and to the right of your navel, which means you either went asking for trouble, or trouble came asking for you.'' Looking away, she added, ''And you're in love with someone named Nora.''

Silence.

"Well?'' she whispered. "Is she your wife?''

Rafe moved around her. He put his gun on the table and retrieved the pair of Randall Bell's pants that she had placed over the back of the chair.

"A lady friend?'' came her voice behind him.

He managed to pull the breeches up over his hips before facing Charity again. Her eyes were wide, her bruised cheek flushed with color.

"I found her tintype. In your things. There.'' She pointed to his few belongings he'd tossed in the corner, then she hurried to his pack, where she dug furiously beneath a shirt and blanket. Her eyes fixed on the oval locket as she raised it toward him. "She's . . . beautiful. You must care for her enormously to carry this with you.''

Rafe took the locket from her and closed his fingers around it. "Right. I've worshipped her since the day I was born. The likeness is of my mother.'' He tossed it onto the blanket.

Charity drank again. Rafe took the bottle from her and put it aside. "This won't help," he told her.

"I beg to differ. Since I began tippling this afternoon I managed to sew you up and forget about my guilt over having nearly caused your death. It's given me the courage to come here with the naïve hope of convincing you to stay. To . . . marry me."

Her eyes looked both embarrassed and hopeful as they fixed on him, waiting, watching for any sign at all that he took her invitation seriously. He cleared his throat and reminded himself that she was both drunk and crazy. She'd been through hell today and was no doubt experiencing emotional desperation. "Like I said," he began gently, "you don't know me. I've done some things in my life that I'm not proud of. I suspect I'll go on doing them until something or somebody stops me. You need a man who isn't afraid of setting down roots. You want to fall in love, Charity, and *marry* the man you love."

"I could learn to love you. I think I already do."

Silence beat about their ears as the impact of her words settled through Rafe's aching body. He shook his head and took a nervous step back.

"It's Nora, isn't it? If you're married, just tell me, Rafe. I may be a lot of things, crazy among them, but I would never pursue a married man."

A lie dancing on the tip of his tongue, he sank against the wall and stared over her head. "No. I'm not married."

"Then there's hope—"

"No! No hope. I don't . . . love you, Mrs. Bell."

"Not even a little? Fondness would do. A woman in my place can't be particular."

He shook his head.

"But the way you touched me earlier—as if you care.

The way you looked at me made me think—''

He glanced at the sleeping baby on his cot, then swallowed. "You thought wrong."

The light in the little room flickered. Shadows danced over the ceiling and across Charity's stricken face as she watched him sink harder against the wall. His body felt crushed under the weight of her pain. If she didn't leave soon, he thought he might slump at her feet—or worse yet, agree to marry her.

She turned away, thank God. He released his breath and watched as she swept up the whiskey bottle, then the baby, and made her way from the room, her shoulder lightly brushing his.

The night wind smelled of impending rain and cooled the fire in his flesh. The whiskey in his veins numbed the rest. The slow burn eased the ache in his chest, but played hell with his head.

He watched the house with its windows glowing with yellow light in the starless night. The back door opened and the widow Bell appeared briefly, her little body swathed in a long white gown that made her look ghostly in the dark. Her pale hair framed her face and tumbled over her shoulders as she flung water from a dishpan into the dirt. She paused, silhouetted against the yellow lantern light, and looked toward the barn. She couldn't see him, of course, not here in the deepest shadows.

He was tempted to call out, but didn't. She hated him now, with good reason. She'd stitched him back together and he'd showed his gratitude by telling her to her face that he held no fondness for her at all.

And he didn't. He couldn't. How could he make her understand? He was a walking dead man. Every day, every hour he remained here, his chances grew slimmer of ever making it to Mexico.

At last, Charity stepped back into the house and closed the door. He watched her through the window as she bent over the table and blew out the lantern.

Bedtime.

He frowned. The memory of her yellow hair spilling over a white embroidered pillow made his brow sweat. Everything about her was cool and pale: her skin, her hair, her eyes. Kissing her would be like sliding under a crystal pool of thawed mountain snow. His body would vaporize; his existence would become as transparent as steam.

Christ, what was he thinking? There wasn't a place in his life for thoughts like that. He'd come too damn far now to let a pretty face and a cute baby upset his goals.

Rafe.

"Ah, God, Nora. Go away. Just go away and leave me alone. You're not really here. You don't exist. You're dead, dammit, and I'm so drunk I can see you, there, in the dark, beautiful as ever."

It has to end here.

"It ended three years ago! It ended when they murdered you and our son. Don't you know what it was like for me to feel your body go cold in my arms? How can you forgive them? They destroyed us."

It has to end here.

"I have nothing without you. I want nothing without you. I feel guilty for being here. For staying here. She needs help, that's all. They'll come for her if I leave. They'll come back and do to her what they did to us.

"She and the boy mean nothing to me. I wouldn't do that to you. They're just . . . helpless. All right, sometimes I get this feeling in the pit of my stomach when I see them; as if . . . God somehow made a mistake in taking you and he's trying to make up for it now by bringing me here. How can I leave them unprotected?

"Nora? Are you there? Don't do this to me. Don't leave me here alone again."

My darling Rafael, open your eyes. You're no longer alone.

"Come back. Ah, Nora. Nora, please . . ."

He turned the whiskey bottle up to his mouth and drank until there was nothing left. Until the dilapidated clapboard shack in the distance blurred into the shimmery image of another—a white house with blue shutters, a solitary candle burning in a window . . . and a child's laughter beckoning him home.

Once he had sufficiently recovered from his injuries, Rafe plowed the ground twice as big as he should have, then three times bigger, then four. By the end of the fourth day he stood with the sun beating down on his shoulders, his hands bleeding, and he followed each deep furrow with his eyes, his mind laying out precisely where each vegetable would grow. When the moon was right, he would plant. Until then, he hoped the building clouds to the northwest would provide enough rain to saturate the ground so that the dung he had added to the dirt would meld sufficiently. It was going to take a hell of a lot of prayers and tending to wring a decent crop out of the miserly soil, but he had done it before; he would do it again.

And when George Peters came calling again—as Rafe knew he would—he would find a thriving farm and a gun barrel leveled between his eyes. If Peters so much as breathed in the direction of Charity and her son, Rafe would kill him.

Rafe sat on the back stoop just outside the widow's kitchen door, eating his meals in silence while listening to the goings-on inside. The baby cooed and gurgled while Mrs. Bell fussed over stews and dumplings and cobblers. Since Rafe had turned down the widow Bell's marriage proposal, she rarely spoke to him, other than greeting him, *Good morning, Mr. Bastitas*, and at the end of the day, *Good evening, Mr. Bastitas,* just before she closed the door against the night, leaving him to sit on the porch step in darkness. Lucky for them both that they had long since grown accustomed to solitary lives. Who the hell needed companionship or conversation when one had the good fortune of sharing space with scorpions and the occasional rattlesnake? She probably would have liked to fire him—send him on his way. But Peters could return at any time, and she knew it.

The stranger arrived on a hot Sunday afternoon, slicked up in his Sunday-go-to-meeting clothes. Standing well over six feet, his body thin as a lightning rod, he stood beside his spotted horse a good five minutes, hat in hand, his gaze drifting between Charity's front door and Rafe. With his heels dug into the dry dirt, Connie yanking at the lines and eager to get on with the plowing, Rafe stared back with equal curiosity. His grabbing for his gun didn't seem necessary. Most hired killers didn't stand around shuffling their feet and wringing a hat in their hands. Nor did they slick back their hair with flowery-smelling oil or spit-polish their Sunday boots.

When it became obvious that the stranger had no intention of making a move before speaking to him, Rafe was forced to peel himself out of the leather straps. The man backed away, swallowing nervously as Rafe and Jackson approached.

"Yeah," Rafe snapped. "What's your business?"

"Name's Ned Williams."

"So?"

"I come to see the widow Bell." He swallowed again as Jackson sniffed his pants leg and boot. "Does he bite?"

"Only if I tell him to."

Ned cleared his throat and motioned toward the house, his gaze still fixed on Jackson, who had begun to show his teeth in displeasure. "I thought I might drop by to share a friendly hello with the widow Bell."

Rafe frowned. He thought of asking Mr. Ned Williams why he hadn't bothered to stop by with friendly hellos when Charity was nine months along and barely able to lug water in from the well.

Ned moved away from Jackson and asked, "Just who are you?"

"The hired help."

Relief flooded Ned's features; his shoulders relaxed. It was then that Rafe realized that Ned's visit was more than happenstance. He'd come calling on the preacher's wife.

"Is she around?" Ned asked.

"No."

"She ain't? Where is she?"

"Off."

"Off?"

"Yeah. Off."

"She ain't moved or nothin'?"

"Why?"

"Who did you say you are again?"

"The foreman."

Ned cleared his throat and looked toward the house. "I suppose I could come back another time. You'll tell the widow that I called?"

Rafe gave a single nod and narrowed his eyes. "Sure, I'll tell her."

With some reluctance, Ned turned back to his horse. At that precise moment, Charity exited the henhouse with an apron full of eggs.

Ned's head snapped in her direction; then his gaze cut to Rafe. Rafe grinned and shrugged. "Oops," he said, then hooked his thumbs over his waistband and slid his weight onto one hip. "Guess I lied."

Ned kneaded his hat brim and bit back his retort as he focused his attention on Charity. She was obviously caught up in her thoughts, little noting the hens and chicks scattering with agitated peeps and squawks from her path. "Hello!" Ned shouted, and lifted his hand like a salute.

Charity looked up. Her eyes widened briefly, and her step faltered. She glanced from Ned to Rafe, who raised one eyebrow, causing her cheeks to flush.

"Mr. Williams," she said in so smooth a tone that the smirk on Rafe's lips evaporated. "What brings you out this way?"

Ned looked accusingly if not outright smugly at Rafe before turning his full attention on Charity. "I come here to see you, Mrs. Bell."

"Me? Whatever for?"

Jackson sat down and stared up at Ned's blushing features. Rafe crossed his arms, eyebrow still raised, making Ned's voice go as dry as Hell's dust. "I was in the area . . ."

"In the area?" Charity almost laughed. "What busi-

ness could you possibly have all the way out . . . oh.'' *Oh,*
her lips silently formed again as realization sank in. One
hand swiftly swept a strand of hair back from her brow.
Her sweat-moistened cheeks turned as pink as dewy
pomegranates. For an instant she appeared femininely
aquiver; then she managed to recover enough to say,
''This is a pleasant surprise. Would you care to go inside
where it's cooler? I've a cobbler just out of the oven.
Perhaps you'll stay for supper?''

Relieved, Ned sauntered toward Charity, his strut lik-
ening him to a banty rooster. ''Cobbler happens to be one
of my favorites. I'd be more than pleased to share it with
you, Mrs. Bell. Can I help ya with them eggs?''

The pair turned toward the house as Ned said, ''I see
yer planning on a sizable plot this year. Me and my
brother Hank ain't got round yet to plowin'. We plan on
doin' that real quick, though, just as soon as Ernest Hayes
pounds us out a new plowshare. If ya don't mind me
sayin', Mrs. Bell, that is a mighty pretty dress yer wearin'.
I don't believe I ever saw ya wear that to the Reverend's
Sunday sermon.''

Rafe watched Ned trail Charity into the house. He heard
her laugh. There came a clattering of dishes, muted conversation as the scent of baked apples wafted through the
open window. Finally, Rafe took a deep breath, flexed his
throbbing hands open and closed and said to Jackson,
''Happened to be in the area my ass.''

Ned happened to be in the area every afternoon for the
next week. By the fourth day Charity had gone through
every decent frock she owned, including one she'd pulled
from a cedar trunk. Alas, she was forced to let out the
seams across the bosom by a good inch. Even then, the

bodice was a tad too snug and caused her breasts to ache. Still, it was a small price to pay. Ned Williams was pugugly and had about as much inborn intelligence as a katydid, but he was male company, without a wife . . . and took her mind off other things—Bastitas being one of them, George Peters another. So far she'd seen or heard nothing more from Peters, perhaps thanks to Rafe's continued presence. Regardless, she kept her shotgun loaded and handy. She'd made the decision not to budge off her ranch, threat or no threat. Yet the burden of worry was unmistakable. It had driven her to make a fool of herself by proposing marriage to a ne'er-do-well like Bastitas.

Arrogant bastard for turning her down—*as if he were some prize himself.* The last thing she needed in her life was any more trouble, and that's exactly what Rafael de Bastitas offered her. She needed stability for her son. Love would come in time. Respect was the utmost quality she needed in a mate at this turbulent and unpredictable turning point in her life. Soft-spoken, patient Ned would suffice. So what if he was ugly? Too skinny. Chewed snuff. And had poor table manners.

Ned didn't make her feel as if she were wound up tight as a bowstring, as Bastitas did. He didn't cause her stomach to feel as if she had just leaped off a tall cliff. His presence didn't cause her mouth to go dry, nor did it stir up the sort of agitation in her mind and body that left her feeling out of sorts and looking for an argument. Ned was idle chitchat. He chitchatted constantly about his farm, his brother who helped him run the farm, and their invalid mother who lived on the farm. Occasionally he reminisced about his poor dead wife—how lost he had been the last five years without her. Lovely, sweet Margaret had been taken from this world too soon.

Ned was companionship, pure and simple. His voice was like the drone of night locusts while she went about washing up after dinner, or caring for the baby, or stitching thin material into tiny sacques in which to dress her rapidly growing son. He droned on and on as she sat near the window, the child's sleepy head resting on her shoulder, and watched Rafael de Bastitas turn sand and rock and manure into dark, rich loam. She watched him break up hard earth with a sledge, and irrigate the dusty furrows with buckets of water he lugged from the well when the much-prayed-for rain never materialized. She watched too as, at the end of the day's work, he sat, exhausted, on the plowshare, elbows on his knees, head down and sweat dripping from his brow and running down his back. It was then that Ned's drone became a pinpoint of noise so indistinct he might have been a solitary cricket whirring a mile away.

Over and over the questions came to mind: Who are you, Bastitas?

What are you?

Most important, why do you remain here?

And who is Nora?

As it had for the last several nights, dinner came two hours late. Sitting on a stump outside the barn, elbows on his knees, body washed of its daily sweat and grime, Rafe felt his gut cramp, not to mention every muscle in his back and shoulders. Yesterday Ned had loaded Charity and Alex into his wagon and had driven them into town. Upon Ned's arrival today, he had again ushered them away from the house after apparently having coerced the widow Bell into packing up a basket of food for a picnic, only to return several hours later, his sunburned face red as the shaved and scalded butt of a freshly killed hog.

Finally, Charity appeared at the kitchen door, plate in hand. He was off the stump and on the bottom step before she could manage to set the food on the porch and escape back into the kitchen.

"You're late," Rafe snapped, noting that the frilly white blouse she wore appeared to be new. He snatched the hot plate from her. "Guess it doesn't make you any difference that after a day of working this hellish dirt a man gets hungry."

She narrowed her eyes and set her obstinate little chin. "I beg your pardon. I wasn't aware I was required to accommodate your stomach at any particular hour."

"I'm accustomed to eating at five o'clock. It's now going on seven. I'm starting to feel nauseous."

"In case you haven't noticed, I have a guest. I've been . . . occupied."

He looked over her head into the kitchen. The table was neatly set with two plates—unfamiliar dishes: white bone china painted with a border of red roses. The cobbler sat cooling on the countertop, sugar-bubbled and golden brown. Ned was nowhere to be seen. Nor was the baby.

"Where's Alex?"

"Alex?"

"Your son."

Her expression became exasperated. "I wish you would stop calling him that."

"What the hell am I supposed to call him? You haven't named him yet."

About that time Ned appeared from the hallway, entering the kitchen with the baby cradled awkwardly in his arms. He stopped abruptly at finding Rafe in the doorway. "Is there a problem, Charity?"

Rafe narrowed his eyes and Charity replied, "Not at all, Ned. Mr. Bastitas just came for his supper."

"You're holding him wrong," Rafe declared.

Ned stared at him blankly.

"The baby. For God's sake his head is flopping like a chicken with a wrung neck."

Ned hurriedly cocked the baby's head upright. The infant squirmed and thumped Ned's shoulder with a fist.

"The baby was crying." Charity hurried to collect her son before he began squalling again. "Ned was kind enough to pacify him while I finished supper."

"He isn't a sack of onions."

She bounced the boy against her shoulder and patted his back, her look at Rafe growing more agitated by the second. "I appreciate your concern, Mr. Bastitas. Now if you'll excuse us, our food is growing cold."

When Rafe refused to budge, Charity hurried to the door and closed it in his face.

"He's a mite meddlesome, ain't he?" came Ned's muted voice. "I don't rightly think you ought to be puttin' up with such behavior from a hired man."

Charity said something in response, but Rafe couldn't make it out. He peered through the slit between the curtains, unable to see much more than flashes of bodies moving around the table, followed by the scraping of chairs on the floor. At length, he forced himself to turn away, to descend the steps to where Jackson sat on his bony haunches, wagging his tail and hungrily eyeing Rafe's plate of stew and bread.

"Forget it," Rafe snapped. "I'm damn near hungry enough to eat you."

Jackson whined and lay down, muzzle on his dusty paws, brown eyes fixed on Rafe as he sat on the bottom step and proceeded to dip his bread into the stew.

Feminine laughter.

Masculine laughter.

Rafe flung his sopped bread toward Jackson, who caught it in midair; then he spooned up a potato.

Lilting, womanly words that babbled like spring water.

An undertow of baritone.

Rafe put the plate on the ground and watched as Jackson lapped up the stew, the dog's body quivering with appreciation.

Charity heaped a bone china plate with meat and potatoes, cut a slab of bread and padded it with soft yellow butter, then placed it on the table before Ned, who licked his lips and flashed her a smile as he caught her wrist in his thin fingers, squeezing lightly.

"I declare, Charity. You must be the best cook south of the Red River. Are all the ladies of Boston as talented with a cookpot?"

"I suppose." She wrist-wiped damp hair back from her brow and smiled a little. "By the looks of you, Ned, I suspect anything would taste good as long as it's filling."

"Reckon I am a bit on the thin side, but you know what they say. It ain't quantity but quality that counts. Besides, a month or so of this sort of fare and I'll be forced to let out my pants." He winked and speared a turnip. "My ma has been sayin' that I've been too long without the benefits of a talented woman. Maybe she's right. Since Margie died five years ago I've been too caught up in the farm."

He popped the turnip into his mouth. It bulged his cheek like a cow's cud as he continued to talk and chew. "Ma's sickness don't allow her to cook no more. If she manages to get to her feet it's a pure miracle. Doc Ritter

declares she ain't long for this world. Course I'm prayin'
that he's wrong. Me and Hank have taken care of Ma
since Pa died fifteen years ago. I just can't imagine the
farm without her.''

Charity turned back to the stove and blinked sweat from
her eyes. The room felt like a furnace. Her dress, freshly
washed and ironed before Ned's arrival, clung to her skin,
as sticky as the strip of flypaper tacked to the ceiling
above the window.

''By the way, I brung a few shirts with me that are
needin' a good patchin' job. Would ya mind to have a
look at them?''

In the distance, Rafe disappeared into the barn. Charity
walked to the door and looked down at the dog, still lick-
ing his chops after his unexpected feast.

''I like my shirts starched real stiff, if that's all right.''

Charity reached for a china plate. She heaped it with a
double helping of beef and potatoes, then ladled the meat
with rich brown gravy.

''There's a social Saturday down by Ernest's livery,''
Ned said. ''Thought you might care to go.''

She walked to the open door, plate in hand.

''Charity?''

She looked around. ''Yes?'' she replied absently.

''I just asked if you'd care to attend the social with me
Saturday.''

''Oh.'' She shrugged. ''Certainly, Ned. It's very kind
of you to ask.''

''You seem mighty preoccupied tonight, Charity. Anything wrong?''

''I was just wondering . . .'' She looked toward the
barn. ''It's not like Mr. Bastitas not to eat his supper.''

"If you ask me, you'd do well to send that saddle tramp on his way."

"Why would I do that?" She stepped onto the porch, her gaze sweeping the sprawling plot of furrowed earth, then focusing again on the barn.

"He gives me the shivers, that's why. Ever' time he looks at me I get the feelin' he's mentally slicin' off my scalp. It's them damned eyes of his, black as perdition. Charity? Charity, where are you? I could use another helpin' of turnips if that's all right. Charity?"

As Charity neared the barn, the sound of hammering came to her. Pausing at the door, she called Rafe's name softly. The dog was the first to appear, pink tongue lolling from one side of his mouth. Then came Bastitas, materializing from the shadows. His sleeves were pushed up to the elbows, revealing thick, muscular forearms shadowed with dark hair. His shirt was unbuttoned to just above his navel, exposing a shocking length of brown skin. His step slowed when he saw her; his black eyebrows lowered.

"I noticed that you gave up your food to the dog. Thought you might be hungry." She offered him the plate.

"Maybe I've just grown accustomed to eating two hours later." He took the food without so much as a thank-you and turned away.

"I heard the hammering." Her gaze drifted down his spine to the small of his back, then focused on the way his body filled out his pants. The worn material hugged each bulge and curve like a second skin. "Doing repairs?" she asked.

"Something like that." He plopped onto a crate, sending puffs of dust into the air.

"The plowing appears to be going nicely."

"If you call bloody hands and bruised shoulders nice, then, yes, the plowing is going nicely."

She leaned against the doorjamb. "You've been scarce lately. I hardly know you're on the place."

"Imagine that."

"You don't like Ned, do you?"

His chewing stopped. Focusing on his food, Rafe took a deep breath before replying. "It's none of my business what you do with your life."

"What's wrong with him?"

"Aside from being an idiot?"

"He's not an idiot."

"You might try being a little more particular."

"Meaning?"

"I mean he's a long way from Chester Muesler."

"It's not like this Godforsaken country has a lot to offer."

"So you'll settle for anything that happens along as long as he's breathing?"

"You're insufferably crass, Bastitas. I don't know why I continue to put up with you."

"True. You could always sweet-talk Ned into plowing that piece of rock you intend to grow potatoes in."

"Perhaps I will."

Shrugging, Rafe put down his plate and wiped his mouth with the back of one hand. "Just say the word, Mrs. Bell, and I'm gone. I'll drop you a line or two from Mexico."

"After you finish your killing, I assume." He stood and walked away.

"Yeah," he drawled and gave her an impertinent wink. "Just as soon as I wash the blood from my hands."

With that he disappeared into the dark barn. Charity

felt unreasonably shaken that he could so easily unravel her sensibilities. Why should she care, after all, if she woke up in the morning to find him gone? Why didn't she just send him on his way to Hell, wash her hands of him once and for all? She didn't need him any more. If she was any judge of men at all, Ned Williams wasn't simply making the long ride over here for food alone. He was a widower. He was lonely. So what if he wasn't particularly handsome, refined, dignified?

The shirt Rafe had worn the day before hung from a rusty nail in the wall. He had obviously put it there to dry. Sweat stains blotched the underarms of the sleeves and the chest, and made a triangle down the back. Charity took it in her hands, briefly closing her eyes as the scent of him washed over her. Her breath caught somewhere in the pit of her chest. She could have dealt with that, but it was the other thing that made her body feel as if it were turning to warm liquid. It was the reason she had done her best to avoid him these last few days.

He aroused her.

He made her breasts ache.

The very thought of him touching her brought on that increasingly familiar pressure that was so unbearable she wanted to scream. Lately there seemed to be no relief from it—except when she was with Ned, of course.

She buried her face in the shirt, relishing the incredible agony.

He appeared at the door, plow collar in one hand. The sight of Charity with her face buried in his shirt made him pause. The encroaching dusk painted his features with shadows, obliterating his eyes. She wanted him to ask her just what the hell she was doing. She wanted to tell him.

She wanted to lift up her skirts and show him exactly what his presence did to her.

But all he said was, "I suspect Ned will be wanting his cobbler about now."

Twisting her fingers into the shirt, Charity waited, experiencing a curious weightlessness in her stomach at the sight of him. Expectancy thrust up against the underside of her heart as she said, "You're welcome to join us . . . Rafe."

The sound of his name hung in the air between them.

"I'm sure Ned wouldn't appreciate the intrusion."

"I could send Ned on his way." She swallowed, hope surging as silence charged the air, bolstering her courage. She took a tentative step toward him. "I've missed talking with you these last few days."

"I've been . . . preoccupied."

"With the plowing. I know. You've done an incredible job. I only wish there were something I could do to repay you."

"Think of me each time you boil up a turnip."

She laughed.

Rafe moved to place the freshly oiled collar on a hook. The brass fittings shone dully in the gloom of the musty stable.

"The baby is missing you," she said.

Rafe rolled down his sleeves, then proceeded to button his shirt. His jaw worked.

"Just this morning as I was bathing him, he heard you whistling and began to squeal and kick. I'm certain he smiled."

"Yeah, well, it was probably gas." Carefully, he stepped around her, making certain to keep a distance between them, then moved to the barn door where he became silhouetted against the gray sky. Hands on his hips, his back to her, he appeared to stare at the house a long while before asking, "What does the boy think about Ned? More important, what does Ned think about him?"

She shrugged. "He has no children—"

"That's not what I asked. Does he hold him? Talk to him? Give a damn that he exists?"

"It's not as if the child is his own."

"What difference should that make?" Rafe took a breath and held it until his spurt of anger subsided; then he focused on the horizon, where heat lightning danced in orange and yellow bursts among the advancing clouds. "I hope to God it rains," he said more to himself than to her. As if in response, thunder rumbled.

Ned stepped from the house and looked toward the barn, hands on his hips in a show of irritation. "Charity?" he called. "You comin' in or what?"

Charity replaced Rafe's shirt on the nail, allowing her fingers to dwell on it momentarily before she moved past Rafe, and without so much as glancing his way, hurried toward the house.

Ned was standing in the kitchen with his hands planted on his hips. The dusk and the gray of the encroaching storm painted dark hollows in his cheeks and eyes as he glared at her, his lips thinned. "You took your good sweet time, Charity. I'm startin' to think that you and that saddle tramp are just a mite too friendly."

"*Friendly* hardly describes Bastitas's behavior recently," she replied absently, then proceeded to tiptoe to the bedroom, where her son slept soundly on her bed.

Ned moved up behind her. "I reckon I'm feelin' a tad jealous," he said.

"No reason to be."

She slid around Ned and returned to the kitchen. "There's a storm moving in. I suspect you'll be wanting to get home before it hits."

"Ain't no way I can beat that storm."

Water boiled in a pot on the stove. She poured the water into the dishpan, then turned back to collect dirty dishes from the table. Ned stood in her way, looking slumberous. "I was thinking to stay here and ride out the storm," he told her.

"But it could rain all night."

"That's a sure possibility."

Her movements slowed as his meaning sank in.

Ned reached around her and took the plate from her hand, setting it on the table again before closing his fingers over her shoulders, making her breath catch in her throat as he turned her to face him.

"I've been ridin' over here ever' night for a week, Charity, and it occurs to me that it's time for the two of us to get better acquainted."

"Meaning?"

"By now you must have figured by callin' on you like I have I must have more in mind than passin' time in idle chitchat. I'm a widower and I'm lonely. Yer a widow and lonely. We both got needs. I need a wife and you need a husband." He raised both eyebrows. "I can see I've caught you off guard."

"You talk of marriage as if it were nothing more than a convenience, Ned."

"Marriage between a man and woman such as us is a natural thing, Charity. Yer a fetchin' woman and should be seen after by someone other than . . . saddle tramps."

"Are you proposing to me, Ned?"

"Yes. In a manner of speaking, I guess I am."

She looked into his face and tried to imagine gazing into the same features for the next fifty years, but the only image to rouse in her mind's eye was Rafael de Bastitas—his haunting, burning eyes, his smirking mouth, and the gun strapped to his hard thigh.

"Are you saying, Ned, that you hold a fondness for me?"

"I wouldn't be proposin' marriage to you if I didn't." His eyes focused on her mouth. He was going to kiss her. Of course he was. He was preparing to press those thin, dry lips on hers and, hopefully, make her heart sing.

Please, she thought, as she offered her mouth to his as if it were some sacred sacrifice. *Please make my heart sing. Please wipe away all images of the dangerous stranger in my barn—the one who needn't even touch me to make my body turn inside out.*

His lips felt like old leather, and his breath smelled of onions. His arms closed around her like a bony trap, rigid, hurting, cutting off her breath while the pressure of his kiss forced her head back. When he at last came up for air, his breathing was hard. "I reckon we're gonna get on fine, Charity. Real fine. Like I said, I figure it's time we get acquainted—if you know what I mean."

There came a knock at the door. Bastitas stood there, peering in at them through the window. Ned cursed under his breath—something about good-for-nothing saddle tramps—while Charity's heart leaped to her throat and the desire to scrub away Ned's taste on her mouth was almost too much to contain.

Ned moved to the door and threw it open just as a clap of thunder crashed somewhere in the near distance. The noise rolled through the room like giant boulders as lightning appeared to dance momentarily over Rafe's shoulder.

"This better be important, Bastitas. You're interruptin' the widow's personal goin's-on here."

Rafe looked directly at Charity. She felt her face flush. The lingering taste and feel of Ned's kiss burned as if it were radiating like a hot ash on her mouth. Ridiculous. Why should she feel guilty because a man had kissed her? "What is it, Mr. Bastitas?"

Ned righted his shoulders. "Whatever you got to tell Mrs. Bell, mister, you can tell me first. I'll relay the message."

Rafe regarded Ned as if he were a bug to be squashed. "This is going to be a bad storm . . . Mr. Williams. I suggest that you leave before things get ugly."

Ned reached for Charity and pulled her close, wrapping his lanky arm around her shoulder while her body became as unpliable as wood. "I believe I'll be remaining here for the night," Ned confessed with an air of superiority.

The brazenness of Ned's actions spurred her mounting agitation. But it was the cold indifference on Rafe's face that kept her silent, made her inwardly fume, caused her to lean her body slightly into Ned's and allow her eyelids to grow droopy with the same look that she had supplied Rafe a time or two. Only then, the drowsy desire had been real. The turmoil in her heart and stomach had been exhilarating instead of nauseating.

Finally, Rafe shrugged, and without so much as a glance at Charity, said, "Just a friendly warning, Mr. Williams. I wouldn't like to see anyone get himself killed for something as silly as a . . . tempest." Then he walked away, his long dark hair and blousy shirt rippled by the escalating wind.

Pulling away from Ned's arm, Charity stepped out on the porch and down the steps, her hands clenched, her heart rapping at the base of her throat. She wanted to shout, *You arrogant bastard. I hate you for not giving a damn about what I do or who I do it with. I hate you for making me feel like a whore because I crave the touch of a saddle-tramp gunslinger instead of a decent sort like Ned Williams.*

She bit her lip instead, and tried to breathe amid the rising hot wind that whipped one way and then the other, driving sand into her ankles like a scattering of birdshot.

$\mathcal{E}leven$

AT LAST THE RAINS CAME, ALONG WITH THUNDER AND lightning and winds that threatened to tear the meager barn walls down around him. Rafe had consumed more whiskey than was prudent, considering his mood. For the last hour he'd made a hundred trips to the barn door only to stare through the black rain at the lantern-lit windows of the widow's house, not overly eager to confine himself in this leaking, stinking swine hole and think about the widow Bell spreading her legs for Ned Williams.

As if he should care what that crazy woman did or who she did it with.

He took another long drink of the bad whiskey he had bought the last time he had ridden into Hell, and did his best to visualize Frank Peters's face, to allow the absolute hate to engulf him, to madden him. And it did. The black beast of loathing roused and uncoiled like a sleepy snake. It slithered throughout his body in a slow, expanding heat that made him sweat.

Withdrawing a crudely hewn flute from beneath his mattress, Rafe sat on the edge of the bed and held the instrument like a god's offering in his uplifted hands.

Play it again, Papa.

Oh yes, darling, please play it again. It's the most beautiful music I've ever heard. So beautiful it makes me cry. Tell me the story of the flute again.

Rafe held the flute to his lips and closed his eyes, focusing his thoughts on the howling wind and rain pummeling the roof and walls; then he breathed softly into the reed. Like birdsong, the sweet tone obliterated the tumult erupting overhead. He played until the numbness overtook him, then gripped the flute fiercely in both hands as he lowered his head and resisted the overwhelming urge to snap it in two. Instead, Rafe closed his eyes and listened to the rain beat the roof and drip into a bucket in the corner. He hardly noticed when Jackson sat down beside him and laid his muzzle on Rafe's leg. The dog whined for attention and licked his hand.

"Rafe?"

He looked up.

Charity stood in the door, hair and clothes dripping rainwater around her feet. Her face appeared pale, her eyes shadowed. The lantern light reflected in her dark pupils as she regarded his features as if mesmerized.

He frowned and tossed the flute on the bed. "Don't you believe in knocking?"

"I did. I guess you didn't hear me." Her gaze drifted to the flute. "The music was . . . hauntingly sad. What is it?"

Rafe left the bed. "Indian folklore—'The White Birds.' The legend of a chief who so loved his wife and son that he turned his back on his warring tribe in order to live with his family alone in peace and harmony." He drank from the whiskey bottle, holding the whiskey in his mouth a long moment before swallowing. "For a while their lives were bliss. Then one day while he was off hunting, strangers came upon their farm and discovered his wife and son alone. When the chief returned home he found his family murdered. He hunted the killers down and avenged his family's slaughter, then he returned to his wife's and son's graves, lay upon them, and willed himself to die. Since that time three white birds have nested amid the stones marking the graves. The belief is that they're the souls of the family living peacefully together at last. Should any man or woman witness the white birds, they're assured of a long, happy and prosperous life.''

"How very sad,'' she whispered.

He reached for the shirt he had removed earlier, then tossed it to her. "Dry off before you ruin my floor.''

She glanced at the dirt floor, then toward the dripping roof where runnels of rain drummed into rapidly filling buckets, then toward the bed. Her eyes became intense, her jaw rigid. She clutched the shirt to her breast, but didn't put it on.

Rafe dropped into a chair and leaned back against the table, his elbow secluding a letter he had earlier attempted to write to his parents. He balanced the cane-seated, ladder-back chair precariously on two legs. "So what brings you here, Mrs. Bell? Don't tell me Ned reconsidered his motives for staying and struck off for home through the storm.''

"I'd appreciate it if you'd stop calling me Mrs. Bell. My name is Charity.''

He raised one eyebrow. "That's rather informal, isn't it? I mean between the hired hand and the boss lady. Ned might not like it.''

"I really don't care what the good folks around here think about me, or haven't you noticed?''

Rafe scratched Jackson behind his ear, his gaze never leaving Charity's. "What are you doing here . . . Mrs. Bell?"

She averted her eyes.

Leaving his chair, Rafe approached her. "You don't strike me as the kind of woman who's afraid of a little thunder and lightning. Have you been tipping the whiskey again, sweetheart? Are you having second thoughts about sleeping with Ned?"

She shook her head and mumbled "Bastard," under her breath; but she didn't back away, just parted her full lips and rolled a look at him that caused a spur of disquietude to dig into him. He rewarded her with an emotionless smile. "I might warn you that my mood of late has been a bit mercurial. If you came here looking to get laid—"

"You're a crude animal." With a look of frustration, she turned for the door.

He caught her arm. "Not so fast. Just what sort of game are you playing, Mrs. Bell? The last few days you've hardly spoken to me. Now here you are like some feline in heat. What's wrong? One man at a time not enough for you?"

She struggled and clawed at his hand. He pulled her close and lowered his head enough to catch the sweet smell of gardenias in her hair. "Is the perfume for Ned or me, Charity?"

Flinging back her head, she glared up at him with wide hysterical eyes, looking like she had the first night he had stumbled upon her giving birth. The insanity was back— the mind-bending pain and desperation. It rattled his anger.

"Just what the hell do you want from me?" he asked through his teeth.

Her lips parted, and in the instant they did he kissed her—brutally. Impassioned. Invaded the sweet, moist cavity of her mouth with his tongue until he felt as if his brain were on fire. Until the reality of her fingernails digging into his shoulders and her wet body molded against his drove like a fist into his groin. She kissed him back, her teeth grazing his lips, her tongue dancing with his, her hands clawing up the back of his neck and twisting into his hair, refusing to allow him to back away.

He managed to turn his face aside. She smothered his neck with kisses, touched her tongue to his chest, slid her knee up the inside of his thigh until he was forced to twist one hand into her hair and wrench her head back. Her mouth looked swollen and angry red in the dim lantern light. Her eyes glittered.

"I detest you," she finally managed in a hoarse whisper. "I detest what you do to me—how you make me feel. That's why I came here—to tell you that."

"You got one hell of a way of showing you detest somebody, lady."

"I'm going to marry him if you don't stop me."

He searched her face, aware that his fingers were painfully pulling at her scalp.

"If you send me back to that house I'll sleep with him. I swear it."

His fingers twisted harder; his jaw tightened. As she leaned her body closer to his, he felt his resistance evaporate. As if in a fog, he reached for her skirt and dragged it up, trailing his fingers along the inside of her smooth thigh until reaching the apex of her legs. Her mound was hot and moist and she spread her legs, thrusting the cleft eagerly against his exploring hand.

Her breath left her in a rush and she made a low painful moan in her throat that sounded like, "Oh God, I've fallen in love with you."

My dear sweet handsome husband, I shall love you forever.

His body stiffened. He pulled away, allowing Charity's dress to slide down her legs. For an instant, she stared up at him blindly, lost in confusion and the drugging effect of her desire for him. "Get the hell out," he groaned as he spun on his heel and slightly staggered to the table to retrieve the whiskey.

She was on him without warning, beating his back with her fists, causing him to ram into the table and knock over the whiskey. "God damn you," she wept as he threw his arms up to shield himself. "Insensitive bastardly coward! Just who do you think you are, rejecting me?"

He did his best to subdue her. She struggled like a hellcat, clawing the side of his face as she sobbed uncontrollably. "How dare you lie to me. How dare you make me think you love me when all you want is someone to cook your bloody meals and scrub your shitty floors. How dare you bring me to this disgusting hellhole to nurture your flawed pietistic flock while you're off sporting at Sally's. I've a good mind to tell them just what sort of man you are. I've a good mind to tell them that their beloved sermonizer hasn't got the guts or the manhood to partake in conjugal acts with his own wife!"

Stumbling back, the palms of her hands pressing against her temples, Charity swayed from side to side as if she would collapse like a house of cards at any minute.

Rafe slowly lowered his arms. The meaning of her tirade settled like lead in his chest.

Finally, as if dragged back to reality by the sound of pouring rain and rumbling thunder, she slowly lifted her head and raised her eyes to his. Her pallor faded white as a sheet before she moved like an automaton toward the door, then vanished into the dark.

The rain continued.

Rafe lay on the miserable cot and stared at the ceiling. He'd dozed once, only to awaken with a start as a crash of thunder shook the walls. Briefly he'd dreamed that he'd plowed his way through the rain to Charity's door, fully intent on stopping her from doing something she would ultimately regret, only to kick in the door to discover another woman and child sitting at the kitchen table—his wife and son, their beautiful faces smiling expectantly up at him, their throats slashed.

Jackson lay on the floor near the foot of the bed. He raised his head suddenly and looked toward the door, the hair on the back of his neck bristling. Rafe reached for the gun under his pillow, at the same time moving cautiously from the cot. The dog padded to the door, sniffing along the edge before sitting on his haunches and looking back at Rafe.

A moment passed before Rafe eased the pressure from the trigger and allowed himself to take a steadying breath. "I'm liable to shoot you if all you got to do is take a hike," he told the dog, who responded with a whine and a thump of his tail on the floor.

Rafe opened the door, allowing the dog to slip out into the dark barn. The cool, damp air felt good on his sweating face and chest. He stood there a long moment, eyes closed, allowing his body to shiver in the draft, his mind trying its best to disregard the impact of his dream. Nor did he wish to acknowledge that he had paced half the night in an attempt not to storm into the widow Bell's house and boot-kick Ned Williams out of her bed.

Jackson barked. Rafe groaned. No doubt the damn dog had cornered himself a coyote or, God forbid, a skunk. Cursing, he moved to the barn door and did his best to see through the dark and rain, only vaguely able to make out Jackson's form in the distance. He had something cornered all right, and it wasn't any flipping coyote.

He drew back the hammer on the gun, aimed the weapon in the general direction of the distant form, and moved cautiously into the rain. Jackson barked and whined, sloshing back and forth in the mud while Rafe did his best to keep his footing in the deepening muck.

The widow Bell sat on her knees in the mud, her naked body shaking as she hugged herself and rocked back and forth. She wept so hard that her body heaved.

"Jesus," Rafe whispered, and lowered the gun. Cautiously, he stooped before her. Her face was hidden behind her drapery of wet blond hair. Her arms made pale globes of her breasts. A sudden rage filled his chest as he reached a tentative hand toward her cheek. "What's he done to you, Charity? Has he hurt you? I'll kill him if he has."

She rocked back and forth and shook her head.

Catching her chin with one finger, he tipped up her face. Rain streaked down her cheeks and dripped from her nose. Her lower lip trembled. "What's wrong with me, Rafe? Why is it I expect so much from a man?"

He tried to breathe through the rain. "What the hell are you talking about, Charity?"

"Something dreadful must be wrong with me, Rafe. I'm sure to have some strange disease that makes me feel so undone in here." She touched her chest—the action revealing her upthrust little breast. Rafe's gaze locked on it before he could force his attention back on her ravaged face.

"Why is it I repel every man I ever cared for? Why don't they want me like I want them? Is it wrong to want to be held, to be touched? Am I so hideous—"

"Hell no," he snapped. "Nothing about you is hideous, Charity."

Covering her face with her hands, she sobbed so hard that her body appeared to draw in on itself.

Rafe sank to his knees in the mud and took her head in his hands. "Hush," he said through the rain. "Don't cry so hard. You're liable to hurt yourself."

"I don't care."

"Course you do. You have Alex to think about. Remember?" Just then a streak of lightning lit the sky. It hit the near horizon with a pop and flash that sent Jackson yelping toward the barn and Charity into Rafe's arms. She clung to him, her body shivering, her face buried against his shoulder.

He lifted her from the mire and ushered her toward the barn, kicked open the door of his room and walked her to his bed. Still, she wouldn't let go; he was forced to peel away her fingers where her nails had dug little bloody half moons in his skin.

Finally, he managed to sit her on the bed. He flung the sheet around her shoulders, but as he attempted to turn away, she grabbed his hand and raised it to her mouth. Her lips felt soft, her breath warm upon his damp palm.

"Charity—"

"Please. I just want to experience a man's hand against my face. I want to know what it's like to feel small and helpless beneath a man's touch." She nuzzled her cheek within the cup of his hand. "It feels so damn good, Rafe. Your hand smells good. And tastes good. Knowing that you got those calluses from plowing my ground makes me want to cry."

He allowed the gun to slip from his other hand. It made a soft thud as it hit the dirt floor. He cupped her face with both hands and swept her tears away with the pads of his thumbs. If he kissed her this time, there would be no turning back.

"You think I'm crazy," she whispered.

He nodded.

"Is it crazy for a wife to want to be loved by her husband?"

"Randall Bell didn't love you?"

"He believed the only proper wife for a man as virtuous as a preacher was a woman pure as the driven snow in both body and soul. I learned too late that my only worth to the Reverend Bell was to be his disciple. I should have realized it the night we were married. I should have run home to my father and mother the instant he refused to share our marriage bed. But there were always excuses: plans to make our journey here, sermons to write, souls to heal long after dark." Charity laughed bitterly. "I was so damn gullible then, and forgiving. I adored everything he stood for—the charity, the hope, the exhilaration of working at his side to lift the spiritually downtrodden. I thought for certain that our married life would become complete as soon as we settled into our new home."

Her fine brows drew together and her features became dark. The fire was back, dancing in her eyes as she focused on Rafe for the first time. Her voice dropped to a hoarse whisper. "But it didn't. As soon as we left Boston he changed. Instead of the angel Gabriel, he became Lucifer. He spouted fire and brimstone and ranted his sermons aloud day and night."

Charity pulled away. Clutching the sheet around her, she left the bed. "It was two years before I finally knew my husband conjugally. And only then because I managed to get him inebriated on church wine. It wasn't an occurrence I was eager to reprise . . . at least with him. I needn't have worried, of course. For the next few months I was cast to my knees before his congregation and emotionally flogged for my depravity. I . . . ceased to exist, since I was no longer pure enough to be the wife of so godly a man as he."

"Is the boy his?" Rafe asked flatly.

Her head whipped around. Her eyes flashed and her fingers twisted in the sheet. She said nothing, but finally raised her chin and set it at that stubbornly belligerent angle he had come to recognize. "No," she replied with a touch of sad haughtiness. "He's mine."

Standing, Rafe said nothing. Charity regarded him coolly, ponderously, before allowing the sheet to slide to the floor. "Will you send me away again?" she asked.

"No," he whispered. "I don't think so."

She walked past him to the bed and lay upon it, her damp, matted hair spilling over the edge of the mattress to brush the floor. She stretched her body like a cat's, lifting her arms above her head so that her hands tangled in her drying hair and her breasts sat upon her chest like peaked cups of snow. Her legs spread unashamedly, revealing her soft gold nest and the apricot lips within.

He removed his pants. Her eyes regarded his aroused

body, yet she said nothing, just moistened her lips with her tongue and rocked her body in invitation.

"Where is Williams?" he asked.

"Sleeping."

He eased onto the bed and settled between her legs. Her body quivered beneath his. She made an agonized sort of moan in her throat and closed her eyes. The sound made his breath catch; his fingers twisted into the old mattress in his effort to keep from burying his body into hers too swiftly. That's not what she wanted, or needed. He knew what she needed, what any woman needed: the touch, the whisper, the murmured adoration that would turn her drab and needy reality world into a moment of sublime ecstasy.

So he bathed her with his tongue: her eyes, her mouth, her breasts, and soft pale belly with its slightly pink stretch marks. He worshipped her with his hands—sliding into places that made her weep with arousal and pleasure. Each cry of delectation brought his own body to a peak of pure bright pain that magnified the hunger in him. Still, he didn't take her, not yet, because the sweet agony was too damn good. He wanted to drive her to the brink, until she begged, until she wept, until the final fragments of control shattered like glass in a windstorm.

He would dominate, because she desired to be dominated.

He would put from her mind all those other men who might have come before him—men who might have used her like most men used a woman, who had left her empty and unfulfilled and feeling like chattel. He would do that for her this one time—just for tonight—before he said goodbye, before he disappeared and became nothing more than a memory to assuage other memories.

She begged and wept at last. She thrashed and fought to breathe. Then he eased into her and watched her body and soul die for an infinitesimal moment . . . only his did as well—unexpectedly. The force catapulted through his chest like a bullet.

When he rolled from her body at last, he lay on his back, breathing hard, her head resting on his shoulder while his heart beat like a sledge at his chest wall. The scent of woman and gardenias floated around them while the rain and thunder continued to fill up the outside world. They lay for an hour without speaking, or sleeping, or moving; then she lifted her head and regarded his eyes.

"Are you in love with me just a little?" she asked.

"You're brazen, Charity. Did anyone ever tell you that?"

"Are you?"

"What if I say no?"

"Then I guess Ned is better than nothing."

"I won't do you any good, Charity. I can't stay here. I'm living on borrowed time as it is. Besides, I came to Hell for a reason."

"To kill someone. Whatever the reason, Rafe, is it worth your life and future happiness? The past is the past. A bullet isn't going to change that."

He listened to the rain tapping on the tin roof, and suddenly felt tired.

Finally, she rolled from the bed and retrieved the sheet from the floor. For the first time he noticed that her knees, shins, and feet were muddy, as were the tips of her hair.

"Then I'll be going," she said, and turned for the door.

"Charity."

She looked back hopefully.

"You're a strong woman. You don't have to settle,"
he told her gently.

"Neither do you," she replied with a faint sad smile;
then she quit the shabby room, leaving the door open behind her.

The dark swallowed her. Rafe rolled from the bed and
followed. By the time he reached the barn entry she had
mounted the back porch steps; she paused, allowed the
sodden sheet to slide to her feet, then disappeared into the
house, closing the door behind her.

Naked, the spray of fine rain spattering on the ground
before him causing him to shiver, Rafe gritted his teeth
and did his best to ignore the fist of discomfort twisting
his insides. The thought occurred to him that he hadn't
bothered to ask her if she had had sex with Ned before
he found her weeping in the rain.

He simply, or not so simply, didn't want to know.

Twelve

CHARITY TIED A KERCHIEF AROUND THE INFANT'S HEAD
to protect it from the unrelenting sun. The ride to Ned's
farm would be a long one. Already the baby was screwing
up his little features and thrashing his arms. He'd suckled
recently, so that wasn't the problem. She'd changed his
diaper and dressed him in the coolest gown she could find.

"That boy ain't goin' to squall the whole trip, is he?"
Ned asked from the bedroom door.

"He's hot."

"So am I, but I ain't bellyachin' about it constantly."

Charity bit her lip and scooped up the squirming child.
"Hush," she whispered, and jiggled him up and down,
to no avail. His fret became an all-out wail of displeasure.
"I don't know what's gotten into him lately. Seems like
he's always in a state."

"From sunup to sunset and half the night." Ned made
a sour face and scratched his head. "I ain't sure my ma
is goin' to be tolerable to such a racket."

"Then maybe it's best I don't go, Ned." Her back to
Ned, Charity smoothed the baby's sweaty head with her
hand, closed her eyes, and waited.

"We're goin' all right," he finally said. "I'll be waitin' in the wagon."

Ned left the house. Charity sank down on the edge of the bed and did her best to swallow. She wanted to curl up on her bed with her son nestled in her arms and sleep away the rest of her life. Except . . . the damnable bed was no longer a refuge. She wanted to burn the mattress and set fire to the memories of the last few nights. Oh God. When Randy had died she had been born. She had planned and dreamed of a future that she alone could build for herself and her son until the right man showed up to fulfill her every fantasy. She had been willing to wait forever, occupying her long nights with rambling conversations with some imaginary, faceless, nameless god of her mind's creation—a man who would shower her with devotion and adoration. A man who would share in her dreams.

But forever had shown up with a gun on his hip and hate in his eyes; he wasn't remotely interested in caring or sharing, not even after she had offered him her body and soul. He simply didn't want her. And Ned did.

At last she left the house, standing on the back porch stoop while her eyes adjusted to the intense light. All traces of the rain a few days before had vanished, soaked into the dry, cracked earth, giving life to an occasional tuft of buffalo grass and inviting the shriveled ground cactus to flower with great yellow blooms that would close during the hottest part of the day.

Since the night she visited Rafe in his room, she had avoided him, choosing instead to watch him from a distance as he mended the barn, sowed crops, and worked on the well pump. How could he go on with his life as if nothing had taken place between them? Why couldn't he care just a little that she now intended to marry another man?

The baby squirmed and whimpered.

Rafe walked from the barn, Jackson following on his heels. He stopped when he saw her, then looked toward the wagon, where Ned was adjusting the harness buckles and lines on a swaybacked horse. Charity took a fortifying breath, then walked toward him. He watched her approach, his features emotionless, his stance slightly arrogant, if not outright cautious. As usual, he was shirtless. He'd tied a blue bandanna across his brow to keep the sweat from his eyes. He looked, she thought, like a savage, and the memory of his body inside hers filled her with a sudden dizziness that made her knees weak.

She stopped a good distance before him and did her best to quiet the fretting child. "You should know that I'm leaving for a few days," she informed him. "Ned thinks it best that I get to know his family before we marry."

Rafe said nothing, just gave her that hooded look that made her stomach tense.

"While I'm gone you'll see after the livestock, won't you?"

"I usually do."

"Of course." She started to turn away, then paused. "You're welcome to use the kitchen while I'm gone. You know where everything is . . ."

"Right." His eyes narrowed and his jaw worked. He focused on her son, who grew more agitated by the second. "What's wrong with the boy?"

"I don't know. I can't seem to do anything to make him happy these days."

"Maybe because you're not so happy yourself."

"That's ridiculous." She laughed lightly. "I have every reason in the world to be happy now. I'm soon to become Mrs. Ned Williams. My days of lonely despair will be behind me."

He approached. She took a quick step back before catching herself and glancing toward Ned. He'd stopped his fussing with the harness and turned his attention back to her. If Bastitas touched her now she would collapse. Then what?

But he didn't touch her. He took her son into his arms and cradled him close, rocked him in the crook of his muscular brown arm and stroked the baby's cheek with his callused fingertip. The infant quieted. A flicker of a smile crossed his rosebud lips, then he cooed.

"Charity!" Ned stomped toward them. "You comin' or what? If we don't git goin' we'll be cookin' by noon."

Charity reached for the baby.

"I hope to hell you know what you're in for, Charity." Rafe surrendered the child, causing the baby to whimper and squirm.

"I don't need you, of all people, offering me advice, especially in light of the mess you've made of *your* life."

"You can go home—"

"*This* is my home. Every rock and cactus and spider. I can't go back to simply being a trinket to be set on a shelf and admired because I dress up a room."

"So you'll spend the rest of your life cooking and sewing for a man who hasn't outgrown his need for a nurse-maid. Christ, hasn't it occurred to you that the only reason for his being here now is because, like George Peters, he wants to get his hands on your farm?"

Breathing hard, Ned walked up and grabbed Charity's arm. "Git in the wagon. I'll be there in a minute." Then he turned on Rafe. "You'd best be makin' plans the next few days, Bastitas, 'cause once me and the widow Bell is married I'll be makin' the decisions around here."

"Meaning?"

"You got no place on this farm."

"We'll cross that bridge when, or if, we come to it." Rafe smiled coldly, and Ned bristled.

"I don't like you, Bastitas. You smell of a killer. I don't like how you look at Charity, and I don't care for your arrogance."

"And I don't care how the both of you talk as if I have no say-so at all in this matter," Charity declared from a distance, her voice trembling with anger.

Ned turned on her. "I told you to—"

"You don't tell me to do anything, Ned. The fact is, we're not married. This farm is mine. It will be mine after we're married—if we marry. Should I choose to employ Lucifer himself to run this farm, I'll do so."

His face going ash gray, Ned glared at her with his mouth open.

She didn't wait for a response, but turned, hesitated while she forced strength back into her knees, then moved to the wagon. Finally, without a word, Ned joined her. Charity refused to look back as they headed for Hell.

Frank Peters put down his poker hand and lifted his gaze toward the saloon door just as Lendon hurried in, his face flushed by the morning heat.

"We got to talk, Frank," Lendon said.

"I told you not to bother me when I'm conductin' business, Lendon."

"Yer gonna want to hear this."

Frank tapped his cards on the table and shrugged apologetically at his fellow players. They groaned and grumbled before shoving back their chairs and departing. Tossing aside his straight flush, Frank pursed his lips. "This better be good, Len. You just cost me ten dollars."

"I just seen the widow Bell ride out of town with that skunk Ned Williams. Rumor is she's about to marry him."

"Bull hockey."

"It's true, Frank. Seems Ned stopped in at the mercantile and was struttin' and crowin' to the boys that he was takin' her home to meet his ma and brother."

Frank reached for the cigar in his pocket.

Lendon sidled closer and lowered his voice. "Are you thinkin' what I'm thinkin', Frank?"

"I'm thinkin' that the widow Bell ain't about to give up that farm of hers to move onto that sorry excuse for a parcel Ned owns."

"Which means Ned will be movin' to Charity's place, lock, stock and barrel."

"Seems good ol' Ned is lookin' to broaden his horizons."

"Looks that way, Frank."

Frank stood and walked to the door. He chewed his cigar. "I'm wonderin' what happened to that guard-dog saddle tramp she had watchin' her back?"

"Still there, as I understand it. Ned was braggin' on how he aimed to get rid of him soon as he and the widow tied the knot."

"Ned ain't got the balls to swat at a snake if it aimed to bite him. Might prove interestin' though. No tellin' what sort of confrontation might arise between them. One of them is just liable to get himself killed."

"Maybe even both," Lendon hurried to add.

Frank smirked as he turned back to the room. "You still afraid of that gunslinger, Lendon? You suspect he's some ghost arisen from the grave to reap vengeance on yer sorry head? Don't it stand to reason that if he was, he would have already cut all our throats?"

Lendon mopped sweat from his brow. "I don't know, Frank. I just don't know nothin' these days since I vowed off the whiskey."

"You still havin' them dreams?"

"Naw, Frank. No dreams."

"You still hearin' flute music?"

Lendon shook his head.

"Don't you think that's a tad coincidental? No whiskey, no booger bears hidin' in the shadows at night."

Slapping at a fly on his neck, Lendon mumbled under his breath about being as thirsty as a mud dauber in a drought; then without looking at Frank, he exited the saloon, pausing to glance up and down the street before heading toward the sheriff's office.

"Idiot." Frank grinned and hitched up his pants; then his good eye locked on a hulk of a man reclined in a chair a few feet away.

The stranger peered up at him from beneath a slouch hat, eyes as pale blue as ice. A bright red beard covered the lower portion of his face and draped like a scraggly bib over his chest. He wore a buffalo hide across his shoulders.

"You got a problem, stranger?" Frank demanded.

"Nope." The man reached for his drink, his gaze still locked on Frank.

"You make a habit of eavesdroppin' on folks' conversations?"

The man shook his head.

Frank hitched his pants again and adjusted the gun belt on his hip. The stranger didn't blink, just set his empty glass down and slowly left his chair, revealing a gun strapped to each massive thigh. Frank took a step back before catching himself. He cursed the fact that he'd forgotten to pin on his badge that morning . . . not that a pitiful piece of corroded tin would intimidate this mad-dog son of a bitch in the least.

As the stranger moved toward the door, Frank stepped aside and asked, "You passin' through or what?"

"Who's askin'?"

"The sheriff."

The man made a sound of amusement and cut his gaze to Frank's. "That's funny," was all he said before stepping from the establishment into the harsh sunlight and the racket of the busy street. Frank thought about plugging him in the back, but changed his mind. Instead, Frank watched the man move in a frighteningly graceful manner, considering his size, toward the sheriff's office. Good. If the brute had a mind to kill somebody, maybe it would be Lendon.

Lendon decided that borrowing a swig of Frank's whiskey wouldn't be a bad idea, considering the time of day and how hot it was. He'd proven to his cousin that he could do without drinking, if he had a mind to. Besides, it was the middle of the day. The dream terrors had only belea-guered him at night. Maybe Frank was right. Since he'd stopped swigging before bedtime there had been no more music, no more creepy feelings that he was being haunted by ghosts.

As Lendon pried the stopper loose with his teeth, the

door swung open. A buffalo filled the entry, causing Lendon's jaw to go slack.

The stranger looked around, his eyes fixing on the wall of yellowed wanted posters. He examined the collection carefully before ripping them down with a swipe of one big hand, crumbling them into a scattering of dust, which he flung at Lendon's muddy boots. "Seems your sheriff don't read his mail often enough. These hombres done rotted in their graves a long time back."

"How would you know?" Lendon gulped. That damned whiskey was looking better by the second.

The man showed his teeth in a smile. " 'Cause I killed 'em," he said.

"You don't say."

"Take Clyde there. I caught him sleepin' one day in the back of a gristmill and cut his throat from ear to ear 'fore he ever knew what hit him. Then there's Schuster King. I nailed him 'tween the eyes while he was humpin' some Mexican gal in Goliad." He chuckled and scratched his chin through his beard. "Deke Betz met his maker on a Sunday afternoon. I tossed his sorry hide in a pit of squirming rattlers out near the White Mountains. I figured it was his just desserts, considerin' what he done to deserve getting his puss on that poster."

Lendon glanced at the whiskey bottle. "What, exactly, did he do?"

"Stole a milk cow."

Lendon coughed. "He got his puss on a poster for stealin' some damn cow?"

"It was my cow."

Finally, the man turned and Lendon moved back, bumping the desk and knocking over the whiskey bottle, spilling Frank's cherished sour mash in a stream to the floor. Gawd, Frank was going to be pissed, sure enough.

"I don't take kindly to cold-blooded murder, Lendon. Fact is, I've made it my purpose in life to make certain to carry through with the good Lord's will—an eye for an eye, so to speak. Besides, collecting bounties on some scum-suckin' no-good frogshit of a pissant ain't a bad way of makin' a living. Saves the government the time and money of tryin' and hangin' em.''

His voice dry as lint, Lendon asked, "What are you doin' in Hell?''

"Waitin','' he replied with a disconcertingly pleasant smile. "Waitin', watchin', . . . and listenin'.''

Charity decided that the only disease plaguing Greta Williams was her immense lust for food and her aversion to labor. The woman weighed three hundred pounds if she weighed an ounce. From dawn until dusk she sat her hulk in a rocker near an open window and looked over her pitiful domain as if she were the Queen of Sheba.

From the moment Charity arrived with Ned, the woman had made no secret of the fact that she didn't care for children or lazy women. Greta herself had given birth to five children, only two of whom were still living. Until her husband's death fifteen years ago, she had slaved her fingers to the bone to provide him with comfort, and in Greta's opinion it was definitely a woman's lot in life to see that her husband's comforts were provided for. Charity surmised, however, that dedication to husband and dedication to sons were two entirely different matters.

By the looks of her pitiful excuse for a farm, Greta Williams had traded in her scrub brush for a comfortable rocking chair in the shade, leaving Ned and his retarded brother to fend for themselves. The fact that they didn't appear to give one iota that the farm was collapsing in on itself didn't concern her a degree. Charity suspected that the barn hadn't been cleaned in eons. At night the stench was so bad she'd been forced to close her bedroom window, only to open it again due to the insufferable heat.

It hadn't taken long for the realization to sink in that her presence in Ned's home had more to do with her passing the grade as a cook and housekeeper than her simply getting to know Ned's family. Rafe had been right, damn him. Ned wanted a nursemaid—someone to take up where his ma had quit: scrubbing floors and cooking.

She had known in her heart all along that Ned didn't care for her any more than she cared for him. A woman who cared remotely for a man craved his touch; she anticipated the moment alone when they would fill up each other's world with passion and bliss. A man who truly cared for a woman made certain that happened. At least . . . that was what she had always believed while married to Randall. It was Rafael de Bastitas, however, who had proven her right. To accept less now from her husband would be a mockery.

Charity mulled over her decision not to marry Ned for nearly a week, however, clinging to the hope that at some point the slightest spark of fondness and desire for Ned and his family would flicker to realization. It didn't. By the evening of the fifth day she had come to the end of her patience. As Ned joined her in the kitchen, she didn't bother to look up as he poured himself coffee, sipped it and shuddered.

"Damn coffee is stout as boar piss, Charity. This crap could melt silver. Why you got to make it so dang strong?"

"Some people like it that way." She punched the biscuit dough with her fist.

"Like that bastard Bastitas?" he asked, causing her to hesitate in her kneading. Ned hissed through his teeth, then tossed the coffee into the washpan. "I reckon that son of a bitch didn't have no problem gettin' you to cater to his tastes . . . did he?"

Charity grabbed up the rolling pin and proceeded to flatten the dough. Ned was spoiling for an argument—had been for some time. She had done her best to avoid any unpleasantness, considering that she and her son were his guests—and until now, she'd held on to the asinine idea that she wanted to shackle herself to a life of drudgery.

"It occurs to me that you get a real closed mouth when I bring up his name, Charity. Why is that?"

"If you're insinuating something, Ned, then do so. Don't beat about the bush."

He moved up behind her and put his hands on her shoulders. She stiffened.

"I'm thinkin' that you and him had a cozy little relationship goin' before I come along. I'm thinkin' that, if you had your druthers you'd rather be marryin' him."

"He doesn't want me," she snapped before catching herself and squeezing her eyes closed. She moved away, only to be brought up short as he sank his fingers into her arm. Pain rendered her motionless as he moved up behind her, pressed his body indecently against hers and said, "You slept with that saddle tramp, Charity?"

"That's none of your business, Ned."

"It's a man's right to know who's crawled between his intended's legs."

"You have no rights. I don't intend to marry you."

He squeezed against her harder.

"I can't imagine why you would even want me, Ned. Your mother detests me—"

"She detests that squallin' brat of yours."

"He comes with me, remember?"

He smirked and cupped her face with his free hand. She did her best to turn away, but he gripped her jaw and forced her head back. "That don't matter, Charity. We'll be havin' our own soon enough."

The blood left her face. Dear God, that possibility hadn't occurred to her.

"I always imagined this place crawlin' with my young'uns. My first wife was barren, God rest her worthless bones. If a woman can't produce, then what the hell good is she to anybody?"

"I can't settle again for a man who doesn't love me, Ned . . . or I him—"

"A bit late to come to that decision, considerin'."

"I made a mistake but I'm not willing to pay for it for the rest of my life."

"Think again, Mrs. Bell. I brung you into my house and introduced you to Ma. That makes our engagement official and I'm not about to let you make me a laughin'stock."

"You can't force a woman to marry you, Ned."

"We'll see about that."

Charity refused to join the Williamses for supper. Instead, she sat on the front porch rocking her son in her arms, listening to the clattering of dishes, doing her best to swallow back the sensation of hysteria clawing at her insides. She was starting to feel crazy again, as if she were going to start screaming and be unable to stop.

What if Ned had put a baby in her?

She covered her mouth with one hand, gripped her son fiercely to her bosom and closed her eyes, listening to the muted conversation in the house.

"Chops is tough, Ned," Greta was saying. "I don't know what you want with a wife who can't cook."

"She's easy on the eyes," Ned declared with a full mouth.

"I suspect she's lazy, too," Greta continued. "Ever' time I see her she's staring at the clouds, her expression distant as an idiot's. I think she's crazy."

"She'd have to be to have married the preacher." Ned again.

"You deserve better, son. Pass them potatoes."

"She makes one hell of a mean bowl of mashed," Ned declared.

" 'Bout the only thing she can do. You want gravy? If you ask me she don't look like she could stand up to birthin' a lot of young'uns. She might end up like Margaret."

"She ain't barren, obviously," Ned said.

"It ain't natural how she spends so much time with that baby. Why ain't she in here with us, anyhow? Something goin' on between you that I should know about?"

"No, Ma."

" 'Cause I can't continue the way I have been, you know. I got to have help. There'll be cannin' come July. It's all I can do these days to walk from my bed or rocker to the table. Before I'm laid in the ground I got to know my boys will be taken care of proper."

"Don't be talkin' that way, Ma. You ain't dyin' no time soon. Me and Charity is goin' to be married just as soon as the justice of the peace makes his way back to Hell."

Charity entered the house, moved to the kitchen door and looked at the family, mother and sons bent over their food like starving coyotes, scraping every last morsel into their mouths.

"There's not going to be any marriage," Charity declared, causing Greta to look up. Ned stared into his plate, his face going as red as the beet on his fork. "I told Ned this morning that I couldn't marry him. I don't love him. I simply ask now that I and my son be taken home."

Greta put down her fork.

Ned wiped bean juice off his chin and sat back in his chair. He slowly raised his eyes. "Don't listen to her, Ma. She's bein' hysterical, is all."

"The only hysteria I feel right now, Ned, is over the thought of becoming a part of this family."

Greta's hand flew to her chest as she took a long, wheezing breath. Ned jumped from his chair, snatching up a napkin and plunging it into her glass of water.

"Don't listen to her, Ma," Ned said through his teeth as he mopped her brow. "We had us a little tiff this mornin', is all. Soon as supper is done I'll set it right."

Charity turned away and, holding her son close, returned to her bedroom and closed the door.

Charity lay across the bed, her head near the open window, her body sweating from the heat.

"I've done something really stupid, baby boy. I've taken on a man and his family that I don't even like, much less love. Rafe was right. I've settled. I settled when I married your father as well. The moment I discovered that heaven would most likely turn out to be hell, I should have washed my hands of it and left. But no one likes to fail, do they?

"I broke my parents' heart, and Chester's as well. How could I have returned to Boston a used woman of a failed marriage? My mother would have been humiliated. I would have been an outcast among my peers."

Charity turned her face toward the window. A breeze touched her brow and caused her eyelids to grow heavy. God, she was tired. Oh, to be home in her own bed, where it was her right to bathe in the middle of the afternoon if she wanted. To lie naked over her cotton quilts and allow the breeze to kiss her aching body cool again. To drowsily gaze out the window and watch Rafael de Bastitas move across her line of vision like some powerful ocean undertow, dragging her heart into some dark, swirling place that obliterated all judgment. Would he still be there when she returned home? When she informed him that she had no intention of marrying Ned Williams, would he be happy?

The baby at last quiet beside her, she allowed her mind to drift. She saw herself lying sublimely across Rafe's cot, his dark body poised over hers, features hungry, erection massive and probing, aching to drive inside but resisting.

Wicked woman.

His hands cupped her breasts and she groaned. They slid over her slick body and she whimpered and opened her legs further. Now, she tried to cry. Do it now before I scream of insanity. But the words wouldn't rise in her throat, which suddenly felt as if a vise were cutting off her air.

Her eyes flew open. She stared up into Ned's smirking face as he pressed his forearm across her neck. Charity gasped and clawed at his arm. The baby beside her wailed in despair.

As she beat his shoulders with her fists, Ned shook his

head and drew up her dress. She closed her eyes and gritted her teeth, wondering in the deep recesses of her consciousness if her son would someday remember this.

"This is gonna teach you to show me up in front of hired help like that sorry saddle tramp you got workin' your farm," Ned declared. "You don't show me up in front of Ma again, either."

She grabbed Ned's ears and twisted. He howled in response and rolled from the bed onto the floor, with Charity still hanging on to his ears, sinking her nails into his flesh and peeling it away in little runnels.

He managed to break her hold and fling her aside before scrambling to his feet. Charity stared up at him, her throat feeling as if it had been crushed. "I'll kill you in your sleep for this, Ned. I swear it," she hissed through her teeth.

As he left the room, hands plastered to his ears to stem the flow of blood, Charity ran for the door, slamming it behind him.

Rafe awakened suddenly, body sweating from the insufferable predawn heat. His head pounded with whiskey. He needed to vomit but he was too damn tired to stumble out back, as he had for the last two nights. Still, he suspected he was going to have little choice in the matter.

Groaning, Rafe rolled from the bed, squeezed his eyes closed and took a deep breath. He'd be damn lucky to make it out back of the barn.

He walked slowly to the barn door, braced himself against the wall and waited for some stirring of wind to encourage him. The house sat black and empty in the distance, causing the nausea in his stomach to rise like a wave. Then and there he decided that as soon as his head cleared, he was bidding *adiós* to this farm. He was going to kill a few people, then set up housekeeping in Mexico—just like he'd vowed for the last three years—before the crazy widow Bell drove him as nutty as she was.

Jackson barked somewhere in the distance. Rafe mopped the sweat from his head with his forearm and did his best to focus on the barking instead of his churning gut. Where the blazes was the dog? A hell of a long way off, by the sound of it. Crazy mutt was going to get himself eaten by coyotes.

Rafe frowned and listened harder. He walked toward the road, thinking that he should go back and get his gun, then decided, what the hell. He was still too damn drunk to hit the side of the barn at ten paces.

Barefoot and shirtless, he moved toward the sound of the dog's barking.

The sky turned gray. Jackson barked louder and closer.

Rafe stopped. An image materialized from the dark. A ghostly sight at first, it appeared to lumber, to sway, to stumble, then to set its course right once again and move forward.

"Charity?"

The baby asleep on her shoulder, Charity paused long enough to regain her bearings. As he approached her, recognition was a moment in coming, then her pale face lit in a relieved smile. "You're still here," she sighed aloud.

"What the hell are you doing?" he demanded, then stared out into the dark beyond her. "Where's Ned?"

"At home with his ma, I suppose." She shrugged and smiled weakly.

Taking her head in his hands, Rafe did his best to search her face, which looked bone-weary even in the dimmest of light. "Have you been walking all night, Charity?"

"It wasn't so bad, though I admit that my arms have grown a bit stiff. I declare this boy put on a pound each mile I walked." She tried to laugh, but her chin quivered.

Rafe reached for the baby.

"No!" She shook her head. "Not yet. He's my strength, you see. He's kept me from falling."

With a muttered curse, Rafe swept Charity and the baby up in his arms and headed the quarter mile up the road to the house.

Her head resting on his shoulder, she asked, "Are you glad we're back?"

"What do you think?"

"Did you miss us?"

"Like a toothache."

"We missed you, too," she whispered near his ear.

Thirteen

THE INFANT'S BED HAD BEEN HEWN FROM MESQUITE wood and was sanded smooth as glass. It swayed from side to side on what had once been the rockers on Charity's rocking chair. With barely a touch of her fingertips, it rolled into an easy rhythm that sounded like little drumrolls on the wood floor. The mattress was a pillowcase overstuffed with goose down. Where Bastitas had found goose feathers, Charity couldn't guess. It didn't matter. At last her son had a bed, and by the looks of him, sleeping contentedly, he wholeheartedly approved.

Charity wept quietly and ran her hands lightly over the scrolled spindle sides and the headboard boasting the carved image of a jackrabbit in full flight. "I believe this is the most beautiful cradle I've ever seen," she whispered aloud, unaware that Rafael had moved to the bedroom door and stood watching her.

"Thank you," he said, causing her to jump and glance at him from behind her curtain of yellow hair. His tone sounded congenial, but his face looked grim and angry.

Charity wiped her nose with a kerchief and continued

to gaze down at her son. "You must have been working on the cradle for days."

"Nights. Look at me, Charity."

She turned away and walked to the window, where the dusk light painted pale shadows on the rug at her feet. "I don't know how I can ever thank you enough, Rafe."

"You can try looking at me."

She touched her cheek and bit her lip.

"There's no point in attempting to hide those bruises, Charity. I sat in that damn chair there for the last eight hours staring at them while you slept. Being a man of considerable imagination, my brain went a little crazy with all kinds of reasons how you might have got them. But I'm also practical. If I'm going to kill a man I've got to be damn sure he's guilty of what I'm shooting him for."

"You're not going to shoot anyone," she responded wearily.

"Think again."

"I don't intend to marry him, so the point is moot. Besides, you've got no stake in this, so why should it matter to you?" Charity sat before her dressing table and regarded the bruises on her neck, jaw and cheek. Her arm throbbed, not to mention her feet, thanks to her long trek home. Then she lifted her gaze to Rafael's reflection as he leaned against the doorjamb, thumbs hooked over the waistband of his low-slung breeches. He regarded her with a thunderous look, then turned on his heels and left the house.

Charity hurried after him. "Rafe!" she called from the porch. He didn't stop, so she ran down the steps and grabbed him. He jerked his arm away, refusing to look at her.

"Get the hell out of my way, Charity."

"I won't unless you promise me you won't go looking for trouble."

"What gives you the idea I'd go looking to harm a hair on Ned's head?" He tried to sidestep her, but she barricaded his way.

"I don't like the look on your face, Rafe. It's terrifying."

"Then get the hell back in the house and you won't have to look at it."

"I could never live with myself if I was the cause of a man losing his life . . . especially if that life is yours." She touched his arm. "You know how I feel about you, Rafe."

He turned on her with so frightening a look that she stumbled back. "Just shut up with that kind of talk, Charity. The fact is you'd love any man who showed you a little consideration."

"That's not so," she countered angrily.

"No? Ned comes sniffing your skirts for a week or two and you're ready to marry him."

"But I didn't love him!"

"Oh, *that*'s reassuring."

"I get lonely sometimes—"

"We all get lonely, dammit."

"But you're not a woman with a little baby. You don't have folks like George Peters waiting out there somewhere to take everything you own. You don't have a child's future to consider."

He turned his dark eyes to hers; his jaw worked. Hands curling into fists, he looked, for a moment, as if he would implode.

More softly, she said, "I don't think I would have gone

through with the marriage for any reason. But a woman has to consider any and all opportunities. Out here, they don't present themselves every day." Swallowing hard, she lowered her eyes and shrugged. "I slept with him—"

"I don't want to hear about it." He started for the barn, yelling back over his shoulder, "What you do with other men is your business. Hell, if you want to fornicate with every man south of the Red River, be my guest. I just don't want to know about it."

"Because you're jealous and you just won't admit it," she yelled back. He spun toward her, spilling black hair into his eyes. He moved toward her like a slow, swirling tornado, causing her to back away and attempt a half-hearted smile. "You can deny all you want to, Bastitas, but if you didn't have a smidgen of feeling for me, you wouldn't still be here. Why would you bother to make my son a bed—"

"It was intended to be a wedding present."

"A baby's bed?" She continued to back away.

"I figured you'd need that extra pot he's been sleeping in to cook for Ned."

She planted her feet and lifted her chin, refusing to cower any longer. "Look me in the eye, Bastitas, and tell me you have no feelings for me at all."

Charity crossed her arms and waited, her foot tapping in the hot dust as he stood before her and fumed. Finally, he turned on his heel again and continued toward the barn.

"Are you telling me that our lovemaking meant nothing to you?" she called after him.

"I'm not headed down that road, lady."

He disappeared into the barn. Charity frowned and followed, pausing at the barn door and allowing her eyes to adjust to the dark. He exited his room with his gun and holster in one hand and started for his horse.

"Fine," she cried. "Go ahead and get yourself killed and see what good that will do me."

Rafe grabbed up his saddle and swung it onto the horse's back.

"Give Sheriff Peters a reason to come looking for you here. While he's at it he just might decide to do his brother a favor and shoot me for harboring a cold-blooded killer." As he adjusted the saddle against the horse's withers, Charity moved up behind him and laid a hand on his back. His movements stopped. His body tensed. "Think of the child, Rafe," she pleaded softly. "You brought him into this world. If it weren't for you we might both be dead. How could I ever explain to him that the man who saved our lives got himself hanged for killing someone? He adores you, Rafe. You're his hero."

Rafe shook his head. "He's too damn young for those kind of feelings, Charity."

"Yours were the first hands to hold him. Yours were the first eyes he looked in. You're the one who gave him sustenance, rocked him to sleep and sang him lullabies. When he hears your voice, his face lights up like a candle flame. You might not give two inklings for me, but will you deny that you feel a fondness for my son?"

He said nothing, just leaned heavily against the gelding and allowed his shoulders to sag.

"Promise me," she whispered. "Promise you won't go gunning for Ned Williams."

An excruciatingly long moment passed before he nodded. "Fine. I promise I won't shoot Ned Williams."

• • •

Ned Williams downed his fifth shot of sour mash and tossed in his ante, then grinned at Frank and George Peters and their cousin Lendon. "It's a true pleasure playin' poker with you boys," Ned said. "Yep, a real pleasure."

George raised his eyebrows and reached for his cigar. He cut his gaze to Frank and grinned. "I do believe the man likes your sour mash, Frank."

"What's not to like?" Frank replied. "Jack Daniels is goin' to put Lynchburg, Virginia, on the map with this ambrosia. Once a man has grown a taste for the best, there just ain't no goin' back to rotgut. Same with women. Once you've had that special one willin' and pantin' in yer arms, goin' back to the ugly ones is a little like humpin' yer own sister. Ain't that right, Ned?"

Ned shrugged and eyed his empty shot glass thirstily. Frank refilled it, then sank back in his chair.

Cards were passed. Bets continued. Ned sucked his glass dry again and fumbled with his few remaining coins on the table.

Frank and George exchanged glances. George leaned toward Ned and plastered a look of condolence on his face. "Rumor is you and that pretty little widow Bell is no longer about to stroll hand in hand into matrimonial bliss."

Ned mumbled and recounted his coins.

"That retarded brother of yers tells us that she up and snuck off in the middle of the night. That was after she insulted yer ma."

"Bitch insulted my whole family," he muttered.

"That's a right shame. She's a mighty attractive lady. Not a man in this town who wouldn't care to cuddle up beside her on a cold night. You're a much-envied man around here, Ned."

Sitting back in his chair, Ned looked from Frank to George to Lendon, whose face looked pale as a fish belly, and proceeded to smirk. "She was brazen, pure and simple. Had no shame about her body. Wanted me to touch her all the time. I shoulda known right then that I was in for trouble. Hell, a wife's place is to lie there and satisfy whether she likes it or not. But I'm tellin' you, she was brazen and demanding—tellin' me when I could or couldn't have a little. I taught her, though. Thought she could turn me away. Thought she could insult my family. I showed her what she was in for once she married Ned Williams. I stormed right into the room and jumped her, that squallin' brat of hers lyin' right there beside her. She fought me like a hellcat. You see these claw marks around my ears?"

Ned tipped his head from side to side, exhibiting his crusty wounds to Frank, George and Lendon, then sat back again and puffed out his chest. "By the time I was done she was whimperin' for mercy. I told her she best get used to it. That was what was goin' to happen ever' time she thought to deny me my conjugal rights."

Frank shook his head and looked at George. "I can't imagine why she would have snuck off like she did, can you, George?"

"You just can't please some women, Frank," George replied; then Lendon spoke up.

"I don't rightly think you boys ought to be sputterin' on about the widow Bell in such a public place, if you know what I mean."

Frank and George rolled their eyes, then George shook his head. "I hope you ain't goin' on about ghosts agin, Len, 'cause this ain't the time nor place. Ned here is sufferin' with an achin' heart."

"Don't matter." Ned nudged his empty shot glass toward Frank and sighed. "She couldn't cook worth a damn anyhow."

Just after midnight, Ned stumbled into the street, grabbed hold of a hitching post for support and did his best to focus on the horse and wagon still parked in front of the mercantile, the bed loaded with supplies his ma had sent him to town that afternoon to collect for their supper.

"Damn," he muttered aloud. "Ma is gonna have my scrawny butt for this." He belched and scratched his crotch, doing his best to focus on the wagon and the excuses he would give his ma for not returning home when he was supposed to. Several men exited the saloon behind him, each slapping him on the back and congratulating him for putting the widow Bell in her proper place. He nodded weakly and looked for some place to vomit.

Frank and George exited then with a half-dozen others, each bawling in laughter so loudly Ned wondered if his head wouldn't pop. They surrounded him like a wave, causing the sour mash in his belly to roll up his throat.

Frank smiled broadly. "No doubt about it, Ned, yer one hell of a man for doin' what you done, 'specially in light of that mad dog she's got protectin' her skirts these days."

Ned blinked and frowned. Sweat popped out of every pore in his body as he tried his best to fix on Frank's words. They must be damn good 'cause the men around him were all staring at *him*—Ned Williams—as if he had just won a war single-handedly.

". . . Bastitas is a killer through and through. If he was to learn what you done to the widow he'd probably castrate you first, then slice off the top of yer head."

"Bastitas?" Ned squeezed his eyes closed and swallowed. Think. *Bastitas*. Damn, he'd forgotten about Bastitas.

"Yep," George agreed. "I admire any man who ain't afraid of retribution. A man who thumbs his nose at certain death. If I was you, Ned, I'd take to packin' a weapon."

"Might try some target shootin' as well," someone else chimed in, causing another burst of earsplitting, stomach-churning laughter. Then someone else added, "When you've sobered up, of course!"

The men dispersed, fading like phantoms into the dark. All but Frank, who remained at Ned's side, smoking a fat cigar and gazing out at the emptying streets. Finally, he looked at Ned soberly. "Best you git home to yer ma, Ned, and stay there a while."

Ned nodded the best he was able, considering that his head felt as if it weighed a ton.

Frank walked off toward his office, his cigar ash winking orange in the dark.

The lights of the closed saloon went out. Ned bent at the waist and tossed up Frank's sour mash until he felt as if his innards were going to rip and his brains ignite. Finally, he managed to stand well enough to make his way toward his wagon, his step slowing as a figure moved from the near shadows. Ned froze, widened his eyes to better see through the dark, then allowed his shoulders to relax.

"Hell, Lendon, you 'bout give me a heart attack. What are you doin skulkin' about this hour of night?"

"The booger bears are back," Lendon said, in such a flat tone that Ned raised his eyebrows.

"The what?" he asked.

Lendon moved toward him. His face looked whiter than it had earlier that evening. "I said the booger bears are back, Ned. Can't you hear them?"

Ned cocked his head and tried to listen. A woman's laughter erupted through an open window at Sally's. A donkey brayed in response. Other than that, there was nothing. Ned shook his head. "Lendon, yer 'bout as drunk as I am. I don't hear nothin'."

"You will. Listen hard."

"I'm too sick to listen hard. You might try tellin' me just what I'm listenin' for. And don't come at me agin with no damn booger bears. What's a booger bear anyhow?"

"My dreams. Frank calls 'em booger bears."

"Gawd, Lendon, you ain't sleepwalkin'—"

" 'Cept they come when I ain't sleepin', Ned. How do you explain that?"

"I'm too damn drunk to explain anything," Ned mumbled, fixing his gaze on the wagon beyond Lendon. "I just want to go home. Ma is gonna kick my butt for spendin' a passel of her kitchen money on cards." He attempted to walk around Lendon, but Lendon grabbed him.

"I'm tellin' you now, Ned, you shouldn't have said them things about the widow Bell. That was plain stupid. You shouldn't have done what you did to her, either."

"Who's gone and made you a preacher?" Ned yanked his arm away.

"*You'll* be hearin' them booger bears now. He don't forgive and forget. He'll drive you crazy as a loon too, if he don't kill you first. He's liable to, you know. It wouldn't be the first time."

"Git out of my way, Lendon, before I hit you."

Lendon stepped aside and watched as Ned clumsily attempted to mount the step board of the wagon. Only when Ned had fallen onto the bench seat and taken up the leather lines did Lendon twist his fingers into Ned's shirt sleeve and shake him.

"Flute," is all he said.

Ned frowned.

"Flute," Lendon repeated. "Soon as you hear it you better fall to yer knees and pray, 'cause it means yer time is comin'. He'll play with you first, though. He'll drive you crazy."

"You're already crazy, Lendon."

"Go on and scoff. Frank and George do. They don't want to believe that the hand of vengeance has been raised and is about to squash us all like we was a lot of cockroaches."

Ned slapped the lines across the horse's rump. He was starting to feel sober again, thanks to Lendon's tirade. By the time he made the two-hour jaunt home, his head was going to be hurting like hell. Glancing over his shoulder, he watched as Lendon's white features faded from sight. Lendon called out, "I'd git yer idiot brother and yer ma and get the hell out of Texas, Ned, 'cause he's gonna come after you. If he cares for the widow Bell like I think he does, he's gonna be after you for sure."

"I wouldn't be callin' somebody an idiot if I was you," Ned grumbled. Elbows on his knees, lines lying loosely in his fingers, he allowed the swaybacked horse to amble down the road toward home.

An hour out of town Ned sobered enough to realize he hadn't taken a leak in nearly five hours and his bladder was about to explode. He managed to clamber down from the wagon and relieve himself against a mesquite bush, his mind fingering through the night's conversations.

Lendon and his booger bears. Hell, if Frank's sour mash whiskey turned men into fruit heads like Lendon, then maybe he'd be wise to stick to rotgut. He'd stick to beddin' Sally's whores as well, instead of sniffin' out preachers' widows who couldn't cook or screw worth a damn. Who wanted a woman who demanded all that dilly-fartin' around before givin' him a poke? What did the sex act have to do with love, anyway? God, what he'd give to have Margaret back. She just laid there and took it, givin' only an occasional little squeak of pain when he first jabbed her. Silly bitch, goin' and hangin' herself like she done. What could she have been thinkin'?

Nope, he sure as shootin' didn't need no woman hamperin' his way of livin'. And he sure as heckfire didn't need no gunslingin' lunatics takin' aim at his gizzard. Not that he was scared of Bastitas in the least. What was it that Lendon had warned him about?

A sound behind him; he looked around. Damn, couldn't he pee any faster? At last he hitched up his pants and turned back to the wagon. Another sound, closer this time. The horse pricked up its ears and looked off in the dark before stamping impatiently and lugging on the braces. Ned scurried aboard and grabbed up the lines, then cocked his head, his breath catching in his dry throat.

A coyote yelped, followed by another.

Ned grinned nervously. Hell, he was gettin' as crazy as Lendon. For a moment there . . . he could have sworn he heard flute music.

$\mathscr{F}$ourteen

❧

CHARITY SAT WITH HER FEET IN THE POOL OF CRYSTAL-clear water and listened to a breeze flirt with the cluster of willow leaves overhead. The shade felt good on her face as she watched Rafe dunk her son up to his chubby chin in the water. The baby squealed and pumped his arms and Rafe began the process again, bobbing the little body into the water, first his toes, then his legs, then all the way to his shoulders. Then he lifted her son high in the air so that he resembled a pudgy pink bird in flight.

"You're spoiling him," Charity laughed. "He'll be expecting you to play with him like that every day."

"There's nothing wrong with spoiling a child," he replied, water dripping from his black lashes. "Makes him feel loved." He exited the water, breeches clinging to his form like a second skin, then dropped onto the blanket and proceeded to towel-dry her son's squirming body.

Charity forced herself to look away, to the cluster of somnolent pregnant cows in the distance. "Eight new calves this spring. Perhaps my luck is turning around at last." She smiled and gazed out over the wide expanse of blue water and surrounding green hills. "Now can you understand my unwillingness to give up my farm, Rafe? Can you understand why George Peters would kill me to get it?''

''What I don't understand is why your husband never built a home here instead of on that plot of rock and dust you live on now.''

She shrugged and watched a minnow nibble at her big toe. ''Randy was a dreamer with no initiative. Or maybe he thought if he prayed loudly enough, God would build it for him. I've imagined building a house there.'' She pointed to a hill in the distance. ''I could see the entire valley from my front porch.''

''No.'' He shook his head. ''There. Atop that knoll. You'd have the hills to block the north wind in the winter. The trees would offer shade in the summer. You'd also have a wider view of the water.''

She smiled dreamily. ''The house would be grand—''

''Two stories with a wraparound porch.''

''White with pale yellow shutters.''

''Half-a-dozen bedrooms.''

''And a library,'' she added excitedly and splashed her feet in the water. ''Walls lined with books.''

''A massive dining room with a view of the valley.''

''A kitchen overlooking the hills.''

''A winding staircase.''

''A bedroom facing the east so I can awaken with the sun in my face. And a fireplace! No more cold winter mornings huddled up to my chin with blankets while I convince myself I must get out of bed.'' Laughing, she fell back on the blanket beside her son and watched clouds tumble over the green hills. ''Someday,'' she said softly, ''everywhere I look I'll see my cattle. When I die, my son will be the wealthiest man in Texas.''

The baby cooed and gurgled.

Charity smiled, then lifted her gaze to Rafe. His eyes were heavy-lidded, his mouth soft as he regarded her and her son, a distant longing reflected in his relaxed features. "A penny for your thoughts," she whispered.

He briefly closed his eyes, saying nothing.

Rolling onto her stomach, her skirt falling to the backs of her knees, Charity propped herself up on her elbows and continued to study his face. "You looked a thousand miles away, Rafe."

He cleared his throat and sat up.

"Is something wrong?" she asked.

"I'm thinking that all this waxing on about houses and such isn't getting our chores done. It'll take half the day to get these cattle up."

"Don't you ever dream, Rafe?"

"Dreams are for women and children. It's a man's job to make them come true." He climbed to his feet and reached for his boots. "Besides," he added, "I never cared much for cows."

An hour later Rafe dismounted his lathered horse while Jackson did a commendable job of herding the stubborn, bawling cows into a submissive huddle near the wagon. "God, I hate cows," he said as he tore his gloves from his hands. "The only good cow is one frying in a skillet." Charity offered him a canteen. He snatched it and poured water over his head. "The only thing more stubborn or dumber than a cow is a jackass. I don't like them either."

"Because you both have so much in common, I suspect." Charity smiled as he pinned her with a look. "You're both stubborn and cantankerous and apt to get in your own way."

"Very funny. This coming from a woman who thumbs her nose at men like George Peters."

"I told you. I'm not afraid of George Peters."

"You should be." He moped his brow and looked around. "Now that I've seen this place I'm convinced that you sure as hell should be."

Rafe led his horse toward the water. Charity called out, "What are you doing?"

"What does it look like I'm doing?"

"But you're not done."

He looked around, frowning.

"You've forgotten one," she explained, and pointed to the distant copse of low-growing trees.

Jackson came streaking through the belly-high grass, his tail tucked between his legs. The gelding snorted and lunged back on the reins, burning Rafe's hand and causing him to curse. What the . . .

His eyes narrowed. His gaze sharpened on the mass of hide and horn emerging from the trees. "Jesus," he hissed through his teeth. "What is it?"

"Bruce." Charity stepped up beside him, her face beaming and eyes twinkling. "I suggest that you keep your voice low. He doesn't take to being yelled at."

The spotted range bull roared and shook his head with its ten-foot span of black-and-yellow horns. He pawed the ground and swished his tail.

"Incredible, isn't he?" Charity said.

"Incredible my ass. That's death on hooves."

"Only if he doesn't like you. You might remain in the wagon if you're in the least bit anxious. Nervousness annoys him."

Charity struck off across the field toward the bull.

"What the hell are you doing?" Rafe yelled after her.

He attempted to mount his horrified horse, to no avail. The gelding was having none of it. "Charity!" Rafe barked, running to catch up. "Get back to the wagon."

"Why, Mr. Bastitas, is that concern I hear in your voice?"

"Right. I'm not spending the next year of my life spoon-feeding that kid of yours if you go and get yourself gored by that." He pointed to Bruce.

"Ah, ye of little faith." Charity laughed gaily and hiked her skirts a bit higher. Rafe fell back, watching Charity move across the meadow, her blond hair swinging around her shoulders and shimmering in the sunlight. The image made him think of a watercolor painting he'd seen once in a museum in Chicago. *Girl in a Field of Daisies,* it had been called. He'd stood for an hour studying the way the artist had portrayed sunlight upon the girl's fair skin and hair, but it had been nothing compared to this.

She walked straight up to the animal and scratched its fuzzy ear; then she caught hold of one horn and proceeded to direct the beast toward the wagon.

No doubt about it. Charity Bell was as crazy as they come.

Upon first seeing the unfamiliar wagon parked outside her house, Charity's first reaction was caution, then dread. Had Ned Williams come calling again? Had he some fiendish idea of getting back at her for humiliating him in front of his beloved ma? She glanced back through the dusk shadows, toward the distant cow pen where Rafe pitched hay and filled water troughs while the tired and hungry cattle bawled and jostled one another for their dinner.

The baby whimpered and rubbed his face on Charity's

shoulder. "Hush now." She bobbed him up and down as she circled the wagon, going to her toes to peer into the bed where a collection of well-oiled trunks were stacked. There was something disturbingly familiar about the chests, but she shook off the notion—or tried to. Still, as she turned woodenly toward the house and approached the back porch, a niggling suspicion settled like a stone in her stomach. It couldn't be. Dear God, it just couldn't be.

She mounted the steps and opened the door. "Oh," she whispered aloud. "Oh . . . my."

Caroline and Claude Hesseltine—her parents—looked at her blankly, recognition took a moment in coming.

Sitting in a chair near the table, her beautiful white face a mask of dismay, Caroline burst into tears. "Dear merciful father, Claude! It was just as I feared. My poor, poor baby. Look what she's become!"

Impeccably dressed is a dusty navy-blue suit, his thinning golden hair a touch windblown, Claude hurried to comfort her. "There, there, my pet. You mustn't allow Charity to see you this way."

They both stared at Charity again, their mouths open and brows screwed in consternation.

"What a . . . wonderful surprise," Charity said softly. "Had I known you were coming I would have . . . dressed for the occasion."

"We wrote you of our visit," her father said, still doing his best to console his distraught wife.

"The mail is unreliable here, to say the least," Charity replied.

Caroline wept into a hanky. Claude patted her shoulder reassuringly; then they focused on the baby as if seeing him for the first time. "What, pray tell, is that?" her mother wailed.

"Your grandson."

Caroline sobbed louder and clutched at her husband. "She never even told us, Claude."

"I fear, my dear, that there is a great deal our Charity hasn't told us." Claude raised one eyebrow and looked around the cramped kitchen. "Or shall I rephrase? There is little that our Charity has told us that's the truth."

Charity took a deep breath and slowly released it. "I suspect you're starving. I'll put the baby down and change. Dinner won't be long. I hope you don't mind warmed-over beans and cornbread." She closed her bedroom door and sank against it, listening to her mother sobbing and her father doing his best to control her.

"Lies!" Caroline cried. "All lies. All those letters telling us about her beautiful home and all the luxuries. Dear Lord, Claude, our darling Charity looks like a waif. And this . . . shack! It's not fit for white trash, I tell you."

Charity placed the baby in the crib and sank down onto the bed. She wouldn't cry. She wouldn't apologize. And she definitely wouldn't lie—not anymore. How could she? The truth was all around her—every tattered rug and curtain, every crack in the wall and every creak in the warped old floor.

The bedroom door exploded open then, causing Charity to scream and jump to her feet. Her mother stumbled into the room, clutching her breast, her eyes round as two green saucers. She pointed toward the kitchen and managed to croak, "There's a barbarian with a gun pointed at your father's head."

Charity ran to the kitchen, skidding to a stop at the sight of Rafe, partially crouched, his Colt aimed directly between her father's eyes. "Oh God," she muttered, and briefly closed her eyes.

"Oh God what?" Rafe snapped. " 'Oh God shoot him,' or 'Oh God—' "

"That's my father. Put the gun away."

Rafe slowly lowered the gun as Charity sank against the doorjamb. What next?

Claude withdrew a kerchief from his suit pocket and blotted his sunburned forehead while her mother continued to sob in the bedroom. "Seems this is a day for surprises," Claude remarked, his smile as stalwart as he could manage, considering the circumstances. "First we discover that Hell, Texas, is exactly that. Then we find that your 'heaven on earth' is more like a breeding ground for vipers and scorpions. You sashay in with a grandchild we knew nothing about, and now . . . this." He wagged his finger at Rafe and sighed. "Now I suppose you're going to tell me this is your husband."

Husband?

Oh God.

"Yes," came the response, before she could bite it back.

Rafe's head snapped around and his face became incredulous. "What the hell are you saying, Charity?" he said through his teeth.

She pasted on a bright smile and hurried to him. "What I'm saying, darling, is that—silly ol' me—I never got around to telling my parents about Randy's death. Subsequently . . ." She laughed lightly and wove her arm through Rafe's, hugging it fiercely. "I failed to mention that I had remarried."

Claude raised his eyebrows. "The Reverend Bell dead?"

"A few months after we came to Texas. He drowned at Rattlesnake Gulch."

Her father looked from Charity to Rafe, whose face had gone wooden. Claude sighed. "So this is the child's father."

"This is the very man who brought your grandson into the world, Papa. I thank God every day for him, because if it wasn't for Rafael, I wouldn't have Alexander."

"Alex . . . ander?" her father said.

Rafe slowly turned his black eyes down to hers. She smiled at him and nodded. "We named him after Rafe's father. I hope you're not too disappointed, Papa. Perhaps we'll name the next boy after you."

Rafe pulled away and turned for the door. Charity hurried after him, glancing back at her bemused father long enough to say, "Perhaps you'd better see to Mama. I'll help Rafe bed down the horse and be back in a few minutes."

Charity ran down the porch steps, catching up to Rafe as he neared the barn. "I realize this is a lot to ask—"

"Forget it."

"If you'll only try to understand—"

"I understand all right. You've been lying to your parents all along. You've been doing your best to snare me the last few weeks and now you think you've got a way to do it. You're sly, Charity, but not that sly."

"I'm certain they won't stay long."

"They can stay until doomsday for all I care. It's no business of mine."

He entered his quarters and began grabbing up his belongings. Charity watched from the door, her voice beginning to quaver. "Yes, I lied to them, Rafe. What else could I do? Had they known about my wretched circum-

stances they would have been heartbroken. Had I written
to them about Randall's death they would have been on
the first stage here and forced me to go home."

"Smart parents. They love you. You might try listening
to them."

She watched as he continued to pack. "Fine then," she
said. "Go. The cattle are up. That's all I needed you for.
I've a few dollars tucked back for an emergency, I'll give
you that."

"I don't want your money, Charity. I want you to do
what the hell is best for that boy . . . and you."

"And that's taking him to Boston—"

"Damn right!" he yelled, then flung a shirt onto the
bed. "Where he'll get an education. Where he'll grow up
with some semblance of sophistication, instead of turning
out like—"

"You?" Her tone was biting.

He hesitated, then, "Yeah. So he doesn't grow up with
his back to a wall, and his idea of heaven is nothing more
than a real bed and getting laid by whores."

Rafe continued to roll up his few clothes while Charity
watched from the door, saying nothing. At last, she sighed
wearily. "Fine then. Go and good riddance."

When he looked, she had gone. He kicked the chair,
then the table, then finally the wall, causing a dauber's
nest to fall from the ceiling onto the bed. Jackson trotted
into the room to investigate, tucked his tail and exited
again. "Traitor," Rafe sneered after him.

By the time Rafe left the barn, dark had fallen completely, interrupted only by the streams of yellow light
spilling through the windows of Charity's house. He approached, hesitating every few steps until he stood on the
porch and peered through the window at the less-than-

joyous scene: Charity frantically mixing cornbread batter while her mother sobbed in the parlor and her father, dapper in his impeccable suit despite the arduous journey that had brought him and his distraught wife from Boston, poised near the stove, regarded his daughter with deep concern . . . and immense disappointment.

Charity beat the batter with a wooden spoon, her shoulders sagging, her head down, allowing her curtain of disheveled hair to hide the fact that she had begun to silently weep. Rafe frowned as the image of her that afternoon roused before his mind's eye, her face flushed with sun and excitement as she dreamed aloud of her plans.

No doubt about it. The instant Claude and Caroline Hesseltine learned that Charity and the child were scratching out a miserly existence—alone—on this pitiful plot of prairie, they would insist that she return to Boston.

Charity stopped her stirring and, reluctantly putting the bowl and spoon aside, slowly turned to face her father, her swollen eyes lowered and her chin quivering. "Papa," she began, "I have something to confess."

Rafe closed his eyes. "Shit," he said, then grabbed for the door.

"Sorry it took me so long in the barn," he announced, flashing a smile at Claude, who regarded him as if he expected Rafe to pull a gun on him again. "That damned horse of mine was being stubborn again about his feed." He walked to Charity, whose face looked as pale as the cornbread batter on the tip of her little nose. He flipped the cornmeal away with one finger and winked. "You look exhausted, sweetie. I'll take over here while you get yourself and Alex cleaned up for dinner. You'll want to spend some time alone with your parents, I suspect . . . maybe tell them about our plans to build in the valley soon."

Her eyes welled with tears.

He touched her cheek and gave her a resigned grin. "Chin up," he whispered. "I'm just a sucker for a pretty face."

Fifteen

CHARITY'S MOTHER RETIRED TO THE BEDROOM WITH A headache, but not until Charity had changed the musty sheets and assured her there were no snakes or spiders lurking under her bed. Sitting on a straight-backed little chair Randy Bell had once called his prayer stool, her lavish laced and lavender skirts pooling around her feet, Caroline regarded Charity sadly as she went about preparing the spare bedroom for her parents.

"My greatest fears have been realized," Caroline declared brokenly. "My one and only child has fallen into the dark and desperate hands of destitution. Not to mention that she's lied to me and her heartbroken father for the last two years. I'm not certain what's worse."

"I lied to protect you, Mama."

"Understandable." Caroline sniffed and glanced around the stack of trunks and crates crowding the tiny room. "Are you certain there aren't savages about? Just recently *The Chronicle* reported that a band of marauding Indians wiped out an entire township, subjecting its inhabitants to unmentionable tortures." She regarded her coiffured blond hair in the mirror. "I visualized my scalp dangling from a lance the entire ride from town."

"Quite certain." Charity plumped pillows and smoothed the sheets. "You'll be comfortable in this bed. Randy considered it the most pleasing mattress he ever slept on."

Caroline raised one pale brow and scanned the chamber. "Your husband slept here?"

Her movements hesitating, Charity bit her lip. "Randy spent most of his nights composing his sermons. Naturally, he didn't wish to disturb me."

"Do you vow to me that he was a decent husband to you?" Caroline watched Charity closely.

"I assure you, Randy was the best husband he was capable of being."

Caroline lifted one lily-white hand toward Charity. "Come here, my darling. Come to mama. Sit at my knee and look into my eyes like you did when you were a child."

"I'm not a child anymore."

"Please."

Reluctantly, Charity eased to the floor and rested her cheek upon her mother's knee. Oh, how good it felt! How stable, how comforting! The perfumed scent of her mother's skirts, the coolness of her soft fingers on Charity's brow roused childhood memories she had desperately tried to forget—recollections of security and love, fables of happily ever after, blessed by abundance and every creature comfort that spoiled children expect from life.

"Look at me, Charity. Why?" Caroline pleaded softly. "Were you so unhappy with us as parents that you would choose this terrible existence over coming home again?"

"No, Mama."

"Did we not instill in you a sense of pride and dignity?"

"Yes, Mama, you did."

"Yet, you remained in this place—"

"I married Randall for better or worse. He was my husband. How would it have looked had I returned to Boston while he was living? A divorced woman in Boston society? I think not."

"But when he died—"

"This farm became mine."

Caroline frowned and shuddered. " 'Tis a despicable place, Charity. There are holes in the walls."

"It's the largest farm in the area."

"And what do you farm? Stones?"

"Cattle."

Her mother smiled sadly as she stroked Charity's head. "My beautiful baby, I hardly know you. Your skin is weathered and your hair is dry. Your eyes are weary, my darling."

"I'm fine, Mama. Please don't worry."

"Worry? Charity, I've heard nothing from you in months; my letters to you have gone unanswered. Is it any wonder why your father and I came to find you? Now we discover that your first husband is dead and that you've remarried and have a child. Why weren't we informed?"

"You ask too many questions, Mama."

"As your mother, I have a right to know."

Charity sighed. "I'm not a child any longer. I'm a mother myself now."

"And some day you'll understand the vastness of a mother's concern for her child."

Charity stood and retrieved a brush and comb from her

mother's open valise. She admired them, smiling as she ran her fingers lightly over the mother-of-pearl handles. "I remember when Papa gave you these. I was ten and it was Christmas. He had them sent from Paris. Such an act seems so extravagant now. I could buy a month's supplies on what this must have cost him."

"He dotes on me. He always has."

"You're very fortunate." She walked around her mother and began to remove the pins from Caroline's hair, allowing the soft gold curls to spill through her fingers. "Your hair is still so beautiful, Mama. It's as fine as a child's."

They remained silent as Charity brushed out her mother's hair, admiring the silken texture and the way the lamplight reflected from it. Then Caroline's hand came up and caught Charity's. She turned and gazed up into her daughter's eyes.

"Do you love him?" Caroline asked.

"Who?"

"Your husband, of course."

Charity turned away and put aside the comb and brush. "That's a strange question to ask. I wouldn't have . . . married him otherwise."

"Poppycock. You didn't love that dreadful preacher."

"Mama!" Charity flashed a look at her indignant parent. "I don't know what you're talking about."

"You were in love with the idea of circumventing our dreams of your marrying Chester Muesler. You were always a rebel, Charity. Far too opinionated and unwilling to submit to the dictates of our social standards."

"Those standards were suffocating. Besides, Papa encouraged me never to settle for anything less than what I felt would make me happy. Personally, I happen to think that money doesn't necessarily buy one happiness.''

"Ah, yes, but money will put a decent roof over your head and food in your child's stomach when he's hungry."

"I have a roof over my head, and my son will never feel hunger, I assure you."

Caroline regarded the threadbare rug on the floor, the neat but well-mended curtains on the windows, then left the chair, swinging her back to Charity. She swept her hip-length hair aside, offering the row of tiny buttons down the bodice of her dress. Charity complied, hoping that her mother would drop the subject of husbands and money as she worked her way from neck to waist, struggling over each little bone button, her chagrin growing at the thought that she, too, once dressed in such a bothersome manner.

"Well?" Caroline pursued. "Do you intend to tell me about this Bastitas person or not?"

Dropping her hands, Charity stared at the back of her mother's head. "What do you want to know?" she asked weakly.

Caroline turned to face her. "Everything, of course. Who he is. Where he comes from. How you met. I want to know about his family."

"His family?"

"He's the father of my grandson. I do believe some knowledge about his lineage is in order. Obviously, with a name like Rafael de Bastitas, he's Mexi—"

"Spanish."

"Whatever. He looks like some plains savage and brandishes that horrifying weapon as if shooting someone between the eyes were perfectly normal to him."

"He was simply concerned about my welfare. He wouldn't have shot Papa."

Caroline pursed her lips, obviously unconvinced.

There came a knock at the door, and her father called, "Enough girl chatter! I care to spend some time with my daughter, if you please."

With a sigh of relief, Charity sprang for the door and flung it open. Claude filled up the threshold, his features feigning agitation, her sleeping son nestled in the crook of his arm. "I find it totally unfair that your mother is allowed to occupy your time to such a degree."

Smiling, Charity went up on her toes and planted a kiss on his cheek. "Very well, sir. It's your turn." She glanced beyond him, to the empty kitchen.

"If you're looking for your husband, he excused himself. Said he had business to do at the barn before cleaning himself up for bed."

Bed.

She chewed her lip. Of course her parents would expect her and Rafe to sleep together . . . at least sleep in the same house.

"You needn't look so worried," her father said. "I'm certain he'll return in due time."

"Don't be vulgar, Claude," her mother called. "Despite how Charity looks, she's still a young lady."

"Undeniably, my dear. She's also a married woman . . . with an incredibly beautiful son." Claude smiled warmly at the baby, his features melting in fondness. "I say, Carol, he looks the spitting image of our Charity at this age."

Caroline rolled her eyes. "You were always a softie for children, husband."

"How can one not be a softie toward his own flesh

and blood. Look how he sleeps. Just like an angel.''

Caroline approached her husband and daughter, her gaze locked on the child. "Yes," she replied at last. "He looks a great deal like Charity."

"Would you like to hold him, Mama?" Charity asked. "No."

Caroline turned away and the smile slid from Charity's lips.

Noticing, Claude shrugged and winked. "I suspect that your mother is either experiencing a twinge of jealousy or feeling a trifle miffed. It's not every day one is faced with the reality that she's old enough to be a grandmother."

Dropping onto the bed, Caroline sighed. "I have no intention of being goaded into an argument, Claude. I'm simply too exhausted and heartbroken. You may take this entire occurrence with your usual lassitude, but I, personally, have no intention of accepting the dreadful circumstance in which Charity now exists. It's my responsibility as her mother."

"Very well then. Charity and I will tuck her son into bed by ourselves."

Claude stepped from the room. Charity followed, closing the door behind her. She trailed her father to her bedroom and watched as he laid the sleeping infant amid the quilts. Alex drew his little legs up under him, sticking his butt in the air so that he resembled a tiny frog. His pink mouth made suckling noises as he slept. Claude studied his grandson silently for a long while, smiling faintly, his hands in his coat pockets. When he looked at Charity again, his eyes were misty.

"I'm glad I came," he said, "or I might never have met him until he was grown."

"I'm sorry I didn't tell you."

"It's not important, as long as you're happy. You *are* happy . . . aren't you?"

She nodded and tucked a stray strand of hair behind her ear.

"And the boy's father . . . he's a good husband?"

Averting her eyes from her father's, Charity approached the crib. As the infant fidgeted, she patted his back until he lay motionless again. Still, she couldn't manage to look at her father. She'd never been able to lie to him; he'd always seen right through any untruth she had thought to spin, and therefore, since an early age, she had practiced total honesty where he was concerned . . . at least until marrying Randall Bell.

"Papa," she began softly.

"I spoke briefly with Rafael," Claude interrupted. He moved to the window and peered into the dark. "Seems like a pleasant enough chap, once he put that damned cannon away. Doesn't say much, but then we *are* strangers to him. He's as stunned to see us camped on his doorstep as we are to find him instead of Randall residing with our daughter."

"Papa, I—"

"He certainly seems to dote on the boy."

Charity smiled. "Yes. He cares very much for Alex."

"A commendable trait. There aren't a great many men who would exhibit their affection so openly before strangers."

"You always did."

Claude shrugged. "A man would have to have the heart of an iceberg not to melt in your presence, my darling child."

"Papa . . . I'm not a child any longer."

Claude gave her a tight smile. "You're absolutely right, my dear. As much as it grieves me to admit it, you're a grown woman with a will and a mind of her own. Still . . . a father has certain prerogatives. It's my lot in life to worry over my little girl, be her age two or fifty-two. You'll see. Someday, when this lad is a strapping six feet tall and walks out your door as a man, your heart and soul will go with him. There will never be a time when you wouldn't lay down your life to protect him. To think of you unhappy or desperate in any way would undo your mother and me."

Charity sank down into a chair near the crib. She clasped her hands in her lap and did her best to swallow the lump in her throat. "I know that finding me living in these 'conditions,' as Mama calls it, is dreadfully upset-ting to you, which is why I never told you."

"We simply want the very best for you, pet."

She nodded, understanding.

"Had she married Chester," her mother said from the doorway, "she would be living like a social queen."

Charity sank back in the chair, closing her eyes. "I wondered how long it would take you to bring up Chester."

"The man adored you. He still does."

Dropping down on the dressing-table stool, Claude fixed his wife with an aggravated look. "Good grief, Carol. I thought we settled the Chester issue before we arrived. You weren't to bring up his name."

Her pink dressing gown whispering around her feet, Charity's mother floated like a pale cloud across the floor, her gaze taking in Charity's personal belongings. "I feel the occasion warrants the subject. Besides, I promised him."

"Promised him what?" Claude demanded.

"That I would inform Charity that he remains heart-broken over her marriage to the Reverend Bell. That I would remind her that to this day he remains unmarried, although that dreadful Charlotte Billingsly-Ford is doing her best to grab him. Simply put, he shan't give in to her until he knows beyond any doubt that Charity won't return to him."

"Good God." Claude jumped to his feet. "How dare Chester make such brazen comments to a happily married woman."

"Is she?" Caroline turned her raised eyebrow on Charity, who frowned in response.

"Am I what?" Charity replied.

"Happily married?"

"For heaven's sake, Mama, what does it look like to you?"

The baby squeaked and bobbed his head. He nuzzled his hand and began to suckle. Charity left her chair, thankful for any diversion from the topic of Chester Muesler, and equally thankful not to have to look into her parents' eyes and lie ... again. Lifting Alex into her arms, she said, "He'll be wanting his final feeding before he settles down for the night."

Claude took his wife's arm and propelled her toward the door. She pulled away at the last minute and returned to Charity, her face flushed with color as she withdrew an envelope from her dressing-gown pocket. "Chester asked me to send this along," she whispered, and slipped the note to Charity before turning on her heels and following her husband into the hallway, closing the door soundly behind her.

Charity sank again into the chair, opened her blouse

and shirt and lifted her breast to her hungry son. As usual, the pull of his mouth on her swollen nipple made her wince at first; then the slow warm and liquid languidness set in, tugging at her heart. Drowsily, she regarded the envelope her mother had pressed into her hand. She recognized the handwriting immediately. Chester's. She'd always teased him that his handwriting was prettier than most women's.

To think he missed her still. That he would risk breaching God's commandment to contact her. That he would entertain the shocking possibility of associating socially with a divorced woman—worse yet, of marrying one.

Of course, he wasn't aware of the child. Or of Ned Williams . . . or of Rafael de Bastitas . . .

Voices sounded in the kitchen—strained pleasantries. Nervous tittering from her mother, then the slamming of a door as Caroline fled to her bedroom. Rafe's voice came to Charity then, deep and smooth as a slowly flowing river, but she detected the strain—oh yes, she knew him that well—he wasn't happy with the ruse she had imposed on him. Why, she wondered, had he agreed to go through with it? Why had he stepped into the kitchen at the last possible moment and rescued her from spilling the bitter truth to her already reeling parents?

"Good night," came her father's words, then silence.

Would he wait in the kitchen until her parents had settled down for the night? Then would he slip away from the house and return to his shabby little room that wasn't fit for an animal, much less a man?

She listened to her heartbeat in the silence and wished she could breathe.

The door creaked open. Charity put the envelope aside,

then hastily pulled the blanket up to cover her nursing son.

Rafe stepped into the room.

Her gaze flew to his.

He eased the door closed and leaned back against it. She noted he'd bathed; the ends of his black hair were still damp. He'd changed into a clean shirt and brushed the dust from his boots. His face looked flushed, his jaw set.

The silence dragged on, electrifying the air as Rafe continued to lean against the door, his unflinching gaze focused on her. Finally, she found enough strength to ask softly, "What now?"

He stared.

"I didn't think, Rafe. I'm sorry. Of course they would expect us to . . . live together . . . as husband and wife, I mean . . . sleep in the same bed. I realize you find the prospect of doing so . . . unappealing, but think of it this way—this bed is much more comfortable than the one in the barn. You might actually get a decent night's sleep for a change."

His mouth curled into a grim smile as he pushed away from the door and approached. With her heart climbing her throat, she did her best to smile as he bent over her, weight braced upon her chair arms as he lowered his face to within a breath's embrace of hers.

"There is no way in hell I'm climbing into that bed next to you," he said flatly.

Charity blinked.

"I'm thinking I gotta be one crazy son of a bitch for going along with this sham in the first place. But I'm not that crazy. Not yet."

She looked at his mouth, her skin turning unbearably

warm with the memory of his lips touching her in forbidden places. "What do you propose that we do?" she asked.

"Soon as they go to sleep I'll leave."

"And in the morning?"

"Far as they know I'm a real early riser."

She nodded. If she were to lift her mouth half an inch, she could kiss him. If she kissed him ... perhaps he would stay. Perhaps she could persuade him to quench the heat in her nether region with his body. Funny she hadn't experienced this desire with Ned—not even a little.

He moved away suddenly. She shifted in her chair, hoping the pressure between her legs would go away—except the rhythmic tug on her nipple seemed to agitate the feeling, stirring it up like sediment in an eddy.

Rafe paced, dragging his hands through his hair. Occasionally, he glanced at the bed, his expression one of mounting aggravation as the sounds of her parents' voices leaked through the thin wall. Her mother was sobbing again, sounding pitiful. Her father did his best to console her.

Having his fill of nursing, Alex drifted to sleep, a bubble of milk on his lips. Charity pressed a kiss to his moist forehead and put him to bed, then poured water from the ewer into the basin and proceeded to cleanse her breast.

Rafe continued to pace, though she saw him glance her way as she gently blotted the water from her skin. His brow had begun to sweat. Moisture beaded on his temples and ran down this jaw.

"Jesus," he muttered. "It's hot in here."

"You're working up a lather pacing like that. You might try to relax, Rafe. I won't accost you, I promise."

She began to remove her blouse.

He frowned. "What the devil are you doing now?"

"Going to bed."

"You're not taking off your clothes . . . ?"

"I don't normally sleep in a dress."

"Do *not* take off your clothes."

"It's not as if you haven't seen me naked."

"Exactly."

She smiled and lowered her lashes, her fingers plucking at her buttons, gradually revealing the simple shirt underneath. "If you think about our circumstances logically, you're bound to find humor in it."

"There is absolutely nothing funny about this."

"I'm not certain I've ever known a man so skittish at the very prospect of marriage."

"Jesus," he muttered again.

She tossed away her blouse, then peeled her skirt down her hips, kicking it aside with her bare feet. With her hips and legs covered in cotton drawers that tied at the waist, she lay back on the bed, nestling her head in a pillow.

The minutes ticked by. Charity's lids grew heavy and the roused feelings inside her mellowed to a warm but manageable ache. She dozed once, only to awaken with a jolt, expecting to find Rafe gone. He wasn't. He sat in a chair near the open window, gazing out on the black terrain, a breeze flirting with his hair. She studied his profile, watched the tension leave his jaw little by little until weariness replaced his aggravation. Sometime after midnight she roused enough to lift her head.

"Do you intend to sit there all night?" she asked.

"If I have to."

"I've not heard a sound from my parents for hours."

"Go to sleep, Charity, and leave me alone."

"What are you afraid of, Rafe?"

He looked at her at last; his eyes were hollow with fatigue, and something else. "You wouldn't understand," he finally said. "If I crawled in bed with you this time . . . I might never crawl out again."

"Would that be so bad?"

"Yes." He swallowed and a flicker of anger returned. "Yes," he repeated. "I have a difficult time already dealing with my thoughts. Were I to let my emotions get involved . . ." He left the chair and stood with his hands fisted at his sides. His face became dark as he regarded her. "Sometimes I think about killing you. Did you know that? I imagine wrapping my hands around your beautiful throat and making you pay for messing up my mind and my priorities, yet here the hell I am still, caught up in your growing web of lies."

"If you want to know the honest-to-God truth," she said wearily, "I'm happy that I lied to my parents about you. Because now I have you."

"No you don't," he snapped quietly. "I can walk out that door right now and never look back. I could be in Mexico by morning."

"You've been telling me that for weeks, yet here you are still . . . wanting me, though you won't admit it. I knew you cared for me when I returned from Ned's. You could have taken the opportunity during my absence to escape, but you stayed. When I introduced you as my husband to my parents, you could have told them the truth. You wanted to drown in this lying pool right along with me." She smiled sleepily and closed her eyes. "I've decided that I'm in love with you."

He crossed the room swiftly and grabbed her by her shoulders, partially pulling her off the bed. He shook her hard, causing her pale hair to fly back and forth. "Stop that," he whispered hoarsely. "That kind of talk is what got you in this trouble in the first place. You thought you loved the preacher. You thought you loved Ned."

She shook her head. "I never loved them."

"And what makes me so different?"

"I don't know. Because you're kind."

"I'm not kind, Charity. I'm a son of a bitch."

"You love my son."

"The hell you say."

"It's all over your face when you hold him."

He shook her again, harder this time, making her bite her lip to stem her cry of pain. "I—don't—love—him," he hissed through his teeth. "I—don't—love—you."

"Then why are you still here?" she hissed back, struggling.

Burying one hand in her hair, he twisted and dragged back her head, forcing her onto her stomach, her face pressed into the pillow. Lowering his weight onto her, he whispered in her ear, "I've slept with a hundred whores, Mrs. Bell. You're just one more who thinks she's special enough to make a difference to me. Think I'm the sort of person you'd care to raise your son? Answer me, damn you."

Closing her eyes, twisting her fingers more fiercely into the sheets, Charity remained silent, feeling his heart pound against her back, his body melt at long last against hers. His arms held her. His warm breath flurried the hair on her neck. As if all anger and resistance had flooded from him, he relaxed into the soft mattress and curled his long legs into the backs of hers.

He didn't move. He said nothing and she realized he was sleeping. Finally, she eased from the bed and left the room, feeling her way to the kitchen, to the pantry where she pulled out the whiskey bottle and poured herself a portion in a glass. All she needed now was one of her parents to come in and find her tippling—she, whose lips had not so much as touched a glass of sherry before she married Randall Bell. Who once believed that all men adored their wives like her father adored his. Who thought that the long hours between dusk and dawn were filled with gentle whispers and tender kisses. How would she explain that the man sleeping in her bed could, with a cut of his tongue, slice the very heart from her? How could she tell her father that she had given her body and soul to a man who thought her nothing more than a whore?

She washed out her glass, tucked the whiskey back into the cupboard, hiding it behind a lopsided stack of chipped china cups, then returned to the bed, where she lay drowning in his presence, weeping silently in his obscureness.

Some time later, Rafe eased from the bed, doing his best not to disturb her. Burying her face in a pillow, Charity listened as he quit the room, fumbled his way through the kitchen, then exited the house.

What if the dawn found him gone?

Would she care?

No. Yes. No.

She thought of Chester's letter. She'd forgotten to read it. A few familiar words of adoration and admiration would be welcome about now. Might take her mind off Bastitas and how, for a singular heartbeat in time she had actually hated him, had actually wanted him dead, had wanted desperately to kill him herself.

Sixteen

SHE AWOKE TO THE SOUNDS OF LAUGHTER AND THE smell of frying ham and baking biscuits. Judging from the hot sun spilling through the window, the morning was several hours old.

Charity dragged herself from bed and stumbled to her son's crib, which was empty; then she turned for the door, pausing as the full effect of strong coffee and cooking food hit her with stomach-turning force.

"Well, well, my little girl rises at last," boomed her father in so jovial a tone that Charity winced.

"Don't tease, Claude," her mother said. "Our Charity needs her rest. Poor dear, she's exhausted. Just look at her."

The bright sun spilling through the windows made focusing on the spectacle before her virtually impossible for a moment. She rubbed her eyes and wished the pounding in her head would subside.

Someone thrust a cup of hot coffee under her nose. She took it, stared into the oily black brew and tried to swallow. Only then did she look up into Rafe's dark eyes.

He smiled. She didn't.

As he turned back to the stove, she said, "Just what the hell are you doing now?"

Her mother gasped. "Charity! Is that any way for a lady to talk? Especially to her husband."

Frowning, she turned her attention to her parents and said, "In case you haven't noticed, I'm no longer a lady."

Splendidly dressed, the pair regarded her with shocked bemusement. Her father, cradling a gurgling Alex in his arms cleared his throat and said, "I fear your husband is attempting to make me look bad. Your mother will be expecting me to wait on her hand and foot when we return to Boston. She simply won't be satisfied until I learn to fry eggs sunny-side up or over easy."

Caroline laughed, her mood vastly improved from the previous day. "I must confess, Charity, that the idea of one's husband running the house is fascinating. Just think of the money we could save by letting the cook go. Instead of carousing the deplorable men's clubs with his cohorts, your father could spend his days concocting recipes. Perhaps he could even form a club for cooking husbands. I, on the other hand, could sit about stuffy offices and prattle about risky investments."

Claude huffed and smiled at his grandson. "Never you fear, my boy. The day will never arise when a woman dons the breeches in the family. A woman's place has been and always will be coddling her husband and raising a passel of children."

Rafe poured coffee into the simmering ham grease, sending a cloud of dark steam into the air, then glanced at Charity. "Breakfast will be ready soon. Why don't you get dressed—"

"I'm not hungry," she snapped; then, noting her parents' dismay at her tone, she did her best to relax.

"Charity dear, Rafe was just about to tell us about his family." Her mother smiled stiffly.

"Oh? *That* should be fascinating."

"The fact that he was born in San Antonio, one of four boys." Turning her attention to Bastitas, Caroline said, "Please do continue, Rafe."

He poured the redeye gravy into a bowl, which he placed on the table alongside a mound of powdery biscuits and a plate of steaming pink ham. Only then did he look at Charity again. "Sit down and eat. Afterwards we'll discuss our plans for the day."

"Don't tell me what to do."

"Fine." He shrugged. "Starve."

Charity turned on her heel and left the room, pausing in the hallway as her mother said, "I'm not certain I've ever seen Charity in such a foul mood. Are you quite certain everything is fine between you?"

"She gets a little out of sorts when she sleeps late, is all. I should have awakened her hours ago."

"She seems so . . . tired and desperately angry this morning."

Claude spoke up. "My dear, I've known you to be a tad sour on occasion—especially if we've had a tiff the previous night."

Charity reentered her bedroom and stood in the middle of the floor with her nightgown pooling around her feet. So he'd done it again—managed to win her parents over as easily as he had won her over, all with that infuriating hypnotic voice and eyes that left one speechless and feeling upended. In the space of hours her mother had gone from frantic to virtually flirtatious—as giddy as some naïve girl. What sort of lies did he intend to spin them about his past? Would he inform them that his reasons for coming to Hell, Texas, in the first place were hardly to plow dirt and burp babies?

The letter from Chester lay on the table where she had put it the night before. Charity picked it up, turned it over and studied the unbroken seal before tugging it open and withdrawing the note embellished with Chester's initials.

My dearest Charity, it began.

She sank into a chair, her eyes following the flowing script. So her mother was right. Chester cared for her still. He beseeched her to return to Boston if her life with Randall was not everything she had hoped it would be. They would deal with her divorce in the most tasteful manner possible. Her friends would understand and support her. If she would only return with her parents, he would build her the finest home in Boston. He would pamper her shamelessly. He would devote the entirety of his life to making certain of her happiness.

Charity closed the note and tucked it away, then walked to the hallway, slowing at the sound of Rafe's voice.

"My uncle died at the Alamo. My mother was captured by Santa Anna but eventually released, along with several of the men's wives and children. A few years later a number of my family were massacred during a Comanche uprising, my great-grandfather included. His entire estate then passed to my father."

"What of your grandfather?" Claude asked.

A moment of silence ensued before he said, "I never knew my grandfather. He was killed when my father was a young man."

"Not by Indians, I hope," Caroline said weakly.

"Carlos de Bastitas, my great-grandfather, believed that a man wasn't truly a man until he became accomplished in the dance of the *toro*—the bull. For generations our ancestors were renowned for their bravery in the ring. Unfortunately, Grandfather was gored to death by his father's prize bull.''

Caroline gasped. "How very tragic, Rafael. Your father must have been devastated.''

"My father considered Carlos a murderer. Carlos, of course, was reminded of his son's death every time he looked in my father's face. They grew to be enemies. My father even refused to attend Carlos's funeral when he was butchered by the Comanches.''

"Tell us about your brothers," Claude said.

"Tomas is married with a son. He and his wife Rachel live on the ranch with my parents. Stephen and his family moved to Austin a few years ago, and Ramon recently received his law degree from Harvard. He'll be practicing in New Orleans.''

Her mother gasped in delight, and Charity rolled her eyes in disbelief and mounting irritation. How smoothly the lies rolled from his tongue. It was one thing to paint such a portrait of family tragedy and bravery—false as it surely must be—but now this. Harvard indeed!

"I left San Antonio a number of years ago, traveled abroad for a while, spent time in Spain where my great-grandfather was raised. Upon returning to this country I considered joining my brother at the university but decided, after the last few years of wandering where I pleased, that cloistering myself in schoolrooms at my age would have been a trifle suffocating. Besides, I enjoy farming. Turning over barren dirt and watching it become a wealth of crops appeals to me.''

"Farming is an admirable pursuit," Claude declared. "But there are no guarantees with farming. Farming will never make you a wealthy man, my boy.''

"My great-grandparents made certain that each of us was financially secure when they died. I needn't turn over a solitary clod of dirt for the rest of my life if I don't choose to."

"Then why do you remain in this despicable little shanty?" Caroline asked. "Why don't you take Charity and the child away from here?"

Charity frowned and held her breath.

"This is Charity's farm, Mrs. Hesseltine. Besides, once you see the valley you'll understand why she's so adamant about staying."

"When do we see it?" Claude asked.

"We can ride out today."

"I'll change immediately," Caroline said.

Charity stepped back as her mother appeared at the doorway. Caroline's eyes widened to discover her daughter lurking in the hall, still draped in her nightgown, her hair unbrushed.

"Charity dear. Rafael has agreed to ride us out to the valley."

"I heard."

Taking a cautious glance over her shoulder, Caroline caught Charity's arm and tugged her toward the bedroom. She lowered her voice conspiratorially and smiled. "He's delicious, darling. Positively enchanting. I must admit that he's far preferable to your first husband, once you get to know him, of course. I'm dreadfully ashamed of my behavior yesterday. But you can imagine how I felt when I first saw this place . . . and you."

Raising one arched brow, Caroline regarded Charity's appearance with a pout of dismay. "I'm not certain what looks worse, this pitiful house or you. Never mind, sweet, I've got just the remedy."

"Remedy for what?"

Caroline nudged Charity into the bedroom and closed the door. She floated to a trunk placed against the wall, dropped to her knees and lifted the lid. "Call it woman's intuition, but I sensed you might appreciate a few things from back home."

Charity moved toward the trunk, her gaze focusing on the contents.

With a flourish, Caroline extracted a butter-yellow dress with flounces and ruches and a scattering of tiny silk bows. She held it up to her chin and spread the skirts across her toes. "Well, daughter? Do you like it? I recalled how the color accentuates your eyes."

Charity swallowed. "What are you saying, Mama?"

"I brought it for you."

She took a step forward, then stopped, forced herself to back away and shook her head. "I . . . can't."

The smile slid from Caroline's face.

"Please understand, Mama."

"Understand? No, I can't say that I do."

"What good will a dress like that do me out here? I can't cook in it, or wash in it, or plow in it. It'll only serve to remind me of what I left behind."

"Charity, just because you've chosen the life of a pauper doesn't mean you must also cease being a woman. It might even put a little spark back into your marriage."

Charity turned away. She sank onto the bed and buried her face in her hands.

Her mother hurried to her. "You *are* unhappy, aren't you, sweet? Don't deny it, it's written all over you. Is it your marriage? Don't you love him?"

"Love him?" Charity sniffed and wiped her eyes.

"Yes," she whispered. "I don't want to sometimes, but I do and I can't even explain why."

"That's the way of it, I fear. On the surface, love comes and goes like the seasons, either blustering or burning. But deep down it's like the roots of a tree. Storms may come and go, they may shred the leaves and peel away the bark, but once planted and given time to mature the tree will withstand almost anything as long as that foundation is in place. It'll take a lot to kill that tree *if* it was healthy to begin with."

"He doesn't love me."

"Pish posh."

"You don't understand—"

"Men can be dreadfully moody—your father included. But I assure you, my darling Charity, that the man in that kitchen fawning over that child is so wrapped up in his role he positively aches. He needs you, Charity. He needs you both. I suspect that before he met you he was a soul afloat with no anchor. You and Alex and this pitiful little house have *become* his anchor. Why else would he be here?"

"This coming from a woman who only last night was aghast at the idea of my marrying a 'barbarian' and living in this dreadful hovel. My, what a difference a night makes."

Caroline lowered her eyes. "I feel dreadfully ashamed of my behavior. I should never have mentioned Chester, and I certainly should not have given you his letter. Your father is right. Chester's attempt to lure you away from your marriage is hardly commendable. While I would thrill to the prospect of your returning to a life that better suits you, I could hardly applaud your walking away from a commitment unless I thought your well-being was at stake. You have a beautiful son to think of. His father adores him. Besides, it's not as if Rafael were some ne'er-do-well with a questionable past. He's practically from Spanish aristocracy!''

Oh God, she thought, her shoulders sinking. No doubt her mother would return to Boston and announce to all that her daughter was married to some Spanish prince. To inform her now that Rafael de Bastitas was not actually her husband—much less in line to inherit a fortune—would send her mother back into a state of vapors.

Standing, Caroline again held up the Parisian creation and smiled. ''There's a hat and shoes to match, and a brand new shirtwaist and petticoats. I'll bet if I dig deep enough I might also find combs for your hair and a bottle of Chateaux Parfum.''

Charity bit her lip as she regarded the frivolous frock, her mind imagining herself ornamented by the dozens of bows, ruches, and flounces as she promenaded down Hell's main street, and she felt ill again—desperately ill.

Rafe took a swig from the whiskey bottle he kept tucked under his bed in the barn, scratched Jackson's head, and read—for the third time—Chester Muesler's letter, which Charity had left on the bedside table in her room.

Then he drank again. Damn, he was getting smashed. Not a good sign. It meant something was eating at him, and, at that particular point in time, there was only one logical reason why he was holed up in this hot, stinking shanty nursing a bottle of bad whiskey. Chester Muesler. Just who the hell did the pompous son of a bitch think he was to seduce a wife away from her husband? He had a good mind to fire off a letter to Muesler detailing exactly what was in store for him if he continued to woo Charity.

Then again, Charity wasn't really his wife . . . was she? What she decided to do, or not to do, about Chester Muesler was none of his business. He could put her out of his mind—get on with his life—forget about her pouty lips and naïve eyes, both of which had begun to get under his skin.

He sensed a movement at the door and looked up.

A young woman stood there, clean blond hair spilling over her shoulders in long ringlets. Her frock hugged her shapely figure a bit snugly, but accentuated her breasts and hips to perfection. Her skin looked like ripe peaches, her eyes like blue porcelain beneath the brim of her floppy feathered hat. She gripped a closed parasol in one gloved hand.

He stood, his gaze locked on her pale face. Charity's mouth looked dreadfully unhappy, as did her eyes. Clearing his throat, he said, "Very pretty. You clean up well, Mrs. Bell. I can see why good ol' Randy lied to get you to Texas. You dress this dump up nicely."

"Why?" she asked simply. "Why have you spun all these lies to my parents?"

"What lies? Aside from our being married, which, I might remind you, started with you."

"All that ridiculous chatter about your family coming from Spanish aristocracy. Brothers who attended Harvard. Heroes who died at the Alamo."

His mouth curled. "How do you know they're lies?"

"A man as cruel as you couldn't possibly have been raised within a decent family. And if, by some remote chance, you are telling the truth, then I pity your mother because her heart must be breaking over what you have become."

Rafe turned away. He looked again at Chester's letter.

"Nice guy, this Chester Muesler. Any man who would try to steal another man's wife would be quite a catch. So tell me, are you going back to him?"

There came an outraged gasp, then Charity was beside him, snatching the letter from Rafe's hand and flooding the air around him with scents of flowery perfume. Her eyes blazed. "How dare you read my mail. Just who do you think you are?"

He lifted one brow and raked her with his eyes. "Your husband, of course. Who else?"

She crushed the letter in her gloved hand. "You're the most arrogant, vulgar man I've ever known."

"More vulgar than Ned?"

His tone dripped innuendo. Charity spun on her heel and headed for the door, her skirts sweeping the dirt floor like a broom.

Rafe said, "At least let me know what story you intend to spin for your parents this time, *Mrs. Bastitas.* Should you decide to return to Boston, do I simply turn up drowned at Rattlesnake Gulch—or do you intend to tell them the truth?"

She didn't so much as hesitate, but swept from the room in a flurry of yellow taffeta and silk, her hat mushrooming from the top of her head like a pale daffodil. His jaw working, Rafe followed her to the door, watched as she stormed across the yard toward the house, scattering chickens that were scratching in the dust. Jackson sat down beside him and cocked his head.

"She's enough to drive a man to drink," Rafe muttered aloud.

Charity and her mother stood on a grassy knoll, looking like a vivid oil painting against the blue sky. "There's nothing that brings a woman out of the doldrums like a new frock,'' Claude declared. "Our Charity looks fresh as a daffodil, don't you think?''

Rafe nodded and fiddled with the reins in his hands. He didn't look toward Charity, but toward the western horizon, where a bank of dark clouds was building rapidly. God, his head hurt. The crucifying mugginess of the hot air didn't help.

"To really appreciate Charity—like her mother—one must realize exactly what sort of woman he's dealing with.''

"You mean stubborn, spirited, moody and just a little crazy?''

"By gosh, you do know her, don't you? How long, exactly, did you say you've been married?''

Rafe glanced at Charity's father. "I don't recall saying at all.''

Claude smiled. "Have you known her long?''

"Long enough to know she's stubborn, spirited, moody and crazy.''

Claude laughed aloud and slapped his knee. "Good man. It'll take a sense of humor to stay on top of the situation. Now then, tell me something about this castle you intend to build my daughter.''

Rafe and Claude left the wagon and sank to their shins in the green grass that rippled in the rising hot wind. They walked to the lip of the knoll and gazed down on the clear water.

For a long moment Claude remained silent; then he took a deep breath and released it. "To say I'm stunned would be an understatement. The valley is beautiful.''

"Two, three thousand head of cattle can graze here easily. The lake will never run dry because it's spring fed, and when the rains come the surrounding hills act like the sides of a bowl, allowing water to run directly into the lake." He pointed to an immense table of flat land on the south side of the water. "You can tell by the vegetation that that particular area sees some occasional flooding. A hell of a crop field could be planted there. All a man would have to do is to construct a dam of sorts with a spillway that can be manipulated to allow for enough water to come through to irrigate when needed."

"Sounds like quite an undertaking, my boy."

"It's not as difficult as it sounds. I've done it before, when Nora and I settled in Kansas..." He stopped in mid-sentence and looked around at Claude who, with his hands in his pockets, was regarding Charity and Caroline with a smile.

"They make quite a pair, don't they?" Claude said. "Get them together and they giggle like girls."

Rafe relaxed. Obviously Claude had been too caught up in his admiration for his wife and daughter to have noted Rafe's blunder.

"Shall we join them?" Without looking at Rafe again, Claude struck off through the grass, his coattails whipping the backs of his knees. Rafe didn't join him. He remained on the ledge, his gaze locked on Charity and the image she made wrapped in butter yellow amid the green grass, her broad brimmed hat with its scattering of flowers and feathers and bows shading her face. He could imagine her sitting like a queen on the porch of her home overlooking this verdant valley. Except that he knew Charity Bell well enough to know that she wouldn't be poised in the shade being waited on hand and foot by servants. She'd be down in the valley with her husband—working at his side, turning the spark of a dream into a blazing reality.

"Forget it, Bastitas," he said under his breath, then turned back to the wagon, where Alex lay sleeping in a basket.

Thunder rumbled.

Rafe glanced toward the horizon, where earlier the clouds had been little more than a splash of dark shadows. An ominous band of black now stretched across the junction of earth and sky and was creeping their way.

He looked toward Charity. Holding her hat on her head with one hand, she had turned her face into the wind to note the building storm. Her features looked calm, but concerned. She spoke to her parents and they started back to the wagon while Rafe mounted and took up the lines, speaking soothingly to Connie, who stomped her feet and snorted.

Claude assisted Caroline into the wagon while Charity scrambled aboard herself. Her face looked chalk-white as she collected Alex into her arms and turned her gaze up to Rafe's. Softly, she asked, "Will we make it back to the house before the storm hits?"

"No," he whispered back. "I don't think so."

Ten minutes from the house, they were hit by a wall of wind and sand that rocked the wagon perilously. Then came the rain, driving like little knives onto their shoulders as lightning danced in fireballs across ground. Charity huddled over her son while her parents crouched the best they could on the floorboard, Claude shielding Caroline with his body. By the time they reached the house the wind and rain had become an earsplitting roar.

Rafe jumped from the wagon and grabbed for Caroline, yelling at Claude, "Get the women in the house. I'll be there shortly!"

"What are you going to do?"

He motioned toward the corral where the cattle were bawling in terror and looking for any means to escape the escalating storm. "They'll survive this better if I release them!" he yelled, then turned and ran toward the pen.

Claude helped Charity and Caroline to the door of the house, then turned back. His wife grabbed him. "Where are you going?" she demanded frantically.

"To help Rafael!" he shouted.

Charity thrust her son at her mother and ran after her father, sinking up to her ankles in water and mud. "Papa! Papa, wait!"

Lightning speared the dark and cracked against the earth a hundred yards away. The terrified animals screamed and surged against the fragile fence, rails splintering with the abruptness of the thunder clattering overhead. They poured through the gap, directly toward Rafe. He sank his heels into the slippery muck and threw himself to one side, rolling into a ball as hooves shook the ground and dug into the earth around him. Pain shot up his back, his shoulder, his arms, and he gritted his teeth and tried his best to bury himself in the mud before the animals could pummel him to death.

Then they were gone, disappearing through the wall of rain. Rafe did his best to lift his head—God, he was drowning in mud—he couldn't breathe! He—could—not—breathe—

Charity fell to her knees and rolled him over. She clawed at his face, raking aside the mask of mud buried in his eyes, nose and mouth. "Speak to me," she screamed. "Look at me, damn you. Rafe!"

He gasped for air. His eyes flew open and he fought to get up.

"They're gone." She did her best to hold him down. "There's nothing you can do now!"

Caroline appeared through the deluge, her hair plastered to her head, her voluminous skirts hampering her efforts to run. Her face looked horrified as she pointed to something in the distance.

Charity looked around. "Oh God," she cried.

Rafe shoved Charity away and climbed to his feet, ripped open his shirt and peeled it from his shoulders and arms as he ran toward Claude and the maddened, terrorized bull. The horned beast wagged its head at Charity's horrified father, pawed the ground and roared before lunging forward.

Rafe threw himself in front of the bull and flung his shirt over the animal's eyes, causing it to stumble and roar, its horn catching the shirt and ripping it in two. The animal spun toward Rafe, his shirt flapping from one horn like some limp dead being.

"Ah, shit," Rafe swore, as the animal ducked its head and, spinning on its massive haunches, drove upon him. He saw a quick flash of blind fury in the beast's eyes before the animal sank one horn into Rafe's thigh and pitched him into the air like some rag doll. Rafe hit the ground hard, rolled and scrambled. But the animal was on him again, driving him into the mud and sinking the bloody tip of his horn into Rafe's shoulder.

There came a sharp crack, then another, and still another, and suddenly the beast was gone. Rafe lay in the mud on his back, rain pouring into his face as he felt himself teetering upon the ledge of the black hole that yawned before him, cold and bottomless. Closing his eyes, he let himself float gently over the edge.

Charity fell onto her knees beside him, tossed his smoking gun near the body of the dead bull, and grabbed Rafe's shoulders. Clutching his head to her breast, she turned her face up and wept, "Oh God, Papa, please do something!"

Seventeen

CHARITY AND HER MOTHER LOOKED ON AS CLAUDE drove a final nail into the new fence rail. He stood back from his handiwork and regarded his accomplishment with a sense of satisfaction. "Good job if I do say so myself."

"Marvelous job, darling," Caroline declared as she carried a pail of cool water and a ladle to her sweating husband. "Now I do wish you would break for a while. You know how easily you burn in the sun. And your back is certain to play havoc with you tonight if you're not careful."

"Pish posh." Claude beamed Charity a smile. "She's spoiled me rotten, you know. I can't make a move without her flitting about me like a mother hen. She acts as if she hasn't ever seen me do a day's work."

"I haven't," Caroline declared. "Now drink your water before you become dehydrated."

Charity watched her parents with a sense of melancholy. After thirty years of marriage they were as in love as the day they were wed.

She returned to the house, stood for a moment in the

center of the kitchen while she caught her breath. She felt bone-weary, and as despondent as the day Randy had died. Half her farm had been blown to smithereens by the storm four days ago. Her cattle had been scattered to high heaven, and Rafe continued to battle an incredible fever and weakness from loss of blood.

Then there was the fact that she had been forced to shoot Bruce. Without Bruce there would be no calves next spring, unless the new bull arrived in time . . . if he arrived.

At last she moved to the bedroom doorway, crossed her arms and watched Rafe sleep. If there had been any hesitancy on her parents' part to accept Rafe as her husband, it no longer existed, not after Rafe had saved her father's life. Over the last few horrible days, as Rafe fought for his life, her parents had been her greatest support. They had taken shifts throughout the nights, mopping his brow, spooning water through his parched lips, holding his hand and assuring him that he would get better very soon, but that he must continue to fight, both for Charity's sake . . . and his son's.

That, of course, had made Charity want to cry. The more they came to care for Rafe, the harder it would be to tell them that he wasn't her husband . . . or the father of her son.

"Charity?"

Charity turned to find her mother at the kitchen door, her face concerned.

"There's a rather dreadful-looking man here to see you. A Mr. Wesley, I believe he said."

"I don't know a Mr. Wesley."

"He's ridden in from town." Lowering her voice, Caroline added, "Get your gun, darling. I don't care for the looks of him at all."

Frowning, Charity reached for the shotgun she kept propped by the bedroom door. She checked the chambers—both loaded—a necessity since George Peters had become such a dreaded nuisance. It would be just like Peters to want to take advantage of the situation caused by the storm. He would look at the damage as another reason why a "woman alone" had no business running a farm in Hell, Texas.

She snapped the shotgun closed, causing her mother to jump in alarm. "Mama, I'd like you and Papa to remain in the house."

Caroline's eyes widened. "Your father is in the barn, Charity, and what do you mean by that? Who is this man?"

"I have no idea. Now do as I told you. Stay here with Alex and Rafe and don't come outside for any reason."

Charity stepped around her mother and moved slowly to the open kitchen door, gun gripped in both hands, the butt caught in the crook of one elbow. Moving onto the porch, she squinted in the sun and did her best to focus on the hulk of a man straddling a dun horse. Her eye went to the pair of guns—one strapped to each thigh. There was a foot-long knife tucked into a scabbard on his gun belt. He wore one dangling earring of what looked like human teeth.

He removed his hat and his matted hair fell partially over his bearded face. His eyes, Charity thought, were as cold as stones. She shivered and tipped up the barrel of her gun.

"Mornin'," he said. "I take it yer Mrs. Bell."

Charity frowned. "Who are you and what's your business?"

He smiled and shifted in his saddle, his gaze darting toward the barn, then again toward the house. "I'm lookin' for a feller, kinda tall, black hair—"

"You didn't answer my question, Mr. Wesley. Who are you?"

"I'm a lawman, Mrs. Bell. Or so to speak. You might say I take up where the law has been a mite lazy. I clean up the scum the law has overlooked or been just a tad haphazard about nabbin'. You know the kind. Them snakes what have a tendency of crawlin' under rocks when they sniff a badge in the vicinity."

"You're a bounty hunter."

He grinned again and hocked on the ground.

"Why are you here?"

He reached inside his buffalo cape. Charity aimed the barrel directly at him. His eyebrows shot up and he chuckled to himself as he withdrew a yellowed paper. As he began to dismount, Charity said, "Don't bother. Pitch the paper over here. And be easy about it. I'm not above shooting a man just on principle."

Wesley shrugged and tossed her the paper. She caught it with one hand, gave it a shake, then cautiously glanced at the faded and crumpled image.

"I'll ask you one more time why you've come here."

"Heard that renegade has been seen in these parts. I also heard you'd hired him to manage yer farm."

"Should you take a good look at Hell, Mr. Wesley, you'd discover that the populace is made up of liars." Managing a dry smile, she added, "Fact is, a man like you could grow wealthy collecting bounties on most of the law enforcement running the town."

"Maybe. But I ain't after their worthless hides right now. I'm after his." He motioned toward the paper in Charity's hand. "That the man you got workin' for you, Mrs. Bell?"

Charity reluctantly lowered her gaze to the sloppily sketched image that was little more than dark scratches on old onionskin. "What's he done?"

"What ain't he done?" John Wesley scratched his jaw and shook his head before replacing his hat. "He's one bad hombre, lady. Done killed four men in cold blood. His hide is worth a thousand dollars right now and I'm aimin' to collect." Turning his gaze onto Charity again, he said, "I wouldn't be disinclined over the idea of sharin' that bounty with the man or woman who helped me catch him. Truth is, that kind of money would go a long way in fixin' up a place like this, and by the looks of yer storm damage you could use it." Scanning the yard, he said, "I see you've managed to rebuild yer fences. You do that, or did yer foreman do it?"

"I did it," came her father's voice, causing Charity to jump and Wesley's horse to shy. Claude stepped around the corner of the house, an ax in one hand, a piece of splintered wood in the other. His once-pristine dress shirt now sweaty and soiled, he sauntered up to Wesley's horse. "The handiwork you see is my doing, sir. Have you some problem with my capabilities?"

"You did it, huh?"

"I did."

"And what about that patch job on the barn roof? You did that too?"

"Correct."

"And the herdin' of them cows too." Wesley hocked

on the ground again, then squinted one eye. "And who are you?"

"Her father."

"You always work in them prissy clothes?"

"I have always been one to feel that a man works his best who looks his best."

Pursing his lips, the bounty hunter nodded and sat straighter in his saddle, allowing for a better viewing of his mud-matted buffalo-hide cloak. "I always reckon that the clothes make the man, myself."

Claude smiled flatly. "Indeed. Now, regarding this 'renegade' who supposedly works for my daughter . . . as you can see, there is no one residing on this farm other than Charity, myself and her mother. However, should we cross paths with this incorrigible we'll be certain to contact you."

They regarded each other steadily; then Wesley tipped his hat and turned his horse away. For an instant, Charity said nothing, then, "Mr. Wesley!"

He looked over his shoulder, his eye barely visible behind his curtain of oily hair.

"These men who were murdered," Charity said. "Who were they and why were they killed?"

"Is there ever a good reason for killin' a man, lady?"

"You seem to think so, Mr. Wesley."

He laughed softly and shook his head. "Folks in town said you was saucy and half crazy. I'm beginning to think they didn't exaggerate."

"What else did the folks in town tell you?"

"Enough to pass on some friendly advice. Keep that gun loaded. There's fellers 'round here that would shoot a priest if they thought it would buy them a way to heaven. Right now that heaven appears to be the thousand or so acres of lowland you got down near Palo Duro Canyon. Now, far as answerin' yer question about the scum who was killed. They was the lowliest bunch of dung crawlers I ever had the misfortune of knowin'. Rumor is they is dead 'cause they murdered themselves a family. A wife and child. Made the husband watch before puttin' a bullet in him and leavin' him for dead. 'Cept . . . he didn't die, and he's out fer blood.''

"Sounds like they deserved what they got.''

"If it's the truth then I reckon they did. Problem is . . . once a man has gotten a taste of killin', there ain't no turnin' back. Trigger gets jest a little easier to pull each time. The reasons for pullin' it get just a little slimmer. Then a feller looks at himself in the mirror one day and discovers he's as lost as the men he loathes.'' His voice trailing off, Wesley focused his eyes on the distant horizon of brush and rock. "Best to just put the poor bastard out of his misery, 'cause sooner or later some mad dog like me is gonna plug him in back of the head. You have a good day, ma'am . . . and my best to that little boy of yers.''

As Wesley rode away, Charity lowered the barrel of the shotgun and did her best to quiet the buzzing in her head. She couldn't swallow. Her eyes felt as if every speck of sand between her farm and Hell had settled behind her lids.

Her father moved up beside her. He slid the crumbled paper from her hand, and Charity looked up, only then realizing that he had caught hold of her arm, offering support to her shaking legs. "Papa,'' she began, but he interrupted.

"I can't imagine why that animal would come here looking for the man on this poster. Daft fellow. Why, as bad a shape as that tattered paper is in, I imagine one couldn't tell for certain just whose likeness that may, or may not, be . . . Mrs. Bastitas.'' His stern veneer cracking, he pulled Charity against him and hugged her close. "Never mind, princess. It'll all work out.''

Her eyes filled. The gun suddenly felt as if it weighed a ton. "Papa, what am I going to do?''

"Have faith, daughter, and listen to your heart.''

He stood removed from the unfamiliar house with its breezy wraparound porch and its trellises of roses and did his best to focus on the misty image of a woman and child. They were huddled around something, whispering in conspiratorial voices, nodding, smiling, laughing like tinkling bells. They looked up as he drew near. They seemed so familiar, and so dear. His heart ached to be near them, yet . . . their faces remained indistinct.

Then the door of the house opened and a woman wearing a frilly hat and a butter-yellow dress stepped out. Her features were clear as a spring morning, her eyes and smile vibrant, causing a gladness to fill him. He wanted to join her on the threshold of that house, wanted to step through the door, but something held him back, some invisible force that drowned his momentary gladness with despair.

"You're free to go,'' came the soft voice behind him. "It's time.''

He looked around. The woman's and child's images were now little more than faint forms as gossamer as smoke. "Go,'' the woman said. "And remember that we love you.''

•   •   •

Rafe opened his eyes. Charity sat at his side, her cool hand on his forehead.

"Go and remember that we love you."

Rafe reached for Charity's hand. She drew away and left the bed. Her back to him, she stood at Alex's cradle, her fingers caressing the carved wood.

"Charity," he called softly.

She turned. Her smile looked rigid, her eyes hollow.

"Something's wrong," he said. "Is Alex—"

"Alex is doing wonderfully."

"Your parents—"

"Papa cooked breakfast this morning. Mama has given up her corset and petticoats and has allowed herself the freedom of walking barefoot in the grass. She may have trouble adjusting again to the old ways once we return to Boston."

Rafe swallowed. "We?"

She nodded. "We. I've decided that Alex and I will join them."

Closing his eyes, Rafe did his best to focus on the throbbing pain in his shoulder and leg, and not on the sudden spasm of panic in the pit of his stomach. "Chester," was all he managed; his mouth was too damn dry. Perhaps he was still asleep. Maybe this was simply another of his out-of-kilter dreams; if so, why the hell should the thought of her returning to Chester bother him one iota?

"You were right all along," came her oddly unemotional voice. "This is no place for a woman to raise a child. I could never feel certain that the next man to ride over the horizon could be a cow thief or land thief . . . or killer."

He frowned.

She lowered her eyes.

Rafe licked his dry lips. "Charity, come here."

"I don't think so."

"Please."

As if drawn against her will, she slowly approached the bed, her eyes still downcast, her lower lip beginning to quiver. God, she looked pretty, scrubbed clean and wearing one of her mother's dresses, but without all those stiff undergarments that made women look so unapproachable. Her hair hung in ringlets over her shoulders, and the air around her swirled with the scent of jasmine.

He reached for her hand and held her hard when she attempted to back away. Sweat formed beads on his brow and trickled into his eyes as he whispered, "Look at me."

She shook her head.

"Dammit, I said look at me!"

"And if I don't? What will you do? Murder me?"

"What the hell are you talking about?"

Turning her face away, Charity shook her head. "I suppose it doesn't matter. You tried to tell me but I was so wrapped up in my own delusional world that I didn't hear you." Her visage softening, she took a deep breath and wearily released it. Her shoulders sank. A look of defeat settled over her being as she reluctantly brought her gaze back to his. Softly, she said, "You cry in your sleep at night. Do you know that?"

He narrowed his eyes.

"I've never seen a man weep so despondently. I thought the grief and pain you were experiencing were brought on by your injuries. Now I know differently."

He pulled her closer. "What, exactly, do you think you know, Charity?"

"Why you'll never allow yourself to love me." Her

voice cracked and she was forced to remain silent while she struggled for control. For a long moment she refused to look at him directly. Instead her gaze skipped along the bed frame, up the wall, then to the hollow of his throat. Finally, she finished: "And I know what brought you to Hell."

His jaw tightened. "Is that right." It wasn't a question.

"Someone murdered your family . . . your wife and child. You've come here for revenge."

Silence swelled in the room. The air became unbearably hot.

Charity leaned upon the bed, her knee sinking slightly into the feather mattress as her body pressed closer to his. Her wide eyes searched his face. "Should you tell me it's all a lie . . . perhaps I'll believe you."

"And if I don't?"

"I . . . don't know."

"I wonder what upsets you more: the fact that I may or may not have been married before—in love with another woman—or because I might be cold enough to slit a man's throat while he's sleeping."

A shudder ran through her, but she didn't move.

Sliding his hand around the back of her head, his fingers entwining in her silken hair, he drew her closer until her lips were close enough to kiss. He watched her lids grow heavy, her lips part, her face flush. "True," he whispered. "All true, Mrs. Bell. I was married. I had a little boy. I was forced to watch as they raped and murdered my wife, then blew my son's head off. They killed me that day as well." He lightly touched his lips to the tip of Charity's nose. "The man you see here, sweetheart, is a walking, talking zombie. They took a farmer and made him a killer as savage as they are. The difference is, they still give a damn if they live or die.''

She looked at his mouth. ''You must have loved her very much—your wife, I mean. Was she very beautiful?''

He frowned. The widow Bell was tapping at a door he had fought to barricade three years ago. Beyond the door, grief swelled like a tidal wave.

''I know now that Nora was your wife. What did you call your son? Was he very much like you?''

Rafe squeezed his eyes closed, then shoved Charity away. He struggled to roll from the bed, the pain in his shoulder and leg no more than an insignificant ember compared to the mounting firestorm pressing against the barricade in his mind.

''Murdering those men won't bring your family back,'' came her desperate voice. ''Don't you see? You've become as violent as they.''

He turned on her, snarling, ''Don't you think I know that? Jesus Christ, I go to sleep every night with those sons of bitches' faces gawking up at me from their graves. But when the vomit rises in my throat, Charity, I see my wife and son bleeding to death in the dirt and I go insane all over again.''

''The insanity is holding on to the pain. The insanity is sentencing yourself to hang for taking the law into your own hands. Is that what your wife would have wanted?''

He hobbled toward the doorway. Charity hurried after him, hands clenched, panic draining the color from her face. She attempted to grab his arm; he yanked it away before falling against the doorjamb in an attempt to steady his spinning-out-of-control world. When she came at him again, he grabbed her and snapped back her head. She cried out and clawed at his hand, to no avail. He gripped her tighter, suspecting her face to shatter at any moment. Fear ignited in her eyes.

"Is this what you want, Mrs. Bell?" he laughed in his throat. "Do you still want to cuddle at night with a cold-blooded murderer? Won't you be just a little worried that you might wake up with a sharp blade against your throat?"

"No," she responded silently.

He smirked and closed his other hand over her soft breast, molded it with his fingers, allowed his thumb to rub the nub of her nipple through the thin material of her blouse. Her eyes fluttered closed. Her breath panted softly between her parted lips. Lowering his head over hers, he whispered, "Will you be so eager to open your legs for a murderer, sweet Charity? Or will the idea of making love to a wanted man be more than even you could bear?"

"I ... don't know," she replied thinly, then added, "but I'm willing to try."

His hand still gripping her jaw, he pushed her against the wall, released himself from his breeches, and dragged her skirt up. Her eyes widened briefly—whether out of fear or anger ... or passion, he couldn't tell. As he slid his hand between her moist thighs he sensed a moment's hesitation, but then, as before, she yielded, became pliant and hot and wet within his palm. Her flesh flushed the color of a desert sunset and radiated a sheen of desire that robbed him of breath.

He forgot his present anger. Forgot the past as well— realizing that over the last few weeks the widow Bell had done that to him time and again—made him forget— dulled the pain—caused him to ignore his murderous priorities. She melted against him, making him moan like a dying man. He wanted to turn away, to absorb himself in the throbbing ache of his body and the crucifying pain of his memories. But her damned, beautiful and seductive body was arching toward him, beckoning, pleading, and he felt like a man scrambling to hold on to a crumbling precipice. If he fell now there would be nothing left to stop his fall. *Nothing.*

He took her, standing. With her legs wrapped around his hips and her arms around his neck, fingers clutching at his hair and bandaged shoulder, her head thrown back, exposing the beautiful arch of her throat, she matched his every desperate thrust with her own—her sobs a litany, her body a blazing, glorious heat that made his blood boil. He wanted to drive her insane with the fury that raged inside him, yet it was himself, not her, who lost that final thread of control. The cry tore from him as his body expanded, exploded into fragments that turned his world red as flames; the flood came, poured from his body into hers, and with it came the final collapse of the wall, folding inward, sending him spiraling into the void.

Eighteen

THE SOUND OF DISTANT HAMMERING INTRUDED ON HER sleep. What time was it? Noon? Her parents would be in shortly, expecting a meal—and here she was tangled in sheets and clothes and sweating in her bed, feeling sick and sore and disgusted with herself. What was wrong with her sensibilities? A short while ago she had made passionate love to a cold-blooded killer. The same hands that had driven her mad with desire had cut a man's throat. Yet . . . God help her, as she lay there in her damp sheets with her skirts hiked to her waist . . . she wanted him again. She wanted him forever—the truth hadn't changed that. If she was honest with herself, she'd admit that the ache in her chest had nothing to do with the fact that he had killed four men. She hurt because—as he'd said—he had loved another. Some other woman had given him a child. She was jealous of a dead woman.

Charity forced her eyes open. Beside her the bed was rumpled but empty. Her heart skipped. A dread wedged beneath her breastbone and cut off her breath. She rolled from the bed, swayed from side to side while the world momentarily spun out of control, then stumbled to the kitchen and flung open the door. The midday heat boiled into the room. It radiated off the dusty ground in waves.

In the distance, her father placed the final fence rail against the post and began to hammer. Her mother, with Alex in her arms, perched on an overturned apple crate beneath the tree and watched her husband toil and sweat. Charity scanned the empty barnyard, then ran down the steps and toward the barn.

Rafe's horse was gone.

She ran back to the house, ignoring her parents' call of concern, took the steps two at a time and flew to the living room, which was semidark despite the hour thanks to the heavy shades on the windows. Interminable seconds passed as her eyes adjusted to the shadows; then her gaze focused on the lopsided mannequin in the corner. Her heart sank, and so did she. She sat on the floor and buried her face in her hands just as her mother entered the house, calling her name.

"Charity? Charity, dear, what's wrong? What's happened?"

Charity sobbed. Her shoulders heaved.

Caroline dropped to her knees, took Charity in her arms and rocked her. "Hush now, darling. Tell mama what's happened."

She shook her head and wept harder.

"Please, Charity, you mustn't weep like this. Claude! Claude, help me. Put Alex in his crib and come quickly. There, there, daughter. Surely whatever has happened can't be so terrible. Talk to me, Charity."

Claude dropped to one knee and took Charity in his big arms. He hugged her close and kissed her forehead, rocked her back and forth and brushed her hair back from her face. Calmly, quietly, he asked, "Is it Rafael?"

She nodded and gulped down another sob.

"Is he worse?" Claude asked.

Shaking her head, Charity knuckled her tears aside.

"Then what in heaven's name has happened?" Caroline cried.

At last, Charity raised her eyes to her father's. "He's gone, Papa."

A cloud crossed Claude's face, but he did his best to smile as nonchalantly as possible. "Perhaps he simply rode to town—"

"He took his gun."

"What are the two of you talking about?" Caroline demanded, her voice rising in panic.

"He took his gun, Papa. You know what that means. He's not coming back," she wept. "He's never ever coming back."

It had been a few weeks since Lendon had so indulged in bad whiskey, but tonight he was feeling pretty damn cocksure of himself. He'd won the last eight straight hands of five-card stud, and had enough coins mounded in front of him to buy five whores, three hot baths and a bottle of the mash elixir Sally kept stashed in the back room for bastards like Frank.

"I quit," he slurred to his disgruntled companions. "I'm takin' what I got and callin' it a night." He proceeded to load his pockets with coins as the mangy group of gamblers cursed and threatened to shoot him. "If you sons of bitches want another crack at me, be here tomorrow night. I'll whoop yer asses agin. And you know why? Cause Lendon Hintz's luck is changin'. I kin feel it in my bones. Sleep tight, you bunch of losers. I'm off to find me the sweetest smellin' woman south of Kansas City."

"And what makes you think she'll lie down for you?"
one of the men snarled.

Len snorted and jiggled up and down, causing the coins
in his pockets to clatter, then clumsily turned on his boot
heel and sauntered to the bar, where he elbowed his way
between two men. Grinning, he looked around, straight
into Ned Williams's drunken face.

"You look like hell," Len said. "You ain't still
moonin' over that preacher's widow, are ya?"

"Mind yer own business," Ned sneered and drank
again.

"Heard she dumped you like piss in a chamber pot."

"Who the hell wants a woman who can't cook anyhow?"

"Who cares if she can cook? Or talk or walk for that
matter. That ain't what a woman's for anyway. What matters is if she can lay on her back and moan and groan a
little when she's poked." Sidling closer, Lendon elbowed
Ned and snickered. "The preacher's widow—what's she
like?"

"Buy me another drink and I'll tell you. I want mash.
Not that crap I've been drinkin'. Hell, I won't be able to
hold my head up tomorrow. Ma is gonna chew on me like
an old bone 'cause I'm hung over."

Lendon yelled at the barkeeper to bring them both a
shot of mash. When the barkeeper narrowed his eyes, Len
flung two coins on the bar top and curled his lip as if to
say, *There, you bastard, and there's more where that
came from.*

"When are you gonna git rid of your ma?" Len asked
as he watched the barkeeper dip under the shelf and with-
draw a fresh bottle of sour mash. "Hell, Ned, you must

be near thirty by now. How long you gonna keep jumpin' when she yells toad?''

"A man can't just boot his ma out of the house. Are you crazy?''

Both men looked on thirstily as the barkeeper poured two mashes, then collected the coins. They sipped the drinks slowly, savoring the smoothness and flavor of the whiskey. Then Len grinned. "Now for the widow Bell.''

"Why the hell is ever'one so interested in what I done with Charity Bell?''

"Is she crazy as folks believe?''

"Crazier.''

"Was she hot for ya?''

"Sizzled like a damn fryin' egg.''

Len let out a whoop, causing men to look around.

"Keep yer voice down,'' Ned ordered. "Jesus, what are you tryin' to do, git me killed? Word gets out that I'm braggin' on humpin' the preacher's widow and that crazy foreman of hers is gonna crucify me.''

Len frowned in confusion.

"That savage she's got workin' for her.'' Ned downed his drink in one gulp. "Hell, I ain't had a peaceful night's sleep since Charity up and took off. He's hot on her himself, ya know. I reckon he's been at her all right. He could just walk up to the door and I could smell her wantin' him.'' His head beginning to buzz, Ned glanced around the crowded room, noting that every head was turned his way. "It's true,'' he announced to the curious spectators. "Ever' time she looked at him her skin got all flushed and her breathin' went ragged. Shit, I'da been less of a man if I hadn't taken advantage of it. Ain't that right?''

"Right!'' the audience shouted.

Someone tapped on Lendon's shoulder. He looked

around, smirking as Della Jones raised one eyebrow and shook her head. "If I was you, Len, I wouldn't encourage your pal to go boastin' too much about the widow Bell. He's liable to get himself killed, if he's not careful. I happen to know Mrs. Bell's foreman, shall we say . . . intimately. He ain't a man I'd care to cross. Got a lot of anger simmerin' inside, if you know what I mean."

Len laughed drunkenly. "He ain't gonna hurt nobody, Della. Hell, he ain't even real. He ain't nothin' but a figment of my imagination. Frank said so."

Della frowned and leaned back against the bar. "Frank wasn't in room number ten with him not so long ago. Honey, I don't know what kind of bull Frank has been feedin' you, but that so-called figment is one hunk of livin', breathin' devil. I'd advise you and Ned not to cross him."

Len's hand clamped around the bottleneck, and he swallowed. Reluctantly, his gaze shifted to Della's blue eyes.

"He's real all right," she said. "I seen him this afternoon. At the edge of town. He was just sittin' on his horse and starin' down the street. Straight at the sheriff's office. He was pale as a ghost."

Slowly collecting two precious bottles of mash, Len glanced around the room, his eyes darting from face to face, his stomach twisting into a rock-hard knot.

"Except there was a difference this time," Della added. "He was wearin' his gun."

"Every man in here is wearin' a gun."

"Ever' man in here ain't got murder in his eye."

Lendon cradled the bottles against his chest and gave Della a shallow grin. "What say you and me go back to my room and share a bottle of this mash?"

"No thanks."

"What's wrong? My money ain't good enough?"

"Honey, there ain't enough money in Hell to get me in bed with you."

With that, Della turned away and wandered through the crowd of boisterous men, her hips swaying from side to side like a willow limb in a breeze. "Fine," Len mumbled. "I wouldn't share my mash with you anyhow . . . stinkin' ol' slut."

He staggered out of the saloon, standing in the pool of yellow light while searching the dark street. Nothing. No ghosts. Just who did Della think she was to get him all jittery again?

He bumped and stumbled his way to the back of the mercantile, used one hand to help drag himself up the creaking stairs until he reached the landing outside his door, then dug in his pants pockets for his key. "Where the hell is that key?" He swayed from side to side, then backward, coming perilously close to toppling off the landing ledge before grabbing at the broken banister. He poked into his shirt pocket, chuckled with relief at discovering his key, then proceeded to aim it in the general direction of the keyhole.

Except he didn't need his key after all. With a slight touch of his hand, the door creaked open. Len's eyes widened briefly before he shrugged and ambled into the hot, musty room, which was as dark as pitch.

The door closed behind him.

Lendon stiffened. Silence and heat swelled up around him like a bubble. Then:

"Welcome home, Lennie."

With a croak of fear, Lendon leaped away, his bottles of mash still clutched to his chest as he rammed his shin against the bedstead, causing him to yelp in pain and topple onto the mattress. The hands came at him through the dark, twisted into his shirt front and easily lifted him as if he were no more than a paper puppet. They pressed him against the wall and closed around his throat so tight that he felt his tongue swell. "Gawd, Gawd," was all he managed.

A match scraped, then flickered, tingeing the air with the smell of sulfur. As the face materialized before him, Lendon closed his eyes and did his best to reason with his inebriated consciousness. This was all simply another one of his drunken hallucinations. He would wake up at any moment with a hangover and a sour stomach; he'd vomit and fall back in bed until the hammers quit pounding at his temples—oh Gawd oh Gawd this wasn't a dream this was real he hadn't ever choked to death in his dreams no matter how shitty he felt—the boogy man was real. Real! Damn Frank. Damn him, damn him.

Bastitas touched the match to the lamp wick, one hand still pinning Lendon to the wall. Then he raised the burning match level with Lendon's eyes, allowing the thin yellow flame to devour the wooden splinter little by little toward his fingers. Len's eyes widened as the fire lapped at Bastitas's skin, scorching the flesh without so much as a flinch of pain from Rafael.

"Scary, isn't it?" Rafe said, bringing Lendon's gaze flying back to his. "I stopped feeling pain a long time ago, Lennie. I'll bet you can guess why, can't you? Come, come. Don't play the idiot with me. We're *compadres*, right? You could have killed me, but you didn't. You simply left me lying there with my son's brains splattered all over my shirt and a bullet in my gut. I suppose you thought bleeding to death was a kinder fate. I wanted to die. I really did. I lay there for days, unable to move, while the corpses of my family rotted around me. I finally told God that he'd better take me, because if he didn't, I swore I was going after the sons of bitches who slaughtered my wife and son, and I was going to kill them. I was never a man to go back on my word, Lendon.''

Lendon wagged his head from side to side. "Didn't do it,'' he choked. "Didn't touch them.''

"True. But you didn't do anything to help them, either, did you, Lennie? You simply sat back like a sniveling coward and watched my wife beg for her life.'' Rafe held up the locket Lendon had kept tucked in a drawer the last three years. It was open, revealing the faces of a woman and child. Lendon's bulging eyes followed it as it swung like a pendulum from Rafe's fingers. "I wish *this* were the image of my family that I carry in my head, Len. But you can imagine what I see when I close my eyes. No smiling faces. No childhood innocence.''

He released his grip on Lendon's throat and backed away, reaching for one of the bottles of mash Lendon had dropped when tumbling onto the bed. He uncorked it, turned the bottle up to his mouth, drinking deeply, until the warmth of the whiskey began to ooze through his body like a fever.

Lendon stared, his body pressed against the wall as if staked there. If he hoped hard enough, maybe this would all turn out to be a nightmare after all.

Then Rafael pulled a flute out of his boot and handed it to Lendon.

Lendon gaped at it and shook his head.

"Take it,'' Rafe sneered through his teeth.

Hands trembling, he took it.

"I'm certain you remember the tune,'' Rafe said.

"Can't," Lendon rasped.

"Try." Rafe pulled his gun and leveled it between Lendon's eyes. "Try real hard, Lennie. Your life depends on it."

Raising the flute to his lips, his gaze locked on Rafe's black eyes and the cold smile curling one side of his mouth, Lendon did his best to conjure enough breath to blow into the instrument. Impossible. He couldn't swallow, much less breathe. "Can't," he whined, and began to cry.

"Tough, huh? Imagine my difficulty trying to play as my wife was being raped. But I managed because Frank said that if I played real pretty he'd let my family live. I played real good, Lennie. The best I'd ever played in my life, but guess what." Drawing back the gun hammer, Rafe pressed the barrel into the sweating flesh of Lendon's forehead. "They killed my family anyway," he said, then pulled the trigger.

Lendon screamed until the realization sank in that he wasn't dead. Forcing open his eyes, he stared into his torturer's amused face.

"Bang." Rafe grinned and drew back the hammer again, this time easing the gun barrel into Lendon's mouth. His teeth made a trembling *rat-a-tat-tat* on the barrel. He tasted gunpowder and metal.

"Wonder how many times I get to pull the trigger before we find a bullet, Lennie? Twice? Three times? Tell me, would you rather get it over with quickly, or shall I give you time to pray . . . or beg? Maybe you'd like a few minutes to think about your miserable life and the lives you destroyed. Speak to me, Lennie. I'm a reasonable man. I don't much care if I kill you now or ten minutes from now."

Lendon shook his head, knocking his teeth against the pistol.

"Now?" Rafe toyed with the trigger and a sound like a calf bawling erupted from Lendon as he braced himself against the wall. "Why not?" Rafe whispered, and pulled the trigger again.

Click.

His body twitching, his eyes rolling back in his head, Lendon melted down the wall and squatted in a puddle of his own urine. He vomited mash and the tough-as-leather steak he'd eaten for supper.

Rafe raised one eyebrow, then drank again from the whiskey bottle. "That's a waste of good whiskey, Len. I don't think Frank would approve."

"It's Frank you ought to be tormentin'," Lendon cried. "Not me."

"I'll be sure to pass on your well wishes when I see him."

Lendon groaned and buried his head in his hands. "I told him. I told Frank our past was gonna catch up to us."

"He should have listened."

His head snapping up, Lendon stared at Rafe wildly. "You ain't no killer. You're a farmer, remember?"

"Not anymore." Rafe moved to the dresser and tugged open a drawer, rummaged through it with an air of nonchalance before swigging again and glancing around the room. "Not anymore," he repeated more solemnly, his words slightly slurring, thanks to the whiskey working its way through his body and brain. Frowning, he focused on the locket pressed into the palm of his hand and touched the faces of his wife and son. "My son's name was Anthony. We called him Tony. He'd be turning seven next month. By now there would have been other children.

Nora loved kids. She wanted a dozen, which was okay with me. Whatever made her happy was okay with me.''

"What about the widow Bell?'' Lendon glanced toward the door, measuring the distance. If he could only make his legs work, he might stand a chance at escape. "Word is you and her were right cozy at her farm.''

Rafe frowned and stared harder at the tintypes.

"Ned Williams says you was the reason the widow walked out on him.''

Cutting his gaze to where Lendon crouched against the wall, Rafe closed his fingers around the locket before sliding it into his pants pocket. He continued to drink from the bottle. He didn't want to think of Charity. Or her son. He didn't want to recall the pleasure of gliding his body into hers, of having her drive him crazy with exasperation one minute, the next with blind and mindless ecstasy. He sure as hell didn't want to acknowledge the ache that had racked him when leaving her bed that morning. But by killing those men before coming to Hell, he had ruined his chances of starting over. The fact that Charity knew about his family—about his killing the men who had destroyed his life—was proof of that. Somewhere in Hell, Texas, his past had finally caught up to him; and bounty hunter John Wesley was out there waiting for him.

Lendon scrambled toward the door. Rafe aimed his gun and cocked it, the triple click of the locking hammer resounding like cymbals in Lendon's ears. He sprawled on his belly and covered his head with his arms as if he could make himself magically vanish into the filthy wood floor. Rafael planted his foot between Len's shoulders and pressed the gun barrel to his nape.

"What else did Ned Williams say about the widow Bell?'' Rafe asked.

"He's down at the saloon right now boastin' on how he had her." Peeking out from under his elbow, Lendon added, "There won't be a man in Hell now who won't be sniffin' after her. If I's you I'd go down there right now and shut his mouth."

"Aren't you the hero, Lennie? Always one to help the ladies out. Somehow I don't think they'll be writing that on your epitaph."

Click.

Lendon squealed and rolled into a fetal position.

"Three down, three to go, Lennie. Your odds are growing slimmer by the minute."

"For God's sake, just go ahead and shoot me," Len howled. "Git it over with."

"Maybe you're right. I'm wasting valuable time when I could be discussing this issue with Frank. All right, Len. If you're sure that's what you want . . ."

Click.

Lendon's body convulsed and he sobbed aloud.

Rafe eased down onto one knee and traced Lendon's ear with the tip of the gun barrel. "Fifty-fifty chance you die now, Len. Or maybe I don't have any bullets in my gun at all. Maybe I have no intention of killing you now. Maybe I'll be back later . . . in the middle of the night while you're trying to sleep but can't, because you'll be thinking every little noise is me coming to slit your throat like I did your cousin's.

"Or maybe I'll just saunter over to the sheriff's office and introduce myself to Frank. Let him know that you didn't follow his orders those years ago. That you allowed one witness to live to tell about his crimes. Somehow I don't think Frank is going to be very understanding of that, Lennie. Do you?"

"Ah Gawd!"

Rafe laughed to himself and thumbed the hammer into place before sliding the gun into the holster. "Sweet dreams, Lennie. Oh, and thanks for the whiskey. You might want to save the other bottle for Frank. I expect him to be dropping by shortly to have a nice family chat."

Standing, Rafe stepped over Lendon's shaking body. He paused at the door, reached into his pocket and withdrew the locket, studied the photos a moment longer, then tossed it onto the floor near Lendon's head. "A few memories to keep you company." Then he opened the door and disappeared into the dark.

Cautiously, Lendon lifted his head and looked around the empty room; then his gaze fell to the open locket. He scurried away, grabbed up his whiskey, then threw himself into a corner, knees drawn up to his chest, his eyes fixed on the closed door . . . waiting. Waiting. Waiting. If Bastitas didn't come back . . . Frank would. Frank would kill him for sure. Any man who would murder a woman was perfectly capable of killing his own cousin.

A sound outside.

Lendon jumped and shook and whimpered as his heart climbed his throat and his blood roared in his ears. But the door didn't open. No boogy man this time.

He drank his whiskey until the world blurred and the fear subsided . . . until he no longer jumped at the sound of a rat scurrying over his floor or a horse whinnying on the street below. Clumsily, he got to his feet, staggered to the dresser and withdrew a rope he occasionally used to keep up his breeches, then dragged his only chair to the middle of the room, climbed onto it and looped one end of the rope over the ceiling rafter, tying it tight. The other he wrapped around his neck.

• • •

Ned needed help in standing up. He stumbled from side to side, egged on by the hooting, hollering men crowded around him. "She's got a heart-shaped mole right here!" He pointed to his buttock and wagged it back and forth. "And her nipples go all flushed when she's horny. I reckon if I was to ride out to her place right now she'd be on me like white on rice."

"Sounds like we were right to give her her nickname, ain't that right, boys?" Max shouted. "Charity Bell, Jezebel. Maybe we should all take a ride out to her place right now and see if we can git a little sweet talkin' from her ourselves."

Hitching up his pants, Ned smirked and slurred, "I'm gittin' her first. I still got a knot on my head from where she hit me. We'll see how sassy she is once I—"

Rafe exploded through the saloon doors and plowed into Ned with enough force to lift him from his feet and fling him halfway across the room. Ned slammed into the bar like a rag doll and howled with pain as Rafe drove his fist into Ned's stomach, then his mouth, shattering his teeth like glass. Rafe managed to bust Ned's nose and jaw before he was grabbed from behind and hauled away, his arms pinned around his back. Someone twisted a hand into his hair and yanked back his head.

"Well, look who we have here," came the familiar voice.

Rafe squeezed his eyes shut briefly, then did his best to focus on the visage materializing before him. The face swam, then sharpened.

Peters stared at Rafe with his one good eye—the other sunken behind its black patch. "If it ain't the widow Bell's guardian angel. 'Cept, he don't look so heavenly tonight, does he? What's wrong, boy? Can't hold your liquor? Or could it be you git a mite testy at our good-natured jokin' about Charity Bell?''

"Go to hell," Rafe said, then spat in Frank's face.

The room went silent. The smirk slid from Frank's mouth, and his cheek began to twitch. He reached for a whiskey bottle on a nearby table, smashed it against the tabletop, then lifted the jagged edge and pressed it against Rafe's face. "Know what I'm thinkin', boy? I'm thinkin' yer just a little too pretty by Hell's standards. As sheriff of this fine town, I think it's my duty to rectify that problem.'' Glancing around, Frank said, "Think the widow Bell would get so hot and brassy if he wasn't so pretty?''

The men mumbled and shuffled nervously, their gazes shifting from Frank to the bottle to Rafe.

Ned stumbled to his feet, one hand plastered over his mouth and nose, which did little to remedy the blood seeping through his fingers. "Cut the son of a bitch," he choked. "Cut him good, Frank. I want to see him bleed.''

Frank slid the sharp edge of the glass across Rafe's cheek, drawing tiny droplets of blood. Rafe didn't flinch, and Frank's mouth thinned. He stuck the daggerlike glass against Rafe's jugular and said through his teeth, "Next time it'll be deeper, boy. Unless, of course, we can compromise. Git on yer knees.''

"Fuck you.''

Someone slammed something across the backs of Rafe's knees. His legs buckled and the world went black for an infinitesimal moment.

Frank glanced at the pair holding Rafe. They forced Rafael to his knees, then Frank waved the weapon before Rafe's eyes. "I haven't liked you since the day you first rode into town, boy. Now you come barrelin' in here accostin' one of Hell's finest citizens. Seems to me you need to be taught some manners." Looking around at Ned, Frank said, "Care to teach him some manners, Ned?"

Ned spat out two teeth. His lips had swollen to the size of purple plums and blood still ran from his pulverized nose. He kicked Rafe in the jaw, then the gut, then planted the toe of his boot into his groin. He hooted in amusement as Rafe's body writhed, despite his attempt not to give in to the pain. Ned was prepared to inflict another kick when Frank shoved him aside.

"Maybe our guest is ready to apologize, Ned. What d'ya say, boy?"

Rafe struggled to breathe, to focus. Finally, bringing his gaze up to Frank's, he said, "I don't beg, you son of a bitch. *Not anymore.*"

A look of fury crossed Frank's features, but as his gaze locked with Rafe's a sudden shadow of uneasiness clouded his face. For an instant he looked like a man who'd just peeked into a grave and discovered that the corpse was himself.

"What the hell is goin' on here?" came Della's voice. She plowed through the crowd, tugging up the straps of her gown in an attempt to finish dressing. "Can't a girl make a livin' without you bunch of losers wreckin' the place?" Her eyes widened at seeing Ned, then she saw Rafael and shook her head. "No point in tellin' me what happened here. Wasn't no more'n an hour ago I told Lendon he'd better shut you up, Ned. As for you, Frank, if you was any kind of sheriff you'd be stoppin' fights instead of instigatin' em."

"Shut up," Frank snarled and continued to stare at Rafe as if he were a coiled rattler. "This ain't yer business, Della."

"It ain't yers either, Frank. Now you tell those boys to let him go. If they don't I'm gonna have Chuck bring out his double-barrel and pepper their breeches."

No one moved.

Hands on her hips, Della pinned Rafe's captors with a look. "Better yet, I'll see to it that none of my girls so much as flutter their eyelashes at you idiots for a year."

They dropped Rafe's arms like hot coals. He fell onto his hands as the floor seesawed beneath him.

"Same goes for you too, Frank. If I've told you once I've told you a hundred times—you leave yer mean, sadistic side at the door when you come in to Sally's Place. And as for you . . ." She turned on Ned, who was forced to breathe through the hole in his teeth. "Go home to your ma and stay there if you know what's good for you. Don't let me see you back here for six months. If I do, you'll be pickin' buckshot out of your ass when you're sixty-five."

Managing to struggle to his feet, Rafe pointed one finger at Ned and said through his teeth, "I'll kill you if you so much as breathe Charity's name again."

As Ned's face bleached of color, Della grabbed Rafe by the arm. "Hush now. Don't be makin' promises you have no intention of keepin'. Now you come on with me and let's leave this bunch of hyenas to feed on one another."

Rafe stood his ground as he turned to Frank, whose one eye looked as round and glassy as a clock face. "You're right about one thing, Frank. I am trouble. Big trouble. More trouble than you're capable of handling."

Della tugged on Rafe's arm. He followed, slowly, each step sending spears of pain down his legs and up his spine. She hooked her arm around his waist and helped him up the staircase, ushering him to her suite, a splash of burgundy-red and purple velvet walls. Oriental rugs covered the floors; damask casings shaded the diamond-pane windows. The air smelled of heavy French perfumes that added to the nausea Rafe felt in his stomach.

She sat him in a chair, then hurried to collect a whiskey bottle and glass. Pouring him a drink, she studied his swollen, bruised face. "I reckon whiskey is about the best medicinal you can get, depending on what's ailin' you, o'course. By the look in your eyes, honey, I got a feelin' you got plenty churnin' your insides. Care to talk about it?"

He snatched the drink from her hand and quaffed it. "Another," he snapped and held out his glass.

Della raised one eyebrow and poured. "Fine. Don't talk. Just listen. Frank Peters ain't the kind of man to forget tonight."

"I know exactly what kind of man Frank is."

Frowning, Della watched Rafe toss back the whiskey as if it were water. "Somethin' tells me there's more between you and Frank than that little tiff with Ned Williams. If I know Frank, he's been up to no good where you're concerned. That what brought you to Hell in the first place? Were you lookin' for a confrontation with Frank?"

Silence.

"Then I'll leave you alone with your friend here while I make certain the lot of jackals haven't turned on one another." She handed Rafe the bottle. "After all, Sally's Place is supposed to be a heavenly haven for its patrons." She chuckled sarcastically and adjusted the corset under her dress. "A touch of heaven in Hell. Now ain't that a kicker?"

With a sway of her hips, Della exited the chamber. Rafe drank while his body throbbed and his head pounded. His jaw felt as if he'd been kicked by a horse, as did his shoulder and leg. His flesh burned. By the raw feel of the wounds, he could tell he'd busted his stitches open. Charity wouldn't be pleased . . .

He focused his thoughts on Lendon—or tried to. But closing his eyes he saw only Charity, touching his feverish face with her cool hands. By now she would have realized that he'd gone—forever this time. He'd taken his belongings and ridden off without so much as a fond fare-thee-well. A week ago she might have wept. But now . . .

Now she knew. She could no longer ignore the reality. He wasn't simply a saddle tramp. He wasn't a ranch hand. He wasn't her hero.

He was a killer with a price on his head.

Wincing, he pushed himself out of the chair. The room swam. The whiskey slammed against the back of his eyes like a cudgel. "Stupid," he muttered to himself. "If I hadn't let Ned Williams make me crazy I could have killed Peters and been halfway to Mexico by dawn." He poured again and drank. "Let's face it, Bastitas, you came to this 'heavenly haven' with every intention of breaking Williams in two. You've wanted to do it since you knew for certain Charity slept with him. You'd want to break any man in two who so much as breathes her goddamn name. If you hadn't allowed her to get under your skin you'd have been out of here weeks ago. But here you are, priorities shot to hell because you can't get her or her son out of your head. Hell . . . you can't even remember your wife's face clearly because every time the memories come flooding back Charity's is there to eclipse it."

The door opened behind him. He dropped the glass and

drew his gun, spun on his heel with barrel leveled . . . and staggered back against the wall.

"Holy cripes," Della cried. "Put that blasted gun away before you kill yourself, not to mention me. What is it about you fellas who think you got to flash your gun at everything that walks by?"

Rafe slid down the wall.

Della kicked the door closed and carried a tray of hot water and bandages to the bed. She shook her head. "Ain't you a sight. Beaten black-and-blue and drunk as a skunk. Ah hell, I guess it don't matter. Whatever it takes to dull what's eatin' at you. Come here, handsome, and let Della make it better."

She hefted Rafe up from the floor, stumbling under his weight as she maneuvered him toward the bed. He sprawled across it on his back.

Nineteen

THE LAST THING CLAUDE HESSELTINE EXPECTED WHEN
venturing to Hell on his own the next morning was to find
his supposed son-in-law holed up in a whore's boudoir.
His first instinct was to pummel Rafael de Bastitas to a
pulp, but someone had obviously beaten him to it.

Rafe sat in a chair, elbows on his knees, head cradled
in his hands as Claude paced back and forth. "I have
always prided myself in being a Christian man," Claude
said through his teeth. "Therefore, the very idea that I
would like nothing more than to crack open your head
like a melon both shocks and disgusts me. The truth is,
I've prayed for patience since arriving at this pit of iniquity, and have therefore managed to maintain a respect-
able sense of diplomacy regarding my daughter's
happiness and welfare . . . and the fact that she buried one
husband and supposedly took another."

Claude stopped his pacing and bent over Rafe, who
slowly sat back in the chair and lifted his gaze to Claude's
furious features. "What are you doing here?" Rafe finally
managed.

"I've come to take my daughter's husband home."

Rafe shook his head. "Then you're out of luck, Mr. Hesseltine, because I'm not—"

"Shut up and listen to me. And listen good. I suspect that you'd be hard pressed to produce a marriage license if I demanded to see one. However, the fact that you passed yourself off as Charity's husband, and slept in her bed as her husband, is, in my opinion, as good as vowing before a preacher. You've broken her heart, you son of a bitch."

"She'll get over it."

"Are you sitting there and telling me you care nothing for my daughter and her son?"

"No. I'm not telling you that at all."

Claude frowned. "Then you had better start explaining yourself."

Rafe laughed softly, then took a deep, weary breath. "You don't scare me, Mr. Hesseltine. I'm not one of Charity's old beaus who trembles at the idea of an upset father. Fact is, I've killed men bigger and a whole lot meaner than you. Shocked? Yeah, I guess you would be. That's what I am now, Mr. Hesseltine. I'm a killer. Cold-blooded. Calculating. Unfeeling. I can watch a man's blood turn dust into mud and not blink an eye."

"Then that story you told about your family in San Antonio was nothing more than poppycock. Is that what you're saying?"

"No." For an instant, Rafe's thoughts drifted to flashes of his family—of years spent wrapped up in safety and love. "My family is very real, Mr. Hesseltine. I'm from Spanish aristocracy. I'm wealthier than most men ever dream of becoming. I have a family who loves me—who would, like Charity, be brokenhearted to see what I've become."

"Then what the blazes happened?"

"I had this idea that I didn't deserve my fortune if I didn't earn it. I wanted a more stimulating existence than raising cows like my father. I wanted to travel. I didn't want ties. In short, I wanted to become my own man. Then I met a woman . . ."

Rafe swallowed. The words wouldn't come. How could they? He had not openly spoken of his wife and son since the day he'd walked away from their graves. "Her name was Nora. We fell in love and married. I bought up some property in Kansas and built us a house. I became a farmer. We had a son. One day a group of men came along and murdered them. They left me for dead. For the last years I've hunted each of them down and killed them. The last two men live here, in Hell, Texas. At last I would finish what they started. Then I happened on Charity as she was giving birth to her son. All of a sudden the man I once was, was digging back out of that grave and gasping for air. I fought him. That man was weak. He couldn't even protect his family when they needed him most. But dreams of murder became dreams of compassion. The stains on my hands became dirt instead of blood. The emptiness of my life filled up with Charity and her baby. In short, Mr. Hesseltine . . . the sun came out after years of darkness."

Rafe left the chair and walked to the window. He looked down on the busy street, watching for the familiar face that had haunted him since he'd put a gun to Jimmy Peters's head and pulled the trigger. "He's out there, Mr. Hesseltine. You know who I'm talking about, don't you? John Wesley. A bounty hunter. Ironic, isn't it. The hunter has now become the hunted. I knew it was only a matter of time before he found me. He's damn good at what he does. Can't you understand that I couldn't stay with Charity any longer? Not for my sake. Hell, the desire to kill just isn't in me any longer. She lanced the festering wound and let the poison out. The bounty on my head is dead or alive, Claude. Wesley would just as soon take me in strapped over his horse than sitting on it. Besides, what sort of father would a cold-blooded killer make for Alex? I'm not exactly something to be proud of, considering . . ."

"You'd make a damned good father, by what I've seen."

Silent, Rafe continued to search the distant faces and thought, *Hell yes, I am—was—a good father. The best.*

"If you turn yourself in, Rafe, I'll help you as much as I can. You've done nothing more than take vengeance on the men who murdered your family. The law will understand."

"Maybe. But what proof do I have? It's my word against theirs, after all. I've got no witnesses, Mr. Hesseltine."

"We'll hire the best attorneys money can buy."

Rafe looked at Claude, but said nothing for a moment. Then, "You're assuming that I'll go back to Charity. That she'll take me back. Do you know for a fact she'll have me, now that she's aware of my past?"

"Son, I wouldn't be here now if I thought otherwise." Claude crossed the room and gently laid his hand on Rafe's shoulder. "The question is . . . are you in love with my daughter? Are you willing to face adversity to make a life with her and the child? If so, let's get the devil out of this place and go home where you belong."

Home where you belong. The sound of the words lit a warm flame of emotion in his chest.

My darling Rafe, look around you. You're no longer alone. You're free to go. It's time.

"It's time," he whispered to himself.

Caroline did her best to quiet the squalling infant, to no avail, as Charity lay on her bed, softly weeping. Walking to the open kitchen door, Caroline searched the distant road, bounced the child up and down and crooned a lullaby in his ear. Where was Claude, she wondered with a rising sense of panic. She should never have agreed to his idea of going into town to hunt down Rafael.

A spot appeared on the horizon, then another. Caroline stepped down off the stoop and marched through the sand to the road's edge, where she cupped one hand over her eyes to block the sun's intense glare. Her heart raced, her breathing quickened. She kissed her grandson's forehead and ran back to the house, taking the steps two at a time.

"Charity! Charity, dear, get up. Time for weeping is over. You have a son who needs you, after all. Up, up, up. Look at your beautiful face. Sponge it with cold water, and brush your hair."

Eyes swollen, Charity frowned at her mother. "I don't care if my hair isn't brushed. Why should I?"

"It isn't ladylike to look slovenly."

"I'm not a lady any longer." She tipped up her chin and sniffed. "There are a number of names that fit me, but *lady* isn't one of them."

"Poppycock, as your father would say. Now I'm still your mother and you are obligated to obey me. Put on that lovely yellow dress and pull back your hair with that yellow satin ribbon."

"I fear you've gone as daft as I am, Mama."

"No doubt. This deplorable heat and countryside is enough to drive anyone mad."

With a weary huff, Charity slid off the bed and proceeded to remove one dress for the other. God, how her head pounded. If her parents weren't present, she'd allow herself the privilege of screaming at the top of her voice. But her mother was right. Time for crying was over. Time for mooning over a man who wasn't fit to wipe her feet on was over. He was gone from her life, thank goodness and good riddance. As surely as the devil had horns, she didn't need a man of his reputation raising her son.

As Charity dressed, Caroline walked again to the kitchen door and watched the riders approach. Charity's weak voice came to her.

"I can't imagine what Chester is going to think of me, Mama. I dreamed last night that the moment he set eyes on Alex he fled in the opposite direction."

"Are you nearly finished?" Caroline called.

Charity dropped into the dresser chair and stared at her reflection: red swollen eyes, blotched cheeks, hair like tangled straw. The frou-frou skirts mushrooming around her waist only exacerbated her unkempt appearance. She sighed. "Of course, Chester or no Chester, I have no future here now that I was forced to shoot Bruce. What little extra money I had I wasted on ordering a bull from England that has yet to materialize. One can hardly breed cattle without a good bull, you know."

"Don't forget the shoes, Charity. I tucked them under your bed."

Charity rolled her eyes and thought about telling her mother what to do with her pointed, too tight, dreadfully uncomfortable little kid-leather boots. Instead, she snatched up a brush and tugged it through her unruly hair.

There came voices.

Her brushing stopped. Her father had obviously returned from town with the much-needed supplies. Except . . . he wasn't alone.

Heat flushed through her chest and burned like match flames on her cheeks. Her hands shook. She tucked them into her lap and reasoned with her flurrying imagination. That was not Rafe's voice. *That was not Rafe's voice.* And even if it was Rafe's voice, it wouldn't matter. She had grudgingly accepted his desertion. She'd applauded it, in fact. She fully looked forward to getting on with her life—with Chester Muesler.

"Charity?"

She spun around. Her father stood in the door, dusty and sweaty from his long, hot ride to and from town. His features were flushed and anxious. "There's someone here to see you."

"Oh?" Her voice came out a nonchalant squeak, so she cleared her throat and tried again. "Oh?"

Claude nodded. "He's putting up the horses."

Caroline stepped up beside him, her arms still cradling the fidgeting infant. Charity looked from her father to her mother. "Is it Rafael?"

They nodded.

Charity turned back to the mirror and tried to breathe. Finally, "I . . . don't want to see him."

"But Charity, darling—"

"I don't want or need a man who has to be tied like a range steer and dragged home against his will."

"I didn't drag him," Claude said. "He came because he wanted to."

"Why don't I believe you?" She slammed the brush down on the dresser top, causing several bottles of toilet water to topple over. Jumping out of the chair, she stormed toward the door. "Get out of my way. I'm going to tell that gunslinging ne'er-do-well exactly what I think about his character and manners, among other things."

Claude and Caroline stepped aside, allowing Charity's passage from the room. She rushed from the house, hesitated as the sun slashed across her stinging eyes, focused on the barn where Rafael stood in the doorway, gun strapped to his hip, shoulders propped against the doorjamb. His black hat was cocked low on his brow, hiding his eyes.

"How dare you," she yelled, and stalked toward him, little fists buried in the folds of her ridiculously full skirts. "How dare you think I would allow you back in my life after everything you've said and done?"

He didn't move, and said nothing.

Stopping feet from him, she set her shoulders and lifted her chin. "A gentleman removes his hat in the presence of a lady, sir."

One corner of his mouth curled sarcastically, causing Charity's chin to tip up that much more.

Slowly, Rafe reached for his hat and removed it. His gaze swallowed her. She felt swept up in a tide of some emotion she couldn't fathom. The struggle to stand her ground overwhelmed her as she backed away briefly, before setting her heels.

"Why?" she whispered urgently. "Why did you come back? To mock me? Taunt me? Make me beg for your adoration? Why? Did my father pay you? Did he? Because if he did—"

"Because I care for you," he confessed softly.

She blinked. She stared up into his stony countenance

as if searching out a lie. "If you cared, then why did you leave?"

"I cared for a woman once . . . and I lost her. I'm damn scared of caring that much again, Charity."

Charity took a tentative step toward him. "But your reasons for coming to Hell—"

"Don't matter any more."

"You're willing to put away your gun? Swear you'll never raise it to another human being again? Are you telling me, Rafe, that you'll give up this horrible vengeance for me and Alex?"

He reached for his gun belt and unbuckled it. It slid off his narrow hips, into his hands. He dropped the belt and weapon into the dirt. Charity gasped and covered her lips with the tips of her fingers. Her blue eyes welled as she moved into his embrace. His arms wrapped around her and held her fiercely. "It won't be easy," he said gently. "I'm in big trouble, Charity. I might even go to prison. If I could take back what I've done, I'd do it. But I can't, sweetheart. I can only promise you that I'll do my damnedest to be the sort of man worthy enough to be your husband, and father to Alex."

"You want to marry me?" she murmured against his chest. "Knowing that I'm crazy? That Ned and I . . ."

"None of that matters, Charity."

She kissed his chest, his neck, his stubbled cheek, and he laughed quietly, folding his arms around her as if she were china. They rocked there together in the sun-flooded barn doorway before returning to the house where Claude and Caroline sat at the kitchen table, their faces concerned.

Charity danced across the kitchen floor and kissed her father's cheek. "We're going to be married, Papa. Isn't that wonderful? He truly cares for Alex and me. He has all along. Oh, Mama, I'm the happiest woman alive!'' She spun on her toes before flinging herself against Rafael again and laughing. ''I feel as if I've been reborn. Nothing will get in the way of my happiness again!''

''I'm thrilled for you,'' Claude said solemnly.

Charity looked from her father to her mother. ''Then why look so glum? I've just told you that I'm marrying the man of my dreams, at long last. Yet you stare at me as if you've just learned that I have thirty seconds to live.''

Claude drummed his fingers on the table. ''Rafe told us about the problem you've been having with George Peters. That he's intent on getting his hands on this farm.''

Charity frowned. ''Must we discuss this now? There are plans for a wedding to be made.''

Rafe peeled Charity's arms from around his waist, then forced her to sit in a chair by her father. He touched her flushed cheek with his fingertips as she raised her curious blue eyes to his. ''Something you should know about George Peters,'' he said. ''It was his brother Frank who murdered my wife and son, Charity.''

Charity sank back in the chair. Her face drained of color. ''Frank is the sheriff, Rafe.''

Claude cleared his throat. ''What Rafe is saying, sweetheart, is that while George's threats have come and gone like the tide, this last time bordered damn near on murder.''

''What your father is saying,'' Caroline blurted, ''is that George Peters is fully capable of killing you should he decide that he wants this property badly enough.''

Charity regarded the expressions on her parents' and

Rafe's faces before saying, "You want me to sell him my ranch, don't you?"

Rafe stooped beside her chair and took her hand in his. "I want you to sell to George, and I want you to move to San Antonio, where I have land. We'll build our own home, Charity. And if I'm forced to spend some time in prison, my family will be there to help see to your and Alex's welfare."

Charity closed her fingers around Rafe's hand, and nodded. "Certainly," she said. "If that's what you want."

Charity's parents looked the other way as Rafe slipped into their daughter's bedroom that night. Charity lay beneath the sheets, breathing gently, her hair scattered like sunbeams over her pillow. He removed his clothes, eased down on the bed beside her, and lay on his back in the partial light of the dimming lantern. He heard her sigh. She shifted and nestled closer. He wanted to wake her. He wanted to wrap her arms around his neck, to slide his body into hers. To take what she would freely give him for the next hours until dawn. But dare he disturb her when she looked so beautifully at peace with her dreams? How could he tell her that he was afraid—so damned afraid of what might well be in store for him soon?

He would marry her tomorrow; then he would ride for Fort Worth, where he would hand himself over to the marshal there and pray that Claude Hesseltine would prove to be right. What was a few years' prison time when it meant that Charity and Alex would be waiting for him at home? Sure, a period of hardship and deprivation would be worth a lifetime of never having to look over his shoulder again for the John Wesleys of the world.

"What are you waiting for?" she whispered.

He grinned. "I thought you were asleep already."

"Never hesitate," she said softly.

He turned his head. Her eyes were large and luminous, her lips slightly parted. "Would you like to make love?" he asked.

"Only if you mean it."

He rolled into her arms and into her body, which opened like a flower in the sun, hungry and worshipful, hot, dew-kissed silken petals that enfolded him in their honey-sweet folds. He became mindless in their magic. He sighed into her mouth. He swam in the pools of her eyes and lost his soul, which no longer seemed significant amid the enormity of the act.

Oh, yes, he meant it.

He meant it.

It was there, the feeling, swelling with the tide of aching desire that burned his skin like a thousand flames. He wanted to yell it. I love you. I love you just for tonight, and tomorrow night, and the next ten thousand nights they would share together.

They rolled in the sheets. Their bodies sweated, strained, quivered, trembled together, became one, merged, body in body, hearts beating in time, gasping for the same air, struggling toward the light until her litany of pleasure sang out as gently as a gust of unexpected wind against his ear. *Follow me*, its song encouraged. *Quickly! Spiral with me to the blue heat, and let us implode together.*

Twenty

❧

CHARITY OPTED TO BE MARRIED IN A GINGHAM SKIRT AND white blouse. She braided her long hair and coiled it around the back of her head. Her mother supplied a cameo brooch and a pair of pearl combs that complemented her pearl earbobs. Charity smiled to herself when recalling that the last time she'd worn the earbobs she had been stark naked and delirious with fever.

She was still delirious, only now with happiness.

Claude regarded Charity intensely before speaking. "Rafe will be in soon. He's hitching up the wagon. He's asked me to stand up with him."

"How nice," Caroline said as she dabbed a bit of French perfume behind Charity's ear.

Charity smiled at her father. "I think it's wonderful that you and Mama are here to see me get married again. In truth, if it wasn't for you, Papa, I might not be getting married at all."

"Never think for a moment that he wouldn't have come back, sweetheart."

"I'll get Alex," Caroline told Charity, and bustled from the room.

Claude took Charity in his arms. "There are a great many things a father should say to his daughter at a time like this, but you aren't a child anymore and there is nothing I could tell you that you don't already know."

"Don't worry, Papa. I know I'm going to be very happy with Rafael."

"It won't be easy for a while."

"I'm accustomed to adversity. And I'm very strong."

"Sometimes it takes more than love to hold a marriage together. You must trust him implicitly. But mostly, you must respect him, and believe in him beyond all else."

"Claude?" Caroline stood in the door, her face pinched and her eyes round. She avoided looking directly at Charity as she focused on her husband. "I'd like to see you outside, please. Now."

"Is something wrong?" Charity took a step toward the door, but stopped short as her mother pinned her with a look so fierce that Charity felt her knees sag. "Mama, has something happened to Alex?"

"Alex is fine, Charity. I must speak to your father—"

Voices drifted into the house.

Charity glanced at her father, then her mother. "Who is out there?"

Her voice dry, Caroline managed to whisper, "There is a posse out there, Charity. They've come for Rafael."

Claude turned on his heel and stormed for the kitchen door. Charity stared at her mother as if not completely comprehending what her mother had just told her.

Caroline wrung her hands. "I think it best, for the time being, that you remain in the house, Charity."

"A posse."

"Someone was murdered night before last. Sheriff Peters believes Rafael might have had something to do with it.''

"Sheriff Peters. Oh, God, Mama, he's—''

"Hush!'' Caroline glanced over her shoulder. "We simply must remain calm.''

"Calm?'' Charity tried to move past her mother. Caroline set her heels and blocked her path. Charity turned on her in outrage. "Peters murdered Rafe's family. The man is a butchering beast. How dare he come here to arrest Rafael when he is—''

"They say Rafael killed a man, Charity. Didn't you hear what I told you?''

"Aside from Frank, who would Rafe murder, Mama? Who?''

"Ned Williams.''

The breath left Charity in a rush. She fell against the wall and closed her eyes. "I . . . don't believe it. He couldn't have. He wouldn't.''

"Who is Ned Williams, Charity?''

She shook her head. "Someone I knew. I . . . considered marrying him . . . he wouldn't have murdered Ned. I don't believe it.''

"Well that posse believes it. They've come to take Rafe to jail.''

"We can't let them. If Frank realizes who Rafael is, and that he came here to—'' She shoved her way past Caroline and ran for the open door. The voices now were rising like a coyote pack, inflaming the sickness in her stomach.

There were a dozen men, half off their horses, but all aiming their rifles on one man lying facedown in the dirt, his hands tied behind his back. Charity stumbled down the steps. Her father appeared from nowhere and grabbed her off her feet. He held her fast to his chest, though she beat his shoulders and cried. "Let me go, Papa. Damn you, let me go to him."

"Hush, girl. He wouldn't want you to see him like this. Don't make it any harder for him than it is."

Frank Peters lifted Rafael from the ground. His front covered with dust, his hair in his face, Rafe stumbled toward his horse as Charity broke free of her father and ran to him. She flung herself against him, twisting her fingers in his shirt as she searched his emotionless features and let the tears spill down her cheeks.

"Tell them you didn't do it," she choked. "Tell them that you didn't kill Ned. Make them believe you."

His black eyes narrowed as he focused on her face. His lips curled. "You think I did it, don't you? You don't want me to convince *them* as much as you want me to convince *you*."

She shook her head. "Oh God, if you killed him because of me . . ." Her words struck her like an emotional hammer, as did the look of shock on Rafe's face. His color faded whiter than the sand on his cheeks, and she stumbled back. "I didn't mean that, darling. I only meant—"

Frank pulled her away while several others ushered Rafe none too gently toward the horse. Charity yanked her arm from Frank and slapped him aside. "Don't you dare put one filthy, murdering hand on me, Frank Peters, or I'll shoot you myself."

"Charity!" Claude moved up and took her arm, squeezing it warningly. "Get back in the house with your mother and son. Do it now."

Frank smirked. "Sorry for the inconvenience, Mrs.

Bell. We all know here just what he means to you. Don't
we, boys?''

His hands fisted, Claude stepped up to Frank's face.
"Careful, Sheriff. I don't happen to be some helpless
woman you and your brother can bully around. I might
remind you that there is no greater or frightening power
than a father's vengeance. Should you hurt my daughter
in any way, I'll kill you with my bare hands. Should you
do anything whatsoever to Rafael that will in any way
harm him while we get to the truth of his disastrous situation, I will make certain that every honest law-
enforcement officer in this country, not to mention in the
courts, buries you so deep in prison that you never see
daylight again.''

"Is that a fact?'' Frank drawled.

"That is a promise.''

Frank gave a short laugh and shrugged, then turned for
his horse. Rafe had already mounted. With his wrists
bound at his back, he stared straight ahead, not so much
as glancing at Charity as the posse moved off.

Frank smoked a cigar and watched George pace the room
like a caged cat. "If it ain't one thing it's another, Frank.
Just when it looks like I'm about to get a break, along
comes the widow Bell's family like they was a goddamn
cavalry.''

"Calm down, George. Yer startin' to git on my nerves
as bad as Lendon did.''

"Speakin' of Lendon. That idiot undertaker is tellin'
me he won't put Len in the ground until I pay for the
casket. Hell, I asked him just what does Lendon need with
a casket? Dig a hole and toss him in. He won't ever know
the difference.''

Frank swigged his sour mash and shrugged. "I always said Lendon was crazy as a loon. He'd have to be or he wouldn't have gone and hanged himself. Jeez, what in Beelzebub was he thinkin' anyhow?"

"By the smell of sour mash in his room, I suspect he was visited by his booger bear agin."

Frank frowned and glanced toward the back of the room and the closed door that led to the pair of jail cells, one of which was occupied by Lendon's booger bear.

George shook his head and muttered, "Fool. If he hadn't got himself so stinking drunk he would have been able to come face-to-face with his demon. He would have seen for himself that Bastitas ain't no ghost from our past." He stopped his pacing and looked at his brother. "Are you listenin' to me or what?"

"Something sure scared the crap outta him, George. Accordin' to the fellers who played cards with him that night, ghosts were the last thing on his mind."

"I also heard he bought up two bottles of good whiskey. Hell, if he wasn't seein' booger bears when he left the cantina, he sure as the devil was by the time he drank that much mash."

Frank slid his feet from the desk and shoved off the chair. His cheek started to twitch, and he fiddled nervously with his eye patch. "I don't want to talk about Lendon's booger bears anymore. I want to talk about what you intend to do now about the widow Bell and her farm. I got a feelin' this whole scheme is gonna backlash on us, George. I think I shouldn't have gone along with killin' Ned and framin' that gunslinger."

His eyebrows shooting up, George laughed. "Yer soundin' like Lendon. When the blazes did you git a conscience?"

"Conscience ain't got nothin' to do with nothin'. What we got on our hands now is some mighty pissed-off papa from back east who has the brains to get us in deep trouble if he has a mind to. It ain't as if we can kill the lot of 'em without questions being raised."

"Naw, but we can kill Bastitas, just like we first intended before Charity's old man stuck his nose in our business." George nodded toward the back of the room. "Right now he's the biggest threat we got. Without him, they got no reason to come snoopin' around here. That old man will pack up his precious daughter and hightail it back east."

Frank thought hard on George's suggestion.

George stuck his face in Frank's. "We haul his ass out back of the jail and put a bullet in him. Alls we got to say is that he tried to escape. End of the problem."

Frank swallowed hard, causing George to scowl. "Since when were you so bothered about killin'?"

"I ain't."

"Yer afraid of somethin', Frank."

"No I ain't."

"You afraid of that gunslinger?"

"Why should I be afraid of him?"

"You tell me."

Frank shrugged and backed away. He walked to the open front door and looked out on the black street.

"Let's do it now," George said behind him. "Git it over quick before that passel of do-gooders come troopin' in here tomorrow."

"Right." Frank fidgeted with his eye patch again.

George walked to the back of the room and peered through the barred window at the shadowed figure slouched in the corner. "If I had been smarter, I'da gone ahead and killed him when I had the chance. Guess I didn't count on his carin' so much about the widow Bell.''

''That was always your biggest flaw, George. You don't think ahead.''

''You'd think he'd have the half-brain to be a little scared now. He just sits there like he's already a corpse.'' Turning back to Frank, he said, ''We killin' him now?''

''Later. I got some thinkin' to do.''

George shook his head, slammed his fist against the wall and headed for the front door. ''I'm goin' to Sally's. You let me know when you work up the innards to git the job done.''

Alone, Frank stood in the middle of the office, shoulders sagging, and stared toward the back of the room. He shoved his hands into his pockets and took a deep breath before moving toward the distant door. He opened it cautiously, as if anticipating Len's booger bear to come leaping at him from the shadows.

Sitting on his filthy cot, Bastitas slumped against the wall, long legs outstretched, fingers laced casually over his flat belly. He'd drawn his hat down over his brow, shielding his eyes.

Frank wrapped his fingers around the cell bars and stared down at his prisoner. ''Look at me,'' he ordered.

Rafe didn't budge.

''I said to look at me, you young shit.''

Slowly, Rafe lifted his head. Frank winced hard to see his eyes. ''I want to see what it is about you that drove my cousin Lendon plumb outta his gourd. It's 'cause of you that he's layin' over at the undertaker's now. I ought to kill you just for that. I might yet.'' He shifted from one foot to the other and gripped the iron bars tighter. ''You ain't no ghost. A ghost could just vanish like smoke in the wind. A ghost wouldn't be wearin' boots and a hat. If Lendon was here now, he'd see yer nothin' more than some worthless piece of buffalo dung who got hot over the widow Bell, just like half the other bastards in this town. No, you ain't no ghost. Ghosts don't get horny.''

Frank listened to himself breathe in the electrified silence; then he forced his fingers from around the bars and walked woodenly back to his office, moved to his desk and picked up Rafe's revolver. "I'll kill him now and git it over with. But first I'm gonna make him beg if it's the last thing I ever do. Arrogant bastard, sittin' there calm as a turnip when he knows his minutes are numbered.''

"Frank?''

He jumped a foot off the floor.

Della laughed and stepped into the office, her arms cradling a bundle of goods. "You're sure jumpy tonight, Sheriff.''

Dropping the gun onto the desk, Frank sank down into his chair. "What do you expect when you come at me out of the dark with no warnin'?''

"Big tough hombre like you? I'd expect a little guts, I guess.''

"I don't like you sometimes, Della.''

"I'll remember that the next time you come sniffin' at my skirts.''

"What the hell do you want?''

She dumped the blanket bundle on his desk and shoved it to one side. Then she plunked herself up on the desk with a sweep of her skirts. "Max asked me to bring you Lendon's personal belongings. He figured Len would want you to have them.''

"Hell, what did Lendon own that I'd want?''

"You always was the sentimental sort, Frank.'' Della

crossed her legs and ran her booted toe up Frank's thigh. "So how's our prisoner? Behavin' himself, is he?"

Frank smirked. "He's got no other choice. One word outta him and he'll git this." He waved his fist in the air, causing Della's eyebrows to go up.

"I'll bet *that* scares him," she said.

Frank frowned and sank back in his chair.

"Mind if I see him?"

"Hell yes, I mind." Mouth screwing to one side, he narrowed his one eye and caught hold of her frilly petticoat. "Course . . . I could be convinced, if you know what I mean."

She made a moue with her mouth. "After I see him."

"What you got to say to that gunslinger, Della?"

"Me and him had a few good times is all. He treated me nice. Paid me well. Thought I'd pay my last respects, 'cause we both know, Frank, that you're gonna kill him before sunup."

Frank dropped her petticoats and set his jaw.

Della leaned toward him, offering him a display of white cleavage. "We both know you and George killed Ned Williams."

"Ever'body in Hell heard Bastitas threaten to kill Ned."

"Frank, you always did have the memory of a pissant. The fact is, Bastitas spent the entire night Ned was killed in my bed."

His cheek began to twitch. "What are you up to, Della?"

"We'll git around to that later. Right now, I want five minutes with yer prisoner, just for old times' sake."

He smirked. "I git it. You want money to keep yer mouth shut. Right?"

She moved toward the back of the room, her hips swaying.

"Della, yer a woman after my own heart."

"I'm after somethin'," she teased and gave him a wink.

"Fine, then. Five minutes and no more."

Frank watched as Della quit the office. His grin melted from his face like hot wax. "Stinkin' bitch," he said through his teeth. "You must be pretty damn dumb if you think I won't slit yer throat from here to Abilene."

He dug for the .45 under Lendon's blanket, upsetting the bundle of belongings in the process. A bottle of sour mash tumbled out and Frank grabbed it up with a grunt of approval and the realization that, according to rumor, Lendon had purchased two bottles of the golden ambrosia. Perhaps his cousin hadn't wasted the other totally before hanging himself.

He'd imbibe a moment in the elixir before showing Della just how stupid she was in thinking she could blackmail a man like him.

There was no second bottle of mash. The idiot had drank the whole blasted thing before hangin' himself, Frank mused. He set the gun aside, removed the bottle stopper and drank as his eye perused his cousin's meager possessions. There was a locket. A black silk coin purse. A crucifix. Several pairs of woolen socks, two shabby shirts, the rope with which he'd hanged himself and a stick.

Frank frowned. What the hell was Lendon doin' with a stick?

He picked it up and rolled it in his hand.

"That ain't no stick," he said aloud and slowly left the chair. "That's a goddamn flute. What was Lendon doin' with a flute?'' His eye socket began to throb, and sweat beaded every pore in his body. His hand shook so hard he missed the .45 as he swiped at it.

Lendon's booger bear was real. The ghost was real.

A sound behind him.

He spun on his heels.

Della smashed the side of his head with an iron rod, and he sank like a stone in a sea of blackness.

It was just before dawn when Charity rolled from her bed. She tiptoed to Alex's cradle, tucked his thin blanket around his shoulders, then joined her parents in the kitchen. Caroline hurried to pour her a cup of coffee while Claude slid on his dress coat and adjusted it over his shoulders.

"I pray we aren't too late," Caroline said. "Frankly, Claude, I can't imagine what your riding to town will accomplish. How can you hope to confront a man like Frank Peters? How can we hope to prove that Rafael didn't kill Ned Williams?''

"I'm quite certain that, if I look hard enough, I will find someone who is aware of Rafe's actions that night.''

"Do you know something we don't?'' Charity asked, studying her father's odd if not outright embarrassed expression. "Because if you do, I want you to tell me.''

Claude exchanged glances with his wife before taking hold of Charity's shoulders. "I suppose you have a right to know. I found Rafe at Sally's Place. He'd spent the entire night with some floozy named Della.''

Charity swallowed, then nodded. "It doesn't matter, if she can prove Rafe's innocence.''

Claude smiled. "That's my girl.'' He looked at Caroline. "Keep the gun by the door. Don't so much as—''

The kitchen door opened. Windblown and sweating, Rafe stepped into the room.

"Oh God," Charity wept, and stumbled around her father. "Oh God."

He grabbed her and held her as Caroline and Claude looked on in speechless shock.

"How—" Charity began.

"Don't talk," he interrupted. "Just listen."

"No. You listen. I'm sorry I doubted you—"

"That doesn't matter now, Charity."

"But it does! I failed you and I'm so ashamed of myself I could cry. Love isn't conditional. Love is faith and believing in one another beyond any shadow of a doubt. But I was so frightened. One minute I was getting dressed to get married, then next I watched you being dragged off to jail for murder. I was frightened for us, Rafe. Not frightened of you. Do you forgive me?"

He smiled. "There's nothing to forgive, sweetheart. Now, I want you to grab Alex, then you and your parents get in the wagon I have for you outside. I want you to ride like hell for Abilene and don't stop until you get there."

"But what about you?" Caroline cried.

"I'll be there eventually."

"I won't go without you," Charity stated flatly.

Rafe took her face in his hands. "Do this for me, please. I can't deal with him if I'm worried over what he might manage to do to you and Alex."

"You two gonna stand there all day makin' moon eyes at one another or are ya gonna travel?" came the voice from the door. Della sashayed into the room with a flourish of dusty skirts. Her straw-colored hair resembled a ratty bird's nest. She lifted one eyebrow as Charity pinned her with a look. "Well if it ain't the widow Bell, face-to-face at last. I guess you got a few things you'd like to say to me regardin' past and present husbands. Well go ahead and git it over with, 'cause the longer we diddle here with bad feelin's, the sooner Frank is gonna come ridin' over that horizon. Believe me, after the knot I put on his head, he ain't goin' to be real happy."

Charity took a deep breath, then shrugged. "I have nothing to say except . . . thank you for helping Rafael when he needed you."

Della blinked, then smiled, then shrugged. "Fair enough. I'll be waitin' out in the wagon."

Charity refused to board the wagon, forcing Rafe to pick her up and set her next to her father. He searched her eyes and laid his hand along the side of her tear-streaked face. "I love you," he said. "I love our son. I've loved him since the instant he fell into my hands. I've loved you since you paraded before me wearing nothing more than a parasol. Your smile restored the sunshine in my life. The idea of holding you until we grow gray with age fills up my soul with hope. I swear to you, Charity, that I'll do nothing to jeopardize our future together."

"Then come with us now," she pleaded.

"In this wagon you stand no chance of outrunning a man on horseback. If I head for Mexico, he'll follow me, not you. When you arrive in Abilene, go straight to the sheriff there and tell him what's happened. With any luck, he'll send out a posse to help."

She bent over to kiss him. Her lips quivered under his and opened to lightly touch her tongue to his—so intimate an action that he felt his breath leave him in a rush. Backing away, he looked at Claude and nodded.

The wagon lurched ahead, stirring up dust into the early

crystalline air. Rafe stood in the road, watching until the wagon became nothing more than a tiny blot on the horizon and the sun became hot on his shoulders. Slowly, he turned and scanned the undulating line of rocks and scrubby trees. He checked his gun.

His lathered horse looked around as Rafe approached. The gelding pinned his ears and showed his teeth, and as Rafe reached for the saddle horn to mount, the contrary animal humped its back and took off at a full run. Rafe hit the ground hard.

He stared up at the morning sky, already washed of color by the intensifying heat, and he began to laugh at the irony of his situation. A dozen times he'd thought of shooting the cranky old horse for food. A dozen times he'd talked himself out of it. A horse was man's best friend. A man's survival often counted on his horse.

Around him the hum of insects pulsated as hens scattered over the grounds, scratching for food. Jackson came padding out of the barn, sleepy-eyed, tongue lolling. He walked over to Rafe and lapped his face.

Rafe got up and went into the house. He poured a cup of cold coffee. He prowled the rooms. He stood looking down at Alex's cradle and traced the carved jackrabbit with his finger. He thought of the years he had spent at Rancho de Bejar, his family home; how he and his brothers sat for hours around an old Mexican named Serafin and watched him whittle treasures from blocks of mesquite wood. He checked his gun again, then sat down to wait.

Just after ten o'clock, Jackson started to bark. Rafe left his chair and cautiously moved to the kitchen window and looked out to see Jackson getting his jollies chasing Charity's biggest rooster. "Cut it out!" Rafe yelled, and Jackson tucked his tail and ran for shelter. "Idiot dog," Rafe muttered.

Frank arrived just before noon.

Rafe didn't see him. He didn't hear him. What he heard instead was the sudden deathly silence that pulsated as loudly as the insects had earlier. Holding his breath, Rafe moved from room to room, glancing out windows and determining that the only place where Frank could adequately hide was behind the barn. He surmised that Frank would be alone; a man with cold-blooded murder in mind didn't bother to bring along witnesses. He might have brought his brother George, but he doubted it. George was a bully, but Rafe also suspected that he was a coward if it came to bloodying his own hands.

No. Frank would definitely be alone.

Good. It would be just Rafe and Frank. As it should be. As he had always intended. *Nora, Nora. Sweet revenge at long last.*

Rafe removed his boots and put them in the corner of the kitchen. He walked as softly as an Indian to the parlor, where he hefted the mangled mannequin up and dragged it down the hallway. He crouched on the balls of his feet and shoved it out the kitchen door.

Frank fired five bullets into it before it hit the ground.

Rafe laughed as the cattle in the nearby pen jostled and bawled. He yelled, "Good aim, Frank! I hope you have plenty of bullets."

"It takes only one bullet, Bastitas. I got one here with yer name on it! The others I'm savin' for the widow Bell and her family."

Rafe took a quick peek out the window. The shots had come from the side of the barn that shielded the henhouse. There was no way that either he or Frank could cross that space between the house and barn without being seen.

"Why don't you just do us a favor, Bastitas, and give yerself up. I promise to do a better job killin' you this time."

Rafe tucked his gun into his waistband and poured himself a glass of water, then sat down at the kitchen table. At least he had food and water. Rafe suspected that Frank wasn't so lucky, which was to Rafe's advantage. By the feel of the heat beating through the roof, the air would soon swelter.

It did. As the hours dragged on, the heat rose in waves off the rock-strewn ground. Rafe's clothes grew sodden. The heat seeped into his brain and made his lids heavy, and he struggled not to doze.

An eternity passed. The blazing sun sank toward the western horizon in a molten sphere, but even as the full moon crept over the simmering landscape, the temperature dropped only slightly. As the first long dark fingers of dusk spread over the house, Rafe moved to Charity's bedroom and, as quietly as possible, opened a window. He dropped to the ground as silent as a cat.

He ran. Making certain to keep the house between him and the barn, he made his way to a distant mesquite bush, where he dropped onto the ground behind it and waited for the last shreds of daylight to sputter out.

Crouched, gun in one hand, Rafe moved from one bush to another, dissolving into the darkness and making a wide sweeping arc around the house and barn. Cautiously, he moved toward the henhouse, senses pinpoint-alert, eyes straining for any movement.

Nothing.

He eased up against the barn, and with his back to the wall he inched along until he came to the door. Inside, the barn was as black as pitch. Instead of entering, he moved through the cattle pen, causing no more than a curious glance from the somnolent heifers.

"Bastitas!" Frank yelled, and Rafe jumped. He flattened his body against the barn and tried to calm his heartbeat.

"Bastitas! You remember how surprised you was to come home to find yer wife and kid with company that day? What if I was to tell you that you could have one more chance to save your family? To undo what was done that day."

Rafe frowned. What the hell was Frank getting at?

He peeked around the edge of the wall, straight at the house . . . just as a lamp flickered in the doorway, illuminating Charity's face.

Sinking against the wall, he closed his eyes. "Wake up," he whispered to himself. "This isn't happening again. Not again. You sent Charity and her family away from here hours ago. This is just a nightmare." *Some perverse trick of his imagination.*

"Say hello to your family, Bastitas. Quickly! While you still have the chance. Before I blow her head off just like I did before."

He opened his eyes.

Charity stood at the bottom of the steps, her son in her arms, light from the house spilling like rich butter over the black ground. Claude, Caroline and Della huddled together at the top of the stoop. Caroline sobbed into her husband's chest.

"Come out come out wherever you are, Bastitas. This cat-and-mouse game has come to an end."

The gun hanging impotently at his side, Rafe stepped out of the shadows and into the light. Frank's face leered like a jack-o'-lantern as he pressed the gun barrel to the back of Charity's head.

"Why?" Rafe rasped, trying to breathe through his horror and shock. "What the hell happened?"

Her eyes locked on Rafe, she said in a stunningly calm voice, "Your horse . . ."

He frowned.

"Your horse caught up to us just after noon. We knew something wasn't right. You wouldn't abandon your horse intentionally. I couldn't leave without knowing you weren't . . ." She gripped the baby to her, and for an instant she appeared to sway unsteadily before collecting herself. "I'm sorry," she whispered.

Frank laughed. "Weird how stuff happens, ain't it? If you had just died that day, we wouldn't be goin' through this agin. You wouldn't be the cause of another family's demise. Tell you what, boy, yer walkin' talkin' bad luck for women, ain't ya?"

"I did everything you asked me to do, Frank, you murdering son of a bitch. You killed them anyway."

Frank reached into his pocket. He threw the flute at Rafe's feet. "Play it agin, boy. Play real pretty, and maybe this time will be different."

Rafe dropped to his knees and gently laid the .45 in the dirt. He rocked for a moment, then reached for the flute, his fingers slightly trenching the sand. His hands shook as he raised the instrument to his lips.

His lips were too damn dry.

There was no air to breathe.

Frank was going to kill them all anyway.

And it was Rafe's fault.

Again.

The cacophony swelled up inside him—blasts of

screams, flashes of torture, cries for mercy. They exploded in his head like cannon fire as he took up his gun and rose to his feet as if on wings. He aimed the gun directly at Frank's head. "Die," he roared, and pulled the trigger.

Frank hit the ground, dragging Charity and the baby down with them. She clawed at his face, ripping the eye patch from his brow and revealing the gaping hole in his head. She clamped her teeth down hard on his wrist as he tried to point his gun at Rafe; he howled and rolled away, dropping his gun in the dirt as he scrambled to his knees, only to be brought up short as Rafe leveled the gun barrel between his eyes.

"Get in the house, Charity." Rafe cocked the trigger.

Claude ran down the steps and grabbed his daughter. He barked something to Caroline and Della, who hurried into the house. Charity refused to move. With her gaze locked on Rafe, she pushed her father away and shook her head. "Rafe, please," she called weakly.

"How do you like it down there, Frank?" Rafe sneered. "I hope you know how to beg real good. Not that it's going to do you any damn good." He started to squeeze the trigger, and Frank howled in fear. "Burn in hell," Rafe told him, and jabbed the barrel into Frank's mouth.

The baby cried.

Rafe raised his eyes to those of the child in Charity's arms. Like two pools of crystal water, they looked up at him with complete unquestioned adoration.

Rafe took a deep breath and slowly released it. He removed the gun from Frank's head and flung it far into the dark. Frank blinked in disbelief. He stuttered twice before managing, "What the hell are you doin'? You aimin' to kill me or what?"

"I made a promise." He focused on Charity and grinned. "I'm not a man to go back on my word."

He took a step toward Charity, too late realizing his mistake. Her eyes flew open wide as she screamed, "Rafe, his gun!"

The blast reverberated through the night air like deep, rolling thunder. Frank's body lifted off the ground and jiggled like a wooden puppet before collapsing in the light at the bottom of the steps. Charity fell into Rafe's arms as Claude and his wife rushed to their side. They stared at Frank's body as if he had been killed by divine intervention.

Then John Wesley stepped out of the dark, his smoking buffalo rifle cradled across the crook of one elbow. He nodded to Charity and acknowledged her parents. "Evenin', folks. Pleasure to see you all agin." He raised one eyebrow at Rafe. "You ain't an easy man to find, son. I figured if I hung around long enough you'd show up sooner or later."

Rafe hugged Charity close and touched Alex's smooth cheek with one fingertip. "I'll ask you for only one thing, Wesley."

"What's that?"

"That you let me marry Charity before you take me to Fort Worth."

Wesley glanced at the family huddled in the doorway, faces anxious, then looked at Rafael. "I ain't takin' you nowhere, boy. Why should I?"

"The charges—"

"Aw, hell, them charges was dropped months ago. Right after I managed to get a confession from Billy after you botched cuttin' his throat. He told me him and his bunch of dogs murdered yer family. Shoot, I just followed you to Hell to collect the bounties on Frank and Lendon.''

Rafe sank down on the porch step.

Clutching Alex to her breast, Charity looked into the bounty hunter's eyes as if unable to comprehend completely the enormity of what he'd just told them. ''Are you telling us, Mr. Wesley, that Rafe won't be going to prison . . . ever?''

''That's what I'm sayin'.''

''And we're free to be married . . . to live together . . . to . . .'' She dropped down on the step beside Rafe. Holding Alex in one arm, she cupped Rafe's cheek with her free hand. ''Did you hear that, Rafe? You won't ever have to leave me now. Ever. Is that all right with you? Do you love me enough to stay with me forever?''

He took Alex from her arms, shaking so badly that Charity was forced to help him. Curling the child into his chest, he bent over and began to cry.

They were married two days later—as soon as George Peters was caught and arrested for Ned Williams's murder. On the way home, a half mile from the farm, Rafe and Charity left the wagon, allowing Claude and Caroline, with Alex in her lap, to drive off alone. Shoulder to shoulder, they walked down the sandy road, saying nothing for a while. Then Charity lifted her left hand and fluttered her fingers, causing the gold wedding band to sparkle with sunlight. She giggled and ran ahead, her bare feet kicking up tufts of sand and making Rafael grin.

Walking backward, she blew him a kiss and made a face. ''Think I'm still crazy?'' she called.

''Yeah,'' he called back. ''I think you're crazy as a Betsy bug.''

''But you love me anyway . . . ?''

He nodded. "But I love you anyway."

"Then I guess that makes you even crazier than me, Mr. Bastitas. Doesn't it?"

Throwing back her head, her hair flying, Charity Hesseltine Bell de Bastitas spun on her toes and laughed. The sound rose like music into the air. It trilled like birdsong and cascaded along the thin stream of white clouds like a scattering of blood-red rose petals.

"I guess it does," Rafe whispered to himself, then joined her as they ran like children down the endless road toward home.